COVER ME

The Donovan Family Series (#5)

MARGARET WATSON

TITLES BY MARGARET WATSON

CHAPTER ONE

The cherry red vintage Mustang flew past Brendan's unmarked as if he were standing still.

He stepped on the gas at the same time as he picked up the radio to call in the plate. "License number HOT CAR 7. Heading north on the Dan Ryan." He squinted, trying to ID the driver, but saw only a dark hoodie pulled up around the guy's head.

He flexed his fingers on the steering wheel. "Driver wearing a hoodie. Could be a banger. Lighting him up now."

Brendan put down the radio and flipped the siren and lights switches as he maneuvered behind the red Mustang going – Jesus – one hundred five miles an hour on the late-night-quiet expressway. The car accelerated, and Brendan gripped the steering wheel, focusing on nothing but controlling his car.

He welcomed the rush. He was scheduled to start an undercover op next weekend, but until then, he was spending his time sitting on a drug house. It was driving him nuts. Surveillance for three days with nothing to show for it.

Recovering a stolen vintage car would make up for his lack of production this week.

He tried to get a better look at the driver, but couldn't see anything. The rush of excitement lit him up. There was some serious shit going on here. That car was worth big money. Would the owner be taking such risks with it? Probably not. But a thief might.

He glanced at the radio, as if that would prod it to divulge information. Heard nothing but static.

Suddenly the car braked, swerved across two lanes of traffic and slowed as it pulled onto the shoulder. On the left side. Maybe the guy knew cops didn't want to approach a car on an expressway with his ass hanging into traffic.

But a banger driving a stolen car wasn't going to do a cop any favors.

Brendan glanced at the train tracks running down the median of the Ryan. Was the driver going to hop the fence and escape out the El station?

The Mustang rolled to a stop, and Brendan's car rocked on its tires and he stomped on the brakes. He stepped onto the cracked asphalt, his hand hovering over his gun. Part of his brain noticed the meticulously restored Mustang and filed away the details for later. Shiny, smooth paint. Pristine bumpers. Even the chrome around the tail lights gleamed.

The rest of him was focused on the driver, now sitting motionless in the car. Had he carjacked the 'Stang? Was he holding a gun on a hostage crouched on the floor beside him?

That would be the scenario in a novel. Terrified car owner, afraid the banger was going to shoot him. Brendan tightened his grip on the gun.

His gaze flicked onto the radio, then back to the red car in front of him. He should wait for dispatch to tell him about the car and its owner. But if he heard a gunshot while he waited, he'd never forgive himself.

Brendan approached carefully, watching for any sudden movement. He tensed when the window rolled down, watching for the flash of metal that meant a gun. When nothing happened, he barked, "Open the door. Keep your hands where I can see them. Step out."

"Pretty stupid cop, aren't you?" The voice was low-pitched, but he had no trouble hearing the taunt over the noise of the cars rushing past.

"Pretty stupid banger," he said immediately. "Driving like a bat out of hell down the Ryan in a flashy red car." He curled his fingers around the grip of his Sig. "Out. Now."

The door sprung open and a slight figure slid out, hands in the air. He turned around slowly to face Brendan.

"Lose the hood," Brendan ordered.

One hand flicked the hood back. A woman stared back at him, all golden skin, high cheekbones and wide eyes. In the faint glow of the halogen lamp above them, her hair gleamed golden-brown. Masses of waves fell below her shoulders.

She matched her license plate - hot woman driving a hot car. He swallowed once. "License and registration, please."

"Okay if I put my hands down?" Her mouth curled into a smirk, and instead of irritating him, it turned him on.

"Yeah. Keep them where I can see them, though." He clenched his teeth. He was the cop. He was in control.

She knelt on the seat and reached toward the passenger side. It highlighted her ass in tight jeans. Brendan's gaze lingered on it. Even a bad night had some positives.

After letting him stare at her ass for far too long, she backed out of the car with papers in her hand. The dark handle of what he assumed was her purse dangled out the door. She extended the papers toward him, then fumbled in her purse again.

"Hands where I can see them," he ordered.

As soon as she withdrew her hands and held them up again, he used his flashlight to study her driver's license.

She even looked good on her driver's license photo. His gaze fell to her name. Priscilla Marini. "Ms. Marini, do you know how fast you were going?"

"One hundred and two miles an hour," she said, her voice cool.

Her unruffled answer pissed him off. "No excuses? 'You didn't realize how fast you were going? Your foot must have slipped on the accelerator? Your speedometer is broken?'"

"Nope. On my way to a call." She turned her right hand and the light gleamed on something metallic. His hand fell to his gun again until she extended her arm toward him.

A detective's badge. Chicago Police Department. "You're a cop?"

"So they say." She tucked the badge back into her purse.

"Why didn't you tell me right away?"

"Why didn't you wait until dispatch told you who was driving the car? Then you would have known, too."

"Figured it was a stolen car," he said evenly. "Carjacked. Maybe a hostage involved. Didn't think it could wait." She'd called him a stupid cop, but she'd been driving fifty miles over the speed limit. The knowledge made him fume.

"You have quite the imagination."

"Saved my life more than once." He dropped his Sig back into its holster. "If you're on your way to a call, why the hell did you pull over?"

"I have a few extra minutes. They're putting up their perimeter and calling in the spec ops guys."

He narrowed his eyes. "What kind of call are you heading to?"

"Hostage situation. I'm the negotiator." She raised one eyebrow. "Any more questions?"

"No. Get going."

He turned toward his car, but she said, "What's your name?"

He glanced over his shoulder. "Donovan. Brendan. Detective. Tactical team, out of the nineteenth." He kept his gaze on her. "What district you in?"

"Sixteenth."

Interesting. You needed a lot of seniority – or clout – to

get assigned to the sixteenth, a relatively low-crime district. "Good luck with your hostage."

"Thanks."

She turned toward her car, and he allowed himself another glance at her rear end. "Any cop bars up in sixteen?" he called.

She turned to face him again, a tiny frown wrinkling her forehead. "Why?"

"I could meet you there tomorrow night. I'd like to know how the hostage situation works out."

Her expression went flat. "Sorry, Detective Donovan. I don't date cops."

"Wasn't asking for a date. Just a beer."

"Same difference." She slid into her car without another look at him and took off. The car leaped forward and the engine rumbled as she accelerated quickly. In less than a minute, she was out of sight.

Brendan stared after the car long after it had disappeared. He wanted to know more about Detective Priscilla Marini. No priss in Priscilla, that was for sure. Tough cop. She'd been cool, in control, very smooth. Until he'd mentioned meeting up.

Then she'd shut down.

He frowned. Huh.

***

He was still thinking about Marini the next evening. Wondering how her hostage situation had gone. And why she didn't date cops. So he sent a text to his brothers Connor and Quinn and his sister Mia, all fellow cops. "Get a beer after shift?"

They agreed on a place and time, and by the time he arrived at Oscar's, Quinn and Con were working on their first beer. "Mia should be here any minute," Quinn said.

Brendan slid into the booth next to Con, caught the server's eye and ordered a Guinness. By the time the server returned, Mia was easing onto the bench beside Quinn. "Hey, guys. What's up, Bren?"

"Nothing's up," he said. "Just haven't seen you lately."

Mia narrowed her eyes. "We had dinner with Mom last Sunday. So what do you want, Brendan?"

He took a drink of the cool, smooth Guinness and plunked the glass down with a sigh. "Fine. Any of you know Priscilla Marini? Detective in the sixteenth? Hostage negotiator."

Connor frowned. "Nope. Never heard of her."

Quinn shook his head. "Me either."

Mia leaned against the back of the booth. "I haven't met Cilla, but I've seen her around. Why do you ask?"

Cilla. That suited her. "Met her last night. Pulled her over for speeding on the Ryan. Didn't tell me right off that she was a cop."

Mia laughed, then turned to the server and ordered her own Guinness. "Made a fool of yourself?"

Maybe. Brendan scowled. "Not at all. She was interesting."

"Translation: you thought she was hot," Mia said with a nod.

"Yeah. That, too."

"Don't waste your time. Cilla doesn't date cops."

"So she said."

"Believe her. She's turned down a lot before you, Bren."

"None better, though."

Connor rolled his eyes. "And he wonders why he has a hard time getting women."

"I can get all the women I want," Brendan retorted.

"Just not Cilla Marini," Mia smirked. "Nobody gets her."

"What's her story?" Brendan asked.

Mia slid her glass of beer from one hand to the other. "She used to work in the twenty-first," Mia said. "She came across a guy in an alley roughing up a woman, and arrested him. Guy told her he was a cop, but she arrested him anyway. Ryan Ward. He claimed he was questioning a suspect. Cilla said he was over the line. Excessive force. Big stink. She was transferred to the sixteenth. Stashed there."

"I know Ward," Brendan said. "His partner is Anson Bates, a guy from my class at the academy. Ward's an okay guy."

Mia shrugged. "Cilla's a good cop. Does things the right way. Smart, too. She has a great record as a hostage negotiator."

"She said she was on her way to a situation last night. That's why she was driving one hundred and two on the Ryan."

Quinn whistled. "Woman with brass balls."

"Drove like it." Acted like it, too. "Great car, too. Vintage Mustang."

Connor slapped him on his back. "Good luck, Bren. Keep us posted."

"Yeah." With a tug of regret that went deeper than it should have, he knew he probably wouldn't run into Cilla again. Once he went undercover, he'd be focused only on the job.

His next sip of the Guinness tasted a little less sweet. "So, what's new with the rest of you?"

***

"I have an update on the hostage situation from last night." Cilla's captain, Pete Francisco, motioned her into his office.

Cilla froze. Was Francisco going to tell her the guy was out on bail? She couldn't imagine any other reason the captain would be calling her into his office.

She lowered herself into the chair in front of his desk and clenched her fists in her lap. Damn it! She hoped they'd at least put the victims in a safe house.

"Nice work on that, by the way," Francisco said. "He's in Cook County Jail, no bail."

Cilla's shoulders relaxed, and she unclenched her fists. Thank God. The guy had held three of his co-workers at gunpoint for several hours, periodically firing shots into the wall. "Good. He'll kill them if he gets out."

"I heard you told him he'd get bail if he sent out the hostages and came out himself."

"I lied."

Francisco laughed. "Why you're a great negotiator, Marini." His smile faded. "How are you really doing? This was your first hostage situation since the last one went bad."

"I'm doing fine, Captain." She held his gaze steadily, ignoring the memory of the nightmare that had woken her, screaming, the night before. All the hostages on the floor. Dead. The hostage taker firing at her. The bullet coming toward her in slow motion.

"Thanks for the update, sir." She put her hands on the arms of the chair and began to rise. "Is that all?"

He shifted some papers on his desk and didn't meet her gaze. "No. There's an undercover job, and I think you'd be perfect for it." He studied her for a long moment. "You still play keyboards?"

Cilla nodded, frowning a little. Why did her captain seem nervous? "Yeah. I can still play."

"I need someone who can play in a band. Modern stuff, oldies, nothing heavy metal or too hard. Background music for a pub." He was speaking too fast.

"I could probably do that," she said cautiously. "As long as I got a playlist before the gig. What's the job?"

The captain shuffled his papers again, then met her gaze. "There's a new drug showing up in clubs. We've had three deaths in two clubs downtown, and one in the Pipe and Shamrock Pub in the Beverly area. A sex drug. An erectile dysfunction drug on steroids. According to the narcotics guys, men who've used it are clamoring for more. Except for the ones who've died."

Where was he going with this? "What am I supposed to do? If I'm in the band, I'm not in the crowd. Can't see what's going on."

"Yeah. But it's perfect cover. Who's gonna suspect a woman in the band is a cop?"

"So I'm supposed to use mind control to figure out who's selling the stuff?"

"Don't be a smart-ass, Marini," the captain said, finally relaxing. Clearly, he'd expected her to turn down the job. "You're gonna have a partner. There's a group of singles that meets there on Friday and Saturday nights. Another cop is starting this weekend. He's going to talk to people, insert himself in the group. You'll start next weekend." He grinned at her. "It'll be love at first sight between the guy in the singles group and the keyboard player."

A guy and his girlfriend were perfect cover for a pair of cops looking for a sex drug. "Clever," she said. "But what about the current keyboard player?"

The captain's eyes took on a predatory gleam. "The current keyboard player has a couple of warrants out on him. We're going to take him into custody and put out that he had an accident. You need to go to the pub and apply for a job before we do that. Today, if you think you can handle the job."

"I'm not a full-time keyboard player, Captain." But the idea interested her. She liked going undercover. Submersing herself in a role. Getting away from the station and flying on her own.

"You don't need to play like a pro. Just keep up with the band. Think you can do that?"

"Maybe. Probably." She'd played in a band in high school. She hadn't knocked anyone's socks off, but she'd been okay. Held her own. "So we're supposed to find out who's distributing this drug at the pub and bring him in. Lean on him for his contact."

"Exactly." The captain beamed at her. "You're quick, Marini. We need someone on this job who can think on her feet." He leaned forward. "It's the perfect set up. There's already a group there looking for hookups on the weekends.

The band is going to have an opening for a keyboard player."

"Okay. I'll head down to the pub and apply. Who's my partner?"

"You've never worked with him. And it's better not to know ahead of time. That way the meet will be more authentic. All he knows is you'll be the keyboard player."

"Sounds pretty straightforward. Why were you nervous about asking me?"

His gaze flickered away. "You ever do undercover work for vice?"

"Yeah," she sighed. She knew what was coming. "I've got...revealing clothes. I'll wear something sexy." She didn't like that part of the job, but she knew it was effective. Flash some skin and guys got stupid.

He nodded, his shoulders finally relaxing. "I trust you to get the info once you're in place." He studied her with a faint smile. "You probably don't need the skanky clothes. You're smart enough and quick enough to get whatever you need. You've got the attitude to pull this off, too. But you need to nail the keyboard job down first. We don't have any other seasoned undercover officers who can do this."

"Right. I'll make sure I get the job."

"Here's the address of the place." Francisco pushed a piece of paper toward her, and she picked it up and shoved it in her pocket. South side was good. She'd grown up in a northwest suburb, so very little chance anyone would recognize her. The job was tailor-made for her.

"You need to focus on the drug case. But FYI, there have been a number of rapes in the Beverly area over the past six months. Captain down there thinks they're connected — same MO, similar descriptions of the guy's height and build. Always wears a mask. So keep your eyes open. You see or hear anything suspicious, call 911. Have the guys from the twenty-second handle it."

"Will do."

She stood up to leave, but the captain held up his hand.

"One last thing." Francisco looked nervous.

"Yeah?"

"Ryan Ward works in the twenty-second. That includes Beverly."

Her stomach clenched. Twisted. But she managed to shrug. "As long as he doesn't come into the pub and recognize me, that's not a problem."

"You sure?"

"Absolutely." She stood up. "I'll apply today and let you know how it went."

Cilla left the office and hurried toward the restroom. Dread made her heart race, and she swallowed to wash away the taste of bile.

Ryan Ward. The reason she'd been banished to the sixteenth.

The door banged shut behind her, and she leaned against it. She needed a moment to put the mask back on.

She hated that she needed it here in the station, around her fellow cops. But after the situation with Ward, there were still a lot of people who either ignored her or were outright hostile.

She'd crossed the blue line of silence. Accused another cop of excessive use of force.

Pushing away from the door, she splashed cold water on her face. Studied herself in the mirror as she blotted dry with a paper towel. Good. Cool eyes. No emotion showing. No chinks in the armor.

Despite the need to dress like a hooker, she wanted this undercover job. It would keep her out of the station for days, possibly weeks. Away from the cold-eyed cops.

And if Ward came into the pub, she'd deal with it. Until it happened, she wasn't going to think about it.

Sooner or later, people would forget what had happened. Sooner or later, her fellow cops would thaw out. But until then, she was happy to go undercover. On this job, she'd only be dealing with one other cop, and he'd be playing a role, too.

Her mind started revving, thinking about strategies and ways of getting the information they needed. Who was the other cop? How would he be to work with?

She was looking forward to finding out.

***

Ten days later, she walked into the Pipe and Shamrock, carrying her keyboard. As she headed for the stage, she glanced around the crowded room.

She spotted her undercover partner immediately. Damn it!

She'd already met him.

Even worse, she hadn't been able to forget about him.

CHAPTER TWO

Her partner beckoned like a neon sign, even though there were thirty or forty people milling around the bar.

Brendan Donovan. Slightly too-long black hair, bright blue eyes, a killer smile. And his body wasn't hard on the eyes, either – tall, lean, sinewy muscles.

She'd noticed everything about him the night he'd stopped her car. Too bad he's a cop had run through her mind. Then she'd forced herself to forget about him. Fellow cops, including delicious Donovan, were off-limits. He was a bright, shiny toy, pretty to look at but far too expensive to buy.

Tonight, he leaned against the bar, nursing a beer and talking to a stunning blond in a short, clingy red dress and four-inch stilettos. She rolled her eyes. Nothing obvious about her.

Brendan seemed to like it.

She snorted as she lifted the keyboard case onto the tiny stage. She'd mentioned meeting Brendan to a couple of the women at her station. They'd laughed and told her to watch her step. He had a reputation.

None of them had met the detective, but they'd all heard the stories. One of three brothers and a sister who were Chicago cops. Another brother who was FBI. Brendan was the youngest brother. He lived to go undercover. A wild man. Adrenaline junkie. The only Donovan brother still available.

A playah.

She'd been irritated with herself for asking, but the words just slipped out of her mouth. In spite of her no-cop policy, Brendan Donovan had made her skin tingle. Other parts of her, as well. The wild, reckless risk-taker she kept carefully hidden at work had rubbed her hands together and smacked her lips. Yum.

She turned her back on the scene in front of her and plastered a smile on her face as she greeted the two men on the stage. "Hi," she said. "I'm Cilla."

The drummer, a guy with long salt and pepper hair and a longer beard, reached over and shook her hand. "Keith." He let his gaze wander from the leather vest that made it look as if she was bare beneath it to the short leather skirt and the high boots. "Hear you're pretty good."

She wanted to laugh. How would he know? She hadn't even auditioned for the manager. He'd taken one look at her skin-tight jeans and low-cut tank top and told her he'd call if they had an opening. "Thanks," she said easily. "I got the playlist. Maybe we can talk about what you guys want from me."

Keith's eyes gleamed.

"At the keyboard," she added, trying to look friendly and clueless. This was exactly the reaction she was counting on. She hoped the rest of the men in the bar reacted the same way. It would make her job a lot easier if they were thinking with their little heads.

"Yeah," he said, tearing his gaze away from her chest. "This is George. Guitar. Phil should be here any minute. He's on guitar, too. Go ahead and set up. We'll talk before we start."

"Great." She smiled briefly at Keith and George, then opened the keyboard case and went to work.

***

Brendan edged away from Tiffany on the pretext of picking up his beer and taking a drink. The blond had been surprisingly aggressive, even for a group of singles who'd gathered for the express purpose of hooking up. She'd strolled over to him moments after he'd walked into the Pipe and Shamrock, standing eye to eye with him. Tall woman. And edging close enough that her very large breasts brushed his chest. "Tiffany," she'd said, her voice high-pitched and breathless.

He hadn't noticed her the week before, and he would have. The way she dressed, her killer body, her height. The blond hair.

Not his type, but he was here to talk to people and make friends. "Hey, Tiffany. I'm Brendan."

He used his own first name as often as possible when he went undercover. Turning to look when someone called 'Brendan' could give you away in an instant. So could not responding to his undercover name. He figured there were enough Brendans in the city that he was safe.

Now Tiffany was plastered to his side as if they'd been super-glued together. If he didn't cut himself loose now, he'd be stuck with her all evening.

"Think I see an old friend from the neighborhood," he said, motioning toward the biggest cluster of people. "Catch you later."

She fumbled in her tiny black purse and pulled out a card. "In case we get separated in the crowd," she cooed as she slid the card into his front pocket. Her hand lingered a moment too long. "Give me a call."

"You have fun this evening," Brendan said.

"Would have been more fun with you," the blond said with a tiny pout. Then she turned away, smiling and stepping close to the man on her other side.

Interesting. No one had ever slipped a business card into his pocket at a meet-up bar.

Brendan took a deep breath and made sure his expression said, "What a great place this is. Can't wait to meet these people." Then he leaned against the bar and scanned the small stage at the front of the pub.

His partner had arrived. The keyboard player was crouched on the stage, brown hair cascading in waves down her back, her tiny black skirt creeping up high on her thighs. He smiled in appreciation at the sight of all that hair and her long legs. Her skin gleamed beneath the lights and her vest rode up enough to display a tiny strip of pale skin. She'd dressed for the job - a woman in tight clothes was enough to make most men lose their powers of thought.

Himself included. Except when he was on the job.

He'd enjoy the scenery, but he wouldn't lose his focus.

She stood and effortlessly lifted one of the keyboards onto its stand, and his smile deepened. She had a fine ass to go along with those long legs and wild hair. He wasn't going to have any trouble pretending they were a couple.

His captain had told him they had the perfect partner for him. Seasoned undercover cop, knew how to play the keyboard, willing to dress for the job.

She'd sounded perfect. They had to act like a couple, completely into each other. And even if there was no spark between them, every undercover cop knew how to pretend.

She turned around for the other keyboard, and his smile froze. Shit. Cilla Marini. The cop in the Mustang. The woman he'd thought about more than once since that night almost two weeks ago.

She wore a black leather vest with nothing beneath it. That short, short black leather skirt. And knee-high black boots. His heart thundered against his chest and all the blood in his body headed south.

He wasn't going to have to pretend with Marini.

He took a too-big gulp of beer, coughing a few times to

clear his throat. Then he took a smaller sip and lowered the glass to the bar.

Had she seen him? Figured out he was her partner on this job?

If he was a betting man, he'd say yes. The night he'd pulled her over, Cilla had been composed. Cool. In control. The kind of woman who'd scan the room the moment she walked in. Assessing the crowd. Looking for her partner.

So, yeah. She knew.

As he watched her get ready to perform, he had to give her credit. She chatted with the other band members as her hands flew over the keyboard, plugging in wires and adjusting her mic. Finally, she pulled a piece of paper from her keyboard case and set it on the amp behind the keyboard. Set list, probably.

Not once had she turned her gaze to the crowd.

She was good. She acted as though her entire focus was on the music she was about to perform.

He edged closer to the stage, close enough to hear the guy with the beard who'd been ogling her earlier, say, "You sing at all?"

"Yeah, I can sing." She stopped fiddling with her mic and glanced over her shoulder with a friendly smile. "Rather not do it tonight, though. I want to focus on getting comfortable with you guys first. That okay?"

"Sure. Plenty of time. Sounds like you're gonna be here for a few weeks."

"That's what the manager said."

Brendan eased back into the crowd, going out of his way to talk to as many people as possible. He dodged the women who eyed him like a juicy filet, but made sure he got their names first.

Finally, after an hour, he spotted a woman whose fingers were white around her glass of wine. Her gaze darted nervously around the crowd. Was she looking for someone? A contact? A customer?

He didn't think a dealer would send a nervous, scared

woman into a club to sell drugs, but maybe it was a cover. Maybe she was playing a role, too.

Picking up his beer, he wandered over and smiled at her. "Hi. I'm Brendan."

She swallowed. "Uh, hi. Barb."

They chatted for fifteen minutes, her shoulders gradually relaxing and her hand loosening its death grip on the wine glass.

She was no drug dealer, unless she was the world's greatest actor. She said she taught third-graders, and he believed her.

Glancing around, he saw a tall, thin blond guy who looked as nervous as Barb had been. Another suspect? Or just another desperate wallflower? He turned to the guy and said, "Hey, have you met Barb? This is her first time at the Pipe and Shamrock."

Ten minutes later, he walked away from Chuck and Barb, smiling slightly. Two people he could check off his list. And bonus points for giving both of them a safe harbor in this sea filled with sharks.

"Thanks, folks. We're taking a short break. Be back soon."

The voice came from one of the guitar players in the band. Cilla stepped away from the keyboard and talked to the three men for a moment. Then she smiled, and it changed her face. Made her light up like a Christmas tree. Her eyes twinkled and he saw even white teeth behind her lips.

She stepped off the stage and wove her way through the crowd. She didn't even glance his way. Good. She knew what she was doing. She hadn't gotten the job only because of her keyboard talent and her looks. Although they were a nice bonus – every man in the bar had stared at her at least once tonight.

As she passed beneath a light, sweat glistened on her face, her neck and her arms. A drop trickled slowly down her throat. When it dropped into the hollow between her collar bones, he wanted to shove past the guys in front of him and lick it off.

Damn. Focus.

Brendan hung back and observed as she reached the bar. He'd watch for now. See who else approached her. Let things unfold in front of him.

Three men converged on her at once, all of them clamoring to buy her a drink.

"No, thanks, guys," she said with a smile for each of them. "Rick's getting me an iced tea."

"You don't drink?" the youngest-looking guy asked in a shocked voice. Definitely a bro. The popped collar on his polo shirt was a dead giveaway.

"Not when I'm working," she answered.

Brendan hid a smile. She was fast. Clever. He liked that about her.

"Then let me buy your tea," the guy on the other side of the bro said. He was maybe in his late thirties, dark hair, wearing a suit. Made him stand out in this crowd. So did the twenty he pushed across the bar for her iced tea, waving at the bartender to keep the change.

"Thank you," Cilla said, giving him what looked like a genuine smile. "I appreciate that."

The third guy, standing behind her, pushed closer. So close he was almost touching her ass. Brendan took a sip of his beer instead of grinding his teeth. She could handle herself. She'd worked undercover before.

"Loved your work on the keyboard," the third guy said. He was a little overweight, and his button-down shirt bulged at the gaps between the buttons. "You're new in the band, right? There was a guy here last week."

Cilla swiveled to face him, discreetly using her foot to push him backward. "Thanks. Yeah, Jerry broke his hand. He'll be out for a couple of months."

"Too bad," Bro Guy smirked. Clearly, he didn't think it was bad at all.

Cilla settled against the bar, her back resting against the

wooden edge. "So, I'm Cilla," she said. "Who are all of you?"

She never even glanced Brendan's way.

***

By the end of the third set, after almost three hours onstage, Cilla's fingers were cramping. But she'd done a decent job. Held her own. Tomorrow night, she'd do better.

As George thanked the mostly inattentive people, she stepped away from the keyboard and scanned the room. The crowd had begun to thin forty-five minutes ago. Lots of people leaving in pairs. Two of the three guys who'd cornered her at the bar after the first set were among the lucky ones. The third guy, the older one with the dark good looks who'd over-tipped the bartender, was still there. Watching her in between watching the crowd.

A guy who looked like that and threw money around? The women should have been all over him. So why was he still here?

Her heart began to pound. Finding their dealer couldn't be this easy. Suit Guy stuck out like a penguin in a desert. But maybe that was the point. Maybe he wanted to look obvious. Wanted to stand out from the crowd. Maybe, if he was their guy, he deliberately chose the successful, smooth look as he peddled his drugs.

An upscale crowd would be careful about where they bought their drugs. A guy who looked like a classier version of themselves would make them comfortable. Willing to shell out big money for the wonder sex drug.

Had Brendan talked to the guy?

Her gaze found him halfway down the bar, deep in conversation with a woman. Average looking. Brown hair. Nice clothes. Nothing flashy, but flattering.

Brendan was standing close to her. Hips almost touching. His eyes fixed on hers.

She swallowed hard, then forced herself to relax. That's what he was supposed to do, idiot. Her captain had said her partner was a good undercover operative. He'd done this before. He wouldn't get distracted by a woman. Even one he was attracted to.

Turning away, she began packing up her keyboard. By the time she was lifting the final piece into its case, the pub was nearly empty. But Suit Guy was still there. Watching her.

Would he follow her into the parking lot? Push her to go home with him?

Did he think the twenty-buck iced tea, and the one he'd sent to the stage during the third set, made him entitled to her?

Would he listen when she said no?

Her heart sped up a little. If he didn't, she could handle him. But she didn't want to. She was supposed to be a musician. Not a woman who knew her way around a street fight.

"Hold on, Cilla, and I'll get your money," George called as he headed toward the office at the back of the pub.

She nodded and stepped off the stage, lifting the cases holding her keyboards to the floor. Out of the corner of her eye she saw Suit Guy stand up.

Okay. He was heading her way. She took a deep breath in, then let it out. She'd handled worse than a pushy guy in a bar.

"Hey, Cilla. May I buy you a drink before you leave?" He smiled, making him look shark-like. "You're not working anymore."

"Thanks," she said easily. "But I'm beat tonight. First night playing with a new band is tough. Maybe another night. Do you come here regularly on the weekend?"

He studied her for a long moment. Finally he said, "I will be, now."

"Great," she said, holding his gaze. "I'm looking forward to seeing you again."

His gaze swept down her once more. He nodded and turned back to the bar and picked up his drink.

Brendan had been lingering at the bar. As soon as Suit Guy moved away from her, he dropped a bill on the wooden surface and headed toward her.

"Hey," he said as he reached her. "Loved what you added to the band. You're better than the guy last weekend."

"Thank you," she said. She glanced at Suit Guy's back, saw him tip back his glass and finish it off.

"Can I help you carry those out to your car?" Brendan asked.

She eyed him up and down. "I'm not going home with you."

"Wasn't going to ask. We haven't even been introduced." He leaned a little closer, and she could smell his fresh, outdoorsy smell. How did he still smell like that after a night in a sweaty, beer-soaked bar? "I wouldn't say no if you asked, though. I've discovered I have a thing for sexy keyboardists."

God, Brendan had earned his reputation. His bright blue eyes twinkled at her, letting her in on the joke. A tiny dimple appeared in his right cheek when his smile widened. And that smile made butterflies dance in her stomach.

"Not gonna happen. Although I won't turn down help with the luggage." She nodded toward the two leather cases and the amplifier next to her. "I always appreciate company to my car at the end of the night."

"Sign me up," Brendan said instantly. "Whenever I'm here, I've got your back." He leaned closer. "And I plan to be here whenever you are."

He spoke loudly enough that Suit Guy heard him. The man jerked around, studied Brendan for a moment, then returned to his drink.

Interesting. She'd expected him to storm out of the pub. From his expression, Brendan had, as well.

George appeared around the end of the bar. He handed

her a wad of folded twenties and said, "You were great tonight. See you tomorrow."

"I'll be here."

Cilla pinched the money between her fingers as she opened the latch of the closest case and slid the money inside. Maybe a hundred bucks. Not much money for more than three hours of work. Good thing she was a cop and not a full-time musician.

She closed her fingers around the handle, figuring Brendan would get one and she'd take the other, but he eased her hand away. His fingers were warm on her skin.

"I've got these. You get the doors."

As they stepped into the crisp, early autumn air, he said, "I'm Brendan."

"Cilla," she said as they rounded the corner and headed into the parking lot. "I appreciate this."

"Glad I could help," he said easily.

She heard footsteps behind them. Her fingers twitched to pull her side piece out of her boot, but she kept up her easy gait.

She glanced over her shoulder. Suit Guy stood behind them, next to a dark car. Black Escalade. She'd noticed it as they walked past. He held her gaze for a moment, then unlocked the door, turned it on and drove away.

He left behind a chill in the air.

CHAPTER THREE

The dark shadows of several other cars were scattered around the pitch black parking lot, but otherwise it was deserted. Cilla headed toward her ancient SUV, popping the hatch before they arrived.

Brendan waited while she slid the amp in, then easily hoisted the long, narrow keyboard cases alongside it and closed the hatch. "Maybe I'll see you tomorrow night."

Cilla smiled. "I'll be here."

She headed toward the driver's door, and Brendan opened it for her. As she slid in, he leaned close and said, "Meet me at Oscar's tomorrow for lunch. 1:30. It's on Halsted."

She nodded. "I know where it is."

Brendan stepped away from the car and closed the door. She didn't have to glance in the mirror to know he watched her as she pulled away. The back of her neck burned. She could almost feel the imprints of his fingers. As if he'd touched her.

God. This job better not last too long. Brendan Donovan was going to push her self-control right to the edge.

She wouldn't fall off, though. She had too much discipline for that.

**

Oscar's was crowded the next day when she arrived ten minutes early, but the hostess found her a booth that was out of the way in a poorly-lit corner. Cilla smiled as she slipped into the seat that kept her back to the wall. Brendan would be irritated. No cop liked to leave their back exposed.

She didn't even glance at the menu – she'd been here before and knew what she wanted. Instead, she scanned the room, looking for anyone overly interested in her.

The restaurant was filled with couples and young families. Anyone trying to get to this table would have to weave their way through high chairs, diaper bags on the floor and over-sized purses hanging from chairs. She wondered if Brendan had picked Oscar's because he knew what kind of crowd ate here on Saturday afternoon.

Probably. He was good at his job, she'd realized the night before. He'd worked the crowd perfectly, blending in seamlessly but touching base with almost everyone.

So, yeah. He'd known Oscar's was a good choice. They'd be just another young couple in the crowd.

As she waited for Brendan with more anticipation than was smart, her phone rang with a familiar chime. Her mother.

"Hey, Mom," she said holding the phone to her ear. Keeping one eye on the front door, she leaned against the booth. "How are you?"

"I'm good, Cilla. How are you?"

Cilla clenched her teeth together. "I'm good, too, Mom, but I'm working."

"Then I'll make it quick. I think my car needs a tune-up. It's been making that pinging noise you told me to watch for."

Not now, Mom. She needed to focus on this case. "Okay, sounds like it needs a tune-up. Can Uncle Donny do it? I'm going to be really busy with a case for awhile."

There was a long pause. "I guess I could ask him," her mother finally said. Her tone said she'd rather pull out her fingernails, but she'd do it for her daughter.

"I'll call you back, Mom," Cilla sighed, resisting the urge to snap at her mother. "I'm meeting with someone in about a minute. I'll check my schedule afterward and let you know if I can do it for you."

"Thanks, Cilly," her mother said happily. "I knew I could count on you."

"Yeah. Talk to you soon, Mom."

Sliding the phone into her pocket, Cilla banged her head against the back of the booth. She didn't need to do the tune up on her mother's car. Her father's old partner Donny would do it happily. But her mother always called her.

Everyone in her family called her when they needed help. That was her role in their small family. Cilla the fixer.

At least her mother's phone call had gotten her mind off Brendan.

As if her internal GPS already had him on its radar, she spotted him as he walked in the door. He smiled at the hostess, said a few words, and the woman turned and pointed in Cilla's direction. Moments later, Brendan was at the table.

"Move over," he said as he slid onto the bench beside her.

"Sit on the other side," she said. His thigh wasn't even touching hers, but his heat rolled over her. Warmed her. She narrowed her eyes and tried to stare him down.

"Nope." His thigh touched hers as he edged closer, and Cilla slid over until she touched the wall. "I told the hostess I wanted a table out of the way because I was meeting my hot new girlfriend." His dimple flashed. "She told me you were already here, and that you asked the same thing. I'm flattered, Marini."

"Don't be." She jabbed her elbow into his side, irritated with the way his dimple made her belly tighten. "It was the easiest way to get this booth."

He shrugged, his smile lingering. "Gotta keep up the role, babe. The hostess is telling our waitress about the cute couple in the back booth."

"Don't call me babe."

His smile widened as he nodded toward the front of the restaurant. The hostess was speaking to a tall African American woman. She glanced at their booth, and both women smiled.

"Waitress will expect to see us plastered together."

The thought made her shiver. She grabbed her purse and plopped it down between them. "She's too busy to pay attention to us." Cilla leaned against the wall. "You just want this side of the booth. You should have gotten here earlier."

He picked up the menu and smiled into it. "I have it now, don't I?"

Yeah, he did. He also had her flustered, which irritated her even more. She was never flustered. Not by a man.

Cilla took a deep breath. "Okay. What did you get last night?"

The waitress appeared before he could answer. She swept a glance at the two of them on the same side of the booth and her expression softened. "What can I get for you folks?"

Brendan set the menu down and ordered a burger. As Cilla ordered the mac and cheese special, Brendan lifted her purse from between them and slid closer to her. The waitress smiled knowingly as she slid her order pad into the pocket of her apron.

His thigh wasn't touching hers. It didn't have to. Its heat burned through the denim of her jeans and sizzled up her leg. She shifted on the bench, but she'd trapped herself when she'd edged into the wall earlier. She couldn't escape Brendan and his distracting presence.

She picked up her iced tea and stabbed at the lemon with her straw before she took a drink. Then she clasped it in both hands and stared into its depths. With any luck, he had some ideas of who their dealer was. God knows he'd talked to enough of the women in the bar last night. "So. Back to business."

***

Brendan glanced at Cilla, surprised by her gruff tone. She was sucking hard on the straw in her tea. Hard enough to make her cheeks hollow. Finally she set the glass carefully on the cardboard coaster advertising a German beer, clasped her hands and swiveled to face him.

Her face was the cool mask of the woman he'd stopped on the Ryan almost two weeks ago. The woman who was in control and hard to read.

He wanted the Cilla from last night. The one who'd laughed and flirted with the customers during the breaks. The one who'd lost herself in the music she was playing.

She'd probably deny it. She'd claim she was paying attention to the crowd the whole time. But he'd been watching her. He'd noticed the way she closed her eyes when she was really into a song. The way her fingers flew across the keys. The tiny smile she couldn't hide when the crowd yelled and clapped after one of her riffs.

Cilla Marini was an interesting woman. Too bad they were working together. His skin prickled when he was close to her. His heart beat a little harder. His fingers itched to touch her skin, discover if it was as soft as it looked.

But he and Cilla had a job to do. So he took a deep breath, let it out, then leaned against the back of the booth. Business.

"Right." Brendan cleared his throat. "The guy in the black Escalade who was hanging around. I ran his plate this morning. Dominic Romano. Clean record. Not even a parking ticket." He drummed his fingers on the table. If he was writing the story, that's exactly how it would go. Fake identity, nothing to arouse suspicion.

Cilla frowned. "No one his age has a completely spotless driving record. You dig deeper?"

He resisted rolling his eyes. "Course I did. Nothing there. A list of previous addresses, mostly suburban. Boring bank accounts with regular paychecks from an accounting company. A mortgage."

Cilla's eyebrows drew together, forming tiny lines on her forehead. "You think someone made him a fake identity?"

She'd read his mind. "Maybe," he said slowly. "He wasn't at that pub to pick up a woman."

"How do you know?"

"I watched him." He wouldn't tell her that Romano's aggressive attempt to buy Cilla a drink had made Brendan's hackles rise. That he'd kept his eye on the guy after that. "He talked to a lot of women, bought a lot of drinks, but didn't really make a move on anyone."

"Maybe he was waiting for me," she said with a shrug. "He tried to buy me a drink at the end of the night."

He clenched his teeth together for a moment, then recovered and smoothed his face. She was the honey pot. She was supposed to have the guys buzzing around her. "Yeah. But what guy wouldn't? You were the hottest woman in the place last night."

To his surprise, her cheeks reddened. "Good," she said, her voice cool. "That means I was doing my job. And it doesn't mean Dominic Romano is our dealer."

"No. But we'll keep an eye on him." It'd be interesting to see how the guy reacted when he and Cilla became a 'couple'.

He'd enjoy rubbing it in Romano's face.

"Moving on," Cilla said. "You talk to anyone who could be involved?"

"Don't think so." He absentmindedly tapped his fingers on the table again. "Talked to one jittery woman, but she turned out to be shy and nervous about being at the pub.

Third grade teacher. Unless she's an Oscar-worthy actress, she's off the list."

"I tried to watch while I was playing." The waitress approached their table with a loaded tray, and Cilla waited until she'd deposited their meals and asked if they needed anything else. "Didn't see anything suspicious," she continued after the waitress walked away. "I'm guessing it'll take a couple of weeks before we see any patterns."

"Yeah. Probably."

"You keep tapping the table." Cilla nodded at his hands. "Almost like you're typing."

He curled his fingers into a ball and slid them beneath the table. "Bad habit," he said, his face heating. "It's my go-to nervous tic when I'm trying to work something out."

"Yeah? You a writer or something?"

He froze for a moment, then shrugged. "As much as every other cop. Spend half my time writing reports." He swallowed. "Spend so much time on the computer that I probably type in my sleep."

He felt her gaze on him, so he took another bite of his burger.

"Yeah," she finally said. "I know what you mean."

She'd caught him off guard. Who asks someone out of the blue if he was a writer? She was a lot more observant than he'd realized. No one else had ever pegged his odd tapping as typing.

They discussed the pub while they ate their meals, but neither of them had seen anything really suspicious. As they pushed their plates away, Cilla reached for her purse.

"You going to be there tonight?"

He scowled at her. "Course I am. I'm your partner. You're there, I'm there."

"Okay. You going to make a move on me tonight?"

"You looking forward to it?"

She flushed. "Just want to be prepared. So I can practice my stupidly smitten expression."

Energy hummed through her. Her foot was close

enough to his that he could feel her tapping it against the floor. Her fingers slid up and down her purse handle. As she slid her wallet back into her purse, her hand trembled.

Almost as if she was nervous about the role she was going to play.

He smiled slowly. If she wasn't attracted to him, she wouldn't be nervous. It would only be a job, and she'd play the role enthusiastically. Probably think about her boyfriend the whole time.

He frowned. "You have a boyfriend?"

"What difference does it make?"

"Just wondering."

"Not relevant to the job, Donovan."

That was a no. "Okay. No boyfriend. So I don't have to feel guilty."

"Guilty about what?"

"When I kiss you."

She slid her purse over her shoulder and nudged his hip with hers. He slid out of the booth, then helped her out with a hand to her upper arm. Her muscles tensed beneath his fingers. "We won't be kissing, Donovan."

"Sure we will." He rubbed the pads of his fingers lightly over her arm. Even through the material of her shirt, he felt the tiny quiver. "We have to convince a lot of people that we're a couple. At some point, you're gonna have to kiss me."

"Let me know when. I'll eat something really garlicky for dinner ahead of time. So we both remember what's real and what isn't." She slid her arm away from his hand and headed for the door. "See you tonight," she called over her shoulder, her expression all gooey as she gave him a simpering smile.

It was kind of scary how quickly she could flip the switch from real to acting.

And the fact that she'd need a reminder their kiss wasn't real? That was interesting.

CHAPTER FOUR

Brendan leaned against the bar, beer in hand, and watched Cilla set up her keyboard. When they'd met for lunch earlier, she'd worn jeans and a thin sweater. Both pieces of clothing highlighted her curves but didn't scream 'sex'.

She might as well have been wearing a neon sign tonight. One that flashed 'available and willing'.

Something glittery on her tight black tee shirt caught the lights and sparkled across her breasts. The shimmer only emphasized her creamy skin and feminine curves, barely hidden by the low neck of her shirt.

And how the hell did she sit down in those jeans? It looked as if she'd painted them on. When she bent to lift a keyboard, the sight of her ass made him choke on a gulp of beer.

As he coughed, a flash of red drew his attention to her long, long legs. Knee-high red boots.

Taking a steadying breath, he glanced around. Most of the men near the stage were staring at Cilla, too. They all looked as if they'd been hit in the side of the head by a brick. Some of them had their mouths open.

God! He knew it was all a show, and even he was affected. The rest of these poor slobs were all fantasizing about peeling those boots and jeans off her legs.

Exactly what she'd intended.

If he was honest with himself, he had a few fantasies about sexy Cilla, as well.

There'd be a stampede tonight at the first break. Half the guys in the bar would try to buy her a drink.

And she'd smile at all of them, chat with all of them, choose one of them to buy her iced tea.

Exactly what the job required.

His hand tightened on his beer glass, and he tossed back the last of it. Cilla was doing her job. He damn well better do his.

He turned away from the show she was giving and studied the room. He recognized some of the people from the previous weekend, some from last night. He pulled out his phone and made a few notes on the log he'd started, detailing who showed up on which night. It was too soon to see any patterns, but he'd eventually find them.

Tiffany from last night was here again, this time wearing a curve-hugging emerald green dress that showed off all her assets. She was talking to a guy in khakis and a polo shirt, someone he hadn't noticed before. As she leaned closer to Polo Shirt, the bartender interrupted Brendan.

"You need another beer?"

Not letting his irritation show, Brendan looked away from the blond and smiled at the gray-haired guy. "Yeah. Thanks." He squinted at the bartender's name tag. "Rick." He slid the glass across the polished wood.

"We don't run tabs." Rick smiled apologetically as he pulled Brendan's beer. "Sorry."

"Right." Brendan reached for his wallet and dropped a bill onto the bar. "Thanks."

The bartender nodded, passed Brendan his Warsteiner, scooped up the money and moved down the bar.

By the time Brendan looked back at Tiffany, she was

sliding her hand out of the guy's pocket. Leaving her card behind?

Brendan narrowed his eyes. Was she an escort? Is that why she was passing out cards in a bar?

He glanced at Cilla, who was now sitting on a high stool at her keyboard. What would her take be?

As he wondered about Tiffany, he was distracted by Cilla's fingers, dancing over the keyboard. He couldn't hear any music, but her hands were graceful. Quick. Flexible.

Would they waltz over his body the same way? Playing silent songs that drove him wild?

He turned his head away, scowling at the distraction. Idiot. He needed to keep his head in the game.

Picking up his beer, he wandered toward the back of the pub. Safer there. He wouldn't be able to see Cilla. Wouldn't be distracted by her. Miss a deal going down in the pub.

Cilla had done a great job getting ready for this gig. Now it was time for him to do his job.

He leaned against a wall and watched Tiffany. She was talking to a woman at the bar, laughing with her as she sipped a martini. That grabbed his attention.

He hadn't seen Tiffany talk to any women last week. She'd focused completely on the men.

Was her friend an escort, too?

Brendan watched for several minutes, until Tiffany set her empty glass on the counter and moved away from the other woman. He waited until Tiffany disappeared into the crowd, then slid into the empty spot beside her friend.

"Hey," he said, setting his beer on the bar. "I'm Brendan."

The woman smiled at him. "Holly," she said. She tilted her head and studied him. "I haven't seen you here before."

"Just found the place last weekend," he said easily. "Liked it so much I came back this weekend."

"Welcome, then." Holly took a drink of her beer. She had medium length curly blond hair and a pleasant face. Not drop-dead gorgeous, but striking. Memorable. A full mouth, wide eyes, a killer smile. "Lots of people here on weekends."

"Yeah? You been coming here for awhile?"

She lifted one shoulder. "Long enough to recognize the regulars." Her gaze slid over him. "Are you going to be a regular?"

He didn't see even a tiny flicker of interest in her eyes. Brendan's gaze sharpened. That didn't fit with this crowd.

"I'm coming back next weekend," he said, keeping his tone easy. "Does that count?"

"Three weekends in a row?" Her eyes drifted over him again, then she turned away to pick up her martini. "Good looking guy like you? I'd say you're in."

"Good to know." Clearly, Holly wouldn't be fighting over him with Tiffany. He settled one elbow on the bar. "So what do you do, Holly? When you're not at the Pipe and Shamrock?"

"I'm a physical therapist. How about you?"

"I work in the IT department of a big company in the loop." He shrugged. "Kind of a boring job."

"Not if you like it." Instead of leaning closer and giving him a view of her cleavage, as he expected, she eased away from him and crossed her arms over her chest. "And you don't seem like a boring guy."

"Hope not. Boring is the kiss of death." Under other circumstances, he might spend more time with Holly. Get to know her. Figure out what made her tick.

Get her story.

But he wasn't here to pick up women. He was here to pick their brains. Without them realizing it.

Holly was apparently indifferent. He'd said he was coming back. She hadn't said she'd like to see him there.

Not the reaction he expected in a pick-up bar.

Instead of flirting, she was distancing herself.

And she'd been talking to Tiffany. What was up with that?

Maybe it was time to stir the pot.

His heart rate picked up, and he tapped his fingers on the bar. Then, remembering Cilla's question about his 'typing', he forced himself to stop.

"What do you do for fun when you're not at the Pipe and Shamrock?" he asked her.

"This and that. I don't spend all my free time here."

"Yeah? Where else do you go?"

"I go to clubs sometimes. Places where I can dance. Let my hair down."

Brendan's heart beat a little harder. "Around here?"

"Most of the good places are downtown."

"You know it." He shifted a little closer to Holly. "I used to go to a club downtown myself. Close to where I work. I liked the noise, the action, the crowd. But a guy died of an overdose a few weeks ago." He shook his head. "Too many cops there now. Asking a lot of questions."

Her hand tightened around her glass for a long moment, then relaxed. "That's scary."

"It is. This place is different. A lot more quiet. Don't think anyone has to worry about overdoses here."

She raised one eyebrow. "You don't have to go to a fancy club to get drugs. You can find them anywhere. Even in this white bread neighborhood."

"Probably true, if you're looking for them."

"Yeah." Her expression was calculating. "You don't have to look too hard, either." She stirred her drink with the toothpick holding its three olives. "You sit and watch long enough, you have a pretty good idea who's dealing."

It couldn't be this simple. "Yeah?" He scanned the crowd in the club, wondering who she was talking about. "Any of them here tonight?"

She snorted as she lifted the martini glass. "I'm not that stupid. You want to buy something, figure it out for yourself."

He'd approached Holly, made conversation with her, given her an opening to flirt with him. But she hadn't taken it. It sure didn't seem like she was here to pick up a guy.

So why did Holly come here every weekend?

He straightened, his fingers tightening on the pint glass. Something about Holly was off. Was she selling drugs? Was she an escort?

He scanned her face again, imprinting it in his memory. He'd point her out to Cilla tonight. Look through some mug shots tomorrow.

He'd keep an eye on her at the Pipe and Shamrock.

He waved over Holly's shoulder, as if someone had signaled him. "See a guy I met last week. I'm gonna go say hi. Nice to meet you, Holly. I'll see you around."

"I'll be here," she said. She leaned against the bar. "Every weekend."

He nodded. He would be, too. And he'd be watching her.

Brendan wandered off, waving as if he was hailing a friend. He glanced over his shoulder and found Holly watching him. He nodded at her, smiled, and waited until she turned back to her drink before he slid through the crowd, hiding himself from Holly's gaze.

The band had started playing. He'd gradually make his way toward the front of the room. Time to solidify his standing as one of the guys crushing on Cilla.

***

As Cilla set up her keyboard and fiddled with her mic, she glanced over at Phil, the guitar player furthest away from her. His eyes looked glassy, and he fumbled as he tried to plug the jack into his guitar.

She leaned toward Keith. "Everything okay with Phil?" she asked quietly.

The drummer shook his head. "No. He's had a few drinks, but he's a pro. Once we start playing, he'll snap out of it. Be okay."

"Hope so," Cilla said, watching the guitar player. Phil had had more than a few drinks. "He's really good, and we have a big crowd tonight. Don't want to disappoint them."

"He won't." Keith adjusted the angle of his snare drum and shrugged. "I've seen him worse."

"Right. You guys know him better than I do."

"Yeah." Keith leaned closer. She wasn't sure if it was to share something quietly or stare at her cleavage. "You did a great job last night, by the way. Not sure if we told you. You want to do any singing tonight?"

"Not tonight," she said easily. "I like to sing, but this is only my second night. Let me get comfortable with you guys first. Learn your style, the songs you like to play. You know? I don't want to step on anyone's toes."

Keith's expression softened. "Think that's the first time I've ever heard that in a band. Most people want to stand out."

She shrugged. "I do, too. But this is your band and your gig. I'm here to support you."

"Nice to hear." He was actually looking at her face. "But jump in anytime."

"Maybe I'll do some harmony tonight."

He nodded. "That'd be great."

A few minutes later, George played the first notes of the first song on the playlist. Cilla glanced at Phil, who seemed to have gotten it together. She jumped in and glanced at the audience. A lot of men were clustered in front of the stage.

She suppressed a smile. Men were so easy. She'd have plenty of guys to talk to at the break.

Four songs later, the crowd in front of the stage had increased. Brendan was there, in the background. His eyes fixed on hers. He lifted his beer and took a sip without looking away.

She shivered, even though the spotlights were hot. What would it be like to have all that intensity focused on her in a more private setting?

Cilla jerked her attention away from him. She didn't have to work to draw Brendan in. That was part of the job, and she was confident he'd play his role. Just like she'd play hers.

She let her gaze drift from one of the men to the next, making brief eye contact with as many of them as possible.

Not Nick Romano, though. She scanned the crowd again and didn't see him. Wonder what Brendan thinks about that?

Maybe he'd noticed Romano somewhere else in the pub. She'd ask him at the break, if she got a chance.

Then she glanced at the keyboard and focused on the music.

They were playing a Tom Petty song, and Phil was taking the lead. He sounded good, his voice strong, his guitar playing masterful.

After the second round of the chorus, though, his voice faltered. As if he'd forgotten the lyrics. There was one awkward moment of silence. Then, without thinking, Cilla picked up where Phil had left off.

Her voice was weak at first, but as she sang, it got stronger. She had been telling Keith the truth – she liked to sing. But it had been a long time since she'd sung in public. Usually, she only sang along to the radio or her iPod.

She pretended that having her sing the final verse and chorus had been the plan all along. Out of the corner of her eye, she caught George's appreciative glance. Keith's nod. Only Phil didn't respond.

He swayed on his seat, his face pasty.

When the song ended, a cheer arose from the crowd gathered at the front of the stage. Keith reached a fist over to her, and she bumped it with her own.

"Thanks for saving his worthless ass," Keith muttered.

George nodded to her. "Nice job," he said quietly.

"Not a problem." She swallowed once, wishing she had a glass of water for her suddenly dry throat. "He okay?"

"He will be." George's voice was hard. "I'll sober him up at the break." He pointed a finger at her, and she straightened her shoulders. Was he going to tell her she'd overstepped? "And you," George said. "We need you to sing. You've got a great set of pipes. And they," he jerked his head at the crowd, "loved it."

Brendan stood behind several people, leaning against the bar as he took another sip of his beer. She had no trouble interpreting his expression. He wasn't even trying to hide his desire as he stared at her.

Answering desire swept through her, and she didn't look away. Their gazes locked for a long moment, then George played the first notes of the next song.

Her face flamed as she dropped her gaze to her keyboard. They were putting on a good show. Exactly as they were supposed to do.

But she was afraid it was more than a show. The heat on her face, the quiver in her belly, felt too damn real. And that was a problem.

CHAPTER FIVE

After she stepped in for Phil, she sang a few more songs and the crowd in front of the stage cheered wildly after each one. She didn't have any illusions they were applauding her vocal abilities.

When she finally stepped off the sage for the first break, Cilla waited for Brendan to approach her, but he couldn't get close. Too many guys had pressed close to the stage. Cilla had to fight her way to the bar, using her elbows when some of them got too close.

All of them wanted to buy her a drink. Ignoring the shouts, she chose one guy at random, drinking deeply when the bartender set an iced tea in front of her. Suddenly, three more arrived and the bartender offered a quick grin.

Her lips twitched. She hoped Rick appreciated the way she was generating tips for him.

She chatted briefly with every guy who was close enough to hear her, sighing in relief when George signaled it was time to start the second set. As she stepped onto the stage, she noticed that Phil's hair was dripping wet. Darker spots dotted the black fabric of his tee shirt, and he seemed more alert. Clearly, George had tried to sober him up.

By the time George set his guitar down for the second break, the crowd had thinned. This time, Brendan was waiting when she stepped off the stage. He held out a hand to help her down, and his fingers tightened on hers for a long moment before he let her go.

"Can I buy you a drink?" he murmured into her ear.

His breath stirred the hair at her temple and made her skin quiver. Heat flushed up her chest and onto her face. She wanted to say it was the heat from the spotlights, but she never lied to herself.

It was Brendan.

Her instincts whispered to move away from him. Instead, she edged a little closer. "I'd love that," she murmured, her voice low and a little raspy from singing.

Loud enough, though, that the other hovering men heard her.

Their faces fell and they retreated to the bar. Rick had her iced tea ready, and Brendan handed him some bills. She took a long drink, easing her parched throat, and then leaned closer.

"You see Romano anywhere tonight?" she breathed into his ear.

"Nope." Brendan tucked a strand of hair behind her ear, and her shiver was real. She didn't have to fake her reaction to him. "I checked a few times. He's not here."

"Too bad. I had hopes for him." She eased away and held his gaze while she fumbled for the plastic glass that held her iced tea. She was afraid the sappy 'thank you' smile wasn't faked, either.

"You never know," he said, his voice strumming across her nerves like velvet on skin. He leaned in a little closer, and she realized the men surrounding them were all listening. "There's still time."

"I guess we'll see, won't we?" She drew one finger down the condensation on the glass, leaving a crooked line behind. "Maybe something will...go down tomorrow night."

Brendan froze. One of the guys behind her groaned.

She pretended she didn't hear him and leaned closer to Brendan.

His eyes darkened as he held her gaze. "I hope you're right."

Cilla put her hand on Brendan's shoulder. His heat burned through the thin material of his blue dress shirt.

"Me, too," she whispered. Her hand involuntarily tightened on his shoulder, then she spotted George and Phil. She let Brendan go and straightened. "Looks like it's time to get back to work."

Phil stepped onto the stage and stumbled, almost crashing into her keyboard. George shoved him toward his seat, saying something to Phil in a low voice. It was impossible to hear what George said, but Phil swallowed and nodded.

"Help you with your equipment later?" Brendan asked, loud enough for other people to hear.

She turned away from George's scowl and Phil's whipped puppy expression and smiled at Brendan. "I'd like that." Then she turned and stepped onto the stage.

Phil had picked up his guitar and was playing some chords. Tuning up, just like she did before she began playing. She leaned toward George. "Everything okay with Phil?"

"Hope so," he said, his voice raspy from years of singing. "Should have dunked the dumb shit again, but I was too pissed off. Was afraid I wouldn't let him up." He glanced at the other guitar player and his mouth tightened. "We're going to have a conversation tomorrow."

"Yeah, sounds like he needs someone to straighten him out."

George eyed her for a moment. "You know any guitar players?"

Her sister played the guitar. But that would be complicated. Olivia was a DA. She'd prosecuted a lot of people. The chance of someone recognizing her might be small, but why risk it? "I know some people," she said casually. "But you and Phil have been playing together for a long time, right? Maybe you should give him a second chance."

George nodded once, and his expression hardened. "We all get wasted once in a while. But the rest of us don't do it before a gig. I'll kick his ass later."

Then he fixed an assessing gaze on her. "No way are you a full-time musician. Or you'd jump at the chance to get your buddy a job. Jump at the chance to sing, too, and we had to twist your arm. You're too nice to be a pro. What's your day job?"

She lifted one shoulder. "I work in an office. In a cubicle. Boring as hell."

"You interested in a long-term gig?"

"I might be," she said cautiously. "But what about your regular keyboard player?"

"You're better than Jerry. And a bigger draw." He nodded to the crowd in the pub. "We should talk sometime."

"Sure."

She turned away to adjust her keyboards, trying hard not to grin like an idiot. She loved being a police officer, in spite of her current status as an untouchable in the department. She had no desire to be a full-time musician.

But, damn! It felt good to be asked.

Two hours later, Cilla was packing up her keyboards and equipment and the pub was emptying. Just like the night before, most people were leaving in pairs.

A woman left by herself. Out of the corner of her eye, Cilla saw Brendan lift his chin at the blond. She took a better look, memorized her features. She'd get the story from him later.

As the blond disappeared through the door, Cilla watched several men heading for the door together. Clearly friends, they were complaining to each other about the poor eyesight and lack of taste in the women at the Pipe and Shamrock.

Two of them had been hanging around in front of the stage, trying to catch her eye. They'd been pissed off when she hadn't taken her up on their drink offers. Cilla bit her lip to hide a smile. Those bros needed an attitude adjustment, but she wasn't going to be the one to deliver it. Her job was to catch a dirtbag drug dealer.

One of the two guys shot her a dirty look as he passed the stage. She smiled at him, which made him scowl. He shoved his buddy into the door frame and pushed outside ahead of him.

Her smile faded. She'd keep her eye on Angry Bro.

She'd mention him to Brendan, too. Guys with anger issues could create havoc on undercover jobs.

Finally, there were only a few stragglers left. She hadn't seen Brendan for a while, and her heart rate quickened as she wondered if he'd found a lead. Had he gone out into the parking lot during the last set? She hadn't seen him leave, but she hadn't been watching every single moment. Occasionally, she'd gotten caught up in a song and realized too late she hadn't been paying attention.

She folded the final stand and put it into the case, then looked around the pub. She didn't want to leave her instruments unattended, but what if Brendan was in the parking lot and needed help?

Swinging the cases onto the stage, she called to Keith, "Keep an eye on these for a minute?"

He waved at her without looking up from the drum set he was breaking down. "Sure."

She was heading out the door when she heard Brendan's voice behind her. "Hey, Cilla. Where are you going?"

She spun around to see him rounding the end of the bar, heading for her. Her shoulders relaxed and she took a deep breath. "Hey," she said. "I figured you'd left and was going out to open my car."

"Told you I'd help you." He drew her to the side, into a corner near the bar so people could go around them. "You weren't running away from me, were you?"

She touched her shoulder to his upper arm and pretended to nuzzle his neck. "Thought you might have gone outside and needed help."

"Yeah?" He wrapped an arm around her waist and pulled her against him. "Thanks for worrying." His mouth brushed her ear, and she swallowed. They were pretending. Putting on a show. But her body hadn't gotten the memo yet.

She was reacting as though it was real. As if this heat between them was more than acting.

Forcing herself to smile and relax into him, she murmured, "Wouldn't want you to get hurt tonight. Not before we..." She put her mouth to his ear and pretended to whisper naughty things to him.

His hand tightened on her waist, his fingers digging into her side as if he really was anticipating a night of passion. "Let's get your stuff in your car."

"Anxious?" she purred.

"You would not believe how anxious I am."

She looked up to see Keith watching them. When she caught the drummer's eye, he looked away. But not before she saw his scowl.

She hoped Keith wasn't going to go all protective on her.

She swung her keyboard cases off the stage and Brendan plucked them from her hands. They walked into the warm autumn air and headed for her car. The shadows were just as dark as last night. The parking lot had the same slightly seedy atmosphere as the night before – broken glass from an empty Jack bottle next to the dumpster, weeds growing up through the fissures in the asphalt, cracked pane of glass in the kitchen window. But there was no sense of danger tonight.

Was it because Romano wasn't watching as they walked to her car?

Or was it because Brendan made her feel safe?

She'd never needed a guy to feel safe. She was a cop. She carried a gun. And she knew how to fight. But having

Brendan at her side felt comfortable. Reassuring.

She'd done undercover jobs alone. It was nice to have a partner this time.

Don't lie to yourself. It was nice to have Brendan as a partner.

The chemistry between them was off the charts. And that was good. Perfect for the job. Still, after the job was over, they'd shake hands and walk away to their next assignments.

Exactly as she liked it.

This time, she might glance over her shoulder as she left. But she'd keep walking.

"Earth to Cilla," Brendan said softly as he stood next to her car, her keyboard cases in his hands.

Hoping the darkness hid the rush of color into her face, she fumbled in the small bag she carried for her keys. Her fingers brushed her side piece, a small Sig P238, and the cold metal steadied her. Reminded her of why she was here.

"Sorry," she muttered, popping the hatch. "Thinking about the job."

Brendan slid the cases into the back and closed the door. He glanced over her shoulder and stepped closer to her. "I watched a group of four guys for awhile," he said into her ear. He slid his hand up her arm. "Two of them are standing next to their car, watching us."

Cilla glanced over Brendan's shoulder. Sure enough, Angry Bro and his friend were glaring at her. "I noticed them inside." She gripped his shirt in both hands. "Maybe you should mark your territory."

One side of his mouth curled up. "My pleasure."

He edged her around the side of the car, putting his hands over hers to keep them on his chest. Once they were silhouetted for the watching guys, he cupped her face in his hands and lowered his mouth to hers.

***

Her lips were smooth. Warm. Soft. She leaned into him, and a lock of her hair fell across his face. Its citrusy scent surrounded him, and his cock stirred. The idiot didn't know this was make-believe.

He didn't want it to be make-believe.

Brendan tucked the long, caramel-colored waves behind her ear and dismissed the thought. That was his cock talking. He didn't want a serious relationship. All his energy went to his job and his...other pursuits. Pursuits he didn't name, even to himself. Naming might jinx it.

He nuzzled Cilla's neck, sucking lightly at the soft skin beneath her ear. She gasped and gripped his shirt more tightly.

Yeah, they would pretend really well. They'd sell it to the crowd at the Pipe and Shamrock, he thought, as he trailed his mouth over her cheek and back to her lips.

He crowded her into the side of the car, slipping one leg between hers. He sucked her lower lip into his mouth, touching his tongue to the vulnerable skin inside her lip. Her breasts flattened against his chest as he pressed closer, and her hard nipples sent blood rushing to his groin.

Cilla let go of his shirt, and he figured she was going to shove him away. But instead, she wrapped her arms around his neck and opened for him.

She tasted like the iced tea she'd been drinking, tart and lemony. He curled his tongue around hers and felt her breath catch. She shuddered, then suddenly she was kissing him back.

One of her legs curled around his, pulling him closer. Her hands roamed his back, dipping down to his hips. Playing with his waistband, as if she might slide both palms inside and over his ass. When he tugged up her sparkly tee shirt, the garment that had taunted him all night, her breath stuttered again.

Her abdomen was smooth and firm. The muscles quivered beneath his fingers, and as he moved higher, she held her breath.

The tiny part of his brain that wasn't focused on Cilla heard a car engine roar to life behind them. The driver accelerated until the engine screamed in protest, then pulled away, tires squealing.

Cilla would stop him now. The need for the show was over. The guys who'd been staring at Cilla were gone.

But she didn't stop kissing him. Instead, she burrowed one finger beneath the waistband of his jeans and tickled the small of his back. He groaned into her mouth and shoved his hand beneath her bra.

She moaned, a needy, desperate sound that traveled straight to his groin. Her breast fit his hand perfectly. Its pebbled nipple burned his palm, urging him to taste it. He wanted to unleash more of those sounds. He wanted to hear her chant his name when her legs were wrapped around his waist and they had far less clothing on.

His hips jerked into hers in time with the strokes of his tongue. He shoved her shirt and bra up to her neck, but it was too dark to see the color of her nipples. He desperately wanted to know. Wanted to see them in the light. Needed to watch her face as he licked them.

Her whole hand was on his ass now, gripping and releasing. Gripping and releasing. He fumbled for the car door. Inside. Back seat. Horizontal. Now.

A car door slammed close by. Keith called, "Night, Cilla. Remember what I said."

He'd warned her about the guys at the pub. That they only wanted to hook up.

Cilla jerked as if she'd touched a live wire and broke the kiss. She leaned back, studying his face. Her chest rose and fell too fast, and her hands tightened on his ass. Then dropped away as if his skin was electrified and had just sent a shock up her arm.

She tugged her shirt down. "Wow. I guess Angry Bro and his buddy got an eyeful."

"Yeah," he said, remembering the way he'd lifted her shirt and exposed her. Regretting the way she'd covered up again. "Sorry. I didn't mean to get carried away."

She lifted one shoulder. "Good that they saw, right? Sends the message." She opened her car door and slid inside. "See you tomorrow night?"

He grabbed the door as she tried to pull it closed. "No. We need to talk. Come to my place tomorrow. Or I'll go to yours."

Her hands gripped the steering wheel so hard that her knuckles whitened. "Nothing to talk about," she said. "We were doing our job. Setting up our cover story. Don't worry about it."

His chest tightened. Had it all been make believe for her? "Not what I was talking about. We need to compare notes on what we saw tonight." He leaned close enough to smell her orange-y shampoo. "But maybe we need to talk about that kiss, too."

CHAPTER SIX

Cilla's hands shook as she drove out of the parking lot. She didn't look in the rear view mirror. She was afraid she'd turn the car around if Brendan was watching her.

As soon as she was out of sight, she let out the breath she'd been holding. She'd forgotten they were playing a role. Forgotten the people watching them from the parking lot.

She'd forgotten everything but Brendan's mouth devouring hers and his hands caressing her body.

Damn it!

When their lips touched, the facade of Cilla the flirty keyboard player had vanished and real Cilla took her place. Real Cilla was the woman who'd wanted him since he'd pulled her over on the Dan Ryan Expressway. The woman who looked at his hands and his mouth and imagined him doing exactly what he'd done tonight.

She pressed the accelerator a little harder. Real Cilla needed to remember why she didn't get involved with cops.

Especially right now. After her arrest of Ryan Ward, she had a target on her back. Maybe Brendan already knew about that fiasco. Maybe he was looking for a little payback.

He didn't seem like the type, but she wasn't going to take

any chances. She'd do her job and she'd keep her distance from Brendan. She wouldn't let him tempt her with what she couldn't have.

Didn't want, even if she could have him.

He was a cop, after all. And her Aunt Jessie's pinched face and her mother's warnings about cops were burned into her brain.

They don't make good husbands.

They'd rather hang at a bar with their cop buddies than come home to a wife and kids.

They cheat.

Cilla tried to block Brendan's image by thinking about the Mustang. Her baby. It needed an oil change. Maybe she'd do that tomorrow. It would be good to get some grease on her hands. Tinker with her engine for a couple of hours. Wipe the memory of Brendan's passion-filled blue eyes out of her brain.

By the time she got home to her apartment in Chicago's Lakeview neighborhood, her heart had stopped racing and the burn of lust had dissipated. A few embers smoldered, but she could ignore those.

Until she was around Brendan again a tiny, irritating voice whispered. Then those embers would flare to life.

She pulled her car into the garage she rented, patted the Mustang's fender as she slid past it, and hoisted the keyboards out of the cargo area of the SUV. She wasn't going to waste another minute thinking about Brendan Donovan.

***

She rolled over when her phone rang. Trying to drag her eyes open, she snatched it off the nightstand and stabbed the button to connect the call. "Marini," she growled.

There was a pause. Then Brendan's familiar voice said, "Well, aren't you Mary Sunshine this morning." His voice dropped to the low purr she remembered all too well. "I bet I could adjust your attitude about waking up."

"You got coffee you can pour through the phone?" She pushed up so she was leaning against her headboard. "'Cause that's the only thing that adjusts my attitude when I'm woken up at the ungodly hour of..." she glanced at her clock, "nine AM."

"Nine?" She could practically hear his grin. "Something keep you awake last night? A lot on your mind?"

Yes. You. "Yeah. I got sucked into a book. Hard to put it down."

"Glad to hear you're a night person." His voice went low and throaty. Sexy. "There's so much fun to be had in the dark."

She ignored the shiver that trailed down her spine. "Cut the crap, Donovan. We're not at the pub. What do you want?"

Another pause. "We need to get together," he said, all the sexy gone from his voice. "My place. Figure you don't want me in your space."

Impersonal, business-like Brendan was back. That was good. That's who she wanted. Not the guy with temptation oozing out of every pore. "What time?" She could be business-like, too.

"How about noon?"

"That works. Text me your address. I'll pick up some lunch on my way. Any requests?"

"How about Chipotle? Carnitas burrito for me. Hot sauce."

She resisted saying he already had more than enough hot sauce. "Got it. See you at noon." The phone disconnected, and she stared at the screen for a long moment before setting it back on the nightstand. She wanted to know how he switched it off and on. She'd like an 'off' button, too.

She'd spent half the night thinking about Brendan and those moments next to her car. Which was why she was grouchy and still sleeping at nine in the morning.

Sighing, she got out of bed and padded into the kitchen to start her coffee maker. She needed to keep her hands busy and her mind engaged this morning. As soon as she gulped some coffee, she'd spend some quality time with the Mustang. Maybe she'd be able to focus on that instead of what had happened with Brendan last night.

***

Brendan lived in an older apartment building, surprisingly close to her place. The building was shaped like a U, with two long wings and a short wing connecting them. A wrought-iron fence and gate stretched across the courtyard, which had been planted with trees, shrubs and flowers. Creamy orange canna lilies bloomed next to a small pond and multi-colored flowers mounded against the building walls.

It was a classy place. Not exactly where she'd pictured Brendan living.

Maybe he had hidden depths.

She pressed the bell next to his name, balancing the two books of mug shots and the bag with their lunch. The scent from the burritos made her stomach growl.

The gate buzzed open a moment later. When she reached the door, he was waiting in the tiny lobby, holding the inner door open with his foot.

"Hey," he said, taking the large binders from her, his eyes twinkling. "You showed up. Wasn't sure you would."

"I said I'd be here." She let the door slam a little too hard. "I do what I say I'm gonna do."

"Good to know." He gestured for her to precede him up the stairs. When she got to the top step, she stood aside and waited for him. He led her down a softly lit hallway with a slightly worn floral carpet to an unlocked door, then pushed it open.

"Come on in," he said.

The apartment was small but inviting. The kitchen had

old oak cabinets and was big enough to hold a tiny table. A faded floral couch sat in the good-sized living room, in front of windows looking onto the courtyard. A half-closed door off to the side was probably his bedroom. She swallowed and tore her gaze away from that door.

Bookshelves against one wall were filled with books, both paperbacks and hardcovers. On some shelves, the books were stacked on their sides, filling the space completely. A desk stood near the bookshelves, a computer standing open on top of it. Framed pictures lined the front of the desk, and she wandered over to study them.

As she approached, she caught a glimpse of the computer screen. She glanced over her shoulder and raised her eyebrows. "You read that blog, too?"

Faint color washed his cheeks and he shoved the lid down on the computer. "Yeah, I read it. Do you?"

"Of course. And there's nothing to be embarrassed about," she said, watching the color recede from his face. "Pretty much all the cops I know read 'Cops and Robbers'."

"Yeah, that's why I was reading it. Heard it was interesting."

"He has to be on the job. No one but a Chicago cop could know some of that stuff." She studied him for a moment, wondering at the hint of discomfort in his expression. "Do you know who it is? Is that why you look like a kid with his hand in the cookie jar?"

He lifted one shoulder. "I don't think anyone knows. And you know cops – nothing they like as much as gossip. If anyone knew, we'd all know. Maybe it's just a guy with a good imagination making stuff up."

Cilla shook her head. "He gets too many details right. Uses language only another cop would know."

Brendan shrugged. "A mystery, I guess."

"And who doesn't love a mystery? The more people talk about 'Cops and Robbers', the more intriguing it gets."

"Maybe." He glanced at the brown bag in her left hand. "You took my lunch suggestion, I see."

He was changing the subject, but she didn't mind. She was hungry. "Yeah. I love Chipotle." She lifted the bag. "Let's eat while they're still hot."

"You want a beer to go with that?" he said as he headed to the kitchen.

"No, thanks. We're working tonight."

"Just thought I'd offer. I have a few cans of soda from the last party. Iced tea. Orange juice."

"Iced tea would be great."

He drew a pitcher out of the refrigerator, poured two glasses and handed her one. She raised her eyebrows when she tasted it. "Brewed tea."

"I knew you liked it. Easy enough to make it."

A curl of warmth unfurled in her chest. "Nice of you."

"Not a big deal."

He pulled out a chair for her, then sat across from her and lifted a burrito and a burrito bowl out of the bag. As she dug into her bowl, Cilla looked around the apartment.

"I like your place. It's not exactly where I pictured you living."

"No?" He took another bite, swallowed it and said, "Let me guess. You had me in some slick, soulless place, all black and white modern furniture and dirty dishes in the sink."

"I hadn't pictured the dirty dishes," she said, her lips curling up. "This place feels comfortable. Homey."

"Why wouldn't it? I spend a lot of time here."

"Do you...are you living with someone?" she blurted. The moment the words were out, she wanted to snatch them back. Her question implied that she cared about the answer.

The corner of his mouth twitched. "You're a good detective, recognizing the feminine touches." His smile widened. "Would you be disappointed if I said yes?"

"I'd feel sorry for the woman," she retorted.

Brendan grinned. "You can save your sympathy. I'm the only one who lives here. The feminine touches are leftovers from my brother's girlfriend Raine. It used to be her place. She left the couch, the kitchen table and a few other things when she moved in with Connor."

"Convenient for you."

"It was. She needed to sublet and I was looking for a new apartment. Worked out great for both of us."

Cilla scooped up some guacamole and black beans from her burrito bowl. "Do you have a big family?"

"Yeah." His expression softened. "Three older brothers and a younger sister. All cops except Mac, the oldest. He's an FBI agent."

"Wow. Talk about a family tradition."

Brendan lifted one shoulder. "My dad was a cop. Killed by a drunk driver while on duty. We were raised with his stories. I guess that's why we all became cops."

A shadow crossed his face, gone almost before she realized what it was. She rested her elbow on the table, propped her chin in her hand and watched him. "Are you sorry you followed the rest of your family into the business?"

He waited a beat too long to answer. "No," he finally said. "I like what I do. I like the hunt. The chase. I like getting the bad guys off the street."

"Sounds like there's a big 'but' in there."

He rolled his shoulders. "I think everyone has second thoughts sometimes about the career they chose." He leaned closer, until she could see the navy blue spots in his aquamarine irises. "You love what you do all the time? Ever regret becoming a cop?"

After she'd arrested Ryan Ward, she'd had a lot of regrets. She took her elbow off the table and clenched her hands in her lap. "Maybe we all do, once in a while."

He nodded. "If you don't, you're probably in the wrong profession."

Cilla blinked and studied Brendan more carefully. That was a surprisingly perceptive statement. Especially from a guy she'd dismissed as a cowboy adrenaline junkie. "Yeah. You're right." But she didn't want to talk about her own dark night of the soul.

She stood up and collected her cardboard bowl and the foil from Brendan's burrito. "Where's your trash?"

"Beneath the sink." The chair scraped against the floor as he stood up. "You have any siblings, Cilla?"

It sounded as if he was as eager to change the subject as she was. She opened the cabinet and deposited the trash in the white plastic bin. "Yeah," she said, closing the door and turning around to find him closer than she'd expected. "A brother and a sister. Olivia is an assistant DA. Sam plays baseball."

"In college?"

"No, on a minor league team."

His expression sharpened. "Sam Marini? Isn't he one of the Cubs' hot prospects?"

She rolled her eyes. "Yeah. We try not to let it go to his head."

Brendan laughed as he picked up a sponge and wiped down the table. "If he has any swelling head problems, I'll talk to him for you. Being a hot prospect for the Cubs isn't that big a deal. Bunch of losers."

"Not for long," she retorted, fighting her smile. "They've picked up some amazing free agents and they're going to be great in the next few years."

"Yeah, great at losing."

"Sox fan, huh?"

"Of course. It's the only professional baseball team in Chicago."

"I'll make you eat your words when the Cubs win the World Series."

"You're on," he said immediately. "Want to put your money where your mouth is?"

Betting with him about the Cubs was implying they'd be...friends down the road. But she was surprisingly reluctant to point out the fallacy in his thinking. "Sure. How much you in for?"

"A hundred bucks says the Cubs don't make it to the

Series in the next five years."

"Done," she said immediately. "That's a sucker bet, because I know they will."

"In your dreams, maybe."

"You better put that hundred aside, 'cause you're going to be giving it to me."

"You keep telling yourself that." He headed toward the living room. "Come sit down. I've got some books of mug shots, too. We can go through all of them."

The abrupt change of direction threw her for a moment. Then her cheeks heated. Looking at mug shots, discussing what had happened the night before, was the reason she was here.

Not talking smack about Chicago's baseball teams or having a 'first date' conversation about their families.

As she began to sit down, her phone rang. She pulled it out and saw Sam's smiling face. "Excuse me," she said. "I need to take this. My brother."

She hit the connect icon as she walked into the kitchen. "Sam. How's it going?"

"Great, Cil. We're in the minor league playoffs. Doing pretty good."

"Yeah, I saw an article in the Trib sports section. Even mentioned you," she teased. "Talked about your game with three strike-outs, Mr. Phenom."

"Ouch," he said, and she could hear the grin in his voice. "Nothing like a big sister to take a guy down a peg."

"Just keeping you the humble Sam we all know and love. So how are you doing otherwise?"

He drew in a deep breath. "Good, except for one thing."

Here it comes. "What's that?" she asked.

"I got a speeding ticket. I was hoping you could do something about it."

"A speeding ticket? Sam, are you kidding me? You're in Iowa. What makes you think I can do anything about a speeding ticket out there?"

"You're a cop. I figured you'd know what to do."

"Were you actually speeding?"

There was a long pause. "Yeah," he finally said. "Twenty over."

"For God's sake, Sam." She was getting tired of being the family 'fixer'. "Plead guilty, pay the fine and ask for supervision. You stay clean for three months and it's off your record."

"Yeah, but..."

"You're already on supervision," she sighed.

"Yeah."

"You know what, Sam? I'm working right now. I'll see what I can figure out and get back to you. Okay?"

"Thanks, Cill. You're the best."

"Damn right I am. I'll talk to you later."

Stabbing the 'off' button, she slid the phone into her pocket and sat down on the couch. Then she grabbed one of the heavy books. "Who are we looking for?"

Instead of answering, Brendan said, "Trouble?"

She glared at him. "I'm sure you heard every word. My idiot brother got a speeding ticket, and he's already on supervision. He wants me to fix it for him."

Brendan's face softened. "You're a good sister, Marini."

"Too good," she muttered. "He needs to figure stuff out for himself." Her mother and sister did, too. But they all called Cilla.

"Tell me what I'm looking for," she said, making it clear that the conversation about her family was over.

"The blond woman I pointed out at the end of the night," Brendan said. "Her name is Holly, although that could have been a lie. She was talking to Tiffany, and Tiffany has ignored every other woman in the pub."

He described their conversation and Holly's obvious disinterest in him.

Cilla raised her eyebrows. "And because she wasn't all over you, you assumed she's there for some nefarious reason?"

Instead of being offended, Brendan moved closer to her.

"I like a woman who uses words like nefarious. That's hot."

His breath was warm on her cheek. She swallowed and fumbled the book open. "Let's see if we can find her."

***

Brendan leaned against the back of the couch and shoved the last book onto the table in frustration. His back ached and a hammer pounded inside his head. "Well, that was a waste of time. Maybe she's never been arrested, but she was at the Pipe and Shamrock for a reason. And it wasn't fun and games."

Next to him, Cilla vibrated like she was holding a live wire. She clearly loved this undercover stuff. "You think she's our dealer?"

He thought about Holly for a moment. He'd kept an eye on her last night. "She wasn't talking to a lot of people," he finally said. "So I don't think so. She mostly sat at the bar, nursing her drink and watching everyone else."

"She talked to you," Cilla pointed out.

"I sat down next to her and engaged her. And she wasn't interested."

"Did she seek Tiffany out? Or did Tiffany go to her?"

"Damn good question." He thought about the interaction between the two women. "I think Tiffany went to Holly."

"Maybe Tiffany thought Holly was a rival. Maybe she was checking her out."

"Possible," he conceded. "But that still doesn't explain why Holly's there."

Cilla shrugged. "Maybe she comes to listen to the music."

"Yeah, that's possible, too." He shoved his hand through his hair. "I guess we need to give it more time."

"It's only been two days." Cilla smiled, softening her expression and lighting up her eyes. Her mouth curved, and he remembered how she'd tasted. How she'd shivered when he'd kissed her.

He remembered the tiny moan she'd made when his tongue tangled with hers.

Damn it. He'd been doing really well this afternoon, focusing on business instead of that kiss last night.

Now Cilla's mouth was all he could think about.

When he lifted his gaze from her mouth, her smile had faded. But her cheeks were flushed and her chest rose and fell too quickly.

She fumbled the book she still held onto the table and stood up, smoothing her hands down her thighs. "I should get going."

He stood up as well and reached for her. She wasn't going to get away until they talked about that kiss last night.

As he touched her arm, his phone rang. Curling his fingers around her wrist, he reached into his pocket for his phone.

Connor. "Hold on a minute. I need to get this."

Cilla nodded as he pushed the 'call' button. "Hey, Con. What's up?"

"You know Jack Murphy, right?"

"Yeah. I've worked with him a couple of times."

"He's been shot. Chest wound. He's at Northwestern."

His stomach clenched and his throat tightened. He swallowed hard and said, "I'm leaving now."

He took a deep, stuttering breath and shoved the phone back into his pocket. Cilla clutched his sleeve. "What's wrong?"

"Cujo's been shot."

CHAPTER SEVEN

Brendan slammed through the emergency room doors, Cilla trailing behind him. He'd told her to go home, but she'd insisted on coming with him. Insisted on driving, too.

She'd woven in and out of traffic on Lake Shore Drive, her foot pressing on the accelerator until his teeth ached from clenching them. But she'd gotten them to Northwestern Memorial in record time. She'd tossed the keys to her SUV to the valet in front of the hospital, stopped long enough to grab her ticket, then ran after Brendan toward the emergency room.

He spotted Connor, standing in the middle of a group of cops from Con's district. Clumps of other cops dotted the waiting room, some in uniform, others in plain clothes. A bunch from his own district stood in the corner, heads bowed, murmuring together.

Cujo was from Belmont. His district.

Instead of heading toward them, he shoved his hands into his pockets and walked toward the group from Town Hall. Con and Quinn and Mia's district.

"Hey." Con's voice was too high. Jittery. "Thanks for

coming, Bren."

"Wouldn't be anywhere else."

Con jerked his head toward the corner. "Belmont's over there."

"Yeah, I saw them. Wanted to thank you for calling me." He'd wanted to see his brother. Reassure himself Connor was okay.

Connor's face softened and he squeezed Brendan's shoulder. "Knew you'd want to know."

"Yeah. Hear anything yet?"

"Not a thing." Connor shrugged, but his foot tapped the floor. "Nurses are a damn close-mouthed bunch."

The doors to the ER whooshed again, and Cilla stepped into the room. A few older guys from the 16th stood on the other side of the room, but she ignored them. Didn't meet anyone's gaze. She leaned against the wall, as if trying to make herself invisible.

Which was a waste of time. Cilla was the most vivid person he'd ever met.

He waited for her to join a group, and when she didn't, he caught her eye and jerked his head, telling her to join them. She shook her head, a short, choppy motion, and looked away.

What the hell? They were partners. Temporarily, but still. Partners stuck together.

He started toward her, but before he reached her, Ryan Ward broke away from a group and headed for Cilla.

Brendan walked faster. He knew what had happened between Cilla and Ward.

He got close enough to hear Ward say, "What are you doing here, Marini?"

She held Ward's gaze and said evenly, "Same as you. Standing with a brother."

"You're not wanted here." Ward flexed his fingers, then shoved his hands into his pockets.

Brendan wanted to step between them, but Cilla gave him a sharp warning glare before returning her gaze to

Ward. "You going to make me leave? Slap me around a little, like that woman in the alley?" She raised an eyebrow. "You must have liked the cuffs last time."

Shit. She was goading the guy. Why didn't she just ignore him?

She stood straight, her gaze locked onto Ward's. Arms crossed over her chest. Daring Ward to come after her.

That was Cilla, Brendan realized. She'd never back down. Would always face a threat head-on.

He was lucky to be her partner, even temporarily.

The room had fallen silent. Quiet enough to hear the squeak of shoes behind the double door into the ER. Everyone stood frozen, but the air hummed with tension. Anger. Suppressed violence.

Cilla and the blond cop stared at each other, neither of them backing down.

Ward took a step toward Cilla, but she stood straighter. Narrowed her eyes. "You're a piece of shit, Ward. But I'd come here for you, too. So go to hell."

Ward sucked in a breath. Then, with a muttered curse, he spun around and stalked away. Brendan stepped in front of him.

Ward raised his arm and pulled it back, but dropped his fisted hand in time. "What do you want, Donovan?"

"No grudges in the ER, Ward. She wants to be here, she's here. She's one of us."

"You fucking her? That why you're defending her?"

Brendan curled his fingers, resisting the urge to smash them into Ward's smug face. "Marini doesn't need me. She's doing a damn good job of sticking up for herself." He shook his head. "Bates deserves better than a partner like you. She's right. You're that stinking pile on the sidewalk everyone steers clear of."

He deliberately turned his back on Ward and found Connor right behind him. His brother watched Ward as he crossed the room, then turned back to Brendan. "Nice job," he said quietly.

Connor glanced at Cilla and jerked his head in the universal sign for 'come here'. She stared at both of them for a long moment, then strolled over to join them.

"I'm Connor. This one's brother," he said, holding out his hand. "Good to meet you, Marini."

Cilla shook Connor's hand. "Thanks. You, too." Her face was pale, and her hands shook. When she saw Brendan staring at them, she shoved them into her pockets.

Brendan grabbed her wrist and pulled her toward an unoccupied corner of the waiting room, away from the other cops. "Why did you stand there by yourself? You're my partner. Partners stick together."

Cilla eased her wrist out of Brendan's grasp. "We're partners on this job. At the pub. With other cops?" She lifted one shoulder. "Standing with me isn't a good idea."

"Good idea or bad one, doesn't matter." He glanced across the room at Ward, who was facing away from him, talking to another cop. He wanted to beat the crap out of Ward. But he wasn't going to start something in the ER waiting room.

Brendan returned his gaze to hers. "Don't do that again, Cilla. Don't think I'm going to shun you when other cops are around. It'll never happen."

She swallowed. Blinked a couple of times. Then nodded. "Thanks, Brendan. That...that means a lot."

"Cops are assholes sometimes."

She managed a smile, although it didn't reach her eyes. "Except for the Donovans, apparently."

He shrugged. He'd had his moments of asshole-ness. "Including me."

"He's right about that." Connor nudged his shoulder. "Guy has pulled some stunts you wouldn't believe."

Connor studied Cilla for a long moment, then nodded. "You have some big cojones, Marini, showing up here. Gotta hand it to you."

"Knock it off, Con," Brendan said sharply.

His brother held up his hands. "Down, tiger. I wasn't

telling her she didn't belong. I was admiring her guts." Connor elbowed him in the side. "Walking into a roomful of already-angry cops was a ballsy move. You're damn lucky to be working with her, little brother."

"Yeah." Brendan exhaled. "I know it."

"So bring her to dinner."

Brendan froze. His older brothers had all introduced their girlfriends at one of the monthly family dinners. His gaze skittered away from Cilla and back to Connor, who was walking away.

"It's not like that," he called after his brother.

Connor glanced over his shoulder. "You do know all of us said the same thing, right?"

"Bite me, Con."

"Said that, too."

Brendan stared after his brother for a long moment. He should be panicking. If Connor thought he had something going on with Cilla, his brothers would be brutal with their ragging. Payback for the way he'd teased them when they'd brought their girlfriends around.

This tightness in his chest didn't feel like panic, though. It felt like...anticipation.

Because he wanted to have sex with Cilla. That's all it meant.

Clearly, Con had noticed.

He swung around to face Cilla again. Her expression was less guarded, and the tension in her shoulders had eased.

"I should get going," she said, clearing her throat. "I don't want to cause problems for you."

"You're not causing problems for me." He spotted a guy standing by himself. Greg Harrison. Cujo's partner. "Harrison looks like he could use some company." Without thinking, he put his hand on Cilla's back to guide her toward the other cop. Dropped it when he felt her tense.

"Don't," she said quietly.

"You didn't seem to mind last night."

She shot him a glare and moved farther away. "Last night we were on the job. Putting on a show. Today we're in a room full of other cops. Completely different message, Donovan."

He'd just wanted to touch her. He hadn't thought about where they were. He sighed. "Sorry. Still thinking about last night."

She stumbled, but kept walking and didn't look at him. "Start thinking with your big head, Brendan. We're in a hospital waiting room. Cujo's on the other side of the door."

That's why he was thinking about sex with Cilla. The whole 'prove you're alive thing'. "Yeah. Got it. I'm an idiot."

She stopped and turned to him. "Don't say that, Brendan. You and your brother just did a huge thing for me." She nodded at the other cops. "You stood for me when no one else would. They're all still watching, but they're not so hostile about it. You and Connor defused that. So thank you."

He shrugged one shoulder. "You're my partner. Okay? Let's go talk to Harrison."

When they reached the tall blond cop, Brendan squeezed his shoulder. "How're you doing, buddy?"

"How do you think I'm doing?" He scrubbed his hands over his face. "Cujo just took off running. I tried to stop him, but he saw the guy we were after and shook me off. It would've taken him three seconds to fasten his vest, but the dumb-ass didn't do it. That's why he took the round to his chest." Harrison turned and kicked a row of chairs, sending them crashing over backward. "Damn cowboy. I'm gonna kick his ass the minute he gets out of here."

He nodded at Cilla. "Marini. Good of you to show up."

Brendan moved closer to Cilla. "Your buddy Ward didn't think so."

Harrison shook his head, his eyes red. "Ward's a hothead. Doesn't think before he acts. Just like Jack." He glanced from Brendan to Cilla. "But if you're standing for Marini, she's okay. You Donovans are solid."

Cilla took a half-step closer to Harrison. "What do you need, Greg? Food? Coffee?"

Harrison ran his hand over his unshaven face. "Coffee would be great. Had some from the machine over there." He jerked his head to a bank of vending machines against one wall. "Hard to believe, but it was worse than the station's."

"I'll get you a cup," Cilla said. Brendan started to follow her, but she shook her head. "Stay with him," she said softly.

Cilla disappeared down a hall, and Brendan steered Harrison to a pair of empty chairs. Both men sat heavily. Neither of them spoke. They stared at the door to the ER.

Brendan closed his eyes. Cujo hadn't taken the time to fasten his vest. Now he was behind those doors, fighting for his life.

That could have been me.

How many times had he done something stupid? Reckless? Too jumped up on the rush to think first?

Too many to count.

The highlight reel of his stop of Cilla on the Dan Ryan a few weeks ago unspooled in his head. He hadn't waited for a license check. Hadn't called for backup. She'd called him a stupid cop, and she'd been right.

He'd been lucky he'd stopped another cop instead of a banger in a stolen car. One day, though, his luck would run out.

Just like Cujo's had today.

Brendan shoved the thought away. "He's a fighter," he said.

"Hard to fight a piece of lead in your chest."

Brendan nudged Harrison's shoulder with his. "You know the docs here are the best in the city."

Harrison bowed his head, let his hands hang beneath his knees. "I should have stopped him," he said, so quietly that

Brendan could barely hear him. "I should have made him fasten the damn vest before he took off."

"Not your fault," Brendan said automatically. But he knew Harrison didn't buy it. Most cops felt responsible when their partner got shot. The ones that didn't? No one wanted to partner with those guys.

"I know how he is. I shouldn't have let him run off without his vest secured."

"What are you, his mother?" Brendan rested his elbows on his knees. "Even she wouldn't have been able to stop him. And you know it, Harrison. He was Mad Dog coming out of the academy, and he morphed into Cujo for a reason."

Brendan knew no one would be able to stop him if the juice was buzzing and he was in pursuit. He slumped in the chair, resting his head against the wall. What if he'd been the one shot? Would he want his partner to carry that guilt for the rest of her life?

He swallowed hard. Of course not. He wouldn't put that burden on anyone's shoulders.

Especially not Cilla's.

The doors to the ER opened and a doctor stepped out. "Family of Jack Murphy?"

Every cop in the room surged toward her, including Brendan and Harrison. The doctor, a short, slender woman with hair escaping from a bun on the top of her head, said, "He's been moved to surgery. The waiting area is on the second floor. Follow the orange signs."

"How's he doing?" someone asked.

"It's touch and go," she said after a moment. "But he's young and strong. That's in his favor." She looked around at the crowd. "He's already received four units of blood, and he'll need more during surgery. If anyone wants to donate, you can check with the receptionist in the surgical waiting area."

Harrison stood up. "Thanks, Donovan," he said, then headed for the orange sign on the far side of the waiting room. In a couple of minutes, the waiting room had emptied except for a mother holding a fretful child and an old man wearing worn and patched clothes, dozing against the wall.

And his brother Connor.

"Where did Marini go?" he asked.

"Getting coffee for Harrison."

His brother nodded. "I'll wait and take it up to him. You probably need to get ready for your job tonight."

Brendan glanced at his watch. Almost four in the afternoon. "Yeah. We do."

He wanted to stand vigil for Cujo. But he and Cilla had a job to do. "Thanks, Con. If we go upstairs, I won't want to leave."

"I'll let you know as soon as we hear anything," Connor promised.

"I know you will." He hesitated. "Do Quinn and Mia know?"'

"Yeah. They're both at a scene in Uptown. I'm keeping them posted."

It was hard to walk away. Especially when he knew it could have been him in that operating room. His brothers and sister and mother, waiting in the sterile room on the second floor that was supposed to look cheerful but instead was smothered in grief and fear and pain.

In his mind, he saw himself on the operating table, blood pouring out of his chest. Spattering the nurses and doctors, running in rivulets off the table. Saw his mother and Mia and Helen, sobbing in the waiting room. His brothers punching stuff.

He cursed his imagination as it churned out picture after picture. Each one more gruesome, more morbid than the last.

He needed to save it for the work at his apartment, the diversion he'd been playing with for a very long time.

What would it take before he got serious about it?

CHAPTER EIGHT

As Cilla walked down the long corridor toward the emergency room, the scent of coffee clashed with the acrid tang of disinfectant. Her stomach rolled.

At least the coffee warmed her cold hands. She'd been cold since Brendan got the call about Cujo. Shaking with it as she drove down Lake Shore Drive toward the hospital.

Frozen by the time she'd stepped into the ER.

She'd known what would be waiting for her. A furious crowd of cops, all looking for a fight.

The glares. The scowls. The deliberately turned backs. None of it was a surprise.

Waiting in the hospital after a fellow cop was shot was emotional. Terrifying. An ugly, wrenching mixture of fear and anger. Would the wounded man or woman survive? Would they catch the shooter?

Would one of the cops in that waiting room be the next one wheeled into a hospital?

She'd steeled herself to stare them all down. So she wasn't shocked when Ryan Ward got in her face. She'd faced him without flinching.

The only surprise was that it hadn't been worse.

She credited the Donovans for that. Brendan and his brother had stepped in. Defended her. Brendan had called out Ward and the cops who stood with him.

Why the hell had he done that?

He'd shouldered her burden without blinking. Simply stepped up and stood with her. Because they were partners.

It couldn't possibly be that simple.

Brendan had acted as though it was.

With the Donovan brothers flanking her, warmth had unfurled inside her. The layers of ice in her chest had begun to thaw, cracking and grinding together as they shrank. She'd wanted to grab Brendan's hand and hang on.

She'd shoved her hands into her pockets instead.

Brendan's brother, too, had acted as if it was no big deal. Connor, who had never even met her. But he was familiar, because he looked so much like Brendan. Same blue, blue eyes. Same dark, slightly wavy hair. Same lean, rangy build.

Connor was more settled than Brendan, though. As if he didn't have as much to prove.

She'd bet he was less reckless than Brendan, as well.

She swallowed the hard lump in her throat as she remembered Brendan stopping her on the Dan Ryan a few weeks earlier. He'd been as reckless as Cujo apparently had been. He hadn't waited for information about her car. Had he even been wearing his vest?

Her stomach clenched. She couldn't remember. But what if it hadn't been her in the Mustang? What if it had been some jumpy, coked-up kid who'd just jacked her car?

She shuddered. He was an adrenaline junkie. How in the hell could she find him so attractive? So tempting?

Her steps had slowed as she reached the emergency room. Before she turned the corner, she took a deep breath and tightened her grip on the coffee.

Stepped into the room, expecting to find fifteen or twenty pairs of eyes focused on her.

Instead, the cops had all disappeared, except Brendan and his brother. Both stood up when they saw her.

"Cujo's in surgery," Brendan said. "Everyone's in the surgical waiting room."

"You going up there, too?" she asked. A small, cowardly part of her hoped the answer was no.

"We can't. We have to get to the pub in a few hours. And we need some time to decompress." Brendan shrugged. "Sorry."

"I'll take the coffee up to Harrison," Connor said. "I'm sticking around for a while."

She hated to hand him the paper cup of coffee. Her hands still needed the warmth. But she extended her arm and let him take it.

"Thanks, Marini," Connor said. He narrowed his eyes at Brendan. "Remember what I said about dinner."

"What?" Brendan frowned, as if trying to remember. "You hungry? Want me to bring you a beef with peppers from Al's?"

"Funny." Connor raised one eyebrow. "Get your head out of your ass, Bren."

Connor turned to Cilla. "Take it easy, Marini. See you soon. I hope." He shot a look at Brendan, then turned and headed for the elevator.

"What was that all about?" she asked Brendan.

He hunched his shoulders. "Just my brother looking for payback."

"For what?"

He looked around the room, as if looking for an escape, then sighed as he ushered her toward the door. "My family has dinner together once a month. On a Sunday. Con wants me to bring you to the next one." He spoke too fast, as if in a hurry to get it out and then brush it away.

She frowned at him, slowing as she walked. "Why would he want you to do that?"

The tops of his ears reddened and he didn't look at her. "All three of my brothers brought their girlfriends to dinner after they started dating. I, ah, gave them all a lot of grief."

"You hassled three women you'd never met?" She stared

at him, wondering if she'd have to revise her recently upgraded opinion of him.

"Not the women," he muttered. "The women are great. My brothers."

Her shoulders relaxed. "Isn't that what guys do?" she asked. "My brother and his friends rag on each other constantly."

"Exactly." He pushed open the door and held it for her. They walked out into a gray sky and a cool wind off the lake. "My brothers are a bunch of nancies. Can't take a joke."

This ridiculous conversation was actually making her smile – something she would have sworn she wouldn't be doing even ten minutes earlier. "Don't they do the same thing to you when you bring a woman to dinner?"

"I've never brought anyone." He glanced at her, then away quickly. "I don't do serious. I don't take women home for Sunday dinner. It's not the way I swing."

That confirmed what Cilla had heard. "Guess you're gonna have to take your lumps like a man, Donovan. Get it over with and move on. I'm game if you are."

His ears flamed again. "They'll make assumptions. My mother and sister will grill you. You don't want to go there," he told her.

"Hey, I took crap from Ward. I think I can handle your mother and sister."

He was finally starting to look like the old Brendan again. Confident. In control. A little cocky. "You have no idea what they're like. They're the best interrogators in the family. You'll be spilling your secrets in about five minutes."

"Assuming I have secrets to spill."

He slanted her a glance as she handed the valet her ticket. "Everyone has secrets."

Before she could respond, the valet pulled her car to the curb. As she walked over to claim her key, Brendan stepped in front of her to press some bills into the kid's hand. "Want me to drive?" he asked, dangling the key from his index finger.

She snatched it away from him. "My car. I drive."

Cilla steered the car toward Michigan Avenue, turned right and maneuvered onto Lake Shore Drive. Now that they were out of the hospital, she wondered how Cujo was doing. Wished she could be in the surgical waiting room, lending support like the other cops.

Good thing she had to work tonight. Sticking around would have been uncomfortable and awkward for everyone.

As if Brendan was thinking the same thing, he asked, "It's Ward, right? Why you do undercover work? Hostage negotiations? Because you can do those jobs alone? Don't have to work with other cops?"

Brendan put two and two together pretty quickly. She shrugged one shoulder. "Since I arrested Ward? Yeah. That's why I take undercover jobs whenever my captain offers them.

"But I like hostage negotiations. Me against the bad guy, one on one. Outwitting him. Getting the hostage free with no casualties. I like using my psychology degree."

"You're using it pretty damn well at the pub. You're psyching out every single guy in the place."

She glanced over at him as she changed lanes. "There's no psychology needed in that situation," she said with a little grin. "Flash some skin and men get stupid."

"Not every guy needs the show." He glanced at her, his eyes dancing. "I was falling at your feet even before you showed up wearing...those clothes."

Warmth slid through her at his words, thawing some of the chill remaining from the hospital. "Yeah?"

"Yeah."

She felt his gaze and risked a glance at him. Big mistake. His eyes had darkened. Desire burned in his gaze, igniting an answering need in her.

Behind her, a horn blared and she jerked her gaze back to the road. Swallowed once. Told herself to hold it together. Especially in front of Brendan, a guy who was a player. And a cop, too. All her relationship no-no's in one package.

She glanced over at him. A damn attractive package. But still.

Not happening.

Five tense, silent minutes later, she pulled to the curb in front of his building. Shifting into park, she half-turned to face him, trying to dispel some of the desire that thrummed in the enclosed space.

"So." Her voice was low. Sultry. She cleared her throat. "You think Romano will be back tonight?"

Brendan stared at her for a long moment. Letting her see that he hadn't forgotten what they were talking about, in spite of her efforts to change the subject. Finally he said, "We'll see. Hope we can shake something loose, or we've got nothing to do for the next four days."

Shrugging she said, "We'll figure something out."

Brendan stilled beside her. Tension hung in the air. He leaned closer. "What did you have in mind, Cilla?"

She swallowed, unable to look away. "Uh, lots of stuff we need to do," she said, stumbling over the words. "All kinds of background work. Check out Romano. Tiffany."

His eyes had darkened to tiny rims of blue around black pupils. "Sure. We could. In our spare time."

Her heart stumbled, then burst into a gallop. Stole her breath. "Spare time? That's our job," she managed to say.

"Our job is finding out who's selling those drugs. Pretending to be a couple, so we can try to buy some of that shit." He leaned closer. "I think we need to practice."

Her mind flashed to the scene beside her car the night before. The desperate want that had flared between them. The way he'd slid his thigh between her legs.

The way she'd pressed closer to him.

"I think we've got that part down cold."

He edged closer. His breath tickled her neck as he nuzzled the skin beneath her ear. "See, that's why we have to practice." His voice was a low rumble that ignited her nerves. "I wasn't cold at all. I was burning up." He drew her lobe into his mouth and swirled his tongue around it. Her heart slammed against her chest. "I want to make you burn, too."

She would have laughed if she could have found her breath. Instead, she sucked in a stuttering gulp of air. "Don't think we need to practice that, either, Donovan," she gasped.

"Yeah?" His voice was a low thrum of pleasure. "That so?"

Instead of sliding her mouth over his, as she ached to do, she murmured, "That's so."

His hand roamed over her back, dipped down to her hip, lingered for a long moment, then moved again. Cupped her nape. Drifted down the bumps of her spine. His fingers burned through the fabric of her shirt. They made her want to rip the shirt off. Feel his hands against her bare skin.

He dipped one finger beneath the waistband of her jeans.

She held her breath as the sensitive skin of her lower back quivered. As heat expanded inside her. She needed to move away from him. She was playing with fire. But she was too turned on to care.

"We both..." She gasped as he sucked gently on her neck. "We don't need to practice." He swirled his tongue around her ear lobe, and she trembled. "I think...I think we'll be convincing."

His lips curved against her throat. "Yeah, I think we will be." His mouth trailed down to lick at the hollow between her collarbones. "But you know what they always say."

She couldn't stop herself from asking. Not when his mouth was doing wicked things to the pulse point on her neck. "What do they say?"

He licked along the edge of her collar bone, as if trying to absorb her flavor. Memorize it. Then, with his mouth against her skin, he murmured, "How you practice is how you play."

Cilla slid her hands beneath her thighs to keep from

reaching for him. "Don't..." A tiny moan escaped as his mouth moved into the vee of her sweater. "Don't think this is what they meant."

"I think this is exactly what they meant." His voice vibrated against her chest and made her squirm. She was so far gone, she didn't even try to hold still.

He slipped the rest of his hand into her jeans, splayed his fingers against her back, and tugged her closer. She felt the imprint of every finger, the ridge of every line on his fingertips. His little finger trailed lower, close to the cleft of her ass, and she sucked in a ragged breath as fire licked through her.

"You're trembling, Cilla." He nuzzled the top of her bra. "Why are you trembling?"

"You're...you're making me nervous."

His mouth curved as he trailed his lips across her skin. "Yeah? Then I'm doing something right."

She slid her hands along his arms. To hold him away? To bring him closer? "We're in a car." Her voice was breathless. Far too aroused. "In daylight. Someone might see us." She hadn't given one thought to anyone walking past her car.

This was a really bad idea. But she couldn't force herself to let Brendan go.

"Would it bother you if someone saw us?" He slid one of his hands over her abdomen. "Or would you like it?" The back of his fingers skimmed the bottom of her breast, and she had to stop herself from arching into his hand. "You liked it last night when those assholes were watching us."

"We wanted them to watch us. That was part of the game," she panted.

His hands tightened on her. "Not a game," he said, his voice a low rumble against her skin. He lifted his head, and she forced her eyes open to meet his gaze. His eyes glittered with need. With desire. The musk scent rising off his skin made her tighten her grip on him.

"This has nothing to do with the job. With the game. I want you, Cilla. Have since you stepped out of that car on the Ryan."

He pressed his mouth to hers and kissed her hard. As if he'd been holding it inside too long and the need to claim her was too much to contain.

As if he'd die if he didn't kiss her.

His desperation triggered an answering craving in her. She needed to touch him. To feel his skin against hers. To taste every inch of him. She was as wild and hot as he was.

The tiny part of her brain that was still functioning knew it was Cujo. His shooting had triggered an elemental need. To prove they were still alive.

That need had crashed through all her barriers. She uncurled her hands from his arms and wrapped her arms around his neck. Tried to get closer.

His mouth was intoxicating. Sweet and spicy and warm. Like something delicious made just for her.

When she slid her tongue along the seam of his lips, he groaned and opened to her. She tasted coffee. The bite of the spearmint candy he'd been crunching at the hospital. Beneath that, a flavor all his own. The cool smoothness of his teeth. The tenderness of the skin inside his lips.

He gasped in a breath when her tongue touched his, then tried to drag her closer. His tongue stroked hers rhythmically and he tightened his grip on her.

Flames licked her skin, and he'd barely touched her. She needed to feel his skin against hers, but the console separating the seats was in the way. She leaned over it until she was laying on top of the console, kneeling on her seat. Brendan groaned and tried to pull her into his lap.

The steering wheel was in the way. He reached around her, fumbling for the lever beneath her seat. The seat flew backward, tumbling her forward into his lap.

Even through the denim of his jeans, she felt the heat of his thick penis against her face. He sucked in a breath above her and held her against him for a long moment, his fingers digging into her back.   Then he lifted her slowly and brought her face close to his, kissing her again.

"We're too god-damned old to be doing this in the car," he said, his voice raspy against her mouth. "Let's go inside."

CHAPTER NINE

Brendan sucked in a lungful of air, then another. They were sitting in a car on the street. The red and orange autumn leaves of the trees on the parkway glowed in the daylight. Less than five feet away, people walked past the car. He needed to calm down.

Cilla moved against him, and he groaned again. Calming down wasn't possible when her heart thundered against his hand. When she was breathing as heavily as he was. When her hands were gripping his back so tightly that she'd leave marks on his skin.

He wanted her. Right now. Right here. And she wanted him, too. When he moved his hand over her soft, silky skin, her taut abdominal muscles jumped against his fingers.

And when he pressed his lips to hers, her hips jerked in response.

"Inside," he muttered against her mouth. "Now."

She drew away and he followed, trying to catch her mouth again. But she flopped back against her seat, pressing her arm across her eyes. "No way am I going inside with you, Donovan. I'm not that stupid."

Brendan shifted, trying to get more comfortable. "You

have to come inside. The sixteenth is going to need those two binders of mug shots you brought."

"Damn it." She drew a deep, shuddering breath and dropped her arm from her face. "I'll wait here. You can bring them down to me."

"No way." He opened the car door and eased carefully to his feet. "I'm not walking up and down those stairs twice. I'll damage my...the goods. Might never be able to have kids."

She raised one eyebrow and smirked as she got out of the car. "You daddy material, Donovan? Never would have guessed that. Who's the lucky baby mama?"

"Don't have one. But you never know." An image of Charlotte, his aunt Helen's baby, flashed through his head. Helen and Jamie were completely besotted. The kid had turned the whole Donovan clan into baby-talking, cooing, grinning idiots.

Not that he'd ever admit he was as smitten as the rest of them.

The car chirped as Cilla locked it, then she walked past him and pushed open the gate to the courtyard. When she turned to watch him walking carefully after her, she bit her lip. He could see the grin in her eyes, though. "Having some trouble there, cowboy? Been on your horse too long?"

"Haven't been on anything," he muttered. "That's the problem."

He was still aching when they reached the top of the stairs. Still painfully hard. Cilla giggled beside him, and he ground his teeth to keep himself from turning her into the wall and showing her exactly what she'd done to him.

His hand shook as he tried to fit his key into the lock of his apartment. When he finally succeeded, he shoved the door open. As soon as Cilla walked into his apartment, he crowded in behind her and slammed the door shut.

He spun her around and pressed her against it. "You thought that was funny, Marini?"

"It was mildly amusing."

Her lips were still bright red. Swollen from the kisses they'd exchanged. Her eyes were still dilated, too. "You like seeing what you do to me?" he asked. He brushed his hand over her breasts, felt her nipples harden against his palm. "I like feeling what I do to you."

His finger toyed with the waistband of her jeans. "If I slide my hand down here, what am I going to find?" he whispered into her ear. When she shuddered against him and grabbed his wrists, he tugged gently on her lobe. "I think you want me, Cilla. Just as much as I want you."

He slid one finger past the waistband over her hot, smooth skin, and she tightened her grip on him. Stuttered out a breath. "I think you're gonna be wet."

"I think you have a big ego," she managed to say. But her voice was hoarse. Raspy with need.

"I have a big something." He pressed his almost painfully swollen cock into her, leaving no doubt about what she'd done to him. "And it's your fault."

Her hips jerked against his, and she slid one leg between his, pressing against his leg. She let go of his wrists and wrapped her arms around his neck.

He slid his lips against hers, finally sucking her lower lip into his mouth. "What do you say, Cilla?" he whispered. His tongue touched hers, waited for her to respond, then slid away. "Should we bet on it?"

"Bet on what?" She chased his mouth when he whispered into her ear.

"On whether or not you're wet."

She didn't answer. Instead, she gripped his hair and found his lips with hers. Her mouth opened, and he swept inside.

She groaned as his tongue tangled with hers, and Brendan wrapped one arm around her to keep her against him.

His other hand fumbled with the button at her waist, then slid the zipper down. When he reached her center, she was hot. Ready for him. He swirled one finger around her clit, and she cried out. Wrapped her legs around his waist.

Her hands fumbled at his waist, then she thrust the button through the hole. Tugged at his zipper. Shoved his jeans down and took him in her hand.

"God, Cilla." He sucked in a breath as his hips twitched. He devoured her mouth until his balls drew up. Until his cock throbbed.

He unpeeled her legs from his waist and pushed her jeans to the floor, yanking them off her legs. His fingernails scraped against her skin, and she bucked against him. His hand trembled as he tore away the scrap of purple silk that covered her. Then he lifted her up and slid into her.

She made tiny cries as he thrust into her, the door rattling rhythmically in its frame. She moaned into his mouth and clutched him tighter. Then, knowing he was close, needing her with him, he put his hand between them and touched her.

She screamed into his mouth as she came, her hips jerking frantically. He clenched her ass more tightly as he followed her over, kissing her deeply as his orgasm went on and on. When they finally stopped moving, he sank to the floor, his arms tight around her. She fit against him perfectly. He tucked her head into the crook of his neck and inhaled the scent of her hair. Something sweet and citrusy. He inhaled deeply. Oranges.

She nuzzled farther into his neck as she sucked in deep breaths, her chest heaving against his. He wanted to lift her shirt over her head, feel her skin against his. As his fingers toyed with the hem of her shirt, she eased away from him.

She stood up, grabbed her sexy purple underwear and tugged it on, followed by her jeans. She hadn't said a word.

When she headed for the couch and picked up the two mug shot binders she'd brought with her, Brendan stood up and pulled on his own jeans. "Cilla?"

She stilled, her back to him. "Yeah?"

"You okay?"

"Why wouldn't I be?" She turned to face him, the books held tight to her chest.

Dread slithered down his spine. Cilla's eyes were cool. Impossible to read. Her expression was carefully blank. She'd thrown up a wall, and nothing of the real Cilla was visible.

The composed, cool woman who'd faced down Ryan Ward earlier that afternoon stared back at him. The woman who allowed nothing of her real self to show. No reactions. No emotions. Nothing.

They'd just had mind-blowing sex against his door, and he felt as if he was staring at a stranger.

"I thought...I thought you were into that as much as I was."

"I was." Her throat rippled as she swallowed. "But I know it didn't mean anything. It was about the hospital. What happened to Cujo. Reminding each other we're still alive. Yada yada." She clutched the books more tightly. "It doesn't change anything."

"Then what's wrong?"

The knuckles of her fingers whitened on the binders. "We shouldn't have done that. We have a job to do, and sex isn't part of that job."

She was probably right. And if he hadn't been so twitchy at the hospital, if he had been thinking clearly, he would have known that, too. But having sex with Cilla had been a better alternative than thinking about ending up in the hospital himself with a bullet in his chest. And once he'd kissed her, he didn't want to stop.

"We can still do our job," he said. "Nothing has to change."

"Once you get naked with someone, everything changes."

"We weren't technically naked," he began, then stopped. He wasn't helping his case here. "I mean, it was a heat of the moment thing. We'll control ourselves better in the future."

"Yes. We will. Because we're not going to put ourselves in this situation again." She brushed past him, careful not to touch him, and opened his door. "I'll see you at the pub tonight."

"I'll be there."

She closed the door without answering him, and he listened to her footsteps receding down the hall. After a long moment, he heard the faint slam of the lobby door closing.

He wandered over to the window and watched her walking through the courtyard. She didn't look back. She simply opened the gate, got into her car and drove away.

The exhaust from her car dissolved into nothing and disappeared. Just like whatever he'd been building with Cilla.

He'd screwed up. Big time. He'd wanted Cilla since the moment she'd stepped out of her car on the Ryan, but he'd been too impulsive. Too reckless. Since the moment they'd left the hospital, he hadn't thought further ahead than getting her into bed.

Hadn't thought beyond the moment.

Maybe it was time he started. Maybe it was time to stop reacting. Stop listening to the adrenaline coursing through his body. Start using his head, instead.

He threw himself onto the couch, leaned back and closed his eyes. Cilla wasn't the kind of woman he normally dated. Those women were shallow. They wanted fun and games and understood the score.

Cilla was a serious woman and deserved to be taken seriously. Deserved to be...to be courted. Wooed into bed.

The kind of woman you made love to all night long.

Not that he had any experience with that kind of woman. He'd gone out of his way to avoid them in the past. But he wanted Cilla. Even more, now that they'd had sex. He wanted her again. Slower this time. More carefully.

Not that he'd ever get the chance. She'd been very clear. One and done. That was Cilla. They'd had their one, and now she was done.

Regret burned in his belly for the mistake he'd made.

After a long time, he stood up and slid into his desk chair. Opened his computer, brought up his word processing program and began to type.

***

He got to the pub later than he'd intended that night. An hour and a half earlier, he'd looked up from his computer and realized it was already seven in the evening. He'd showered, thrown on his 'work' clothes, and gulped down a turkey sandwich before running out of his apartment.

Traffic was a bitch, and by the time he reached the pub, the band was already playing. As he yanked open the outer door, the sound of Cilla's singing voice, low and sexy, echoed in the small vestibule, reminding him of the raspy murmur of her voice that afternoon, when she'd been pressed so tightly against him.

Hell, no. He wasn't going there.

Except that he had to. His hand tightened around the door handle. He was supposed to be infatuated. Hot for her. Stupid over her.

He'd been stupid this afternoon. Tonight, he was going to use his head. Be the partner she needed.

He clenched his teeth until his jaw ached, then threw back his shoulders and yanked open the inner door. Show time.

Cilla sat at her keyboard. He had a perfect view of the honey-colored waves of hair curling over her shoulders. As well as the backless shirt she wore. The two edges of the dark green, silky material hung close together, but they shifted as she moved. Every twitch of her shoulders revealed a flash of skin, hidden again the next moment.

Not a bra strap in sight.

It was a shirt designed to bring a man to his knees. And judging by the number of men clustered near the door, where they had a perfect view, it was doing its job really well.

With clothes like those, Cilla had clearly taken her job in vice very seriously.

Unless those were the clothes she wore on dates.

Jealousy, hot and fierce, flashed through him like lightning.

He closed his eyes and squashed it. He had no right to be jealous.

He loosened his hands, shook out his fingers and elbowed his way through the crowd of men. He wanted to tell them all to wipe the drool from their mouths. Instead, he muscled up to the bar and gave the bartender the order for his usual – Warsteiner Premium, a non-alcoholic beer.

It looked as if he was drinking, just like everyone else in the pub, but he could keep a clear head. And as a bonus, it didn't suck like most non-alcoholic beers.

Once he had his beer, he turned away from the band. He didn't want to be one of the crowd of lust-struck hopefuls gawking at Cilla. If he did, he'd have to think about how he'd screwed up.

So he headed to the back of the bar to do his god-damned job and check out what was going on.

He spotted Tiffany right away. It wasn't hard. She wore another rainbow-colored dress – yellow, tonight – and glowed golden in the subdued light of the pub. She was deep in conversation with a tall, thin man with sandy hair. The guy wore a shirt with a dizzying mixture of blues, reds and purples. Brendan watched for a while, then glanced away when Tiffany patted Loud Shirt's arm, smiled brightly at him, then walked away.

What the hell did she do with all these guys she connected with? Give them her cards? Hook up with them later? They'd searched the database for known call girls, but hadn't seen her.

Maybe she was a new player who hadn't yet been arrested.

Holly was in the same chair at the bar, nursing a martini

and watching everyone around her. Another mystery. She hadn't shown up in any of the books or databases, either.

Why was she here?

Cilla had suggested she might come for the music, but it didn't look as if Holly was paying any attention. Could she be their seller?

He'd put her low on the list. He'd never seen her initiate a conversation. Hard to peddle drugs when you didn't talk to anyone.

He'd still keep an eye on her, though. Maybe chat her up later.

He recognized more than a handful of other people. Clearly, a lot of regulars came to the Pipe and Shamrock on weekends.

His gaze lingered on groups of people, but he didn't see anyone doing more than talking or laughing. Nothing that looked like a business transaction – nothing changing hands, no money being flashed.

He turned to head back to the front of the pub and spotted Dominic Romano off to the side. He was leaning against the wall, a mixed drink in his hand, watching the crowd.

Just like the last time he'd been here.

He sure wasn't acting as though he were here for some action. Maybe they needed to look more closely at him as their seller.

As Brendan studied him, a woman approached Romano, smiling. She clearly introduced herself, because she held out a hand. Romano shook it, the serious expression falling away to reveal a smiling man who was now indistinguishable from every other guy in the place. Looking for a beautiful woman and a good time.

Brendan watched discreetly for a few minutes, but saw nothing more than a flirting couple. He kept his eye on Romano and the woman, now deep in conversation, as he moved casually, just another guy trolling the crowd. Brendan hadn't been able to get a good look at the woman's face, and he was positioning himself to get a better look. Tomorrow, he'd look through the mug shots again.

Just as Brendan got close enough to see her face, she leaned into Romano and whispered something. Romano's gaze flicked to the people sitting at the bar. Then the woman headed in the opposite direction, toward the stage at the front of the bar. Brendan still hadn't gotten a good look at her.

Had it been deliberate?

His imagination was working overtime tonight. Why would the woman have even noticed him?

But his spidey-sense was tingling. So Brendan followed her, keeping one eye on the mystery blond as he stopped to talk to a few people he'd met during his time at the pub.

By the time Romano's woman reached the front of the bar, the band had stopped for their first break. He lost her in the crush of men trying to get close to Cilla.

As usual, Brendan's partner was smiling at all of them, talking to the closest men. Choosing one to buy her iced tea.

Standing on the edge of the crowd, Brendan watched her work. She was good. Every single guy in that mob thought he had a chance with her.

As Cilla's gaze swept the crowd, she spotted him. Her smile faltered for a split second, then was firmly back in place. She held his gaze a moment too long, then moved on. But several men had noticed.

They turned, scowling when they saw Brendan. Most of them recognized him by now. Another suitor for Cilla's favors. The guy who got to carry her instrument out to her car.

Angry Guy was one of the crowd. When his gaze met Brendan's, his eyes narrowed. He remembered what he'd seen last night.

Brendan held his gaze. That's right, asshole. She's mine. Don't you forget it.

The guy's mouth thinned. For a moment, Brendan

thought the bro was going to come after him. Then he turned away, slammed his glass on the bar and called loudly for another Bud Light.

Cilla was getting ready to head back to her keyboard when the door to the pub slammed open and banged into the wall. "Help!" a woman screamed. "My boyfriend! I think he's dead!"

CHAPTER TEN

Cilla froze for a split second. Then, as the woman sobbed, Cilla turned instinctively toward her. Cop reflexes. Out of the corner of her eye she saw several people with their phones to their ears. Calling for help. So she grabbed the woman's arm and dragged her out the door. "Where is he?"

"In the...in the car," the woman sobbed, wringing her hands.

"Show me." As Cilla ran toward the dimly lit parking lot, towing the woman with her, gravel crunched beneath their shoes. Another fainter set of footsteps trailed the woman. Brendan?

Probably. His instincts would make him react just as she had.

She glanced over his shoulder. Even though he was in deep shadow, she knew it was him.

Her pulse jumped, but she ignored it and ran faster. The dome light of a car in the lot illuminated her way. And highlighted the open rear door.

"That where he is?" she asked as she ran.

"Yes." The woman's voice caught on a sob. "I...I didn't

know what to do."

As she reached the car, Cilla saw a pair of legs dangling out the back door. The man was prone on the seat. Unmoving.

His chest was bare. His jeans were unzipped and pulled down, exposing a huge erection.

He'd taken the drug.

Otherwise, his erection would have faded by now.

Sprinting around to the other side of the car, she yanked open the other rear door and put her fingers on his neck. Pulse was thready, but it was there. He was still alive.

"Do you know CPR?" she asked the woman.

"I took a class once. You push on his chest, right?"

Cilla wriggled onto the floor between the front and rear seats, kicking aside a flashy, bright shirt. She watched his chest for a moment. No signs of breathing.

She began chest compressions, counting to six, then pinching his nose as she blew into his mouth. As she started the second set of compressions, Brendan reached the car. "You compress," he said, already lowering his face to the unconscious man's. "I'll breathe."

She nodded and began counting out loud. She stopped, watched the man's chest rise and fall in as Brendan breathed for him, then began compressions again.

It felt like hours until she heard the sirens, but it had only been minutes. Intense ones. When the door to the ambulance opened, she didn't even look up. Couldn't stop yet.

"We've got it now," a female voice said. Cilla pressed once more, Brendan blew into the guy's mouth one more time, then both of them stepped away. The EMT and her partner, a tall, wiry man, climbed into the back of the car. The woman fixed an Ambu-bag over the victim's mouth and began to squeeze it, while the man compressed his chest. The male EMT stopped after a moment, checked the guy's pulse, then nodded to the woman.

"Still has a pulse. Let's get him loaded."

The woman glanced at Cilla and Brendan, who were standing out of the way at the front of the car. "You two probably saved this guy's life. Nice work."

"Thanks," Cilla said as she rolled her aching shoulders. "Keep him alive."

"We'll do our best."

The two EMT's loaded the gurney into the ambulance, and the girlfriend scrambled in after them. Moments later, their siren wailed as they pulled out of the parking lot. When the bus turned right, it revealed a police car near the entrance to the pub, its light bar flashing.

"You see the guy's boner?" Cilla asked, watching the police officers talk to the crowd gathered near the door. "Even after he passed out? He must have taken the drug."

"My guess, too." He kicked at the gravel. "Damn it. Right under our noses."

"I know," she said quietly. "Burns my ass, too."

Standing next to Brendan, Cilla watched the crowd outside for a moment. She needed to think what to do, but she was too close to him. Their arms brushed whenever one of them moved, and she could smell his distinctive scent. She edged farther away and rubbed her hands up and down her arms.

"Sore?" Brendan murmured as he wrapped his hands around one of her arms. He massaged it gently, his fingers pressing into exhausted muscles, then let go and did the same to her other arm.

When he finished with her arms, he turned her and began to squeeze her shoulders. He knew every place where the muscles were tight, and Cilla couldn't suppress the tiny moan.

His hands stilled. Then he let her go. Stepped farther away from her. Nodded at the two police officers now talking to the crowd. "You recognize either of them?" he asked quietly.

"No. You?"

"Don't know them." He angled away from the car so he

could see her face. "How do you want to play it? Identify ourselves? Or keep cover?"

Warmth stirred in her chest. Even though he had a lot more undercover experience, he'd asked instead of telling her what they'd do. Treated her as an equal partner.

"Keep cover," she said immediately. She glanced at his cool, assessing eyes and the warmth faded. That had been a test. "Number one rule on a job – don't tell anyone you're a cop. Even another cop."

"You're right. Just wanted to make sure we're on the same page."

Her stomach twisted. With anger. Not hurt. "You don't trust me, Donovan?"

"Course I trust you. Local cops could be some help, though. They'd know the local dealers. Might point us in the right direction."

"You ever get the locals involved on an undercover job before this?" she asked, keeping her voice even.

"Haven't needed to." He shoved his hands into his pockets and stared at the two police officers in the distance.

"So why now?" she pressed.

"Damn it, Cilla." He scowled, shoving his hand through his hair as he watched the pair of uniforms. "I'm frustrated. We're no closer to knowing who's selling those drugs than we were three nights ago. Some poor schlep almost died tonight. And we've got nothing."

"I've worked undercover before, Brendan."

He finally looked at her. "I know you have." He studied her for a long moment, then grabbed her arm and hauled her toward the front of the car, where they'd be out of sight. "Cilla, I'm sorry. We're partners, and I trust you. To have my back. To cover for me. I'm just impatient. I want to make some progress."

She exhaled, reading the truth in his gaze. She wanted to reach for him. To tell him she was frustrated, too. Just as impatient as he was to get this done. But not after this afternoon. No more touching. "Yeah, I get it."

He took her hands and slid his fingers between hers. She froze, but he didn't let her go. Instead, he rubbed his thumb absently against the back of her hand. As if he didn't realize he was doing it. "I didn't mean to imply I didn't trust your work. You're a good cop, Cilla. Thorough. Careful. Aware. I'm just..." He closed his eyes and shook his head. "I'm impulsive. Too reckless. I'm trying, but it's a work in progress." He squeezed her hand and let her go. "I need to check my instincts against yours."

He touched her cheek, and she wanted to lean into him. Instead, she held carefully still. "Like this afternoon," he sighed. "I wanted you so bad. I didn't stop and think. Didn't think of you. Didn't think about what you deserved. I'm sorry for that, too."

The regret that had chilled her since she walked out of his apartment began to thaw. "I was right there with you, Brendan. I think that was pretty obvious."

"Yeah, you were, and it was so hot. Made me feel like a sixteen-year-old kid with no control. But you deserved better than a quickie against the door. I should have taken my time with you. Should have at least made it to the bed."

"It wasn't a 'take-your-time, in-a-bed' kind of thing, Donovan," she said, struggling to keep her voice light. Nonchalant. "It was a reaction to someone getting shot."

"Yeah. So you said." He tucked a strand of hair behind her ear, and it was far more intimate than a kiss. "I'll do better next time."

Next time? She sucked in a breath as her heart jolted and began to pound. "There's not going to be a next time."

"After what happened this afternoon? Most amazing sex ever?" He drew a finger down her cheek, onto her throat, down to the neckline of her shirt. "You gonna be able to resist?"

She couldn't stop the shudder of desire that rocketed through her. But she'd had plenty of practice at hiding her reactions. "We have a job to do. And that job doesn't include sex."

"It involves making other people believe we're having sex."

He tugged at the neck of her shirt once, then let it go. The brush of the silk against her skin made her long for his touch. She swallowed once and stared at him. She wasn't going to back down. Wanting him was a weakness, and she wouldn't let him see that.

"I want you, Cilla. I'm not going to lie. It's going to be hard to keep my hands off you." His voice was a low rasp in the darkness. But she saw his eyes, focused only on her. As if she was the only thing he could think about.

Her stomach fluttered. Desire blossomed deep inside her. But she managed to say coolly, "Good. That will make our fake romance easier to sell."

"Our personal life is separate from our work life." He took a step closer, and it took all her strength not to back up. Never show weakness. It was a lesson she'd learned well since she arrested Ryan Ward. "We could get together as Cilla and Brendan, not the keyboard player and the single guy trolling for chicks. We could have a lot of fun."

"Yes, we could." Sex that afternoon had been unlike anything she'd ever experienced. Before, it had been pleasurable. Controlled. Nice.

With Brendan, it had been explosive. Earth-shaking. More pleasure than she'd ever felt in her life. She shoved away the mental picture of herself and Brendan, rolling around in a bed. Not going there. "But I don't date cops. Especially not cops I'm working with."

He frowned. "Why not?"

"Lots of reasons." She remembered her mother, comforting her aunt when her Uncle Joe had missed another family event. When her Aunt Jessie had found out Uncle Joe had a girlfriend. "But let's just say I don't mix business with pleasure, and move on."

He smiled, a slow, predatory curve of his mouth that made her swallow. "Bet I can change your mind."

"Really, Donovan?" Her voice sounded too breathy, and

she cleared her throat. "You think you can sweet-talk me? Do you know me at all?"

"I'm working on that. On knowing you." He slid his hand up her arm and down again, then twined his fingers with hers. The sweet, innocent gesture made her throat swell.

"When you do, you'll know I won't change my mind," she managed to say.

"Oh, I get it," he said, leaning closer. His breath lifted the hairs on her neck and made her shiver. "You're gonna be sweet-talking me."

She gathered her wits and elbowed him. "In your dreams, Donovan."

"Oh, you'll be in my dreams, all right." His voice was a low rasp of sex and sin and temptation. "Every night, Cilla." He slid his hand into the open back of her shirt, his fingers burning hot against her skin. "Will I be in your dreams?'"

Reaching desperately for her composure, she smoothed her hands down the front of her shirt, knowing her cheeks were flaming and she was breathing too hard. As she shoved him away, she heard shoes crunching over the gravel.

She and Brendan turned toward the sound. Both of them reached for their weapons, as well. Exchanged a glance when they realized they didn't have them.

The female uniformed officer appeared between the two cars, her hand on her gun. "Who are you two and why are you still back here?"

"I'm Cilla Mason, the keyboard player for the band." Cilla cleared her throat to get rid of the rasp in her voice.

"I'm Brendan Patton. A customer."

"We were getting ourselves together," Cilla said, taking a deep, shuddering breath. True, but not for any reason she would share with this cop. She wiped at her eyes, hoping she was selling it to the uniform. "Pretty upsetting, to see something like that."

"How did you two get to the victim so quickly?" the

officer asked. Her hand was still on her gun.

Smart woman. Smart cop. Cilla glanced at her badge. Officer Sobieski.

Cilla began, "Our band had just taken a break when the guy's girlfriend ran into the pub. I was standing right next to the door, and since I know CPR, I went out to see if I could help." She glanced at Brendan.

"I followed Cilla out the door. I know CPR, too, and I figured that's where she was going." He jerked his chin toward the other patrons who were still outside. "Saw a bunch of them on their phones, figured they were calling 911."

"You two know each other?" Sobieski's voice had sharpened.

"Only from the pub." Brendan gave the woman what was probably supposed to be a smarmy smile. "I like the way Cilla plays the keyboard."

Sobieski began to roll her eyes, then glanced at her notebook.

Cilla smiled to herself. The cop would write Brendan off as a jerk who was trying to get into Cilla's pants.

Her smile disappeared. Which would be perceptive. Because he already had. Due to her own stupidity. And the fact that she hadn't had sex with an actual guy for way too long.

Sobieski interrupted Cilla's thoughts to ask, "How do you know the guy was the woman's boyfriend?"

Cilla jerked her attention back to the present. She shrugged. "That's what she said. That her boyfriend had died."

Sobieski wrote in her notebook, then asked, "What did you find when you got to the car?"

"He was lying on the back seat," Cilla began. "Unconscious. No shirt, his pants were around his ankles and he had an erection. He had a pulse, but I didn't see him breathing. So I started CPR." She nodded at Brendan. "He took over the breathing and I compressed."

She sounded too calm. Too objective. Like a police officer giving a report. So she made her voice wobble as she asked, "Is...is he going to be okay?"

Sobieski gave her a sharp, assessing look, then shrugged. "He was alive when they loaded him into the ambulance. Hopefully he stays that way."

"Did anyone know what happened?" Brendan asked.

"A few of the onlookers had theories."

"Yeah? Like what?" Cilla knew the officer wouldn't tell her, but she figured most people would ask.

"Sorry. Can't share that with you. Can I have your phone numbers?"

Cilla rattled off the number of the burner phone she'd gotten at the start of the job, and Brendan did the same.

"Thanks," Sobieski said. "If we have any more questions, we'll be in touch."

The woman walked toward the other officer, who was taking a statement from one of the men clustered outside the door. He finished with a guy, walked over to Sobieski, talked for a moment, then they got into their car and drove off. The people standing outside the pub watched the car until it was out of sight, then they trickled back inside.

Cilla and Brendan were the only ones left in the parking lot. Neither of them moved. Finally, Cilla started walking. "The sooner the band starts playing again, the sooner things will get back to normal in the pub."

"Yeah." Brendan fell into step beside her. "Interesting to see if anyone is gone."

She glanced at him, surprised at how quickly flirting Brendan could morph into Detective Donovan. "Do you recognize enough people to figure out who isn't there?"

"I might. We'll see. We'll talk afterward." He put his hand on her back, sliding it beneath the edges of her shirt. His big, warm hand settled at her lower back like he'd set up camp there.

Damn it! When she'd chosen to wear this shirt tonight, she hadn't planned on being so close to him. She tried to wriggle away from him, but he merely flattened his palm against her muscles until she felt each of his fingers. Every twitch of his hand.

Her heart thudded in her chest. She got the message. Brendan wasn't giving up that easily.

She straightened her spine and stepped away from him. Neither was she.

As they reached the front door, Brendan slowed. He curled his fingers around her wrist to slow her, as well. "At the end of the night, we'll put on a show again, then you get in your car and follow me. Like we're going home together. You can come back to my place again."

"Right." She rolled her eyes. "Like that's gonna happen. We'll find a neutral place. We can figure out which one later."

He nuzzled her hair, and she could feel him smile. "Worth a try."

"I thought you were supposed to be Mr. Smooth, Donovan. What happened to your game?"

"You talking to people about me, Cilla?" He bent closer. "I'm flattered. And my game? You stole it the moment you stepped out of that hot car on the Ryan."

He let go of her wrist, cupped her ass and squeezed. When she knocked his hand away, he kissed her on the neck and swung the door open. "See you after the show."

CHAPTER ELEVEN

By the time the last note of the band's last song faded away, Cilla's nerves were strung as tightly as the strings on George's guitar. Everyone in the pub had been subdued. They'd stood around in groups, talking in low voices. Gesturing. They hadn't paid much attention to the band.

A few guys had wandered over at the second break, looking for a chance to buy her tea, but most of the men hung back. As if chasing a hot woman was inappropriate on a night when someone might have died in the parking lot.

She'd asked the guys clustered around her at the bar if anyone had heard about the guy in the parking lot, but they all shook their heads. No one knew a thing.

The pub emptied more quickly than usual, too. Now there were only a few clusters of people left. She'd caught only glimpses of Brendan from time to time. Maybe he'd have some information.

He hadn't reappeared by the time her keyboards were packed and ready to go. She curled her fingers around the cases, wondering what she should do. Take them out herself? Wait for Brendan?

What would the hot keyboard player do?

Hot Cilla didn't wait for anyone, she decided. So she hefted them into her hands and headed for the door.

"Lover boy find someone else?" The male voice behind her sounded both cocky and arrogant. "Good riddance. I'll carry those for you tonight."

Cilla set down the cases and turned to find Angry Bro too close. Another step and he'd be plastered against her.

"What's your name?" she asked.

"Mike. Mike Smith," he smirked.

She barely resisted rolling her eyes. Really? He expected her to believe that was his real name? But she flashed him a quick smile. "Thanks, Mike, but I've got them."

The smirk became angry glare, complete with clenched jaw and slashes of red on his cheeks. "What? You'll spread them for that pretty boy, but nobody else gets a chance?"

Cilla set the cases carefully on the stage. Where 'Mike' couldn't kick them. "You're an unpleasant guy, Mike. No wonder you leave here alone every night."

He clenched his fists and took a step closer. She smelled the alcohol on his breath and the ripe scent of a male who'd perspired too much. "You're pathetic," she said. She braced for a fight, although she was pretty sure it wouldn't happen. Bullies operated in the dark. Where no one could see them. Not in front of twenty other people. "Get out of here."

Out of the corner of her eye, she saw the bouncer approaching. "Everything okay, Cilla?"

"Fine, Andy. Mike here was just leaving."

Andy folded his massive arms across his chest and stared at 'Mike'. Mike stared back. After a few seconds, he shoved past Cilla and out the door.

"If he shows up again, watch him," she told Andy quietly. "He's got some anger problems."

"Want me to keep him out?"

She hesitated. She didn't think he was their dealer – too hot-headed. Too much anger. Not calculating enough. But she couldn't rule anyone out yet. "Nah," she finally said. "He's an idiot, but that's not against the law."

"I'll give him another chance. But if he gives you any more trouble, he's gone."

"Thanks, Andy. You're a sweetheart."

The bouncer blushed. "I'd do the same for any of our people."

'Our people.' The simple acknowledgement made her smile after this difficult night. "Good to know you have my back," Cilla said, bending to pick up her keyboards.

"Want me to walk you out?" Andy asked. "In case he's waiting for you?"

She was about to say yes, but a disturbance in the air current told her someone was behind her. Brendan.

She wasn't sure how she knew – he hadn't said anything. And the smell of spilled beer in the almost-empty pub hid his scent.

But it was Brendan.

"I'll walk her out, Andy," he said easily, touching her back. "But thanks."

Andy studied Cilla. "That okay with you?"

"It's fine. Thanks again."

Andy nodded and moved away. Brendan lifted the two cases from the stage and headed for the door. She opened it, held it for him and walked out behind him.

"What happened?" he asked as the door closed behind him.

"I'll tell you later," she said in a low voice. She suspected 'Mike' was waiting somewhere.

Brendan moved a step closer. The instinctive protectiveness should have irritated her. If Mike was around and looking for trouble, she knew how to take care of herself. She didn't need protecting.

But instead of pissing her off, Brendan's unconscious gesture made a warm glow flutter in her chest. She wasn't alone. She had a partner who would stand with her. Have her back.

The way she'd have his back.

The parking lot was deserted. They didn't see anyone by the time they reached her car. She popped the hatch and Brendan swung the cases into the storage area. Then he drew her to the driver's side of the car, as if planning on helping her get in.

Instead, he pressed her against the cold metal of the door and braced his hands on either side of her head. "You gonna tell me what happened?" he said, brushing her mouth with his.

To anyone watching, they were a pair of lovers, cranking up the anticipation of how the night was going to end. She draped her hands over his shoulders and ruffled the hair at his nape. "Our Angry Bro. Mike Smith, or so he says. He wanted to carry the keyboards. Didn't like hearing no."

Brendan eased his body closer, until only a breath of air separated them. "Do I need to straighten him out?"

She nuzzled his ear and carded her fingers through his hair. "Took care of that myself. Then Andy showed up, watched him leave."

Brendan scowled. "If he comes back, I'll kick his ass."

The possessiveness that filled his expression gave her a tiny thrill.

She was an idiot. "I'll be fine. He can't be that stupid."

"Never underestimate a man's stupidity when his cock is involved."

"Is that right?" A car engine cranked in the parking lot, and when she heard its tires crunching the gravel, she moved closer to Brendan. Show time. "And you know this from experience?"

"Hell, yes." He slid one leg between hers and cupped her face. "Let me demonstrate." He drew her against his body and molded his mouth to hers.

It was a game. Part of the job. It wasn't real.

But the way Brendan's mouth moved over hers didn't feel like pretend. Didn't feel like a game.

She told herself to play along, at least until the car left

the parking lot, but the car slowed and the crunch of the gravel stopped. Someone was watching them.

She'd put her money on Mike Smith.

"Can you see who it is?" he murmured against her mouth.

"No. Bad angle."

Without warning, he swung her around so that she was facing the parking lot. He backed her toward the cyclone fence that enclosed the lot, as if trying to get out of the light.

She saw a dark sedan, newer model, and a pale face watching from the driver's side. The driver stared for a long time, then gunned the engine and sped out of the lot. Pieces of gravel sprayed against the parked cars with tiny pings.

"Anyone else?" Brendan's voice was a rough murmur against her neck. The vibration made her pulse speed up and her body flush with heat.

"You can back off now," she said, hating the breathless way the words came out. "He's gone."

"Don't know who else is out there," he murmured, nipping at her ear. "We want to be convincing."

She was convinced. And yeah, she knew it was a show. Nothing about this was real.

But it felt real to her. As Brendan captured her mouth, she curled her leg around his and pressed closer. She'd regret it tomorrow. But she'd worry about that later. Right now, she let her reckless side slip its leash and rise up to meet Brendan's out-of-control mouth.

By the time she pulled away, she was breathless. Panting. Aching for Brendan. Thank God they were in a public parking lot.

Because every nip of his teeth, every glide of his tongue, every caress of his hand had sure felt real. So had the way her pulse raced for him. The way her body wept for him. Needed him.

She eased away, putting her hands on his chest to keep him at a distance. "That was convincing. Let's get out of here."

Instead of moving away, Brendan moved closer. "Sure as hell convinced me. How about you, Cilla? Are you convinced?"

"I'm convinced it's time to go."

"Hmm, I think it's more than that." He slid the pads of his fingers over her throat, lingered on her racing pulse. "Your heart's beating really, really fast."

He dragged his hand lower, brushed her breasts. Lingered over a nipple until she wanted to arch into him. "Your nipples are hard."

His hand drifted lower. "What would I find if I lifted that indecently short skirt?" His fingers played with the hem. "You want me to guess?"

"I want you to stop," she managed to stay, untangling her leg from his and stumbling backward.

"I don't think you do." He caught her hand and tugged her closer. She held her body rigid, refusing to budge. "I think you want me as much as I want you."

"You're delusional, Donovan."

"You want to bet on who's going to break first?" Even in the darkness, she saw the way his eyes danced. How his mouth curled. "Cause my money's on you."

"Really?" she scoffed. "I've got more self-control in my little finger than you've ever had. I'm betting on you, and I'm going to win."

"You think so?" He got closer, and she closed her eyes as his scent washed over her. "What are the stakes?"

"There are no stakes, because I'm going to win."

He grinned at that. "We'll see, Marini." He trailed his hand down her back, finding the space between the fabric. His hand was big. Hot. His fingers curled around her side and brushed the outer edge of her breast.

She shrugged him off and sucked in a ragged breath when he let her go. All he had to do was touch her and he ignited the desire that had been on a simmer all evening.

He bent close and used his teeth to tug on her earlobe. "Want to make a side bet on a time frame?"

"I don't bet on 'when hell freezes over.'"

"Okay, Detective. Thought I'd offer you an out. You might want one after you're the first to cave." The laughter in his voice made her want to lean into him again. Feel him laugh against her neck.

"You keep telling yourself that, Donovan. We'll see what happens."

"We certainly will." He let her go, his hands sliding away as if he could hardly bear to break contact with her. "We need to talk about tonight. My place?"

"Nice try. But no. I'll meet you at Oscar's. It's usually quiet this time of night."

His smile disappeared. "You go there a lot this late at night?"

"Once in a while." She raised one eyebrow, trying to reclaim the upper hand. "It's a good place to...decompress."

"I know better ways to do that. I'll explain them sometime."

"Looking forward to hearing them." She opened her car door. "See you at Oscar's?"

He stared at her for a long moment, then nodded. "I'll be there."

***

Brendan drove down the Ryan at the speed limit, not bothering to look for Cilla's car in his rear view mirror. He was too jacked up. He needed to concentrate on the road in front of him.

Damn it! He'd meant to keep it light. Meant to be all business behind the pub, hidden in the dark.

He'd tried. But one touch, one taste, and he remembered everything about Cilla. The way she tasted. The way she felt, all soft skin and soft curves and eager woman. The tiny sounds she'd made when he kissed her. The small gasps when he touched her. The way her breath stuttered when he pressed his mouth to her neck.

Police officers got involved with their partners. It happened. It wasn't the smartest move, but some couples made it work.

He wanted her like he'd never wanted another woman.

She'd acted as though she was equally hot for him.

They could make it work. After all, they had to sell themselves as lovers. Make everyone in the pub believe it was true.

And they wouldn't be partners for long. Once this job was over, they'd go back to their own districts. Their own assignments. They might continue to see each other for awhile, but it would taper off. Finally end. That was his M.O.

He ignored the tiny pang at the thought. He'd get over her. And she'd get over him. That was how he liked it. Have fun, then move on.

He accelerated as he got off Lake Shore Drive, then caught himself and stomped on the brakes. Slowed until he reached Broadway, making a few turns until he spotted Oscar's down the block.

There was an open parking space three doors down. He almost left it for Cilla, but that would be a waste. It'd be gone by the time she got here.

Locking his car, he yanked open the door to the bar and walked inside. The air was warm with the smell of macaroni and cheese, burgers and beer. Comfort food. He let his shoulders relax and flashed a smile.

He needed to sell the 'lovers' story here, too. You never knew who might be watching. So he asked for the booth in the back corner. Out of the way. Quiet.

The beaming hostess showed him to the same booth he and Cilla had shared the last time they were here. He smiled and thanked her.

No one would overhear them. They could keep an eye on the door. Talk business and not be disturbed.

He could sit close to her. Inhale her sweet, spicy orange scent. And if he sat a little too close? Made her a little nervous?

That was part of the game, too. They were going to be the most convincing set of lovers the department had ever seen.

When she walked in the door ten minutes later, he sat up straight. Watched her gaze find him at the back of the bar.

She squared her shoulders, smiled at the hostess and nodded toward him. Even from a distance, though, the smile seemed tight. Forced.

As she wound her way through the tables, every man she passed swiveled his head to watch her. She'd put on a sweater over the delicious shirt, but her skirt was still short. Sexy. And the black boots that covered her long legs, exposing only the pale skin of her thighs, were the killer finish to her outfit.

Clearly, the rest of the men in Oscar's thought so, too.

Swallowing hard, he stood as she approached the booth. Motioned her onto the bench facing the door, then slid in after her.

"Really, Brendan?" she sighed. "You have to sit next to me again?"

"We're trying to sell something here."

"No, we're not. We're trying to sell it at the Pipe and Shamrock."

"So we're practicing here." He slid a menu across the varnished wood table. "You hungry? I'm getting something to eat."

He felt her gaze on him as he studied his own menu. Finally, edging away from him until she was plastered against the wall, she pushed the menu away and picked up her glass of water.

"Drop the act. Okay? It's been a long day." She took a long drink of the ice water, and he watched her throat ripple as she drank. "Let's just take care of business."

Dark shadows smudged the skin beneath her eyes, and she'd clenched her teeth, as if trying to hold it together. "What happened on the way here?" he asked. Because something sure as hell had.

She spun the water glass around with both hands, staring at it. Then she lifted her gaze to him. "I got a phone call. From my sister. She needs my help."

CHAPTER TWELVE

Icy fear washed through him, and Brendan slid closer to Cilla. "Is she okay?" Water sloshed out of the spinning water glass, and Brendan put his hand on it, stilling its movement. "What happened? Do you need a ride to the hospital?"

She finally glanced at him and shook her head. "No, but thanks for offering." Her tense mouth softened. "Nothing like that. It's a problem in her personal life." She tried to spin the glass again, slid her hands into her lap when her fingers glanced off his. "A problem that affects her work life."

"Never good to combine the two," he said, and then wanted to kick himself. It was exactly what they'd done that afternoon. He needed to think before he opened his mouth.

She glanced at him out of the corner of her eye, and a tiny smile curved her lips. "You're right. Only an idiot would do that."

His shoulders relaxed. Okay. She was teasing him. "Yeah. Or a dumb-ass."

"Which are you, Donovan?" she said, and this time the smile extended to her eyes.

"Think I have to plead the fifth on that."

Her gaze dropped to her hands in her lap. "Olivia's a smart woman. She wouldn't do what we did."

Shame flickered through him. What we did. She made it sound like a complete screw up. Careless. Thoughtless. The kind of mistake a couple of clueless kids might have made.

She was right. It had been a reaction to Cujo's shooting, but it was still a bad call. Unprofessional. A few minutes of sex, even though they were spectacular minutes, had jeopardized their partnership. He glanced at Cilla out of the corner of his eye. "I'm sorry."

Her knuckles whitened. "I know. I am, too." She looked up at him. "I like working with you, Brendan. I don't want to wreck that."

"Me, either. And we won't." He needed to touch her. To reassure her. Himself, too. So he nudged her shoulder with his. "I like working with you too much to mess it up. Okay? I'll think before I act from now on."

"That would...that would be good." She narrowed her eyes to a fierce glare. "And you'll wear your damn vest from now on, too. Fastened. Even for a damn traffic stop."

Remembering Greg Harrison's shattered expression, he nodded. "Yeah. I will. Every time."

"Good. Thank you."

She was thanking him for doing what anyone with any sense would do automatically. "No. Thank you. Someone needs to slap me around sometimes."

That hint of a smile finally flickered across her face as she relaxed her shoulders. "I think I can handle that assignment."

"Great. You're hired."

She picked up her water glass and drank deeply, then set it carefully on the table. Taking a deep breath, then letting it out, she straightened. "So. What did you find at the pub after they took the victim away?"

"You sure you want to do this tonight, Cilla? We can

118

put this off until tomorrow if you want to see your sister."

"No." she shook her head, and caramel-colored waves shivered over her shoulders. "We're here, let's do this. I...I may have to work on some other stuff for a while tomorrow."

"Okay." He wanted to help her. But he didn't want to intrude on family problems. He fidgeted with the menu to keep himself from reaching for her. "So after we went back into the pub, I checked all the people I'd been watching. All still there. Tiffany – the blond," he clarified. "Holly, the woman who sits and drinks alone. Romano. Only one missing was the woman chatting Romano up. Who, by the way, went out of her way not to let me see her face."

Cilla's gaze shot to his. "Really? Could they both be involved?"

"He moved higher on my list," Brendan admitted. "There's something off about the guy, and when the woman went to so much trouble to keep her face hidden, it set off some alarms."

She leaned against the back of the booth and took a long drink of water. "I'm betting you eventually got a look."

"Course I did. What am I, a rookie?" He gave her a half-smile, happy that in-control, business-like, competent Cilla was back. The vulnerable, upset Cilla made him want to take care of her. Help her. And that made him nervous. "Not a full-on view, but enough that I can probably spot her in a picture."

"You going to take care of that tomorrow?"

"Yeah. First thing. I tried to get a photo of her to run through the facial recognition software, but I couldn't get a good angle." He frowned, still trying to figure it out. "Interesting though. Right before the break, that woman walked away from Romano. I never saw her again. But Romano went over and talked to Holly."

One eyebrow rose. "Yeah? Had he ever talked to her before?"

"I've never seen them together."

"Okay." Cilla drummed her fingers on the table. "Maybe we'll get lucky and find a picture of her." She shifted in the seat and half-turned to look at him. "What about the report from the cops and the EMT's? See any of that yet?"

"No, but I figure Sobieski and her partner are probably still on patrol. EMT's might be on another emergency. I'll check tomorrow. I did call the hospital. The guy is still unconscious. Got a name, though. Steven O'Dwyer. The girlfriend is Penny Adams. I'll run them tomorrow, too."

"Let me do that. You'll be busy looking for Romano's mystery woman."

He shook his head. He wanted to touch her, offer some comfort, but he curled his hand into his lap. She was focusing on the case.

He should be, too. And after his promise to act more professionally, touching her was the last thing he should be doing.

"I've got the stiffy and his girlfriend. You'll be busy with your sister," he said. "It's about time I put in an honest day's work instead of hanging around a bar and watching a beautiful woman."

"Yeah? Tiffany's that attractive?" she said.

She actually smiled as she said it, and he took a deep breath. If she could joke with him, her sister's situation couldn't be that bad.

"Didn't mean the blond, and you know it." His burger arrived, and he cut it in half, then began eating. "You need to leave?" he asked after swallowing the first bite. "I don't mind eating alone."

"Thanks," she said, her voice soft. Her eyes were soft, too. "I appreciate that. But I'll stay. Keep you company. And if I stay here for a while, let myself calm down, maybe I won't go off half-cocked tonight. Which would be good. Prevent some bloodshed."

He paused with the burger halfway to his mouth. "You're planning on inflicting bodily harm on your sister?

120

What the hell did she do?"

"Not my sister. The douchebag." She pressed her lips together, closed her eyes and shook her head. "Sorry. Wasn't going to dump that on you."

"Go ahead and dump. I have a sister, too. I'm the one she calls when she needs to download crap."

"Yeah? Why you?"

"I'm the next youngest. And I screw up regularly. She knows I won't judge."

Cilla glanced at him, a laugh lighting her eyes. "You? Screwing up? Can't imagine that."

"Hard to believe, I know. But somehow I manage."

Cilla played with the rolled-up napkin holding silverware, spinning it around until it jumped off the table. She caught it and shoved it across the table. "There's this guy. One I don't like. And he did something to my sister tonight that makes me really, really angry."

"Shit." He dropped the burger on his plate, wiped his hands and raised one, scanning the area for their waitress. "Did he hurt her badly? Do we need to arrest his ass?"

"What? No." She pulled his hand down, but left hers on top of it. She slid her fingers between his for a moment, then let him go. He missed her touch and wanted to snatch her hand back, but he pressed his fingers into the table instead.

"Then what did he do? If you want to talk about it. It won't go any farther, Cilla. I promise. But if you need an ear...?"

She sighed and shoved a hand through her hair. The waves tumbled over her shoulders, and she looked as though she'd just gotten out of bed.

Brendan closed his eyes. This 'being responsible' business was going to be tough.

She hadn't noticed his reaction, thank God. She was staring at the table. "He went through her briefcase," Cilla sighed. "Said he was looking for her phone because he thought he heard it ring. But Livvy isn't buying it. She's not sure why he was in her stuff, but she's angry. Upset. Nervous about what he might have found."

"Which is...?"

"She had files from the office. Cases she's working on. Stuff that shouldn't be seen by anyone outside the State's Attorney's office."

"So what did you tell her to do?"

"To kick the guy out. Which she said she'd already done." Her fingers tightened into a fist. "I know where he lives, though. Which is why I want to stay here for a while. So I don't do something rash."

"Something done in defense of your sister is never rash."

"It is when you're a cop," she said wearily.

He took another bite of his burger, but his eyes never left her face. "What's the plan, then?"

"I'm going to her place early tomorrow, before she leaves for work, and I'm getting the names from all the cases in those files. I'm going to look them up, then see if I can connect any of them to the douchebag."

He frowned, glanced at her as he chewed. Once he swallowed, he said, "Can't she do that herself? If she's an ADA, she has access to the same databases we use."

Cilla rolled her shoulders and kept her gaze on the table. "I've, ah, always kind of looked out for Olivia. Sam, too. Our mother...," She sighed. "Our mother's sister needed a lot of help when we were young, and our mom was usually at Aunt Jessie's. My dad was always working. So I kind of got used to being the go-to person."

"She's an adult now," he pointed out.

She glanced at him. "Yeah. But some habits are hard to break."

For Cilla? Or for her sister?

"Okay. You need some help with the grunt work? I'm good at that."

She smiled briefly, but it looked forced. Weary. "Not sure Livvy wants to get anyone else involved."

She got you involved. "Doesn't hurt to ask. If she's okay

with it, I'm good to go. We have all day tomorrow, and it won't take long to find the reports from last night and look for the mystery woman."

"Okay. I will. Thank you." She took a deep breath, let it out slowly, then closed her eyes for a long moment.

When she opened them again, the shadows had receded. She eyed the half of the burger and few fries remaining on his plate. "You gonna eat that?"

He pushed the plate toward her. "Help yourself."

***

The next morning, Cilla took a deep, settling breath outside her sister's door. Then she rapped softly.

A few moments later, Livvy opened the door. She wore a ragged tee-shirt that said Miami Ohio and a pair of old running shorts, and her hair, so similar to Cilla's, was uncombed. "Cill?" Her eyebrows rose. "What are you doing here at this ungodly hour? You look exhausted."

"Yeah, late night, but I wanted to catch you before you left for work." She peered into her sister's cup. "You have any more of that coffee?"

"Yeah. Come on in. I was just getting into the shower."

"Go ahead. I'll make myself at home and enjoy your apartment."

Olivia slipped into the bathroom, and Cilla poured coffee and wandered over to the balcony door. Her sister lived in a high rise with a view of Lake Michigan, and Cilla never got tired of the scenery. The early autumn morning was warm, and even at 7AM there were sailboats dotting the lake's calm surface. Sunrise had splashed pinks and oranges on the mirror-like lake, and she sipped her coffee and let the panorama calm her.

Twenty-five minutes later, Livvy emerged from her bedroom, dressed in a black suit and emerald green silk shirt. "Looking sharp, Ms. Assistant State's Attorney," Cilla teased.

"And you look like a grease monkey," Livvy retorted, letting her gaze drift over her sister's clothes. "Really, Cill? Jeans and a white button down? Could you be any more bland?"

"I'm at my desk today. No one is going to care what I wear. And I am a grease monkey. When I get the chance." The Mustang needed some work. She'd make time to get it done this week.

"Have you gotten tired of being a cop yet? You could use your psychology degree as a lawyer, too. Go to law school at night and then come work for us. Help us put the bad guys away."

Cilla had had this argument with her sister before and didn't have the energy for it this morning. After only getting a few hours sleep last night, she just shook her head. "Come on, Liv. Are you forgetting that no bad guys get put away until the cops catch them?" She set her coffee on the coffee table and threw herself onto the couch. "Tell me what happened last night."

Olivia nodded, acknowledging the unspoken 'not now'. She settled into the chair across from the couch and wrapped her hands around her coffee mug. "I was in the bathroom. When I came out, James was going through my briefcase." A muscle in her jaw twitched as she glanced at the black leather bag on her desk. "Really pissed me off."

Cilla bit her lip to keep from telling Livvy what she thought of James Dugger. Her sister already knew. Cilla hadn't hesitated to share her opinion of the jerk. "What made you think he was going through your papers?"

"The dumbass said my phone rang. I checked it, and I hadn't gotten any phone calls. So I told him to get out. He said it must have been the neighbor's phone." Livvy rolled her eyes. "He was in my briefcase, and he wasn't even smart about it. He left, but not before I told him not to come back." She shoved one hand through her still-wet hair. "I'm really afraid he got a look at those files, Cill."

"How long were you in the bathroom?"

"Not long. A few minutes, maybe." She flushed. "I was getting ready for... taking off my make-up."

"So he probably didn't have time to see much. It would have taken a while to find the file he was looking for. Then read it."

Her sister sighed, her body shuddering with it, but Olivia suddenly looked lighter. "Yeah. I hope so."

"If you can give me the names from the files, I can check and see if any of them have any connections to the douchebag."

"Don't call him that," Livvy said wearily.

"Why not? That's what he is." Cilla closed her eyes. "Sorry. That wasn't respectful."

"He doesn't deserve respect. Not after what he did last night," Olivia admitted.

"I know he doesn't," Cilla said. "I meant it wasn't respectful of you. You were dating the guy." She frowned. "What did you ever see in him?"

"He liked taking care of me," she said quietly. "It felt good to come home from work and not have to worry about fixing dinner. It felt good when he pampered me."

"I guess even douchebags have their moments," Cilla said.

Livvy stared at her sister for a moment, then both of them laughed. "Okay," Cilla said, grinning. "I won't call him douchebag in front of you."

"Deal," Livvy said. "But you don't need to spend your time on this. I can go through the databases myself."

"Do you have the time?" Cilla asked, raising one eyebrow.

"I have a lot to do today," Olivia admitted. "But I'm the woman who was dating him. I'm the woman who should clean it up."

"I should have an easy day today. So let me do it."

"Isn't it about time I took care of stuff like this myself?" Olivia asked quietly. "Time to stop letting you take care of me?"

"And screw up the natural order of the universe?" Cilla teased. She wanted to agree. She was tired of shouldering everyone's load. She wanted to let Livvy deal with her own mess. But the habit of taking care of her sister and brother were too ingrained. Too knee-jerk.

Who would take care of them if she didn't?

Livvy sighed. "I shouldn't let you do this. I know that. But I have a trial coming up and I'm behind on my prep. So just this once. Okay?"

It was always just this once. Cilla pushed the thought away. "Right. Next time, you're on your own. Sink or swim." Cilla hesitated. Finally she asked quietly, "How did I become the family fixer?"

Olivia stopped arranging her briefcase and looked at her sister. "I'm not sure, Cill. We all leaned on Dad. Maybe because you spent so much time with him, working on Betsy, we automatically turned to you."

"Yeah. Maybe." Cilla forced a smile. "And then I became a cop. I guess I live to serve."

"It doesn't have to be that way," Livvy said. "You can come to me and Sam and Mom, too, you know."

"I'll do that next time I need a shoulder," Cilla said lightly.

Fifteen minutes later, she had all the information she needed from her sister. Before she stood up to leave, though, she said, "My partner and I will be working together today on some paperwork. He'd be willing to help with this," she touched the notebook in her hand, "if it's okay with you."

"Partner?" Livvy stopped with the coffee mug halfway to her mouth. "Since when do you have a partner?"

"I'm on an undercover job. He's working with me."

"Anyone I know?"

"Brendan Donovan. He's a detective on a tactical team. Usually does vice."

Livvy tilted her head. "He have any brothers?"

"A bunch of them. A sister, too. All of them cops or

FBI."

"I've heard of the family. I worked with a Donovan a while back. A homicide detective. Can't remember his first name. Good detective, though. Heard all of them are. Brought me a solid case."

The casual praise from her sister shouldn't have made Cilla so happy. She shifted on the couch. "Must run in the family. Brendan's doing great work on this case."

"Go ahead and let him help, then. As long as he's discreet. Don't want him blabbing to anyone else about how my cases were compromised."

"He won't." Cilla stood up and set her mug on the kitchen counter. "I'm sorry about James, Liv. I know you liked him. I know it had to hurt."

"Yeah, it did." She shook her head. "Maybe your approach is right. Don't stick your toe in the dating pool. Then you avoid this kind of crap."

Cilla felt her face redden. "Not sure that's the answer, either." Maybe if she was dating someone, she wouldn't be so susceptible to Brendan.

She headed for the door, but her sister spoke behind her. "Wait."

Cilla stopped, but didn't turn to face her sister. "What? I need to go."

"You're seeing someone."

Her way-too-observant sister was a lawyer for a reason. "It's casual, okay. Nothing serious."

"Are you sleeping with Detective Donovan, Cill?" Livvy grabbed her arm and spun her around. "You are! It's written all over your face."

"It was one time," Cilla muttered, feeling her face heat. "And it's not going to happen again."

"Why the hell not?"

"Because...because it can't. We're partners. That's a script for disaster."

"You said yourself you're partners only for this case."

"He's a cop, Liv. Don't you remember what Mom and

Aunt Jessie always said? Cops make lousy boyfriends. Even worse husbands. And right now, a cop is the last person I should get involved with."

When Cilla, Olivia and Sam were growing up, their mom had spent more time at Aunt Jessie's than at their house. Holding her hand. Helping with Jessie's kids. Seeing her through the drama that came with being a cop's wife.

Why would Cilla voluntarily sign up for that kind of drama herself?

"You don't think he's looking for revenge for that asshole Ward, do you?"

"No," she admitted. "But it's just too complicated."

"Only if you want it to be."

Cilla opened and closed her notebook. Did it again. "I'm gonna go, Liv. I'll call when I have any information."

"Okay." Livvy gave her a knowing look. She knew exactly why Cilla was running away. "Stay safe in the seamy underworld."

"Not so seamy." Remembering the rush of singing as she played the keyboards, the satisfaction when the guys gave her a turn in the spotlight, Cilla grinned at her sister. "I'm in a band. Playing keyboards. It's actually pretty cool."

***

When Cilla walked into the nineteenth district station half an hour later, Brendan was already there. He sat at his desk, his feet up on the corner, typing away at the computer on his lap. "Hey," she said. "You're here early."

"So are you." Brendan set the computer on the desk, swung his long legs to the floor and stood up. So did the dog she hadn't noticed lying next to her desk.

"Where did the dog come from?" she asked, staring at the black, tan and white animal.

"This is Franny." He bent and slid his hand over her back, and the dog's rear end wiggled in delight. "My brother's fiancée's dog. They're going to visit Lizzie's brother, and he's allergic to dogs. So I offered to take her for a few days. Mac and Lizzie dropped her off this morning. Figured no one would mind if I kept her here until I can take her home at lunch. She's a well-behaved dog." He bent and rubbed her head, crooning, "Aren't you, Franny? Who's a good girl, hmm?"

The dog wiggled again and pressed against Brendan's leg, and Cilla felt a pinch in her chest. It was very hard to resist a man who loved animals. "What kind of dog is she?"

"She's an Aussie. An Australian Shepherd." He rubbed Franny's head again. "I've always wanted one. Once I get...if I'm ever home more, I'm going to try and convince Lizzie to breed Franny so I can have one of her puppies."

Cilla bent over and extended her hand to the dog. Franny sniffed her, then butted her hand until Cilla petted her.

When Cilla stood up and pulled over a chair from an empty desk, Brendan pointed to the floor at the side of her desk. "Franny, bed." The dog curled up on the red blanket Cilla hadn't seen.

Then he scooted over so Cilla could see the monitor screen. "Got a few things. O'Dwyer is still unconscious. So no help there on who he got the drug from. The girlfriend claimed she didn't know a thing. Didn't see him buy any drugs, she didn't ask him to get pharmaceutical help for any bedroom issues, he never told her he'd used anything. She did say, however," he pulled a sheet from the manila file folder on the desk and read from it, "that she was pleasantly surprised by his performance before things went to hell. And that they'd never had sex in their car before, but he didn't want to wait until they had more privacy."

"He used the drug," Cilla said, reaching for the sheet of paper and scanning it herself.

"I agree. They're still waiting on toxicology, but I'm betting it'll be the same one involved in the deaths." He leaned forward. "I'm guessing this would have been another death if the girlfriend hadn't freaked and come running for help. And if the ambulance hadn't arrived so fast."

"Yeah." She swiveled in her chair and stared at the screen, which held pictures of blond women. "Looking for Romano's friend?"

"Yeah. Nothing. These two," he touched a pair of pictures, "were possibles, but both of them are currently guests of the state."

She eventually moved to the desk next to Brendan's. They worked for two hours but couldn't find anything on Dominick Romano, no matter how deeply they dug. And with no mug shots matching Tiffany or Holly, and no last names, they couldn't go much farther.

Cilla got up and poured two cups of coffee and set one down in front of Brendan. "You ready to take a break from this? I could use some help with my sister's situation."

"She said I could help?" he asked, lighting up like she'd just given him a gift.

His eagerness to help her made her chest tight. "Yeah. She worked with one of your brothers. Said he was a good cop."

"Then fill me in. This drug case is frustrating. I'm ready for something new."

When Cilla bent over to pull her notebook out of her bag, Franny lifted her head and studied her. Cilla scratched the dog's ear, and Franny made a tiny whining noise.

Smiling, Cilla pulled out her notebook. "These are the cases that my sister had in her briefcase," she said, setting the list in front of Brendan. "This one's a murder. This one an embezzlement. The other two are drug cases."

Brendan studied the names. "Don't know any of them."

"I don't either. Livvy said to put the murder case last. It's a domestic, the guy didn't make bail, pretty much open and shut case. The embezzlement is an older suburban guy. We should check him out, make sure the douchebag isn't his kid or his nephew. The other two cases are drugs."

"Does the douchebag have a name?"

"James Dugger."

Brendan typed in his name. Shook his head. "A couple of speeding tickets, a handful of unpaid parking tickets, but that's it."

"I wasn't expecting much on him. Livvy wouldn't have dated him if he had a record."

"Does she check before she goes out with a guy?"

"Probably." Cilla shrugged. "She's gotta be careful."

"Okay." Brendan studied the two names. "I'll run Dugger, see if he's related to the embezzler, then I'll take the first drug case. You take the second one. Let's see if we can find a connection to the douchebag."

An hour later, Cilla smiled as she studied the screen. "I found something."

CHAPTER THIRTEEN

Brendan rolled his chair closer to a triumphant Cilla. Her eyes sparkled, and she was practically bouncing up and down in her seat. Her excitement was contagious and he wanted to hug her. But they were in the middle of a room full of cops, and he'd promised himself last night to keep his hands off Cilla. So he asked, "Whatcha got?"

She had a Facebook page displayed on the screen. "Dugger's list of friends. He doesn't have a huge number, like a lot of people his age. Looks like mostly close friends. So it was easy to run all their names."

"Nothing on Dugger's page linked him to Blaine. They're not Facebook friends. But one of his other friends is friends with Blaine, and that's where I found it."

She tapped her computer screen next to one name. "David Blaine and James Dugger were at Illinois State at the same time. And Mr. Blaine has an arrest record in Normal, where ISU is located. Dealing drugs. Mostly pot, some prescription pills. Ecstasy."

This was what he loved about police work. The rush when the pieces all began to fall into place. Just like writing a story. "So Dugger was trolling for info on Blaine's case."

He studied a picture of Blaine and Dugger that Cilla found on another guy's Facebook page. Their arms were around each other's necks, they both held beers, and they grinned into the camera. "You think Dugger was involved in the case in Normal?"

"I'm gonna find out."

She picked up the phone and called the campus police at Illinois State. He rolled his chair back to his desk and kept working as she talked and took notes. Finally she hung up and turned to him, her face full of satisfaction. "Bingo."

"What did you get?" He could watch excited, happy Cilla forever.

"Dugger was Blaine's roommate in an off-campus apartment. Blaine was arrested a couple of times for dealing drugs, but they could never make a solid case against him. The witnesses always changed their stories. They suspected Blaine was threatening them, but couldn't prove it. Both times his slick lawyer got him pled down to possession and Blaine got off with community service."

"What about Dugger?"

"The guy I talked to said they were sure he was involved. The operation was too smooth to be just one guy. But they never had any evidence against Dugger. Never caught him with anything, no one ever implicated him." Her mouth curved. "Officer Plank told me he'd put money on Dugger being part of the operation. Told me he hoped we could take the son of a bitch down."

Brendan saw the anger boiling beneath Cilla's calm, professional expression. "Blaine's still in County Jail, right? Couldn't make bail? When did your sister start seeing Dugger?" he asked quietly.

Her mouth tightened. "About the same time Blaine got arrested, damn it."

"I thought you said she checked guys out before she dated them."

"Yeah, she would have checked, but probably wouldn't have gone this deep. And if Blaine and Dugger are still in business together, they've probably kept their distance from each other since their college days. At least in public."

"You going to tell her?"

Cilla stabbed at her keyboard and the Facebook page closed. "I'll tell her it's the Blaine case. Other than that?" Cilla shrugged. "She's a smart woman. She'll figure it out herself."

"I'm sorry, Cilla."

She lifted one shoulder and gave him a smile that didn't reach her eyes. "Not your fault."

"Maybe I'm apologizing for my gender."

This time her eyes smiled, too. "Think that's a lost cause, Donovan. You go down that road, you'll be apologizing for a long time." She slapped both palms on her desk. "Let's pick Dugger up and have a chat with him."

She stood up and started to walk away, and he grabbed her hand. Let it go as soon as she stopped, although he let it slip through his hand a little too slowly. "We need to let someone else pick him up and handle the interrogation," he said quietly. "We don't want him to see us. Don't want to blow our cover. It would be a huge coincidence if Dugger is involved in our case, but stranger things have happened."

Cilla sank back into her chair. "You're right. Why didn't I remember that?"

"Because you're angry. Upset." He smiled. "I was beginning to wonder about you, Marini. You're a scary good cop. Haven't seen you put a foot wrong yet. Good to know you're human."

She'd been all too human yesterday afternoon in his apartment. Cilla must have been thinking the same thing, because a flush of color came and went in her face. Her throat rippled, then she nodded once.

"Now that we've established that I screw up like everyone else, can we get someone else to handle the interrogation?"

Brendan pursed his lips. "Julia Cooper and Alex Jennings," he finally said. "They're from the twenty-third,

homicide, not vice, but they've got a great vibe together."
He smiled. "Cooper does a hell of a bad cop. Jennings is a
mellow good cop."

"Okay. Let's call them and ask them if they'll do it."

***

Three hours later, Brendan sat beside Cilla outside one
of the station's interrogation rooms. Her leg jiggled as she
watched James Dugger sprawling in the chair at the table,
and Brendan wanted to put his hand on her knee. Help her
settle. Dirtbag Dugger was smirking, as if he had a secret
'get out of jail' card in his back pocket.

He wore an expensive, probably imported suit. Had a
two hundred dollar haircut. Fancy Italian shoes. All more
expensive than a lower-level manager at a bank could afford.

Brendan smiled grimly. He loved it when research he
did on his own time, for his own reasons, paid off at work.
Especially with slick numbers like Dugger.

"Pretty fancy clothes for a guy who makes forty or fifty
thousand a year," he said, watching Dugger examine his
image in the two-way mirror.

Cilla swung around to face him. "How do you know
how much his clothes cost? What are you, some kind of
fashion plate on your own time?" She glanced at his jeans
and worn dress shirt. "Because you sure don't look like it."

"Research," he said, lifting one eyebrow. "I do my
research."

Cilla narrowed her gaze as she stared at him for a
moment longer, then she turned back to the glass. A muscle
in her jaw worked as she watched Dugger. He knew what
she was thinking. Her sister had trusted this asshat. Gotten
involved with him. And the whole time, he was using her.

Brendan wanted to flatten the guy for her. Kick his ass
like he was booting a field goal at Soldier Field. But he was
practicing patience. Not being impulsive. So he stayed in
his chair.

When he saw Cooper and Jennings heading for the box, he called them over. "You all set?" he asked them.

Julia Cooper tucked a stray strand of her red hair behind her ear. "Yeah. We read Blaine's sheet, saw the stuff you got from the campus cops in Normal. Anything you need to add?"

"Yeah," Brendan said. "Don't take your kid gloves in there with you. We want him shaken up. In fact, I wouldn't mind seeing him piss himself. We need anything you can get about that new sex drug."

"We'll do our best," Cooper said with a smile. "You know I like being the bad cop, Donovan."

"Have a ball, Cooper," Brendan said, jerking his head toward Dugger.

Dugger didn't move from his sprawl when Cooper and Jennings walked into the room. They stood staring at him for a long moment. Dugger kept smirking back, and then suddenly Cooper kicked the leg of his chair. Dugger grabbed the table to keep himself from falling.

"Guys who are looking at serious time should be a little more respectful," she said, her voice calm. "They should acknowledge the major charges being filed against them right now."

"Major charges?" Dugger scrambled to sit up straight in the uncomfortable chair. "What charges? I thought you just had a few questions for me."

Cooper pulled out a chair and Jennings sat beside her. She laid her folder on the table and leaned toward him. "Your buddy Blaine doesn't like Cook County Jail. He's rolling on you like a dog with fleas. He can't give us the details fast enough. Looks like he's gonna get a plea again. And you'll get a cage."

"What are you talking about?" Dugger's gaze swept from Cooper to Jennings and back to Cooper. "There are no details to give. I'm not involved in what he did."

Cooper shook her head. "We're not the Uni cops from Normal, Illinois, Dugger. We're not dazzled by your slick.

You're just another low-level dirt bag. Blaine has agreed to tell us everything, including your role in his little operation. So unless you want to rot in prison, you'd better start talking."

"I...I don't know anything."

He looked scared, Brendan thought with satisfaction. There was no trace of his former smirk.

Cooper opened the folder, scanned a piece of paper in it, then slammed it shut. "Let's start with the sex drug that's making its way around the clubs. You guys selling that?"

"No." He narrowed his eyes at Cooper. "Did Dave say that?"

"Nope." She smirked at Dugger. "Just testing you. If it's not you and Blaine, who is it?"

"I don't know." Dugger shoved his hands through his hair. "No one knows. It's not Dave. I'd know..." He pressed his lips together. "It's not Dave. Word is that the guy is someone big. Untouchable. Someone with serious protection. A guy you don't want to mess with."

"Some banger?" Cooper shook her head. "Gangs don't scare us, Dugger."

Dugger shook his head violently. "Not a gang. I don't think. Someone that scares the crap out of all the players in the business. Even the gangs."

Brendan glanced over at Cilla, who turned to stare at him. "Cops?" she murmured.

"Possible," he said, equally quietly.

They watched Cooper and Jennings work over Dugger for another half-hour. Cooper was careful not to ask questions that would make Dugger ask for a lawyer. When he and Cilla were finally convinced he knew nothing more, Brendan rapped on the door to the interrogation room. Moments later, Cooper and Jennings emerged.

"You get what you need?" Jennings asked.

Brendan shrugged. "No, but it's more than we had before."

"Why don't you show him some pictures? We put a few

arrays together. Let's see if he recognizes anyone," Cilla said.

Brendan handed the three sheets to Copper. They'd put a picture of Romano in with a few other men. Holly and Tiffany were in arrays with other women. Cooper and Jennings went back into the box.

Dugger didn't recognize any of the women. But when he saw the photos of the men, his eyebrows rose. "Is this a joke?" he asked, tapping the photo of Romano. "That asshole is a narc. I saw him make a bust in a club a year or so ago."

"You picked up in that bust, Dugger?" Cooper asked.

"Nope. Just out having a good time." From the way the smirk returned, Brendan figured Dugger had managed to slip away before he was caught in the net. "But that guy was wearing a badge and carrying a gun. Vest said DEA."

"Make yourself comfortable, Dugger," Jennings said, standing up. "You want coffee or a soda?"

"I want to get out of here." Dugger stared at the two cops, and the smirk fell away. All that was left was anger that Brendan realized had been simmering beneath his surface the whole time.

"Damn good thing your sister dumped him, " Brendan said to Cilla in a low voice.

"Yeah." He watched her curl her fingers around the arms of the chair. "Livvy needs better instincts when it comes to men."

"Maybe you should give her lessons, Marini."

"Me?" She turned to look at him. "Why would she listen to me?"

"You saw through my bullshit, didn't you?"

Her expression softened. "Yeah, but you're basically a good guy. Dugger's problems are bone deep."

A weight lifted from his shoulders. "You saying he's bad to the bone?" He had a hard time controlling the smile that curled his mouth. "And I'm not?"

"That's what I'm saying." She studied him, a smile

lurking in her eyes. "Maybe we'll play that at the pub this weekend."

"As long as you don't dedicate it to me."

"Don't worry, Donovan. I'll keep your name out of it."

The sound of footsteps on the stairs had them pushing their chairs away from the window and turning to face Julia Cooper and Alex Jennings. "You done with this guy?" Cooper asked.

"Yeah. Thanks. I owe you one. Both of you."

"You know we'll collect." Cooper jerked her head toward the window. "What do you want us to do with Mr. Charming?"

"Let him sweat for awhile, then cut him loose. Tell him you have to consult your captain before you make a decision on charges, don't leave town, yada yada. You know the drill."

"Got it." Cooper nodded at him, glanced at Cilla. "Good luck with your case, whatever it is. Take it easy, Donovan. Marini."

Brendan waited until they were gone, then said, "Franny needs to go out. Want to take a walk with me?"

"Yeah. Let's get out of here."

***

The sun beat down on Cilla's back as she walked beside Brendan toward a local park, loosening her muscles and banishing the residual cold that had crept over her while she watched James' interrogation. Thank God he was out of Livvy's life. Cilla would make it a point to do thorough background checks on every single guy Livvy dated from now on.

If her sister found out, there would be a fight. A big one. Olivia would insist she could take care of herself. But Dugger was proof she couldn't. So it was up to Cilla to protect her sister.

Franny walked at Brendan's other side, sticking close,

even when they passed another person walking a dog.

A woman walked toward them with a dog on a leash and smiled at them. Cilla realized how they must look. Like a couple. Taking their dog to the park.

A warm flutter in her chest made her catch her breath. A couple. With a dog.

Is that what she wanted? She'd told herself she was happy with her career, happy the way she was. But deep down? Yeah. She wanted someone in her life. Someone to come home to at night. Someone to share her burdens with. Someone who could share his burdens with her.

Just not a cop.

The rule she lived by. She glanced at Brendan, saw him patting Franny's head. Murmuring to her.

It was a good rule. Right?

The woman with the dog passed them, and Franny wagged her tail. The other woman yanked her leash as her dog lunged at Franny. The woman grimaced at them in apology. Franny didn't budge from Brendan's side.

"She's well behaved," Cilla said.

"Lizzie trained her really well." Brendan grinned. He set his hand on the dog's head for a moment. "When you meet her, get her to tell you how Franny saved my brother Mac's life. Lizzie's too, for that matter."

When she met his brother and his fiancée.

He spoke like it was a matter of when, not if. Like there was no question she'd be spending time with his family.

Butterflies swooped in her stomach. That implied she and Brendan would be...something, even after the case was closed.

Did she want that? To get involved with Brendan outside the job? Meet his brothers and sister and parents?

Last week, she wouldn't have had to think about it. The answer would have been a quick no. Not interested. When she joined the force, she'd made a conscious decision never to get involved with a fellow cop.

Now, though?

She glanced up at Brendan. They'd reached the park, and the dog plopped her butt on the ground and stared at Brendan, quivering with excitement. Brendan pulled a bright yellow tennis ball out of is pocket, then heaved it as far as he could. Franny raced after it, a streak of black and white against the green grass.

She leaped into the air to make a twisting, acrobatic catch, then galloped back toward Brendan. He laughed as he watched her, the wind lifting his wavy black hair. She wanted to smooth it down. Run her fingers through its silky weight, explore the shape of his skull.

She wanted to kiss him again. Do more than kiss him.

"Isn't she great?" Grinning, he glanced at Cilla as he took the ball from the dog and threw it again. Then shoved his hands into his pockets and watched Franny run.

Yeah, she was attracted to Brendan. More than attracted. Intrigued. Fascinated. There were depths to him that she wanted to explore. But changing the rules she'd made for herself would be scary.

She could be setting herself up for the same heartbreak that had nearly destroyed her aunt. Setting herself up for nights of crying herself to sleep and days of regret.

She could also be opening herself to something fantastic.

She took a deep, shuddering breath. They were working together. She didn't want to add the emotions of attachment and sex into the mix of their job. It was too much to think about. Too complicated.

It could be life-changing.

A nightmare or a dream come true.

She glanced up at him. "Brendan," she began, unsure of what she was going to say.

At the same time, he threw the ball for Franny and said, "Thank God we had the excuse of walking Franny so we could get out of the station," he said, watching her. "I didn't want to discuss this around anyone else."

"You think it's a cop. Romano." Cold dread washed over her, and she pushed all thoughts about her and

Brendan out of her head. They had to focus on this case. Everything else came second.

"Don't you?"

She stared at the dog, wishing everything could be as simple and straightforward as tossing a ball to a dog. You threw it, the dog retrieved it. It should be the same with the cops. They were the good guys. They protected the citizens. Caught the bad guys.

The cops weren't supposed to be bad guys.

"We have to consider it," she finally said. "Seems pretty coincidental, him showing up at the pub."

"I hate the idea as much as you," Brendan said quietly. "But it kind of makes sense. There hasn't been a whisper on the street about who's selling this drug. Even after all those men died. All the vice guys have checked with their snitches. No one knows a thing." He shook his head. "That's not typical. Someone always knows. Or at least has a pretty good idea."

"Yeah." Cilla kicked at a stone in the grass, watched it bounce away. "I've been playing the same reel in my head. Romano would know how to do this. How to distribute the drug, how to keep the reins in his own hands. Most of all, how to keep it a secret."

"Maybe it's complete BS, but we've got nothing so far. We need to pursue this."

"Agreed." Brendan looked at her, and his eyes reflected anger. Sorrow. Determination. The same things she knew he'd see in her eyes.

"So where do we start?"

"We've got a few days before we have to go back to the pub," he said, throwing the ball again. He followed the dog with his gaze as he spoke. "Maybe we should do some clubbing. Go to the places where men have died. See if Romano's there."

"Or anyone else we recognize. We can't assume it's Romano. It could be another cop."

"Can't hurt. Maybe even pay a visit to the pub during

the week." She rolled her shoulders. "Have a beer and hang out together. Make sure everyone sees us, knows we're a couple. Look for our regulars. Keep an eye on them."

"Yeah, let's do that, too." He threw the ball again. This time, after catching it, Franny laid in the grass, panting, the ball between her front feet. "Franny, come," he called. The dog stood up, picked up the ball, and trotted to them.

"She's had enough," Brendan said, taking the ball. "Let's go back. Maybe work somewhere besides the station."

"Sounds good."

They were half-way back when her phone rang. Her captain. Cilla pressed the button. "Marini."

"We've got a hostage situation. Where are you, Marini?"

"I'm at the nineteenth. Working on something with Donovan."

"Get moving and I'll text you the address. It's a bad one."

CHAPTER FOURTEEN

Cilla's hand tightened on her phone. "A domestic?"

"Yeah." He hesitated. "Three kids in the house."

Oh, God. Bile rose in her throat. Her heart jack-hammered in her chest. This was getting back on the horse with a vengeance. "Okay." Thank God her voice sounded steady. Calm. "You getting all the information together?"

"You know it. Throw the gumball on that red car of yours and light it up. You've got the magic touch with domestics."

I wasn't magic on the last domestic. She clenched her teeth. Three people had died. One of them a four-year-old girl.

"Right. I'll be there as soon as possible." Cilla slid her phone into her pocket and began to jog toward the station. "That was my captain," she said over her shoulder. "There's a hostage situation. I need to go."

Brendan trotted alongside her, snapping his fingers at Franny, who stayed beside him. "Want me to drive you there?"

She glanced at him. "Probably not a good idea. It could be hours, and you'd be stuck there." Her heart hitched a little. "But thanks for the offer."

"Where is it?"

"Edison Park." They reached the building and she yanked open the door, then ran up the stairs for her bag.

She grabbed it from Brendan's desk and turned to go, but Brendan was blocking her way. "We all know how domestics can be. You sure you don't need a ride?" he asked, his voice low. "Might be easier to focus if you didn't have to pay attention to traffic."

She shoved her hands through her hair. She'd never had a partner during a hostage call. But a ride might be nice. She could use the time to prepare. "If you didn't have Franny, I might say yes. But it wouldn't be fair to keep her in a car for what could be hours." She allowed herself to touch his arm. "If I get another one while we're still partners? I'll take you up on it."

She wanted to reach up and kiss him. Instead, she slung the bag over her shoulder and slid around him.

"I'll call you later," he said.

She waved as she ran out the door.

Her apartment was close to the 16th, so it took only a few minutes to drive home. She parked the SUV and grabbed the keys to the Mustang. It was stupid and superstitious, but she always took it to hostage calls. The car was built for speed. And afterward, she opened all the windows and drove to one of the Lake Michigan beaches, blowing off the stink and tension from the job.

The address the captain had texted was less than fifteen minutes away.

Two blocks away, she spotted the blue lights flashing, reflecting off bungalows and two-flats on the quiet, tree-lined street. She slowed as she approached the first blue sawhorse, but the uniform stationed in front of it recognized her car and pulled it aside.

She had to park a half-block away, and as she hurried toward the scene, she scanned the neighborhood. The hostage negotiation van was parked in front of one of the bungalows. She spotted a sniper on the roof directly across the street. Another one on top of the house behind the bungalow.

Uniformed officers dressed in protective gear crouched behind squad cars and several unmarkeds parked at random angles on the street.

Nothing was random about a hostage negotiation, though. Everything was designed to keep the hostage-taker calm, keep the police officers unharmed and facilitate the safe release of the hostages.

She swung into the van and tossed her bag in the corner to find her captain sitting in front of the computer. "What's the situation?" she asked.

He spun the chair around and stood up, holding it out for her. "Hostage taker is Zeke Marshall. He's got wife Patty Marshall and kids Josh Graham eleven, Justin Graham nine, and Mattie Marshall three. 911 caller identified guns and knives in the house."

"The wife call it in?"

"No." Captain Francisco's mouth thinned. "One of the boys. Said the guy was hurting his mother."

She scanned the information on the screen in front of her. "The two boys are the HT's stepsons?"

"Yeah. Marshall got out of the army six months ago. Three tours in Afghanistan. No priors. Not even domestics. No one's talked to him yet. Waiting for you."

Pressure settled on Cilla's shoulders, pushing her into the chair in front of a headset. The computer behind it had a picture of Marshall in his dress uniform. Short, dark hair. Brown eyes. Tanned, serious face.

A former soldier. PTSD, probably. She closed her eyes, drained all the fear and nerves from her body, then took a few deep breaths. When her mind was clear of everything except Zeke Marshall and his family, she adjusted the headset and dialed the phone.

"Yeah?" A man's voice. Nervous.

"Zeke?" Cilla asked, her voice calm. Casual, as if they

were having a friendly conversation.

"Yeah, this is Zeke." She heard him draw a shaky breath. "Who're you?"

"This is Cilla. I want to help you resolve this situation."

"There is no situation. I didn't call the police." His voice was rising. "I don't want them here. Tell them to go away and everything will be fine."

"I can't do that, Zeke. Someone called 911 and said there was a problem. That they were scared. So we have to figure out how to solve it."

"Nothing to solve," the man said. Cilla heard him swallow over the phone. "If everyone would just fucking leave me alone, we'd be fine." His voice rose until he was screaming into the phone.

"I want to help you make everything fine again, Zeke," Cilla said calmly. Sweat poured down her sides. "We want to help you. Can you work with us?"

"Work with you how?" His voice was still shaky, but at least he wasn't screaming.

"Are there weapons in the house?"

The line was silent. "Zeke?"

"Yeah," he finally said. "I have guns."

Guns. Plural. Cilla closed her eyes and took a deep breath. "Anything else?"

"A knife."

"Can you put them on the porch for me, Zeke? Where they can't hurt anyone?"

"I'm not giving up my weapons."

No one ever wanted to give up his weapons. "My guys out here are nervous, Zeke. Knowing there are guns in the house makes them jumpy. They're trying to do their jobs, you know? Just like you did your job in Afghanistan. But they want to go home tonight. They don't want anyone to get hurt." Cilla pushed the mute button on the headset and drank a few gulps of water. Cleared her throat.

Unmuted the headset. "Can you do me a favor, Zeke? Put the guns and the knife outside? That would make me happy. It would make the guys out here happy, too."

The phone went dead. Sweat slid down her back as she watched the SWAT members edge a little closer to the house.

Suddenly the front door opened. A hand appeared, shoving several guns and a knife across the porch. Cilla had no illusions that he'd given up all of his weapons, but it was a start. She collapsed back into her chair. Dialed the phone again. "Thank you, Zeke," she said when he picked up. "That was great. I really appreciate that favor. So do the rest of the guys."

"I wouldn't want Mattie to get hold of a gun," he finally said.

"Of course you wouldn't. That's smart thinking. We want to keep Mattie safe. Keep Patty and Josh and Justin safe, too. And you. We want to keep you safe, Zeke."

He breathed into the phone, unspeaking. But at least he hadn't hung up. "So what can we do for you, Zeke? What do you need?"

"I want everyone to go away."

"If you want us to leave, you need to send Patty, Josh, Justin and Mattie outside. Once they're outside, we can leave."

That was a lie, of course. But she'd say anything to keep the dialog going. Say anything to keep this family safe and unharmed.

"They're staying right here," Zeke said immediately. "As soon as I send them out, you're gonna storm the house and kill me."

"No, we're not," Cilla said calmly. She glanced toward the house, where SWAT members were crouched in the bushes lining the front of the bungalow. "That's what happens in movies. This is real life, Zeke. Nobody needs to die. Help me here, will you? Help me help you."

"No one can help me."

The despair in his voice made Cilla take a deep, calming breath. The last HT, the one who'd killed his wife and daughter before taking his own life, had sounded despairing, too. "You're wrong, Zeke."

Cilla knew sympathy had crept into her voice. She hoped Zeke heard it. "Tell me how we can help you. All you have to do is ask. Reach out and take it."

***

An hour later, Cilla gulped some water for her parched throat as the SWAT commander stepped into the van. Zeke had hung up the phone a few minutes ago. "The sniper has him in his sights," the commander said. "He's holding the little girl."

"Like a human shield?" Cilla asked, her stomach churning. She thought she'd made progress with Zeke Marshall. Connected to him. They were waiting for a pizza delivery right now.

"No. He doesn't think so. The kid started to cry, so the HT picked her up. The kid has her head on her shoulder. She's sucking her thumb."

"Okay," Cilla murmured. The little girl wasn't afraid of her father. Cilla could use that.

The back of her shirt was soaking wet. Dark spots of moisture covered the front, too. The interior of the van was sweltering hot. She hadn't wanted a fan, afraid it would make it harder to hear tiny sounds from inside the house.

"Pizza's here," a cop called from outside the van.

Cilla picked up the phone and called again. "Hey, Zeke," she said when the HT picked up. "I've got your pizzas. How about we leave them at the front door?"

"You gonna shoot me when I open the door to get them?"

"Of course not." She glanced at the commander, and he shook his head. "We'll put the pizzas by the door. You get 'em, eat 'em, then we'll talk some more."

"All right." Zeke sounded tired, and Cilla closed her eyes. Maybe they'd still be able to avert a tragedy. Maybe after they all ate, she could convince him to let his wife and kids go.

One of the SWAT guys set the pizzas on the porch, then backed down the steps. Other team members stood behind him, their guns focused on the front door.

It opened slowly, and Cilla watched all the cops tense. Lift their arms higher as they pointed their rifles. One of the boys reached out and tugged on the boxes until they bumped over the door jamb. Then the door closed behind him.

The men pointing the guns stayed that way for an excruciatingly long minute, then they retreated. Cilla's stomach jumped and her head pounded. She hadn't eaten anything since that cup of coffee at her sister's and another two cups since she got here.

Someone shoved a piece of paper on the desk in front of her. Zeke had been treated in a VA hospital. Traumatic brain injury from a roadside bomb. He'd been released six months ago.

Cilla closed her eyes. God. This poor guy.

In spite of the heat, she shivered. Why hadn't Zeke gotten the help he so clearly needed? Was it that warrior mentality, thinking he could conquer everything on his own? Was it the safety net for ex-military that was full of holes? Was Zeke's PTSD making him see the enemy everywhere, even in people trying to help him?

The weight of her responsibility sat on her chest like a stone. The longer this went on, the less positive the outcome. Which was cop shorthand for 'the more likely people would die'. Her hand felt heavy as she dialed Zeke again

"Everybody finish their pizza?" she asked.

"Yeah. Thanks for getting it," Zeke said.

Cilla needed to find out about the girl. "Did Mattie eat any of it?"

"Yeah. She ate a piece." His voice sounded calmer. Cilla could hear the affection in his voice.

150

"So she liked the pizza?"

"Yeah, she's a good eater. Not picky, like Justin."

"How about Justin? Did he like the pepperoni?"

"No. Too spicy for him. He ate some of the cheese pizza, though."

"Good. So now everyone's eaten, why don't you send Patty and the kids out the front door? Then we can focus on helping you."

"I can't send them out. If they're not here, you're going to kill me."

"I promise you, no one has to die today. Just send them out so we can talk about what you need."

"I want a car. So I can get away from here."

"Send them out, and we'll discuss it."

After a long minute, the front door opened a crack. A crying woman pushed two little boys out the door, then turned and spoke to someone inside the door. Sobbed and reached out, but the door slammed in her face.

SWAT team members had grabbed the boys and carried them down the street, away from the house. As their mother stood on the porch, trying to get back into the house, two more black-clothed men pulled her gently away.

Cilla watched, her heart aching for the distraught mother. She took a deep breath and pushed the sympathy away. She didn't have time for emotion. After another calming breath, she called Zeke. "Why didn't you send Mattie out?"

"She stays with me." Cilla heard his voice catch, as though he was fighting tears. "She's the only one who doesn't give me shit."

"Do you love her?" Cilla clenched her hands so hard her nails dug into her palms.

"Course I do. She's my kid."

"Don't you want to do the right thing for your daughter?"

"That's why she's staying with me. Girls need their fathers."

"They need their mothers too," Cilla said quietly. "And it's hard to focus if you're trying to take care of a baby. Why don't you send her out so we can talk?"

"I'm good to talk." The sounds of a child crying came through the phone, as well as Zeke's voice, trying to soothe Mattie.

"She's crying," Cilla said gently. "Let her go, Zeke. Open the front door, put her on the porch, then shut the door again."

"You'll shoot me if I do."

"I promise you, no one's going to shoot you," Cilla assured him. "Just put Mattie on the front porch."

The phone went dead, and Cilla's heart thundered. This was where the last hostage scene had gone bad. Seconds after the HT had hung up the phone gunshots had thundered in the house.

Either Zeke was going to let Mattie go, or everything was going to hell. Right now.

In the distance, a woman sobbed. Captain Francisco's voice soothed, and the sobs quieted.

The front door inched open. A tall man set a small girl down, kissed her and went back inside. As soon as the door closed, a SWAT guy ran up the stairs, grabbed the girl and took off.

Determined to press her advantage, to keep Zeke working with her, Cilla barely glanced at the reunion of mother and daughter down the street. Instead, she adjusted the headset once more. In the distance, she heard Patty's muted sobs.

"Thank you, Zeke. Now tell me what you need and we'll figure out how to get it for you."

"I need a job. A car, so I can get to that job. I need to make money. Those kids eat everything that isn't nailed down. I can't afford to feed them anymore."

"Kids are expensive. I know that. What else do you need, Zeke?"

"I need...I need to see a doctor." His voice caught.

"Something is wrong in my head. But we can't afford a doctor."

"We can help you with that. We'll get a doctor for you. We'll make sure you get the help you need." She swallowed. "You let everyone leave the house, Zeke. No one's going to hurt you now. If you come out with your hands in the air, we'll take you downtown and get you some help."

"I know how this goes. You'll shoot me the minute I open the door."

"No. We won't. In fact, I'll meet you myself." She glanced at her captain, who frowned and shook his head. "Open the door and come out with your hands above your head. Walk slowly. No sudden moves."

She removed the headset and walked toward the door of the van. Her captain caught her arm. "You can't go out there, Marini. What if he comes out shooting?"

"I'm wearing my vest. But he's not going to shoot." She shook off his hand. "He's a veteran who's been injured. You heard what he said. There's something wrong in his head. He wants help. Now I'm going to cuff him and put him in a car."

Francisco reached for her again, but she twisted away from him and walked to the front of the house. She tugged on the straps of her vest, making sure they were tight. She swallowed as she waited. Please, God, not a head shot. Zeke could be in the house, aiming a weapon at her. But she was pretty sure he wasn't.

Finally the front door opened and a dark-haired man with a few-days-old scruff stepped outside, hands in the air. The SWAT members behind her raised their rifles.

"It's okay, Zeke. They're not going to shoot. Walk slowly down the stairs. Keep your hands in the air."

He stumbled on the first step and reached for the railing. Cilla turned around and barked, "No. Wait."

Zeke regained his balance and walked down the rest of the steps. He stopped two feet in front of her. "Can I put my hands down now?"

"Not yet, Zeke. I need you to put your hands on the back of your head and lie down on the ground."

"I already gave you my guns."

"I need to double check that. You probably did a lot of double-checking in Afghanistan. I'm big on double-checking, too. I always need to be sure."

Zeke knelt on the ground, then lowered himself to the sidewalk. Cilla stepped behind him and put the cuffs on his wrists. Then she helped him stand, put on gloves and patted him down.

He had a knife and a gun in his pockets. A uniformed cop handed her two evidence bags, and she slid the weapons into them, one by one. Then she read Zeke his rights and led him toward a squad car.

"I thought you were going to help me," he said, sounding hurt.

"You'll get all the help you need, and I'll personally make sure you do. But not tonight, I'm afraid. We have a lot of paperwork to do first."

He stared at her, confused, and Cilla felt a rush of sympathy for him. He needed to be in a psychiatric ward, but it would have to be at Cook County Jail. "I'll visit you, okay? Make sure you're getting what you need."

"Okay." He exhaled. "That...that would be nice."

As they drove Zeke away, Patty threw herself at Cilla. "Thank you," she sobbed. "You saved my children. I can't believe you got him to talk to you. He hasn't said much in weeks."

"Has he been treated for PTSD?"

Patty took a shaky breath. "The doctors tried, but Zeke said there wasn't anything wrong with him. Refused to go to counseling, refused to see a doctor, refused to take any medication."

"We'll try to help him," Cilla assured her. She looked at the two boys. "Which of you called the police?"

"I did." It was the older boy. Josh.

"You did a very brave thing, Josh," Cilla said, crouching

154

in front of him.

"He was whaling on her again. It made me angry." His lip wobbled. "But it was worse when the police came. Maybe I shouldn't have called."

"You did the right thing," Cilla assured him. "You saved your mother and your brother and your sister. And yourself."

"I think you're the one who saved us," Josh said shyly.

"We did it together, Josh."

She squeezed the boy's shoulder, then stood up and pulled a business card out of her back pocket. She kept a stack of them in the Mustang's glove box. "This is a social worker. Emma Sloan. She's very good. She can help you. You might want to give her a call." Cilla pressed the card into Patty's hand.

Patty clutched it tightly. "Thank you. I will."

Several cops surrounded the small family and led them back into the house. They would take Patty's and the boys' statements, then help them get whatever they needed.

Other than the paper work, her job was done.

She rotated her shoulders, feeling the burn in her muscles from hunching over the desk all afternoon. Her stomach rumbled, reminding her she hadn't eaten anything. And she was exhausted. She'd gotten to bed late and gotten up far too early to catch Olivia before she headed to work.

She stepped into the trailer and grabbed her bag, then turned to go. Captain Francisco nodded to her. "Good work, Marini." He nodded at her. "You were great with Marshall. Now go home and unwind."

"Yes, sir. That's the plan."

She swung out of the trailer and sucked in deep breaths of fresh air. Twilight was creeping over the trees that lined the street. Her red Mustang was a beacon in the distance. She closed her eyes, took one last deep breath, then let it out as she hurried toward her car.

Slowed to a stop as she got closer and recognized the tall figure leaning against the fender. "Brendan? What are you doing here?"

CHAPTER FIFTEEN

He uncurled his tall body from her car and stood up straight. "Figured you'd need a little help unwinding after that." He jerked his head toward the bustle of the hostage scene. "Thought I'd volunteer."

She remembered his offer to help her 'unwind' the other night. A bitter taste filled her mouth as she unlocked her car and tossed her purse on the back seat. Had she been so wrong about Brendan?

She stood in the open door, staring at him across the roof, her chest aching with a pain that she told herself was exhaustion from the day. "Really, Donovan?" she said when she was sure she could control her voice. "You want to help me unwind?" Her fingers slashed through the evening air in vicious air quotes.

He shrugged. "You didn't get lunch today because of that asshat Dugger. I'm sure you didn't stop on the way here. Figured you'd be hungry. Ready for a beer and a burger."

"Wait." The pile of bricks sitting on her chest tumbled to the ground. "You came here to take me to dinner? Not to..."

157

His mouth twitched. "Get your mind out of the gutter, Marini. I was offering food. An ear, if you want to talk about it." He held her gaze steadily. "That's it."

Her legs were cement-heavy as she slammed the back door and opened the driver's door. But everything else suddenly felt lighter. More free. "Get in, then. I'm starving."

He opened the door, then hesitated. "Want me to drive? You look wiped out."

She'd alternately sweated and shivered in the hot trailer. Now she felt like a dishrag left in the sink too long. Wet, cold and gross. But happier than she'd ever been at the end of a hostage negotiation. "I didn't let you drive the SUV. What makes you think I'll let you drive Betsy?"

"'Betsy?" He swung into the passenger's seat. "Your car has a name?"

Her face flamed as she flicked on the ignition and turned the car around. She'd spoken without thinking. That's what happened when her defenses were weakened. "My father named her," she muttered. "It kind of stuck."

"Betsy." He half-turned in the seat to study the back seat, then let his gaze wander over the dashboard. "That's not what I'd name a hot car like this."

"Yeah?" Her shoulders melted into the seat back as she drove east on Northwest Highway, the tension draining away. Brendan was good for her. "What would you name her?"

"Hmmm." He glanced at her, his mouth curling into a tiny half-smile. "Priscilla?"

"Lame, Donovan," she managed to say above the pounding of her heart. "Really lame. What are you, in high school?"

"Just trying to be a good partner," he said. He fiddled with the window crank. Opened and closed the glove box. "Trying to protect you from jerks who might laugh about your muscle car named Betsy."

Trying to protect you. "I think I can handle it. And so

can Betsy."

She didn't need protection. She'd always taken care of herself. But the fact that he wanted to, felt...good. Comforting. Like working on Betsy in her garage, music blaring from her iPod. Holding the worn tools she'd gotten from her father. Adjusting, aligning, until her car was perfect.

"She's been Betsy for a long time. Too old to change."

He glanced at her, and she felt the weight of his stare, even though she kept her gaze focused on the street. "No one's ever too old to change."

They were veering onto shaky ground, so she said lightly, "That include you, Donovan?"

"Change? Me?" She heard the grin in his voice. "Now why would I want to mess with perfection?"

***

Brendan watched her roll her eyes as she turned a corner, and he relaxed into the seat. It had gotten a little too heavy there for a moment. Heavy was the last thing Cilla needed after that hostage situation.

Brendan had arrived a couple of hours before it ended. He'd stood with a few uniformed guys as he studied the scene. Tension had swirled in the warm air, fed by the black-clad SWAT team surrounding the house. The snipers on the roofs of nearby buildings. The ominous-looking black trailer.

Even the uniformed guys keeping the crowds away stood rigidly straight. On edge. Hands too tight on their weapons. Glancing toward the house every few seconds.

Brendan had leaned against Cilla's car and talked to them, getting the story. Cilla was a great hostage negotiator, they'd said. She was calm, in control, empathetic. Kept the HT talking. She was almost always successful.

Except for a recent hostage situation. It had ended with three people dead, including a kid.

No matter how this one ended up, Brendan had figured she'd be strung out afterward. She'd need someone to lean on.

That would be a new role for him. A little scary. But Cilla was worth the uneasy flutter in his belly. Having Cilla depend on him had felt...right. He was her partner. That was his job.

He needed to make sure she was okay.

So he'd found out where she was and tapped one of his buddies for a ride to Edison Park.

"You mind if we stop here?" Cilla interrupted his thoughts. She nodded at a chain restaurant that specialized in gourmet burgers.

"Yeah, that's good. They have decent burgers."

They pulled into the parking lot, but Cilla didn't leap out of the car. She stood slowly, as if stiff. Achy. Brendan walked around the car and hovered, unsure what to do.

In the end, he trailed her to the restaurant door. She stumbled on the door jamb, and he grabbed her elbow to steady her.

"Thanks," she said, glancing at him over her shoulder. Purple circles beneath her eyes looked like bruises, and her mouth was tight. Strained. She looked completely wiped out. He wanted to snatch her up and wrap her in warmth. Comfort her.

Instead, he steadied her as she dropped into a booth in the half-empty restaurant, then slid into the other side and watched her. She leaned against the seat and took a deep, shuddering breath. When the waitress came by, she asked for an iced tea.

"No beer to celebrate?" he asked, raising his eyebrows. "Sounded as if you had a happy ending there."

A ghost of a smile flickered over her mouth. "Yeah. It was good. But I haven't eaten much all day, and I have to drive home."

Neither of them spoke until the waitress brought his beer and Cilla's tea. Holding it with both hands, she gulped down half the glass, then pushed it away and slumped against the seat. He saw her hands shaking violently before she pressed them into the table.

"Adrenaline burn wearing off?" he asked, nodding at them.

"Yeah." She swallowed. "Sometimes I have to pull over, wait it out." Her gaze softened as she studied him. "Thanks for showing up. Nice to have company."

He wanted to pump his fist in triumph. He'd been right. She'd needed him. Instead, he took another sip of beer.

He suspected it was hard for her to admit that. Admit that she needed a little help. "Course I showed up," he said, tilting his head to study her. "I'm your partner."

"Only temporarily," she said quietly, closing her eyes.

He heard regret in her soft voice. An offer to start a different kind of partnership after the case was over trembled on the tip of his tongue. He bit down on it. Not what she needed right now.

"You want to talk about it?" he finally said.

"No." She took another drink of iced tea, pushed the glass away, and exhaled a long, shaky breath. Crossed her arms over her chest and tucked her hands into her armpits. Like she was cold. "There were three kids. The oldest is the one who called the cops." Her mouth trembled for a moment, then firmed again. "His stepfather got out of the army six months ago. Traumatic brain injury, now has PTSD. Needed help, but wouldn't get it. Finally snapped."

Brendan sat a little taller. She trusted him enough to talk to him about it. His brothers teased him about being a screw up, but they could go to hell. Cilla trusted him.

"You got everyone out of the house safely," Brendan reminded her. He wanted to reach across the table and take her hand, but he didn't want to break the mood. "He'll get help now. Put his life back together. He's in jail, but he's alive. Unhurt. And so is his family." He leaned across the table. "You did a hell of a thing tonight, Cilla. You saved those kids and their mother. You saved their father, too."

She shrugged. "Why we wanted to be cops, right? To help people."

He knew he waited too long to answer. But he wasn't sure that's why he became a cop. "Yeah," he finally said. Too complicated to get into right now. He'd held his secrets for a long time, and wasn't ready to give them up just yet. "The glamorous side of police work, right?"

She huffed out a laugh, and he relaxed a little. She was getting back to normal. She unwrapped her arms from her body and picked up the iced tea again. "The hostage thing will probably be on the blog," she said. "Cops and Robbers. Don't you think?" When he didn't answer immediately, she tilted her head and studied him. "I know you read it. I saw it on your computer that day at your place."

His hand tightened around the glass, then he lifted it and swallowed a gulp of beer. "Yeah, I've seen it. Maybe it'll be there. Who knows how he or she picks what they write about?"

"It has to be a cop. Or someone related to a cop. That guy knows too much."

He stared at her for a long moment, wondering if she suspected. Then he lifted one shoulder. "Even if it is, there are a lot of cops. Probably always be a mystery." Time to change the subject. "So what do you want to do tomorrow?"

Before Cilla could answer, the waitress slid their plates onto the table. Cilla swirled a fry in ketchup, ate it, then cut her burger in half and took a bite.

When she'd eaten half of it, she leaned back. "Sorry. I was really hungry."

He grinned. "I like a woman with a good appetite." Predictably, she rolled her eyes. Exactly what he was going for. "So. Tomorrow?"

She picked up the other half of her burger and took a bite before answering. "What kinds of crowds are in the clubs on Tuesdays?" she finally asked.

"Probably not a lot of people. Thirsty Thursday would

be better. We should probably wait until then to hit the clubs."

"Okay." She'd made steady progress on the burger until only a bite was left. "Pub tomorrow night?"

She leaned back and wiped her hands with the napkin, and Brendan exhaled with relief as he studied her. She looked less pale. Less beaten down. A little more like the Cilla he knew.

"Brendan?" She frowned, as if puzzled. "Tomorrow?"

Pay attention. Stop staring at her. "Yeah," he said easily. "Tomorrow we'll check out the pub."

***

Cilla sank into the worn leather of Betsy's driver's seat as Brendan closed the door behind her with a solid thunk. She watched him walk around the front of the car, then slide in beside her.

His familiar scent, all woodsy and smelling of the outdoors, filled the Mustang. She inhaled deeply, trying to capture it inside her.

She was so glad he'd come to the hostage scene.

She'd expected to go home, maybe order Chinese, and spend the evening in an exhausted daze. Watching television without really seeing it. Or maybe just staring out her window.

Instead, he'd been waiting for her. Because they were partners and she might need him.

No one ever thought Cilla might need help. Or support. She was the one who helped everyone else. Talked her brother through his baseball crises. Solved her sister's problems. The one her mother called when she needed to unload on someone. Cilla was the family fixer.

Brendan snapped his seat belt into place, and she started the car. As she exited out of the parking lot, she said, "Brendan?"

"Hmm?" he answered, examining the vintage seat belt

that only went over his lap.

"Why did you really come to the hostage scene today?" Had he needed something from her? "Did something happen with our case?"

"Nope." He swiveled his hips on the seat so he was half-facing her. "I just...hostage negotiation is a tough job. I remember when we studied it in the academy." He shuddered. "I screwed it up every time. Afterward, I'd be jittery for hours, and it wasn't even real." He shrugged. "No matter how it went, I thought you might want some company."

She wished he'd been there after her last domestic went so horribly wrong. Reaching across the console, she grabbed his hand and squeezed it. His fingers were warm. Reassuring. When he slid his fingers between hers, she felt little calluses on his fingertips. "I'm really glad you're here."

He put his palm against hers. "I'm glad I came." He twined their fingers together. "What would have happened to your leftover fries if I hadn't been there?"

She smiled and drew her hand away, stepped on the clutch and shifted gears. "Yeah, they would have gone to waste. Would have been a shame."

He'd told her she'd done a good job. Saved a family. Even though she already knew it, it had been nice hearing him say it. Hearing him appreciate what she'd done.

Without looking at him, she said, "I usually go to one of the beaches after a hostage negotiation. To unwind. The lake, the water, the squawking birds really help. You really helped tonight."

"So you're saying I'm better than a bunch of seagulls?"

"Much better." She smiled. "And you didn't try to steal my food, either."

"I've seen you eat. And you're wearing your gun. No way was I going to mess with your dinner."

She laughed. "I like a man who pays attention." When was the last time she'd laughed after a hostage crisis? Brendan was good for her.

Instead of thinking about that, she asked, "So where do you want me to drop you off? The station? Your apartment?"

"My place is fine. I have to take Franny out for a walk."

"Okay." She made a turn, then another. Ten minutes later, she pulled into a parking spot at his front gate.

She turned to look at him. A streetlight a few cars down shed weak light into the car. He was watching her, an uncertain expression on his face.

"What?" she asked.

"You're exhausted. You probably want to get home. But I was thinking...you want to walk Franny with me? Get some fresh air? You were cooped up in that trailer all afternoon."

She should go home. Shower off the sweat and tension that coated her skin and permeated her clothes. Unwind in peace.

But suddenly that sounded depressing. Lonely and quiet. Company sounded perfect. Not just company. Brendan. "Yeah, I'd like that," she heard herself saying. "Walking would be good."

His face lit up with a smile. "Great. Let's go get her. There's nothing like being greeted by a dog when you get home."

He hurried around to her side of the car, and Cilla waited for him to help her out of it. Having help felt...good.

When they walked into his apartment and he flicked on a light, Franny rushed over, her whole body wiggling. She acted as though Brendan had been gone for days, instead of just a few hours. And after she finished greeting Brendan, the dog bounced over to Cilla.

"What a good dog you are," Cilla murmured, rubbing Franny's ears. "What a smart puppy."

"Franny. Walk?" Brendan said.

The dog sat abruptly, her rear end still moving. Brendan picked up her leash and snapped it to her collar. "Okay. Let's go."

Once again, Franny heeled perfectly as they walked to the small park a few blocks away. When they stepped off the sidewalk, the canopy of trees overhead hid the moon and muted the surrounding streetlights. Dead leaves covered the grass, and when Brendan unsnapped the leash, Franny dashed through them, snapping at the leaves she stirred up, racing across the grass.

Just like earlier in the day, taking Franny for a walk felt – intimate. Something a couple would do when they got home from work. Walk the dog. Talk about their day. Discuss what to do about dinner.

It was a mirage, Cilla reminded herself. Something shimmering on the horizon, drawing her in, but not really there.

Just like she'd created a mirage for Zeke today. Gotten him to believe it was real. Now they had to make it real for him.

It could be real for you, too, a tiny voice whispered. All you have to do is reach for it.

She wasn't sure she knew how. And even if she did, it wasn't smart to do it with Brendan. Yeah, he got her going like no one ever had before. Yeah, he was a great guy. He had depths she hadn't expected.

But he'd told her he didn't do serious.

And he was a cop.

A cop who'd been there when she needed him.

As they walked back to his apartment, they were close enough that their hands brushed. Each time sent a tiny jolt of electricity up her arm. Reminded her of what Brendan's hands had felt like on her skin.

She didn't want to go home. She wanted to stay here with Brendan. Unwind with him. All night.

Maybe Brendan wasn't a good bet for a long-term relationship. But was there anything wrong with short term? Yeah, partners on the job shouldn't get together in their personal lives. But they had some solid leads on this case. It wouldn't last much longer. There wouldn't be time to get too wrapped up in Brendan. When the case was over, they'd go their separate ways.

Until then? Maybe it was time break her own rules.

CHAPTER SIXTEEN

Cilla saw the Mustang, gleaming red in the faint light of the streetlamp, as soon as they turned the corner onto Brendan's block. She closed her eyes. She'd forgotten about Betsy.

She wanted to stay, but she couldn't. She needed to take the car home.

The little flicker of relief made her frown. The whole 'breaking the rules' thing didn't last long, did it, Marini?

She fished in her bag for the keys, ignoring the taunting voice calling her a coward. Turning to Brendan, she said, "Thanks for coming to get me." She lifted a hand and touched his face. His whiskers tickled her fingertips, and she remembered the way they'd felt, scraping against her skin as he'd kissed her throat. Wanted to feel them again, in other, more sensitive places. "I really appreciate it."

"I'm glad I did. And you don't have to leave." The rumble of his voice sent sparks shooting through her body. "Why don't you come up and hang out with Franny and me?"

Because she was afraid she wouldn't be able to hide herself from Brendan. Afraid he'd strip away her walls and leave her bare and vulnerable.

She glanced at the car she loved. The car that had been a gift from her father. No one had really seen her since he'd died.

She knew what would happen if she let Brendan see her. After this case was over, after they went their separate ways, she'd be raw. Exposed. It would take a long time to rebuild the walls around her heart.

"I'd like to, Brendan, I really would, but I can't leave Betsy on the street. I have to lock her in the garage."

A shadow of disappointment flickered across his face, then he shrugged. "Yeah, you don't want to leave a beauty like that alone. Maybe another time?"

"Sure. I'll take a rain check."

He shoved his hands into his pockets and stepped back as she slid into the car. Waved as she drove away. When she looked in the rear-view mirror as she turned the corner, he was still watching her.

"Damn it." She slapped the steering wheel. "Betsy, sometimes you're a real pain in the ass."

It wasn't Betsy who was the pain in the ass. It was her insecurities. Her need for control. Her fear of being hurt. "Sorry, baby," she muttered, smoothing her hand over the steering wheel. "Not your fault I'm such a wuss."

The alley leading to her garage was illuminated at the street, but shadowed in the middle where her apartment was. She bumped over the broken piece of cement as she drove in, and the headlights flashed skyward. Like a beacon, showing her the way.

When the Mustang was safely locked in her garage, she trudged in the darkness up the back stairs to her apartment on the top floor of the two-flat.

Even after she turned on the lights, her apartment felt cold. Empty. Too quiet. Damn it, she didn't want quiet tonight.

The echo of her footsteps bounced off the walls as she walked through the kitchen, around a corner and into her bathroom, stripping off her clothes as she went. After a hostage scene, she always took a bubble bath and had a glass of wine. Relaxed.

Not tonight. Energy fizzed through her. She flipped on the lever for the shower and stepped into the stream of hot water. Her mind drifted to Brendan as she washed her hair. Remembered the way his hands felt as she scraped a washcloth across her body.

Fifteen minutes later, as she wrung out her hair, then towel dried it, she sighed. It felt good to be clean.

It would have felt a lot better to be at Brendan's place.

You chickened out earlier, but no reason you can't go back.

The tiny voice in her head made her freeze, the towel draped over her head. Why hadn't she stayed with him? Betsy had been a convenient excuse. She'd been afraid to let him see the real Cilla.

Afraid of losing control.

It didn't have to be such a big, freaking deal. She was a grown-up, attracted to Brendan. He was attracted to her, too. Why shouldn't she act on it? She didn't have to bare her soul to him. They could have fun, and she could walk away intact.

She ignored the tiny voice that said it might be too late for that.

She shook out her hair, felt the waves settle around her face. She didn't want to be 'responsible Cilla' tonight. She wanted to have fun. Be reckless. Take a chance. She wanted to wrap her arms around Brendan and taste him again.

Do more than taste him.

She dropped the towel on top of her dirty clothes and yanked open her underwear drawer. Chose a deep purple bra and matching panties. Then put on clean jeans, a light green sweater and slipped into a pair of shoes.

As she drove her small SUV toward his apartment, she spotted Frosting, a gourmet cupcake shop on a brightly lit block of Belmont. Cupcakes were fun. And with a parking spot right in front of Frosting, she took it as a sign and pulled over.

It was eight o'clock, and the shop on the busy street was still open. The bell above the door chimed as she stepped inside. She inhaled deeply, savoring the smells of chocolate, vanilla and cinnamon. The cupcakes in the glass display case were beautiful. Some had flowers piped onto the frosting. Others had sparkly sprinkles. One had a piece of chocolate embedded in the white frosting.

She picked one with sprinkles and one with the chocolate piece, paid the smiling clerk and took the box. As she slid it onto the floor of her car, she saw a pet store a few buildings down. Smiling, she hurried down the street and bought Franny a gourmet rawhide bone. Then she got back in her car and drove to Brendan's.

The parking spot in front of his gate was taken, but she found another a block away. Clutching the cupcake box and the bag with the rawhide, she hurried through the darkness toward the soft gleam of the lights in his courtyard.

Once there, she tugged on the gate and realized it was locked. A panel on the fence held a list of names with a buzzer beside each one.

Her finger hovered over 'Donovan'. What if he was gone? Worse, what if he wasn't alone?

She closed her eyes and took a deep breath. She knew one certainty about Brendan. He wouldn't have had sex with her if he was seeing someone else. And if he was gone?

When did you become such a wimp, Marini? If he wasn't here, she'd go home and have a cupcake. Maybe both of them.

Before she could talk herself out of it, she pressed the buzzer for Brendan's apartment. Moments later, his tinny voice came out of the speaker. "Yes?"

"Ah, hi, Brendan. It's me. Cilla." She wiped one sweaty hand on her jeans. "I, um, ditched Betsy and came back. Unless you're busy, or you've..."

171

The lock buzzed, and she pulled the wrought iron gate open. By the time she reached the front door, Brendan was waiting for her.

"Hey." His eyes gleamed in the dimly lit entranceway, and he took her hand to pull her inside. "I'm glad you came back." His gaze fell on the cupcake box. "With presents, too."

"We didn't have dessert." Her hand shook, and she heard the tiny plinks of sprinkles falling onto cardboard.

He took the box from her and tucked it beneath his arm, never taking his gaze off her face. "I love dessert," he said, his voice low. Raspy.

Heat swept over her, settled low in her belly with a pulsating beat. "I hope you like the flavors I got."

"Oh, I'm sure I'll love your flavors." His eyes were heavy-lidded. Dark, dark blue. "They'll be perfect."

As they stared at each other, someone pushed open the outer door and it bumped into Cilla. She stumbled forward, and Brendan took her hand. Warm and strong, it wrapped around hers like a promise. He tugged her up the stairs and around the corner. Ahead, she saw a triangle of light spilling into the hall where he'd left his door ajar.

Franny sat next to the open door, her stumpy tail wagging. "See," Brendan said as he pulled her inside and shut the door behind her. "Franny's excited, too."

"Should I give her the bone I got?"

His face softened. "You got my dog a bone?"

"Well, not your dog," she teased, regaining some of her game. "The dog you're borrowing. Or maybe trying to steal."

"Me? I don't steal anything. I only take what's freely given." He leaned against the door, his eyes fixed on hers, and the highlight reel of her last visit unspooled in her brain. The way Brendan had kissed her. Touched her. Held her against that door.

The desperate need that had gripped both of them.

From the heat in his gaze, he was watching the same

film.

She flushed and stepped away from his touch. If she didn't, she'd embarrass herself. "Is it okay if I give Franny her dessert?"

"Sure." He pushed away from the door. "Franny, sit."

The dog plopped herself on the floor, staring up at Brendan.

"You have to make her work for it," he said to Cilla, his mouth curling up at one corner as his eyes darkened even more.

Heat swept up her neck and flashed over her face. Her voice was raspy as she said, "Oh, I'm going to make everyone work for it tonight."

He leaned closer. "Is that a promise, Cilla?"

She let her gaze hold his. "Guess you'll have to find out, won't you?" Franny barked once, and Cilla took a deep breath. "Someone's impatient."

His gaze swung back to Cilla. "Yeah. Someone is. And you're a tease, Marini." He leaned closer. "Where's the bone?"

She glanced at the bulge in his jeans, opened her mouth, then closed it again. Fumbled in the bag and held out the rawhide. "Okay, what do I do with this?"

"Balance it on her nose."

She glanced at Brendan again. Big mistake. The heat in his dark gaze washed over her in a wave. Her hand quivered, and it had nothing to do with the dog.

Finally, Brendan put his hand over hers. His fingers were warm. Steady on top of hers. He balanced the bone on the dog's nose, then pulled both of their hands away.

Twining their fingers together, he said, "Wait, Franny."

The dog sat motionless.

"Get it," he said. Franny tossed the bone up high, snapped it out of the air, then dropped to the floor, gnawing on the rawhide.

"She'll be busy with that for a while," he said, drawing her toward the couch. "Let's see what kind of surprises you brought for me."

He opened the box and smiled as he saw the two cupcakes. "Oh, yeah," he murmured. "Red velvet. My favorite."

He dipped his finger in the frosting and brought it to her mouth. "Try it," he coaxed.

She opened her mouth and took his finger inside, swirling her tongue around his fingertip. The sweet, cool icing was delicious.

Brendan tasted even better.

His throat rippled as he watched her. When she finally released his finger with a tiny pop, he put it in his own mouth and licked it. "Sweetest flavor ever," he whispered.

His tongue curled around his finger, and she stared at his mouth. She wanted his tongue on her. Drawing lazy circles on her skin. Driving her crazy. "I got all the frosting on your finger," she said, barely able to form the words.

"Wasn't talking about the frosting." He kept his gaze on her as he dropped the box onto the coffee table. "You want to watch TV, Cilla?"

"No," she whispered.

"Play cards?"

"Nope."

"Play some other kind of game?"

Her eyes wanted to flutter closed, but she kept her gaze on his. "You're getting closer."

"What me to guess?"

"Yes." She moved toward him, as if they were opposite sides of a magnet, drawn inexorably closer. She ached to feel his skin beneath her hands, the shape of his muscles, the scrape of his five o'clock shadow against her skin.

Brendan was one surprise after another. Impulsive and reckless. Thoughtful and kind. Fun.

She needed fun tonight.

No. She needed Brendan.

"Cilla." His hands slid into her still-damp hair, lifting it away from her face. He leaned closer, until she could see the thin ring of blue around the black centers of his eyes. "Tell me what you want."

"You, Brendan. I want you."

He let out a breath, and she shivered as it feathered across her skin. "I want you, too, Cilla. So much." He smoothed the hair off her face, tucked it behind her ears. "I've been burning for you since the night we met. On fire to taste you again since we made love."

Made love. He hadn't said they'd had sex. Eyes prickling, she curled her fingers around his ears and drew him closer. "I didn't want to want you. I have rules..." She closed her eyes and shook her head. Opened her eyes again. "You break every one of them."

"What are your rules, Cilla?" He smoothed his thumbs over her cheeks, and that simple touch made her body flame.

"It doesn't matter. They don't matter. Not with you." She clutched the soft material of his shirt in her fists to pull him closer, fumbled at the first button.

He grabbed her wrists and held her hands at his mouth, kissing first one, then the other. "Is this a one-time thing, Cilla? A reaction to what happened today? You needing to blow off steam?"

No. She'd told herself she just wanted fun, but in this intimate moment, she knew she'd lied. She pressed her fingers against his lips, shivering when he nibbled on them. "Would it matter?"

He rested his forehead against hers and took a deep, shuddering breath. "Yeah, it would matter. I don't want this to be a one time thing. It would kill me to have only one night with you. But honestly?" He lifted his head and the heat in his gaze burned. "Don't think I could say no to you."

His words burrowed into her chest. Squeezed her heart. If he hadn't been holding her, she would have melted at his feet. "No." She pressed her mouth to his, tasted the faint sweetness of the frosting on his lips. "Not stress. Not an 'I won' celebration. Not just one night. It's you, Brendan. Just you."

Her heart constricted with a tiny pang. Their time together was limited. The women in the CPD talked, and 'love 'em and leave 'em Donovan' was legendary. He didn't do 'serious'. She told herself she was fine with that.

He tugged her closer and rubbed his lips against hers. They were soft and warm, and she sucked his lower lip into her mouth. Traced it with her tongue, then nibbled at it.

He groaned and lifted her onto his lap, wrapping his arms around her. She felt safe in the cocoon of his embrace. Protected. Everything else fell away. Their case, her sister, their jobs at the pub – none of it mattered.

His hands sliding beneath her sweater were the only reality. His warm palms on the hot skin of her abdomen was all she felt. Forgetting her reservations, her reluctance to let herself go, she squirmed against him. Panted into his mouth. Pressed closer, needing his touch on her breasts.

Needing more, she shifted on his lap until she faced him, her thighs gripping his. His eyes were closed, and his hands trembled as they tightened around her. Swallowing hard, she shifted until his hard cock pressed exactly where she needed it. Holding nothing back, kissing him with wild abandon, she felt for his shirt buttons. But her hands shook too much to push them through the holes.

Suddenly Brendan surged to his feet. She clutched his shoulders, but knew he wouldn't drop her. Wrapping her arms and legs around him, she buried her face in his neck, drinking in his scent. Fresh. Like the outdoors. Musky with arousal.

He held her tightly as he walked into his bedroom, kissing her as they moved. He tore his mouth away from hers as he set her on the bed, then knelt down in front of her. He stroked his fingers over her skin as he unbuttoned and unzipped her jeans, making her shiver as he tugged them down her legs. Then he slowly lifted her sweater, kissing her abdomen, her chest, her breasts as he pulled it over her head.

He sucked in a breath as he studied her purple lingerie. "I think I have a new favorite color," he whispered, smoothing his fingers over the satin cups of her bra. She arched into him, but he grinned down at her and slid his hands lower. He dipped his fingers into the waistband of her panties, making her squirm, but didn't go any farther.

"Never knew you were a tease, Donovan," she said, reaching for him and unbuttoning his shirt. "Two can play that game, you know."

He leaned over her on the bed, his face so close that his breath feathered over her cheek. "That so, Marini?" He nuzzled her neck, nibbled at her earlobe. "Bring it on."

His heart thundered against her hand when she pulled him closer. She managed to undo all his shirt buttons, and she shoved the sleeves down his arms. While he was trapped, his arms caught behind him, she unbuttoned his jeans and peeled them over his narrow hips.

His cock moved against his boxer briefs, and she smiled as she kissed him through the cotton. As he struggled to remove his shirt, she slid one finger into his waistband, touched the hot, swollen head of his cock, swirling her finger around it. Then curled her fingers around him, smiling into his chest as he jumped in her hand. She was affecting him as much as he was affecting her.

His hips jerked against her, and she withdrew her hand, letting the waistband snap back into place. Then she leaned back on the bed, unhooked her bra and let it fall away. She cupped both of her breasts in her hands, watching Brendan flail at his shirt as he watched her.

Finally freeing his arms, he flung it away from him, stripped off his jeans and boxers and crawled onto the bed. Pinned her hands to the quilt and sucked her earlobe into his mouth.

"You're doing my job," he murmured, nipping at the sensitive skin beneath her ear. His hands covered her breasts, sliding over her nipples. When he bent to take one in his mouth, she moaned, wrapping her legs around his waist.

"Supposed to be slow," he panted in her ear as he stripped off her panties. "Remember? That's what I promised last time. But you're making me crazy, Cilla." His hips twitched into hers, sliding his cock along her folds. "You want me to break my promise?"

"I'm begging you to break your promise," she said, sucking on his neck.

His mouth curved against her skin. "I love it when you beg. I'm going to make you beg a lot tonight."

"Bet I can make you beg, too," she whispered.

He lifted her up, yanked back the comforter and blanket, and laid her on the cool sheets. Then he reached toward his night table, opened the drawer and pulled out a foil packet. Before he could open it, she put her hand on his. "If you want to use it, that's fine. But I'm on the pill. Got a clean bill of health at my exam last month."

"You trust me that much?" he asked, frozen above her.

She did, she realized. He'd tell her if there was a reason he needed a condom on top of the pill. "Yeah," she whispered, nuzzling his neck. "I trust you."

He dropped the packet on the floor and wrapped her in his arms. Buried his face in her hair. "I won't hurt you, Cilla. I swear."

There was a good chance he would hurt her. But it would be her own fault if she let herself get too attached to him. So she drew him closer and lost herself in his kiss. When her body was aching for him, when she couldn't wait another second, she drew him closer. "Now, Brendan. I need you now."

He kissed her as he slid inside her. Kissed her as they began to move together. Kissed her when she came apart in his arms.

Kissed her as he followed her over.

They lay entwined together, arms and legs wrapped around each other, until her breathing slowed and her body began to cool. He eased to the side, then pulled her against him. He buried his face in her hair and smoothed his hand up and down her back, as if trying to memorize every inch of her skin. She snuggled closer, reveling in the strength of his muscles, the smooth skin of his back, the fine hairs on his chest, the powerful legs he'd wrapped around her.

After a long time, he eased away from her and brushed her hair out of her face. "You ready for some dessert?"

"Isn't that what we just had?" she murmured, cupping his cheek and brushing her mouth over his.

"First round of dessert," he answered, his eyes twinkling. "I think it's time for some cupcakes."

CHAPTER SEVENTEEN

Brendan strolled out of his bedroom, glancing over his shoulder to see her eyeing his ass. "Like what you see, Marini?"

Instead of being flustered, she gave him a slow smile that made his cock twitch. "Oh, yeah, Donovan. Get over here so I can like it more closely."

He loved that she was so direct about sex. That she'd come over here, intent on seducing him.

She hadn't had to work very hard. He grinned as he picked up the cupcake box. Sex with Cilla was fun. Playful. Intense.

Rock his world, earth-shaking amazing. She made every woman he'd ever known disappear. All he wanted was Cilla.

He grabbed the cupcake box from the end table and hurried back into the bedroom. Cilla was half-sitting, leaning against the head board. She had the sheet tucked beneath her arms, exposing only her shoulders.

He bit the inside of his cheek to keep from laughing. "News flash, Marini." He curled one finger into the sheet. "I've already seen it all." He tugged, and the sheet puddled across her lap.

"Maybe I was cold," she said, leaning into his warmth.

Her long, wavy hair brushed his cheek and surrounded him with her scent. Oranges. Spicy and sweet at the same time. Just like her.

Pink whisker burn colored her neck, and her mouth was swollen from his kisses. It had been less than a half-hour, and he wanted her again.

He wrapped his arm around her and pulled her close. Kissed her. Murmured into her mouth, "I can take care of that for you."

He felt her smile against his mouth. "Counting on it," she murmured as she deepened the kiss.

He continued to kiss her as he fumbled inside the cupcake box. His tongue stroked hers as he curled his hand around her breast. Dabbed a blob of frosting on her nipple.

She flinched, and he eased away from her, running his tongue over the inside of her lip. "Easy, Marini," he said, nibbling on her neck as he made her way lower. "Just preparing dessert." He put another dab of frosting on her other breast, letting his hand linger.

She giggled when she saw the frosting on her nipple, and he smiled against her skin. He really liked giggling Cilla. He'd make it his mission in life to draw that sound from her mouth as often as possible.

He moved lower and drew the frosting into his mouth, swirling his tongue around her pebbled tip. She twisted into him, murmuring incoherently. All he could hear was, "Yes," and "right there," and "Brendan." God was mentioned, as well. She wrapped one leg around his thigh, trying to draw him closer.

"Hey," he said with one final swipe of his tongue. Then he moved to her other breast. "Show a little patience here, Marini. Let me enjoy my dessert."

Her hips were pumping against him now, as if she couldn't help moving. Her hand patted the bed. Looking for the cupcakes, probably. "My turn for dessert," she said, her voice breathy and trembling.

"Uh uh. Not done with mine yet." He closed his mouth over her nipple and sucked, tasting the frosting and Cilla. He'd never tasted anything as sweet.

She squirmed against him, panting. When he finally let her nipple go, he knew she was close by the uneven, scattered rhythm of her hips. Then she surprised him by swinging one leg over him and trapping him beneath her hips. His cock twitched, needing to be much closer.

He smoothed his hand over her face, then tried to pull her closer. "Can't wait, Marini?"

"No," she murmured, holding his gaze. Her eyes were dark, the irises barely visible, and a red flush covered her face and chest. He felt her trembling beneath him. "I can't wait. I want you so bad I would have taken care of it myself if you hadn't stopped."

He stared at her, stunned. His hands tightened on her hips, trying to pull her closer. He needed to be buried in her. But she was resisting.

"Inside you, Cilla. Right now," he said, swallowing hard. "You can't say things like that and not expect me to go crazy."

She smeared a line of frosting across his abdomen, right below his navel, then grinned up at him. "I haven't had my dessert yet." She was panting, too. Her hips jerked against his leg But she was loving the tease. The fun. She bent over him, her silky hair tickling his chest and abdomen, and began licking at the frosting.

After she'd licked off all the frosting, she moved lower. Closer to his cock. Knowing he'd explode if she went any farther, Brendan gripped her hips and pulled her higher, until she was right over his cock. "Enough," he groaned. "I need you. Now. Or I'm going to embarrass myself like I haven't since high school."

She slid onto his cock, pressing her mouth to his. She shuddered when he began to move, and it took only a few thrusts before she cried out, sobbing his name.

Which was a good thing, because he couldn't hold off

for another second. He came so hard that he shook with it. When he finally took a long, shuddering breath, he tightened his arms around her, holding her so close he felt her heart beating against his.

"Brendan," she whispered.

"Yeah?"

"That was..." There was a long silence.

"Horrible?" he said into her sweet-smelling hair. "Disappointing? Blah?"

Her arms were still wrapped around him, and she squeezed more tightly. "Amazing," she murmured. "I was going for amazing."

He swallowed. Nuzzled aside her hair so he could kiss her neck. "Yeah. It was amazing. I think I felt the earth move."

Time to lighten this up. It had been the most incredible, mind-blowing sex of his life. He didn't want to go all serious on Cilla. "Or maybe Chicago just had an earthquake."

She giggled again and burrowed closer, and he reached down and pulled the sheet and blanket over them. He fell asleep with her body wrapped around his and her scent calming him. His last, unbidden thought was, 'mine'.

**

The chatter in his head woke him at three AM. Cilla was tucked in beside him, her head on his chest and her arm curled around him. He lay beside her, his eyes open, listening to her breathe, feeling the slow rise and fall of her chest. He wanted to snuggle into her, to fall back asleep with her in his arms. But he knew sleep wouldn't return until he quieted the noise.

He eased her head onto a pillow, missing her weight immediately. Untangled her arm. She murmured in her sleep, but didn't wake up. He brushed aside her heavy, silky hair, kissed her cheek, then slid out of bed.

Silently throwing on sweats and a hoodie, he hurried into

the living room and booted up his computer. Franny raised her head from her bed, watched him for a long moment, then lowered it again. She'd seen him get up in the middle of the night and sit down at his desk the last time he watched her. She knew it didn't mean a walk was coming.

His fingers flew across the keys, the pictures from the hostage scene unspooling in his head. Everything else faded from his consciousness – the light in the courtyard, the dog close by, the woman in his bedroom.

All he saw was the tense, nervous officers. The SWAT team surrounding the house. The black van, hiding the hostage negotiator trying to make a happy ending.

He typed about the delicate dance hostage negotiators performed. Getting the HT to release his hostages. Getting him out of the house safely. Getting him help.

He wrote about the bond that negotiators forged with the HT, no matter how despicable they were. How their only goal was to get everyone out of the house without any violence. How they put everything they had into resolving the crisis without any casualties.

As he wrote, he thought about Cilla. About the exhaustion on her face as she'd walked toward him. The stiff, careful way she moved, as if she'd been sitting, tense and still, for far too long. Her clothes, rumpled and soaked with sweat. The scent from the inside of the van that had clung to her – old sweat, cold coffee, the yeasty, sour smell of a stale donut.

The toll her job had taken on her.

He changed some of the details. Made other things fuzzy. Put nothing in the story that could identify the neighborhood or anyone who'd been at the scene.

His hands moved faster as he wrapped up the blog entry. Finished with his usual line, paraphrased from some television series his parents watched when he was a kid. 'Stay safe out there.'

When he stretched, he bumped into someone. Cilla. He closed his eyes. In his writing fog, he'd forgotten all about her.

Forgotten everything except the words spilling out through his fingers.

As he looked over his shoulder at her, ready to apologize for abandoning her in his bed, she wrapped her arms around him. "Brendan." She pressed her mouth to his cheek. "What you just wrote, about the hostage thing today? It was incredible. So well done." Her mouth curved against his cheek. "I was there, and it almost made me cry."

"That's because you're a sap, Cilla." He spun his chair around, pulled her into his lap, nuzzled her neck. She wore the shirt he'd discarded, the top buttons undone, and nothing else. His cock was interested. But it would have to wait.

She cuddled into him, drawing her bare legs onto his lap, fiddling with the tie strings from his hoodie. "Who else knows you're the Cops and Robbers blogger?"

"No one."

"Really?" She sounded shocked.

"Not a soul. I don't want anyone to know."

She tilted her head up to study him. "You know I won't say a word to anyone. Ever."

He nodded. "Okay."

No one knew about any of his writing. He hadn't intended to tell Cilla, either. But he'd been so into what he was doing, he hadn't sensed her behind him.

In the past, when he'd spent the night with a woman, he'd gone to her place. Precisely so this wouldn't happen.

He was okay with Cilla knowing, he realized. He believed her when she said she wouldn't tell anyone. "I trust you. If you say you won't talk about it, I know you won't."

She lifted her head from its spot between his neck and his shoulder and gave him a soft smile. "Thank you. It means a lot, that you have faith in me."

"I do." The words made him freeze for a moment. Then he swallowed. Smiled at her. "Want to go back to bed?"

"Will you come with me? Or are you going to..." She wiggled her fingers at the computer screen, "do more of that?"

"Nope." He reached around her and saved his work, then closed the laptop. "I'm done for the night."

He lifted Cilla off his lap, took her hand and led her into the bedroom. Unbuttoned his shirt and slid it down her arms. Stared for a long moment at naked Cilla, standing in front of him.

"You're beautiful," he said. He touched her cool cheek, slid his hands down the silky skin of her sides, then her legs. "Perfect." And mine, that little voice said again. For now, he retorted. To shove that unsettling voice out of his head, he added, "And really hot."

She smiled, a faint blush coloring her cheeks. But her eyes were soft. Tender. "Take off those sweats, Mr. Writer. I want to see your beautiful, perfect and really hot body, too."

Brendan shucked the baggy sweats and faded hoodie, then drew Cilla onto the bed. He worshipped her body with his mouth and his hands, making her come twice before he slid inside her.

They made love slowly, their mouths fused together, their movements synced perfectly, as if they'd been making love for years instead of a couple of days. When he felt Cilla tightening around him, he let go himself. He held her close as their breathing steadied and the sweat on their bodies cooled.

"What do your brothers think of you writing that blog?"

He lifted himself on one elbow to look down at her face. Moonlight illuminated the bed, making her skin look pearly. Glowing. He smoothed her tangled hair away from her face. "They don't know."

"Really? I figured, when you said no one knew, that it excluded your family." She sat up and leaned against the headboard, then reached for his hand and twined their fingers together. It felt...right. He scooted up to sit beside her. "You guys are so close. They'd keep your secret, wouldn't they?"

"Yeah. 'Course they would. It's not that. It's..." He swallowed. Could he reveal his most closely held secret to her?

"It's okay," she said softly, squeezing his hand. "You don't have to tell me." She smiled up at him. "Have to keep some of the mystery, right?"

"In my family, real men become cops. They're not writers," he said. "I think if I tell anyone, they'll look at me differently."

"Being a writer isn't better or worse than being a cop. It's just different," she said softly.

"I know. But it's complicated." Weariness settled over him like a wool blanket. "I'll tell you about it, but not tonight," he said, feeling his eyes closing. "We both need our sleep if we're going to the pub tomorrow night."

"Yeah, you're right." She kept his hand as she slid beneath the covers. "You wore me out, Donovan."

"I aim to please."

"Mmmmm," she murmured. "You did. Several times."

"Lost count, did you?" He'd steer them back into lighter territory.

She must have sensed his uneasiness with the heavier conversation from earlier, because she opened her eyes and grinned at him. "Oh, I know exactly how many times. But I'm not about to feed your ego."

"I'll get it out of you in the morning."

She cocked an eyebrow. "I'd much rather you get it into me in the morning."

His cock twitched, and he groaned. "Oh, my God, Cilla. You better not say stuff like that when we're working, or I'll be walking around with a permanent hard-on."

"Suck it up, Brendan."

"I'd much rather you suck it up."

They stared at each other, then both of them burst out laughing. He was still smiling, wrapped around her, when he fell asleep.

CHAPTER EIGHTEEN

Cilla walked through the front door of the Pipe and Shamrock, smoothing her hands down the thighs of her skinny jeans. Brendan followed her, resting his palm on her back. It was a signal that they were a couple. They'd scripted their appearance carefully, trying to anticipate all possible scenarios. Brendan's hand on her was the first scene in the act.

The weight of his hand felt ridiculously good through the thin material of her silk shirt. Warm. Reassuring. Comfortable.

And yes, possessive.

She wouldn't let herself think it was real. Brendan was out for fun. Just like she was, she reminded herself.

This was merely window dressing for their show. In spite of that, a secretly sappy part of Cilla savored it for a moment, pretended it was real.

Then she squared her shoulders and shoved those feelings deep inside, where no one could see them. Especially Brendan.

Last night had been incredible. Intense. Powerful. She couldn't wait to repeat it again tonight, but she didn't have any illusions.

Brendan wasn't looking for long term. He'd told her so himself. And she wasn't going to fool herself into thinking she'd be the one to change his mind.

Here at the pub, though? She needed to act all smitten with Brendan, and she could admit to herself that it wouldn't be much of a stretch. As she reached for the inner door to the pub, she closed her eyes and slipped into 'besotted girlfriend' mode. Then took a deep breath and stepped into the noise and movement of the pub.

Brendan curled his arm around her waist and bent close. "More people here tonight than I expected," he murmured into her ear. "I see a few people from the weekend, but lots of new faces, too."

"Yeah." Cilla smiled at him as if he'd been whispering sweet nothings in her ear instead of risk assessments. "There are two seats at the other end of the bar, in the corner, where we can see most of the room. Let's grab them."

As they slid onto the high stools, the bartender glanced at them, then did a double take. "Hey, Cilla," he said, walking over with a smile. "Can't stay away from this place, huh?"

"I thought I'd see what it's like from this side of the stage." She leaned into Brendan's shoulder, pleased when Rick's gaze settled on them for a long moment.

"Iced tea for you?" Rick asked.

"Nope. I'm not working. I'll have a Warsteiner's Premium."

Rick frowned. "That's non-alcoholic. Might as well have iced tea."

"No, the Warsteiner is good," she said, smiling at Brendan. "I want to remember everything about this evening."

Rick shook his head, a tiny grin curling his mouth as he turned to Brendan. "How about you?"

"I'll have the same." Brendan picked up Cilla's hand and

kissed her palm. "Same reason."

He leaned closer, as if the words were meant only for Cilla, but Rick's eye roll as he set the beers on the bar told her he'd heard, as well. Which was exactly what they'd intended. Pleased, she rested her elbows on the bar and studied the room. Tightened her hand on her glass when she spotted the unpleasant guy from the weekend. "Mike Smith, the angry guy, is here."

She looked away quickly, but she was pretty sure Mike had seen her, too. "He's on your right," she murmured. "Looking this way. Probably spotted us."

"Good. Maybe he'll get the message that you're off the market."

She let her gaze drift in Mike's direction again. "Those kind of guys rarely get the message. Even when they do, it doesn't matter. They want what they want." She leaned closer to Brendan as Mike turned his head toward her. Stared at her for too long, his gaze flat.

He finally turned away, and Cilla shivered, fumbling for Brendan's hand. "He gives me the creeps," she admitted.

Brendan smoothed his thumb over the back of her hand as he frowned. "Maybe we need to add him to our list of possibilities. I could see him as a drug dealer."

Cilla glanced down at their joined fingers and watched as Brendan drew pictures on her hand. As if he didn't even realize he was doing it. Swallowing once, she said, "He's certainly arrogant enough for it."

They finished their beers and ordered another round, acting like lovers completely absorbed in one another. With Brendan so close, Cilla had a hard time remembering they were acting. She forced herself to keep watching the crowd.

They were halfway through the second beer when Cilla said quietly, "Romano just walked in."

"I see him. He's headed this way." He took a sip of beer and turned toward Cilla. "I don't want him to see our faces, at least not right away. Can you pretend like you really dig me?"

She leaned closer. "It'll take all my acting skills," she said as she nuzzled his neck. "But I'll do my best."

His laugh ruffled her hair and his warm breath skimmed her ear. "God, you're good at this."

"At pretending?" She pressed one hand into his chest and eased back to simper at him.

His hand tightened on hers. "At the whole undercover thing. You play it exactly right." He tugged her close enough that the curtain of her hair partially hid both of them. "I know you weren't pretending last night, though. I could tell by the way you screamed the third time you came," he whispered.

Memories from the previous night flashed through her, making her clench her thighs together. "Careful, Brendan." She pressed into his side, and felt his little gasp. "Or I'll drag you out to the car and have my way with you."

"Later, Cilla." His low voice promised all sorts of things that made her warmer.

"I'll hold you to that." Out of the corner of her eye, she saw Romano, weaving his way through the bar like he had somewhere he needed to be. "Romano's heading this way. Looking for someone, maybe. I doubt he'll notice us, but don't turn around yet."

A few moments later, Brendan eased away from her. "He disappeared into a dark corner in the back. A little alcove. Semi-private. I've seen couples making out in there."

"He came in alone. Maybe he's meeting someone." She didn't turn around to look, in case Romano was watching them.

"Maybe." Brendan squeezed her hand before he let go. "I'll head to the washroom. It's in that direction."

Her heart pounded, and she grabbed his wrist. "Be careful."

"Hey, nothing to worry about. There's a steady stream of guys heading for the men's room every evening in a bar." He pressed a kiss to her cheek. "Nice that you worry,

192

though."

He was right. It was normal to go to the restroom in a bar. But she was worried. That was bad.

There was a good reason couples weren't supposed to work together. Emotion got in the way of doing their job. Made it more dangerous.

So she'd do her job and not worry about Brendan.

She picked up her beer, ignoring the stubborn pinch of anxiety in her gut, and studied the people around her. The pub was more crowded now, and she saw a few familiar faces. She'd ask Brendan to take a look when he came back.

Her phone rang, and she scowled when she saw the screen. Her sister, damn it. If she didn't answer, Liv would just keep calling.

She stabbed the call button on her phone. "Hold on for a minute, Liv. I'm at work."

Cilla leaned toward the bartender, who was only a few steps away. "Hey, Rick."

He walked over. "Need another beer, Cilla?"

"No, I got a phone call I have to take. When Brendan comes back, will you tell him I went outside to take it? I'll be back in a few minutes."

"Sure, Cilla. No problem."

"Thanks," she said as she slid off the bar stool.

She wove her way through the crowd, saying, "You still there, Liv? I'm almost outside."

Bursting through the door, she walked to the side of the pub, but now the rumble of trucks and cars down the busy street made it difficult to hear. So she rounded the corner to the back of the pub, where the building would block the traffic noise. "Okay, Liv, we're good. What's up? I'm working right now and I can't talk for long."

"You didn't call earlier. I wondered if you figured out which case James was interested in."

Damn it! With the hostage negotiation, she'd forgotten to call her sister. "Livvy, I'm sorry. I got called out on an emergency and didn't have a chance to call. It was the

Blaine case. I'll give you the details later. I have to get back inside."

Gravel crunched behind her, and Cilla spun around. Mike Smith was rounding the corner. And he was looking at her. The smile on his face made her grip the phone more tightly.

"Liv, this is important. Hang up and call this number." She rattled off Brendan's burner phone number. "Tell him to get his ass out here. Now. Rear of the pub. Trouble." She disconnected, turned on the voice recorder and slid the phone back into her purse.

Then she turned to face Mike.

"What are you doing out here, Smith?" She straightened her back, held her purse loosely at her side, tensed her leg muscles. "Heading home?"

"I saw you leave. Came looking for you," he said. As he got closer, she saw a stomach-churning gleam of anticipation in his eyes. And a bulge in his jeans. "Thought you might like some company."

"Thanks," she said, trying to sound calm and unconcerned as adrenaline washed through her and her heart began to thunder against her chest. "But I finished my phone call. I'm heading back inside."

She didn't back up as Smith approached. Didn't show any fear. She stepped aside and tried to go around him. Before she got past him, he grabbed her upper arm. Dug his fingers in hard enough to hurt.

"You're not going anywhere. The party's just getting started," he said, his eyes glittering.

She swiveled her body to the side, lifted her arm and broke his hold. "Don't touch me again." She had this. She'd trained for street fights until muscle memory took over and her moves were instinctive.

She heard a tiny snick as he brought his hand up. A switchblade. The sharp edge of the blade caught the faint beam of the flood light at the corner of the building. It flashed as he moved the knife closer. She backed away, gauging the distance she needed for a kick to his chest.

He followed. "I'm going to be doing a lot of touching." He reached for her and she used a clenched fist to knock his hand away.

"You planning on raping me, Smith?" She spoke loudly, hoping the voice recorder had caught her words. She circled around him, keeping herself on the side away from the knife. Scanning the back wall, looking for a place she could use to take Smith down. "Is that why you came out here?"

He gestured with the knife. "Take off your shirt." His gaze held hers, giving her no opening to attack. "Jeans, too."

"I don't think so." She braced herself for his attack, watching the hand with the knife.

He stabbed at her, but she'd seen him tense his arm a moment before he struck, and was able to dance the other way. A dark blue dumpster was at her back now, and broken glass crunched beneath her shoes. The sour, stomach-churning smell of decay filled her nose.

She sidled toward the end of the dumpster, and Smith lunged at her again. "I've seen the games you play," he said, almost panting with excitement. "With that guy who's been feeling you up out here after your shows. Tonight, I'm going to have some fun with you."

His hand shook a little, catching the light again. It wasn't fear, Cilla realized. It was excitement.

Bile rose in her throat, and she swallowed. She knew how to defend herself against a knife. She wasn't going to let this guy rape her. But he was closing in, and if he grabbed her again, she was in trouble.

"You need to get busy with that shirt."

Cilla stared at him, unmoving, and he suddenly lunged. The knife caught in her shirt, and as he yanked it away, the knife sliced through the silky material.

She spun away from him, feeling the cool air on her bare skin. She sucked in a breath, then another.

Smith's face twisted with rage. He lunged for her again, and she leaped aside just in time. The knife blade scraped against the side of the dumpster.

She began to back toward the light, and Smith followed her. "Run," he whispered. "Please. I love it when they run."

They? Oh, God.

She took a deep breath, then feinted as if she was going to do just that. Run. When he lunged for her, she slid in the opposite direction and stuck out her leg.

Smith stumbled over her and fell toward the dumpster. She swept her leg toward him, trying to trip him again. But he put his hands up to stop his fall and shoved himself upright quickly. Ran at her, knife extended.

She twisted away from his knife side, but she planted her foot on a piece of the broken glass, and her leg slipped sideways, throwing her against the dumpster. Smith was on her before she regained her balance.

He pressed her against the cold metal, his fingers digging painfully into her breast. He brought his right hand to her throat, pressed the tip of the knife against her jugular. Pressed a little harder when she flinched.

She froze, and he ground his erection into her. "You should have run when you had the chance."

She never would have run. She knew how to handle herself in a knife fight. One slip, though, had changed her odds.

As skilled as she was in fighting, in self-defense, he was a male. Heavier than her. Bulkier, even though he was only a few inches taller. More muscular.

Now he had her trapped against the dumpster, and her moves didn't matter. Neither did her knowledge or her smarts. Smith used his size to control her, and she couldn't dislodge him.

She was helpless, and the realization brought a punch of panicked fear. She couldn't get out of this by herself. Unless Smith was stupid, she was in deep, deep trouble.

He wasn't stupid. I love it when they run. He'd done this before.

Keeping the knife at her throat, he fumbled with her blouse. Finally, apparently frustrated with the tiny buttons, he yanked it, and the fabric gave way with a dull ripping sound. He tore it off her body, leaving her in the lacy black bra she'd worn for Brendan. The shirt she'd imagined Brendan removing was puddled on the dirty ground.

Smith's hand, holding the knife at her throat, was rock steady. He'd have to take it away at some point, so she'd wait to make her move.

Until then, she'd stay perfectly still. Planning her moves. Figuring out the best way to take him down. Always aware of that blade, digging into her neck.

She took shallow breaths to avoid making the knife dig any deeper. She was prepared for this fight. She knew what to do. But fear spread through her, making her hesitate. A knife at her throat was a checkmate to all her self-defense training.

Smith fumbled with the button of her jeans.

Oh, God. She was in trouble.

This is what happened to other women. Women who weren't prepared like she was. Women who didn't know how to fight like she did.

But she'd stumbled, and Smith had taken advantage of it. Put his knife to her throat and taken all her power. Made her vulnerable. Helpless.

Now she was just another woman who couldn't outmuscle a man. Another woman who was going to be brutalized. Degraded. Raped.

A woman who'd had all her power taken away by a man stronger than her.

Smith took his knife away from her throat for a brief second to unbutton her jeans. She stomped on his instep as hard as she could, but as he jerked backward, he brought the knife to her throat again. Pressed hard against her skin, and blood spilled down her chest.

God. Where was Brendan? Had Olivia gotten through to him? Had he heard his phone ringing?

Smith was yanking her jeans down her legs when Cilla heard the sound of a safety being released. "Drop the knife, Smith."

Brendan. She closed her eyes in a silent prayer of thanks.

Smith didn't move. "You gonna fire that gun at me?" The sneer in his voice said he didn't think so.

"Oh, yeah." Out of the corner of her eye, Cilla saw the gun get closer to Smith's head. "I would love to splatter your brains over that dumpster."

None of them moved. Cilla couldn't see Brendan. Smith smirked at her, as if Brendan's gun was a toy that couldn't hurt him.

She couldn't move her head. Couldn't take a chance. The knife blade was still firm against her skin.

In the distance, a siren wailed. Getting closer. Smith yanked harder at her jeans. "You want to watch, pretty boy?" he said.

"The only thing I'm watching is you going down," Brendan said. She heard the rage in his voice. "The cops will be here any moment."

The pressure of the knife on her throat lessened. Smith turned, as if watching for the squad car. As soon as she couldn't feel the knife, Cilla jerked her knee into Smith's groin.

He turned at the last moment, the knife flashing in the light as he stumbled sideways. His head hit the dumpster with a hollow thud. He slid to the ground, conscious but dazed.

Brendan slid around Cilla and stepped on Smith's hand until he released the knife. Then he kicked it away. It skittered beneath the dumpster with a metallic clang.

"Cilla. You got..."

"No." She interrupted Brendan. He was asking for cuffs, and she didn't want him to expose their status as cops. "Use your belt. We need to get him secured." No. Don't say that. It's not what a civilian would say.

"Right." As he spoke, Brendan yanked his belt out of

the loops of his dress pants. It cracked in the air with the force of his tug as he used his foot to shove Smith onto his belly. Brendan wrapped the belt around Smith's wrists, then yanked until it was as tight as he could make it.

"Sure it's tight enough?" Smith's mocking voice made Cilla clench her teeth, but she yanked on her jeans, pulling them up as Brendan handled Smith. The now-tied-up man tried to stand, but Brendan put his foot on the guy's back and held it there.

"I left it loose," Brendan growled. "You move again, I'll show you how much tighter it can be."

Holding the end of his belt, Brendan reached for Cilla and pulled her into his arms. "My God, Cill." He eased away from her and scanned her body. His eyes darkened as he studied her side. He let her go and ripped off his green polo shirt and dropped it over her head, leaving him in his white tee shirt. It glowed in the darkness of the parking lot.

"You're bleeding." His voice was flat. Cold. "Your side. Your neck. Where else did he hurt you?"

"I'm okay," she said, reaching out from beneath the shirt to grip his hand. She needed him close. Needed to hold onto him. Finally, she forced herself to let him go and struggled to get her arms into the sleeves of his shirt. As she pulled her hair from the collar, warm liquid trickled down her neck.

"I'm okay, Brendan," she repeated. She was. But she needed to wrap herself around him and cling. Hold him tight.

She told herself she was a police officer. She needed to act like it.

But she couldn't make herself step away from Brendan. She needed to touch him. To know he was close. Leaning into him, she said, "He ripped my shirt. Cut me a little. I can't even feel it. That's all he did." She smoothed her hand down Brendan's chest. Felt his rock-hard muscles beneath her hand.

She glanced at Smith, who was struggling to stand up.

She needed to switch into cop mode and out of needy girlfriend mode. But she couldn't quite do it.

Smith lay in the garbage on the ground, his hands behind his back. She was safe.

Cilla began to shake. In spite of the polo shirt, warm from Brendan's body, she was ice cold.

She wound her arm around Brendan's waist and burrowed closer. His muscles were solid against her side. His skin was warm through his shirt. His scent helped to block out the stench coming from the dumpster.

Brendan's arm circled her shoulders and he pulled her close. Cilla flinched when he pressed against the bruise Smith had made.

Brendan untangled himself from her and pushed up the sleeve of the polo shirt. Stared at the bruise for a long moment, then kissed it and smoothed the sleeve back into place.

"We'll make sure he doesn't get bail," he said quietly as he pulled her close again. Caressed her arm. "He'll spend a lot of years in prison. He won't be able to hurt anyone else."

He pressed a kiss to the top of her head. "And if we're very lucky, he'll irritate his cell-mates wherever he goes." Brendan kicked the sole of Smith's shoe. "You're not going to have any fun in prison, dirtbag."

"You think I'm going to jail? Not happening. I know people." Smith sneered up at them, pushing against the dumpster to get to his feet. Brendan put his foot on Smith's back and forced him to the asphalt.

"That right?" Brendan tightened his grip on her and stared down at Smith. "I know people, too. I'll have them talk to your people. They'll make sure you get the accommodations you deserve at Cook County Jail."

The sirens were closer. Smith realized it, too, because his sneer vanished. For a moment, a panicked expression flickered across his face. He shoved away from the dumpster, dislodged Brendan's foot and rose to a crouch.

Brendan yanked at the belt around his wrists. Smith

screamed in pain and stumbled to his knees. Brendan pushed him face down again. "Please try that again," Brendan said, his voice colder than Cilla had ever heard. "I'm begging you."

Smith stayed quiet on the ground. Didn't move. Brendan rolled his shoulders as a squad car crunched on the gravel.

Cilla stepped away from Brendan to summon the officers. As soon as she separated from him, she missed his warmth. His support. She took a step toward the squad car, but stumbled on the rough stones of the parking lot.

"C'mere." Brendan wrapped his arm around her waist. "Give yourself a minute."

The beam of a flashlight bounced in front of them, and a few moments later a police officer came into view. She shined the light on Cilla and Brendan both, then studied the man on the ground.

She turned the light off, and Cilla could see her more clearly. It was Officer Sobieski from the night of the overdose. "I recognize you two," the officer said. "The 911 call was unclear. Want to tell me what's going on?"

CHAPTER NINETEEN

Brendan tightened his arm around Cilla, trying to control the rage boiling through him. "This guy tried to rape my girlfriend."

He hadn't intended to say 'girlfriend'. The word just fell off his tongue, as if it were true. Which was good, he told himself. That's who they were here at the Pipe and Shamrock. It was smart to stay in their persona.

Cilla had noticed. She'd stilled against him. Tensed. Then relaxed, as if she'd remembered they were acting, as well.

He curled his fingers around her waist. They pressed into her skin, sliding beneath the fabric of his polo shirt. He glanced at her pale face, and hatred for Smith spilled over him like a scalding splash of acid. "He came after her with a knife." He pointed to the remnants of Cilla's silky shirt on the ground. "Tore off her shirt."

Sobieski shoved the notebook into her pocket. "Are you hurt?" she asked Cilla

"I think my neck is bleeding." She reached for the wound, and Brendan took her hand to stop her from touching it. "He had his knife pressed against it."

"Has a cut on her side, too," Brendan said, clenching his teeth to keep from launching himself at Smith.

"May I see?" Sobieski asked.

"Yeah."

Sobieski positioned herself between Cilla and Smith, blocking Smith's view, then gently drew the bottom of the polo shirt up. Studied it for a moment. "It'll probably need stitches," she said.

She let Cilla's shirt fall, and took the radio from her vest to call for an ambulance. "Are you able to talk now?"

Brendan watched Cilla gather herself, amazed at her toughness. "Yeah. He cut my side. Not my tongue."

Sobieski hid a tiny smile, and Brendan pulled Cilla closer. He needed her weight against him. Needed to feel her breath fanning over his neck.

Beneath the flashing lights of the squad car in the parking lot, gapers were gathering. People were coming out of the pub to see what was going on. His hand tightened on Cilla. They needed to be out of sight.

"Cilla needs to sit down," he told Sobieski. He tugged her closer, so they were plastered together from shoulder to thigh, and realized it was the truth. Shivers wracked her body every few seconds. If she hadn't been leaning so heavily against him, she'd have trouble keeping her feet beneath her.

He wanted to beat Smith senseless. Pound him into the ground. Grind him into the asphalt for reducing his strong, confident Cilla to this trembling woman.

He wanted to crush Smith like the cockroach he was.

He wrapped one arm around her carefully, avoiding the bloom of blood on her shirt where Smith had cut her. He pressed his face into her hair, inhaling her scent. She leaned into him, wrapping her arms around him.

"Can you put that asshole," he nodded at Smith, "in the squad car? Maybe we can sit in my car and talk."

Cilla opened her mouth, and he knew exactly what she was going to say. That she was fine standing up. She could give the officer her statement out here in the parking lot.

He tightened his hand around her waist until she glanced up at him with a puzzled frown. He shook his head, a movement barely more than a tic, and stared at her until she nodded. Thank God his partner was quick.

Sobieski watched him and Cilla for a long moment, then walked over to Smith. He was lying quietly on the ground. Brendan's jaw worked as he watched. Asshat was pretending to be hurt.

He took a step closer to Smith. "Not so brave when you're outnumbered, are you, Smith?"

Sobieski shot him a warning look, then put a hand beneath Smith's arm and hoisted him to his feet. Smith's carefully coifed hair was mussed, and a flattened piece of hamburger bun smeared with ketchup stuck to the side of his head. A dark, oily stain covered the front of his light blue shirt. Fierce satisfaction sliced through Brendan. Cilla had done that. She'd won.

Smith glanced from Brendan to Cilla to Sobieski. Then back to Cilla. His eyes were dark. Glittering with hatred. Anger. But he didn't say a word. He kept his gaze steady on Cilla.

Footsteps crunched on the gravel, and another cop appeared. Sobieski's partner was tall and broad, with close-cropped blond hair. He looked like a football player and had a confident demeanor. Brendan allowed himself to relax a little. With four cops surrounding him, Smith wasn't going anywhere.

"What have we got, Katya?" her partner asked.

She frowned at him for a long moment. Wondering where he'd been? "Rape attempt." She stepped in front of Cilla, blocking Smith's view of her. "Assault and battery. Knife wounds on her neck and her side."

"Huh." The man, Officer Johnstone according to his name tag, exchanged a long look with Sobieski. Then Johnstone pulled a pair of blue latex gloves from his belt. "Let me pat this guy down, then we'll get him in cuffs."

He fished out another, smaller knife in Smith's pocket and dropped it into an evidence bag he dug out from his belt. Smith didn't even glance at it.

Cilla cleared her throat. "The knife he used on me is beneath the dumpster."

"Yeah?" Johnstone turned to her. "How did it get there?"

"I kicked it out of his hand," Brendan said. "After Cilla tried to knee him in the balls."

"That so?" Johnstone's eyes sharpened as he glanced at Cilla. "The guy had a knife to your throat and was trying to rape you and you were able to knee him?"

Brendan felt her tense. Whatever she wanted to say, he'd follow her lead. He didn't want to jeopardize their operation, but he'd do it in a minute to protect Cilla.

"He was distracted when he heard the siren." She tightened her hold on Brendan. "Supposed to hit him where it hurts, right?"

"Yeah." Johnstone studied her for a moment, then unlooped Brendan's belt from Smith's wrist and dropped it on the ground. In one smooth motion, Johnstone snapped cuffs out of his belt and slapped them around Smith's wrist.

Cilla straightened beside him without moving away. "The other knife was a switchblade."

Sobieski dropped to the ground and turned on her flashlight. Then she reached behind her for the blue gloves sticking out of her belt, pulled them on and slid part-way beneath the dumpster.

When she emerged moments later, she held the switchblade in her gloved hand. "You got another bag?" she asked her partner.

"I'll get another one." He hurried toward his car.

"Grab a bunch of them," Sobieski called after her partner. Then she turned to Smith. "This yours?"

Smith shifted his gaze from Cilla to Sobieski for a moment. Didn't answer. Then fixed his stare on Cilla again.

Brendan watched Smith's gaze lock onto Cilla, anger

simmering in his eyes. The asshole better not get bail. Because this wasn't over. If Smith was free on bond, he'd come after Cilla.

Johnstone trotted back, clear plastic evidence bags clutched in his hand. He opened one and Sobieski dropped in the switchblade. Then she reached into Smith's pocket and pulled out his wallet. Flipped it open and trained her flashlight on his driver's license. "Mike Welles. That you?"

Nothing.

Brendan glanced over her shoulder, memorized the bastard's address. Just in case.

Sobieski dropped the wallet into another bag, then nodded at her partner. He took Smith – Welles – by the upper arm and led him to the squad car. As he was walking away, Sobieski picked up Brendan's belt and slid that into another evidence bag.

The whine of an ambulance siren got closer, and moments later it pulled into the parking lot, parting the watching crowd. Two EMT's jumped out. The one carrying a large bag called, "Where's the victim?"

"Right here," Brendan said.

Cilla moved stiffly, as if all her muscles ached. But she slid away from him, as if trying to prove she could stand on her own.

God! He glanced at the squad car, where Smith was a silhouette in the rear seat. He wanted his hands around that bastard's neck. Wanted to squeeze slowly, until he saw panic in the asshole's eyes. The same fear Brendan had seen in Cilla's eyes.

If he thought he could get away with it, he would pick her up and carry her to the bus. Instead, knowing she needed to reclaim some of her power, he took her hand and walked slowly toward the ambulance.

Brendan glanced at the crowd around the squad car. The flashing blue and red lights swept over the faces, illuminating them with a pulsating glow, but he didn't see either Romano or the two men he'd spotted in the pub. He helped Cilla into the back of the bus, then crowded in behind her. When the EMT guided her down onto the gurney, he nudged her until she swiveled, keeping her back to the open door.

She'd read his signals perfectly. Thank God.

As the EMT cleaned the small wound on her neck, covered it with antibiotic ointment and bandaged it, Sobieski stepped into the back of the bus. "Okay if I talk to her?" she asked the EMT.

"As long as the victim doesn't mind. This other cut could take some time. Might need stitches."

"I'm not a victim," Cilla said in a low voice. "My name is Cilla."

Brendan took her hand. Leaned closer. "Damn straight. You're the strongest woman I know."

Sobieski watched them for a moment, then pulled out a notebook and a pen. "Can you give me a statement? Or would you rather wait until Dumb Ass here is finished?" She jerked her head toward the paramedic.

The paramedic flushed. "Sorry," he muttered.

Cilla didn't glance at him. To Sobieski, she said, "Yeah. I'm good."

Sobieski nodded, then nudged the EMT. "Give her a bottle of water. She's probably thirsty."

Cilla murmured her thanks when the EMT handed her a bottle, uncapped it and took a long drink. Then she fumbled for Brendan's hand. He curled his fingers around hers, grateful she'd reached for him. That he could comfort her.

"I came out here to take a phone call from my sister," Cilla began. "It was too noisy in the pub. As I was saying goodbye to her, I saw Smith coming around the corner. I told my sister to call Brendan and get him out here."

Sobieski stopped writing and studied Cilla. "Why did you do that? Was Welles threatening you?"

"Not at that point." She swallowed again, and the muscles in her throat rippled. Brendan tightened his grip on her hand.

Smith's knife had put a small puncture in her neck. Cut her side. But if Brendan had been slower to arrive, if Cilla hadn't been so fast, Smith might have cut her throat. Brendan could have found her bleeding out next to a filthy dumpster.

"If he wasn't threatening you, why did you tell your sister to call your boyfriend?" Sobieski asked.

Her boyfriend. He glanced down at Cilla, but she didn't react. She kept her grip on his hand and her gaze on the police officer. "I've met him before. He was here every night last weekend while my band played. He, ah, asked me out. More than once. I turned him down each time. He didn't take it well."

"Okay. Back to tonight. What happened next?"

Cilla described what Smith had said, how he'd swiped at her with his knife. How she'd tripped and stumbled, how Smith had grabbed her. Held the knife to her throat, kept it there while he ripped off her shirt and fumbled with her jeans.

Her voice was even. Steady. As if she was talking about a stranger who'd almost been raped. Finally, she drew in a deep breath. Held Sobieski's gaze.

"He told me to run," Cilla said quietly. "He said, 'I like it when they run'."

"Really." Sobieski froze for a long moment, then she scribbled something in her notebook. She glanced toward the squad car, where Johnstone was herding the crowd back toward the pub door. "We always take a DNA swab in attempted sexual assault cases. I'll try to get it expedited. Anything else?"

"I turned on the voice recorder on my phone when I saw him coming," Cilla said. "It was in my purse, but you should be able to hear what he said to me." Cilla looked around, then said, "I must have dropped it back there."

The woman leaned out of the ambulance. "Derek, Cilla dropped her purse. Could you find it?"

Then she turned back to Cilla. "Pretty cool under fire to turn on the voice recorder on your phone. Why didn't you just run?"

"Because he blocked the way back to the pub." She'd kept herself pressed against Brendan the whole time. She was still shivering, though. Brendan slid his hand up and down her arm, trying to warm her. "Smith has given me the creeps since the first time I saw him. I was just...just listening to my instincts."

"Pretty good instincts," Sobieski said. She glanced at the EMT. "How's the cut?"

"She needs a few stitches. Wound's a little deep for a butterfly. We'll take her to the ER."

Sobieski studied him and Cilla. "Okay," she finally said. "Can you come into the station afterward and answer a few more questions? And we'll need you to sign your statement and sign the complaint."

Cilla started to speak, but Brendan squeezed her hand. "Can we do it tomorrow? Who knows how long it'll take at the hospital? And afterward, I want to get Cilla home."

Sobieski studied both of them, her gaze going from him to Cilla and back to him. "It's better if we get her statement right away," she finally said. "Before she forgets anything."

"She's got everything he said on her phone," Brendan answered. "You can listen to it and ask any questions tomorrow."

"Okay," Sobieski finally said, bouncing her pencil on her notebook. "We'll do it tomorrow. Give me your contact info first, though."

Brendan recited his cover name and address and the number from his burner phone. Cilla did the same. Then Johnstone leaned into the bus and handed Sobieski Cilla's purse.

"We'll need to keep your cell phone," she said to Cilla.

"You can't," Cilla said, and Brendan heard the hint of panic in her voice. "It's my only phone. I need it."

"There's evidence on this phone," Sobieski said. "I have

to keep it in my control, or it's not going to be admissible in court."

Cilla glanced up at him, and he knew exactly what she was thinking. They'd realize it was a burner. Realize she only had a couple of contacts in it. How would they explain that?

If she insisted on keeping the phone, it would weaken the case against Smith. Potentially let a rapist slither away from justice.

He smoothed his hand over her back, over and over. To reassure her. Telegraph that they'd figure something out. Finally she nodded. "I guess I can do without it tonight. Can I get it back tomorrow, though?"

"We'll let you know when you come in." Sobieski pulled out a card, handed it to Cilla. "This is one of the detectives in our crimes against persons unit. She's good. She'll be handling the case. Call her in the morning and set up a time to meet with her."

"Thank you. I will."

One of the EMT's leaned in the open door and said, "We're ready to roll." He looked at Brendan. "You can meet us at the hospital."

"I'll ride with Cilla."

"Family only." He stared at Brendan until he raised his hands and backed away.

He needed to stay with her. Hold her hand. Trying to keep his voice casual, he said, "I'll be right behind you." He pressed a kiss into her palm and added, "Will you be able to handle being without me for ten minutes?"

"I can probably survive," Cilla said, leaning toward him to brush a kiss over his mouth.

As he climbed out of the ambulance, Brendan glanced back at her. He'd survive ten minutes away from Cilla.

He just didn't want to.

***

210

Brendan glanced at Cilla as he turned out of the hospital parking lot and headed for the Dan Ryan Expressway. The EMT's had rolled Cilla's gurney directly into the ER treatment area. A doctor had looked at the wound, cleaned it, sutured it and bandaged it. Unbelievably, they were out of the hospital in less than two hours.

Wearing a dark blue hospital scrub shirt to replace Brendan's polo shirt, which they'd cut off in the ER, she sat staring out the window. Her hands curled into fists on her thighs. Her expression revealed nothing.

"How are you doing?" he asked softly.

She roused herself to look over at him. Smiled, but it didn't reach her eyes. "I'm thanking God that my sister got through to you. That you came out when you did. That all I got was a tiny scratch that took about ten minutes to suture."

"That was all you, babe. You kneed him in the family jewels. All I did was use my belt to tie him up."

"Didn't quite hit the family jewels," she said, not looking at him. "You got him on the ground. Kept him there. Called 911. Got Sobieski and her partner there fast."

He glanced out of the corner of his eye. She'd slid her hands beneath her thighs. "Hey, that's what partners do. Back each other up. Cover each other."

"You didn't just back me up. You saved me. From being raped."

"You would have taken him down, Cilla. Even if I wasn't there."

"No." Her throat rippled as she stared out the windshield. "I wouldn't have. He had me. And you know how it happened? I slipped on a piece of glass. Stumbled. As soon as I did, he grabbed me. Put the knife to my throat."

He started to speak, to reassure her, but she spoke over him. "I've always been strong. Fast. Good at hand to hand. Kicked the asses of a lot of guys in training. But real life is different."

She swallowed. Hunched her shoulders, as if she was going to be sick. "Men are usually bigger than women. Always stronger. And when a guy is trying to rape you, it's not like training. He's not going to play fair. He's going to use everything he has to control you. Hurt you. And if he has a weapon, there's not a damn thing you can do about it."

"Yeah. You're right." He reached over the console, fumbled for her wrist. Tugged her hand from beneath her leg. "It's a crappy fact of life. And I'm so sorry you had to experience it."

Her hand lay in his, unmoving. At his words, she curled her fingers around his. "Now I know how all those women feel. The ones whose husband or boyfriend beat them up. The ones who are raped. The ones who aren't lucky enough to have a partner to cover her."

She squeezed his hand more tightly, but didn't let him go. "And I don't like it. I don't like knowing I'm weak."

"You're not weak, Cilla." He'd gotten off the expressway and stopped at a red light at the bottom of the ramp. He turned to face her. "When you saw the moment, you kicked him. You began the takedown."

"I needed you, though. I couldn't have done it by myself."

He twined his fingers with hers. "It doesn't make you weak to need help once in a while, Cilla. To lean on another person."

Was he offering to be that person?

He glanced at Cilla. Maybe. Possibly.

And maybe it was okay for him to need someone else, too. Not someone. Cilla.

"Yeah." She studied her hand, pressed against her thigh. "Maybe you're right."

Her fingers tightened around his as a horn blared behind them. He glanced out the windshield and saw the light had turned green. Hit the gas too hard, and the car lurched forward.

"Looks like you need a green light spotter," she said, untangling her fingers from his. She wasn't quite smiling. But the sadness in her eyes had retreated.

"You volunteering?"

"Guess I have to. One of us has to pay attention. Right," she paused, "babe?"

He thought she'd missed his little slip. "Sorry. Just kind of popped out," he said as he turned onto a side street that led to his building.

"Don't apologize." Her voice was soft. As if she might actually like him calling her 'babe'. "It's okay."

"That's it? You're not going to ream me a new one?" Was she actually okay with it?

Was he?

"People say a lot of stuff in the heat of the moment," she said. "Just like when you called me your girlfriend in front of Sobieski."

"You think that was something I said in the heat of the moment?"

"Yeah. But it was the right thing to say. When we're at the pub, that's what we are. I'm your girlfriend. You're my boyfriend."

"Makes us sound like we're in junior high," he muttered. "Has to be a better word."

"There is. Partners. Which is what, in fact, we are."

He reached for her hand again. "Cilla, I liked calling you my girlfriend. It felt good. Right. Kinda scared the shit out of me."

"Good thing it's just temporary, then."

"Don't," he said softly. "That's not what I meant, and I think you know it. This thing between us is new. Unnamed, so far. My last 'girlfriend' was in high school. It felt weird saying it. That's all it meant.

"I never get too deep in a relationship. I don't have time. I work a lot. I spend my spare time writing. I've always gone out with women who wanted the same things I did – a good time, fun, no ties. That's not how I feel about you."

"Yeah?"

"Yeah." He took her hand, tried to smooth out the tension in her fingers. "You know about the blog. You found out accidentally, but that's because I broke one of my hard and fast rules. I never bring women to my place. Because I often get up in the middle of the night to write, and I never wanted anyone to know about it."

"Then why did you let me come over last night?"

"I wanted you there. And I guess, on some level, I must not have minded if you knew."

"Okay. That's, ah, good. Yeah."

He could read her perfectly. That, itself, should scare the crap out of him. She thought it had been the stress. The worry. He'd meant it.

Just like he'd meant it when he'd called her his girlfriend.

A tiny flutter of alarm churned in his gut. Girlfriend. Babe. Not ready to examine that. Time to focus on their case. "Do you remember when I told Sobieski you needed to sit down?"

"Yeah, I did." She clenched her fist on her thigh. "I knew I was shaking. Made me feel like an idiot."

"That wasn't it, Cilla. I was trying to get us both out of sight." He slowed to pull into a parking spot near his building. "As I was coming out of the restroom, I saw Romano. He was watching two guys in the back of the pub."

"Yeah?" She frowned. "Who was he watching?"

"Ward and Bates."

CHAPTER TWENTY

"Ward and Bates?" Shocked, Cilla swiveled to stare at Brendan in the darkened car. The faint light from a street lamp illuminated the planes of his face, the hard set of his mouth. The pain in his gaze.

"Yeah," he answered grimly. "And before you ask, yes, I'm sure."

"Wasn't going to ask that." She reached over the console and curled her fingers around his wrist. He'd steadied her during the ordeal at the pub. Wrapped her in warmth when she shivered with reaction.

Understood how much she hated being a victim. Made sure she knew he didn't think of her as one.

She knew how much Brendan hated this knowledge – that fellow cops might be involved in distributing the drug that had killed several people.

She hated it, too.

Now she wanted to offer Brendan a shoulder to lean on. "Maybe it was a coincidence."

"You really think so, Cilla?"

No. She didn't. But she had to offer up the possibility. She wouldn't be doing her job if she didn't. And Brendan deserved at least a little hope that fellow cops were no part of the distribution of this deadly drug.

She did, too. "I don't know, Brendan. But we can't jump to conclusions."

"Awfully coincidental that Romano was watching Bates and Ward. Is he dirty? Working with them? Or does he suspect them of something?" He glanced at the deserted street, then swung out of the car. "Let's go inside. I don't want to sit out here."

Cilla stepped into the cool autumn air and reached for Brendan's hand as soon as he came around the front of the car. She held it tight, and he didn't try to disengage when he fumbled with the gate.

"You okay?" she asked as he struggled to unlock the gate.

"I'm fine," he said gruffly, finally twisting the key in the lock. "I should be asking you that question."

"Thanks to you, I'm feeling better."

He wrapped his arm around her shoulders and pulled her against him for a brief moment. Then he let her go. "You're tough." He glanced down at her as they walked through the crunch of dried leaves on the sidewalk. "Maybe I'm not so tough. Maybe I need to know you're okay."

She curled her arm through his and laid her head on his shoulder for a moment. "I'm so glad you were there," she whispered. He'd made the whole humiliating mess so much easier.

"Me, too." He glanced down at her. "No one should have to go through that alone," he said gruffly.

Cilla stepped a little closer. "I'm glad it was you, specifically," she said quietly. "Made me feel a little better."

"I wanted to kill him, Cilla." Brendan's voice was barely a whisper in the darkness. "Me. A cop. I'm supposed to preserve order. Arrest the bad guys. Treat everyone equally. And I wanted to pull that trigger so bad."

"But you didn't." She stopped and pulled him around to face her. "You didn't kill him. You didn't lay a hand on him. If our roles had been reversed..." She shoved a hand through her already tangled hair. "If it had been my sister, and I'd been the one with her, I don't know what I would have done," she admitted.

"Same thing I did," he said immediately. "You would have done the right thing."

"I hope so."

"Think of the alternative. Spending time in a cell with Large Marge?" He nudged her shoulder with his. "'Course you would have stopped yourself."

A tiny bubble of laughter escaped as they reached the door. Two hours ago, that would have seemed impossible. Brendan made her...lighter. More free. More open and relaxed.

He was good for her.

Her smile faded. She hoped she was good for him, too. Up until now, though, she'd mostly given him attitude. Made him defend her in front of a bunch of his peers.

Discovered his deepest secret.

As they walked down the hall to his apartment, she twisted to face Brendan. "You're good for me, Brendan. But I've been giving you crap since we met. I have no idea what you see in me."

He held her gaze, his eyes steady. "You're tough, Cilla. Smart. Kind. A really good cop." One side of his mouth curled up. "And you see through my bullshit." He brushed his mouth over hers. "Not to mention you're seriously hot."

Instead of deepening the kiss, he unlocked his door. Franny came over when he switched on the light, stretching first her front legs, then her back. Brendan finally let Cilla go, then bent to ruffle Franny's fur. He pressed his cheek against the dog's head for a moment, then stood up.

"I need to take her out," he said. "Just into the courtyard." He nodded toward the window. "Not a walk." He stepped into the kitchen, returned carrying a plastic bag. "We'll be right back."

She wanted to go with him. To curl her arm around his

waist and let him lean on her, the same way she'd leaned on him. But before she could offer, he and Franny were heading toward the door. "I'm not going anywhere," she called after them.

She stilled. Tonight. She'd been talking about tonight. Maybe she wasn't.

Brendan paused in the doorway and held her gaze for a long moment as her heart jittered in her chest. What was he thinking? Was what he'd said earlier true, and not just words to make her feel better? Could he possibly want more than tonight?

Finally, after staring at one another for what felt like hours, he nodded. Stepped out the door with the dog.

Cilla watched Franny and Brendan in the dimly lit courtyard, their dark shapes wandering over the grass, until Franny took care of business. When Cilla heard their footsteps in the hall, she opened the apartment door.

Brendan rubbed Franny's back, then unhooked her leash. The dog trotted off toward the kitchen, and moments later Cilla heard her slurping water from her bowl.

As Brendan hooked the leash over a coat hook on the wall, Cilla headed toward his kitchen. Brendan would want to talk about Bates and Ward, and nervous energy suddenly zinged through her. "You want a beer or something?" she called.

He followed her into the kitchen, a tiny smile curving his lips. "What're you doing? I'm supposed to be making you tea. Patting your hand."

Cilla turned and stepped into him. She wrapped her arms around his waist and rested her head on his shoulder. "We've both had a bad night. I was trying to take care of you."

He turned his head, and his mouth brushed her hair. "Thank you, Cilla." He kissed her head, then held her hands and stared down at her. "Last time someone wanted to take care of me, it was my mother and I was fifteen."

The nervous energy sizzling through Cilla's veins

transformed into a different kind of heat. A dark curl of arousal slid through her. "I'm not your mother."

"I'm not fifteen anymore." His eyes darkened as he watched her.

"That's good," she managed.

"Yeah."

They stared at each other for a handful of seconds, desire consuming all the oxygen between them. Then Cilla dropped his hands and stepped away. No. Not going there tonight.

"You have anything worth drinking in that refrigerator?"

"Depends on what you consider worth drinking." His voice was lower than usual. A little hoarse. "Goose Island okay?"

"Sounds good."

He opened the refrigerator, and she saw eggs, milk, some apples that looked as if they'd seen better days, and an unopened package of lunch meat that she'd bet was expired. One shelf held several bottles of beer.

"Take your pick," he said.

She reached for an IPA and her stomach churned. She'd been drinking beer before she'd gone outside to take her sister's phone call. Dropping her hand, she said, "I think I'd like water instead."

He took the bottle of IPA she'd been eyeing and set it on the counter. Then he filled a glass with ice, added water and handed it to her.

After opening his beer, Brendan took her hand and led her into the living room. He settled into a corner of the couch, trying to tug her down next to him, but she let go of his hand. She couldn't sit still. Couldn't think about Brendan and what she wanted to do right now.

Instead she paced in front of the couch. "So. Bates and Ward."

He stretched his legs in front of him and took a drink of his beer. "Yeah."

She lifted the water to her mouth and drank greedily.

She hadn't realized how parched she'd been. How dry-mouthed. She should have, though. Adrenaline rushes were no strangers. Neither were the crashes afterwards.

Every other time, though, it had been part of the job. This was the first time she'd been the one in trouble. The person at risk of injury or worse.

This time, she'd been the one who'd needed help.

She buried that thought deep inside. Time to focus on the job. "Tell me what happened after I went outside."

"Right. Ward and Bates. So, I spotted them as I was walking out of the restroom. I got the phone call from your sister a moment after I sat down at the bar. I told Rick we had to leave, threw money on the bar and took off. But out of the corner of my eye, I saw Bates off to the side, talking to Tiffany. Ward was in a booth. Romano was talking to a woman, pretending not to watch them."

"Do you think it's Bates and Ward?" she asked. "That they're the ones selling this drug?"

Brendan's jaw worked. "I don't want it to be Bates. I was in the academy with him. He's a great guy."

Cilla resumed pacing. She couldn't sit down. Couldn't relax. She was too wired. "Maybe it's Ward," she said. "Maybe there's a connection between the woman he was roughing up and this drug case." She stopped and swiveled to face Brendan. "We need to find that woman. I have her name and address in the report. I can do that tomorrow."

Before she'd started this undercover job, she'd been furious with Ward. She'd arrested him for roughing up a suspect and he'd gotten nothing but a hand slap and a wink. He and his buddies had made her life miserable.

Back then, a tiny part of her would have smirked at the idea that Ward was distributing this drug. Now, though, she just felt contaminated by the thought of him being a dirty cop. Soiled. As if everyone on the force was tainted now.

"Just because he's a jerk doesn't make him a criminal," Brendan said quietly.

"Yeah. I know." She set the glass carefully on his coffee

table. "Just like the fact that Bates was a nice guy in the academy doesn't make him a nice guy now."

Brendan slammed his fist on the table next to the couch. Water sloshed in her glass, and a tall pile of books vibrated. The top two fell to the floor. "Damn it! I don't want it to be someone on the force."

"I know!" She kicked at the wastebasket next to Brendan's desk. "I don't either. Not even Ward."

Brendan glanced at her. "Maybe it's Romano. He was right there."

"Doesn't make him involved," she said reluctantly. "You said he was talking to a woman."

"I didn't get a good look at her." He stared into the distance, as if trying to conjure her in his mind. "Could be the woman he was talking to last weekend. His cover, maybe, for a meeting with Bates and Ward. Can't count him out."

"Yeah." God. She hated this. "DEA guy working with the cops?"

"It's a cliche for a reason." Brendan straightened the books and walked over to pick up the two that had landed on the floor. He didn't look at her as he lined the stack of books up evenly. "Sorry, Cilla. I shouldn't have brought it up. Work is probably the last thing you want to talk about right now."

Cilla stopped pacing and watched Brendan tidy the books. A couple of weeks ago, she wouldn't have guessed that reckless, impulsive Brendan Donovan was so thoughtful. So considerate.

Warmth fluttered through her, and she reached for Brendan before he could sit back down. "Thank you. But talking about work is good. Normal, you know?"

"Yeah. Like working on a puzzle. Takes your mind off other stuff."

"Exactly." She watched him sit on the couch again, then turned to stare into the courtyard. A cool breeze from the partially opened window blew across her skin as she watched a couple walk down the sidewalk, heading for the entrance across from Brendan's. Their arms were twined around each other, and his head was bent to hers, as if listening raptly to something she said.

Too bad her night and Brendan's couldn't have ended the same way. Heading up to his apartment, arms around each other's waists. The moment they stepped inside his door, they would have been wrapped around each other. Kissing. Touching. Stumbling into his bedroom.

Their night had taken a darker turn. And now she couldn't relax. Couldn't slow down. Didn't want to lie in the dark and relive Smith's attack on her.

"You think Smith is part of the drug business?" she asked.

He frowned. "I'm liking him for the serial rapist operating in that part of the city. Not sure how that connects to the sex drug."

"Let's go to your station and look him up," she said, grabbing for the purse she'd dropped by the door. "See what kind of record he has. Check on those rapes from the Beverly neighborhood."

"We can do that tomorrow, Cilla." He watched as she paced. Frowning. As if not quite sure what to do for her.

"Yeah, but I need to do something. Move. Act. Figure something out."

Brendan straightened on the couch. "You need to get your mojo back."

She stopped moving. Felt her shoulders relax. He understood. "Yes. Exactly." She swallowed as he set his beer on the table. Stood up slowly. "It's been a long night, though." She forced a smile. "I can do this myself. You stay here and keep Franny company."

"Hell, no. We go together." He stepped to a dark wood cabinet by the door, opened a door and spun the dial on a small gun safe. Took out his badge and his gun. "We'll swing by your place so you can get your stuff, okay?"

Cilla watched as he stepped into his bedroom, put on a

long-sleeved shirt, tucked another belt through the loops on his jeans and attached his badge. Then he shrugged on his shoulder holster and covered it with a jacket. "Let's go."

CHAPTER TWENTY-ONE

Brendan nodded to the handful of night shift cops in the station as he and Cilla made their way to his desk. The smell of stale coffee, sharp and acrid, hovered over the bull pen like a cloud, but it was quiet this time of night. The patrol cops were out, and the on-call detectives were either in the field on a case or at home, waiting for a call.

He snagged a chair from the desk next to his and rolled it over, turned on his computer. "Piece of shit takes a year and a half to boot up," he muttered to Cilla as they both stared at the dark screen.

Finally the log-in page appeared, and Brendan typed in his user name and password. Then went to the search option and typed in 'Michael Welles'.

Cilla leaned closer, and the scent of her hair wafted over him. Hard to believe, after tonight's events, her hair still smelled clean. Citrusy and fresh.

He wished they were back at his place, where he could gather the cool mass of her hair in his hands and bury his face in them. Hold her close and try to forget about what had happened tonight.

They weren't at his place, though. And neither of them

would forget about tonight anytime soon. So if Cilla needed to work, needed to burn off some energy, that's what they'd do.

But if he was going to sit in front of a computer, he'd rather be at his desk at home. Typing a blog entry. It wouldn't be easy to write about what had happened tonight, and even harder to read. But the words were making his fingers twitch. Filling his mind, leaving little room for everything else.

Focus. The blog would be there when he got home. And he wouldn't forget the words. They were burned into his brain.

This was about Cilla, and what she needed.

He and Cilla both leaned closer as the little wheel stopped spinning and words appeared on the screen.

"No record," Brendan said. "Not even a parking ticket."

"He's a lawyer," breathed Cilla.

"Yeah." Brendan typed another request, leaving his fingers on the keys while the computer worked. Clenched his jaw when the results popped up. "Criminal defense."

Brendan scrolled through a list of the people Welles had represented, his heart pounding as a pattern appeared. "He almost always gets his cases heard by one of two judges. Peter Drake and Glen Larson."

"And an awful lot of them are found not guilty." Cilla looked at Brendan. "Judges are assigned randomly," she said in a low voice, glancing around to see if anyone was close by. "No way is this random."

"Holy crap." Brendan shoved his hand through his hair as he stared at the evidence on the screen. "Your attempted rape just got a lot more complicated. Crooked judges? Crooked bailiffs too? This is FBI territory."

"You said one of your brothers is an FBI agent."

"Yeah. He's on the east coast. Visiting his fiancee's brother."

"Franny's owners."

"Yep." Brendan glanced at his watch. It was one AM.

Too late to call Mac tonight. "I'll call him tomorrow."

"Let's go take a look at Welles's house," Cilla said suddenly, jumping up from the chair. Her foot tapped the floor, and he was pretty sure she didn't realize it. Her body vibrated with tension. Nerves.

"What good would that do?"

"I don't know." She tucked a lock of hair behind her right ear. "Just a feeling. You know? See what we can see."

"Why now? Why not in the morning?"

"Neighbors would see us in the morning," she said immediately. "Might call it in. That neighborhood?" She pointed at the Beverly address he'd written on a post-it note, "Expensive houses. Suspicious of strangers. Better to do it now, when most of them are asleep."

"Okay." He stood up and led her toward the stairs. "Good thing you're a cop and not a crook," he said, opened the stairwell door for her. "You'd be a scary criminal."

"Why I'm a good cop," she said, flashing a smile over her shoulder at him.

As they walked toward the car in the darkness, Brendan forced himself not to take her hand. They were close to the station. Not a lot of cops around now, but there were a few. If someone saw him holding Cilla's hand, the gossip would be in every district by morning.

The crap with Ward was bad enough. Cilla didn't need her co-workers making kissy sounds behind her back. Because that's what would happen. A police station was the biggest middle school in the world. And the female officers were usually the targets.

Once they were in the car, Brendan headed for Lake Shore Drive. "All those rapes happened in or near Beverly," he said quietly. "His neighborhood."

"Rapists like to hunt in their own backyards," she said, staring out the windshield.

"We didn't look up the details of those rapes," he said. "I bet he used a knife. Maybe didn't let them see his face. Probably wore a condom."

"He's smart enough not to leave any DNA behind," Cilla said quietly.

"The guys who think they're smarter than the cops are usually the guys who make a mistake," he said. "We'll see if his DNA sample gets any hits."

"He let me see his face," Cilla said, her voice barely above a whisper.

"Yeah. I know." He'd hoped she wouldn't realize that, but she was too smart. "Maybe it was a mistake. The kind an arrogant asshole like Welles would make."

"Maybe. Maybe not." Cilla swallowed and turned to look out the side window.

"Damn it." He banged his fist on the steering wheel. "I hoped you wouldn't think about that."

"Of course I thought about that. Was he going to kill me?" She swallowed, and her throat rippled. "I don't know. But it seems uncharacteristic for a smart guy to make such a big mistake." Her voice wobbled a little. He reached over the console and took her hand. It was ice cold.

"We'll make sure he doesn't get bail."

"How? A guy like that, you can bet he has the best attorney in Chicago on his speed dial. And he's got a 'get out of jail free' card in his pocket. What do you want to bet he gets either Larson or Drake as his judge?"

"We'll make sure he doesn't." He glanced at her. "Call your sister. There must be something she can do."

She finally turned to look at him. "You're right." Her dark eyes burned into him. "I've been taking care of Livvy's messes for a long time. It's her turn to give me a hand."

"Call her."

Cilla opened her purse, then stopped. "I don't have my phone."

"Use mine." He rolled to a halt at a stop sign and reached into his pocket, handing the warm phone to Cilla. A car behind him honked, and he waved in apology as he pressed the accelerator.

Cilla punched in numbers, then put the phone to her ear.

Her knuckles whitened around it. Brendan counted six rings before it was picked up.

"Liv, it's me. Cilla. Sorry to wake you up, but this is an emergency. Get a piece of paper and a pen."

The female voice on the other end of the line began to speak, and Cilla interrupted. "Get the paper and pen."

A few moments later, her sister spoke again. Cilla said, "Write this down. Michael Welles." She spelled his name and read off his address. "He's an attorney. He tried to rape me tonight."

Her sister burst into speech, and Cilla held the phone slightly away from her ear. "Liv. Stop! I'll explain everything later. He didn't rape me, thanks to your call to Brendan. He's sitting in jail, I hope, but there's a problem."

She sketched out the details, then said to her sister, "It's really, really important that he doesn't get Peter Drake or Glen Larson as his judge for the bond hearing." She waited for a moment. "You know them?"

Her sister must have said yes, because Cilla answered, "Good. Now go into work tomorrow morning, and make sure Welles doesn't appear on either of their dockets. His lawyer will scream. But I suspect you know how to handle that."

Her sister said something else, and Cilla's hand tightened. "I don't have time to explain it now. But if this guy is freed on bond, he'll rape someone else. Might come after me again, as well. And those two judges might let him go. So I need you to take care of this. And make sure you don't tell anyone I'm the victim. I don't want anyone to know a cop is involved. Okay?"

He could hear her sister speaking. Then Cilla said, "Great. I'm counting on you, Liv. And just to warn you, Welles is going to have a damn good attorney."

Cilla smiled as she listened to her sister. "You know it, Liv. Now go kick some fancy lawyer's ass."

Cilla pressed the 'off' button, and stared at the now-dark screen. "She'll get it done."

She rubbed at a smudge on the screen, then tucked the phone into the cup holder in front of the console.

Brendan glanced at Cilla's pale face and wished like hell he wasn't driving right now. Her hands shook, and when she noticed him watching, she gripped her legs to stop the trembling.

"She said she knew how to handle it," Cilla said. "That she'd make sure his bond hearing didn't go to either Drake or Larson. That she'd ask the DA who gets the case to ask for no bail. At least until the DNA results come back."

"That was smart," Brendan said. If Cilla's sister didn't come through, he'd see what connections Mac had.

Cilla nodded. "Livvy was right. She is a good attorney. Smart. Quick."

He needed to distract her. "What did you mean that you've cleaned up her messes?"

She didn't say anything for a long time. "I shouldn't have said that," she finally answered.

"Hey. You know my deep, dark secret. You can tell me yours. I won't spread it around."

"I know you won't." She reached over and wrapped her cold fingers around his wrist, squeezed then let go. "The story doesn't make my family look good. Me, either."

"Cilla. Nothing you can say would make me think less of you. Nothing. Do you understand me?"

Cilla was silent as he turned onto the ramp to Lake Shore Drive. Once he'd merged, he glanced over at her. Her gaze was fixed on him. Unreadable. Then she turned to stare out the windshield.

"My dad was a mechanic," she began. "He had his own shop, which he eventually expanded into a chain of car repair places. He worked a lot of hours and wasn't home much.

"There was a lot of...drama at home, so I hung around his shop. Learned about repairing cars." Her mouth curved into a slight smile. "He gave me Betsy. He'd bought her from a guy who needed cash and who hadn't kept the car maintained. We worked on Betsy together for more than a year, restoring her. I know how to rebuild an engine, take a transmission apart and put it back together, fix brakes." She shrugged. "Just about anything to do with cars. That's my blog," she said. "What I do to relax. I work on Betsy."

His mouth curved into a smile. "Never would have taken you for a grease monkey."

"Exactly what I am." Her shoulders relaxed. As if she'd been afraid he would make fun of her. "Anyway, my father wasn't home much, but the drama always was. My mom's sister leaned on her. Aunt Jessie's husband was a cop. Joe Ferrell. A good one, I think. I loved his stories about being a cop, about his cases, about catching the bad guys." She glanced over at him. "That's probably why I became a cop."

As he drove past the Loop and the museum campus, he listened to Cilla and drank in all these insights about her life. She was revealing pieces of herself, and he'd bet she didn't share this with many people. Pieces he wanted to know. Badly.

"Uncle Joe was a good cop, but a really bad husband. I found out later that he cheated on my aunt pretty much their whole marriage. He didn't spend much time with his family because he preferred hanging out in a cop bar with his buddies. And the badge bunnies."

She slanted another glance at him. "So my mom was busy dealing with my aunt. My father was busy at work. My sister and brother and I had to take care of ourselves."

"And you became the fixer of messes," he murmured. It explained why her brother called about a speeding ticket. Why her sister called so much. Why Cilla had rushed to help her fix the problem with her boyfriend.

Maybe why she was so guarded. So careful. She didn't want to become anyone else's fixer.

"Yeah. I was the go-to person. Olivia had a finely honed sense of right and wrong, and she didn't bother to sugar coat it. So she got into trouble for mouthing off to her teachers. Got into trouble with her friends." Cilla shook her head.

"Do you have any idea how petty and mean teen-aged girls can be? Dad was at work, Mom was at Aunt Jessie's. I had to fix a lot of her messes."

"What about your brother?"

She smiled. "He was Dennis the Menace. Thank God he found baseball. It focused him. Kept him too busy to screw up. When he did, I was the one who figured out what to do."

"And they're still calling you." He kept the judgment out of his voice.

"Yeah. My mom calls, too."

He tapped out a restless rhythm on the steering wheel. "You know you're not doing them any favors. Right?"

"Yeah," she sighed. "I do. Hard habit to break, though."

"I know." He'd learned that the hard way. But he'd save the story of his family for another time. He glanced over at her. "You're a good sister, Cilla. A good daughter."

"Thanks. But you're right. I have to stop being the family fixer."

"Maybe you could fix something for me?"

She stilled. "I'm out of the fixing business."

He mentally kicked himself. He should have realized she wasn't in the mood for jokes.

Fumbling his phone out of the cup holder, he handed it to her. "I was talking about our route. Can you get directions to Welle's house? We're getting close."

She exhaled. Actually smiled. "Yeah. That I can do."

He was glad he'd gotten her to talk about her family. Her leg wasn't bouncing anymore, and her hands weren't curled into fists on her thighs. It was temporary, but she'd forgotten what happened earlier. Brendan would call that a win.

Fifteen minutes after exiting the Dan Ryan Expressway, they pulled to the curb on a quiet, dark street lined with beautiful old homes. They were set far back from the street and were well-cared for, with tidy yards and thoughtful landscaping.

"Nice neighborhood," Cilla said, scanning the area. Brendan kept the car running. "Looks like they have alleys. Maybe we should park behind Welles's house."

"Too suspicious," Brendan said at once. "Who parks in an alley at this time of night? Only people up to no good."

He watched her study Welles's house. It was a colonial. Red brick with white trim. Professionally landscaped. The plantings had a paint-by-number feel, as if they were some landscapers go-to bushes and flowers and trees. Welles probably paid someone to maintain it and mow the lawn.

The porch light was burning. The yellow glow from the back of the house meant there were lights there, too.

He could feel the nervous energy pouring off Cilla. "Let's go take a look," she said, her fist closing around the door handle.

"We're not parking here." Brendan shifted into gear and began driving away. "People in this neighborhood know when a car doesn't belong. We passed a big park a couple of blocks back. We'll leave the car there and walk."

He glanced over at her. "You sure you want to wander around his property? You know we don't have a legitimate reason for being there."

A tiny alarm had been ringing insistently in his brain. They were police officers, but that didn't mean they could trespass. It wouldn't be good for Cilla's case against Welles if they were caught.

"I just want to take a look." She glanced at him, and he saw the knowledge in her eyes – she knew they'd be trespassing. And didn't care. "You don't have to come. You can wait in the car."

"No. I can't." He pulled into the deserted parking lot at the park and parked in a spot behind the field house. Shoved the door open a little too hard and climbed out. Closed it more carefully. Slamming doors meant bad things this time of night. "We're gonna make this quick, Cilla. Down and dirty and out of here."

"Of course." She took his hand, twined their fingers

together as they jogged back to Welles's house. "I know you don't want to do this," she said softly. "But you're doing it anyway. Thank you."

He'd do anything for her when she looked at him like that. Soft. Open. Letting him see parts of her that not many people saw. "You're welcome."

He glanced at her. She'd changed her clothes at her place. Dark pants, dark shirt, dark hat covering her caramel-colored hair. "Looks like you've done this once or twice."

A tiny laugh bubbled out of her throat. "Played a lot of Night Games when I was a kid. I learned early to wear dark clothes if I didn't want to get caught."

Did she realize she was revealing so much of herself tonight? His hand tightened on hers. "This isn't a game."

Her smile disappeared. "I know."

As they approached the house, she let go of his hand. Thick bushes separated Welles's house from the ones on either side, he noted. Good cover if something went wrong.

Cilla avoided them as she peered into a window. Brendan stepped up, as well. It was a living room. Couch, a couple of chairs, big flat-screen TV. A few bookcases on the walls. Three paintings. Nothing out of the ordinary.

They circled the house, keeping in the shadows, looking in all the windows. By the time they reached the front of the house on the opposite side, Brendan's nerves were jumping. Time to go.

As they looked in at what appeared to be an office, they heard footsteps scuffing on the concrete front porch. Brendan froze. Grabbed Cilla's hand and tugged her close to the wall. Thank God for their dark clothes.

The front door opened. The sound of footsteps vibrated through the window. A light went on in the office. As they crouched in the darkness, the footsteps inside the house approached the window.

CHAPTER TWENTY-TWO

Cilla listened to the sounds coming from the room at her back – the rolling wheels of a desk chair. The slide of a drawer opening. The rustling of paper. The cold, rough bricks of Welles's house pressed into her back through her black sweatshirt. Her fingers gripped the sharp edges of the bricks, her nails scraping against the mortar.

On the other side of the window, Brendan was moving. Making a run for it?

No. He was leaning toward the window. As if he was going to look in.

She wanted to shout no. Yell at him to stay hidden. But she couldn't speak. The window was open a crack. If she could hear the rustling of papers in the room, whoever was in there would be able to hear her voice.

Brendan hadn't wanted to do this, and he'd been right. It was risky. Dangerous. Now they were inches away from being spotted.

She should have used her revved up, twitchy energy for something else. She glanced at Brendan. Something a lot more fun than standing outside Welles's house, hoping they wouldn't be seen.

Now Brendan was caught up in her idiocy. Trying to see who was in that room. Taking stupid chances. For her.

She wanted to leap for him. To drag him behind the thick, heavy shrubbery that separated Welles's house from the one next door. To keep him safe until whoever was in that room was gone.

"Take this shit out to the car." The crinkle of a paper bag sounded as loud as a gunshot in the quiet of the night. "Then come back. I'll get the rest of the stuff."

Brendan lifted his head above the windowsill. Stared inside for a few seconds, then slid to the side again. A handful of heartbeats later, the front door opened. Footsteps retreated, becoming faint before they disappeared. Cilla leaned away from the wall and watched a tall man cross the street to a dark, late model car parked two houses down. He popped the trunk, tossed a bag inside, then shut it carefully. Clearly trying to muffle the sound.

She flattened herself against the wall again, turning her head as the footsteps got closer. Hiding the pale oval of her face from whoever he was.

As soon as she heard the house door close, she sprinted for the street. Brendan sucked in a breath as she started to run, but she ignored it. She needed that license plate number. Needed to see if the guy had left the trunk unlatched.

Her footsteps were almost soundless on the concrete as she dived behind the car. She listened for a few seconds, and when no one shouted, no footsteps pounded closer, she exhaled slowly. Steadied herself.

She peered around the back of the car. Brendan was still at the window. Staring inside again. The two men were still in the office.

She crept around the car and tugged on the trunk. Locked. Tugged again, just to be sure. Then she crouched to see the license plate. Smiled grimly. The guy had a vanity plate. Made it easier to remember.

ATTYNO 1. Attorney number one. Had to be Welles's

personal attorney.

What the hell was he taking out of Welles's house?

An owl hooted close by. She lifted her head, listening, and saw Brendan gesturing frantically. They were coming out of the house.

She duck-walked as fast as she could across the grass to a clump of greenery in front of the house across from Welles's. She threw herself behind it just as Welles's front door closed. The juniper bush had prickles, and they scratched her hands as she separated the branches to get a better view.

She didn't recognize the man in front. He was older, dressed in a suit with an open overcoat flapping as he walked. He carried a paper bag with the Trader Joe's logo.

As he reached the car, he handed the bag to the guy behind him, turned and got into the car. She sucked in a breath, then slapped her hand over her mouth.

Derek Johnstone. The cop from the pub tonight. Sobieski's partner.

What the hell was he doing here?

Johnstone opened the trunk, tossed in the second bag, then got into the front seat. Moments later, all that was left was the red glow from the tail lights of the BMW, disappearing around a corner.

Brendan had been watching, too. As soon as the car disappeared, he sprinted across the street. As she stepped away from the bushes, he grabbed her hand and ran toward the park.

Just before she stepped off the curb, Cilla stumbled over a circle of rocks around the base of a tree. Brendan tightened his grip on her, but he didn't slow down. Didn't look over his shoulder at her.

He let go of her hand and slowed to a jog once they rounded the corner. Their cover, she realized. A couple out for a jog late at night. A little odd, but not suspicious.

When the reached the darkened field house in the park, Brendan trotted past his car. Stopped in the playground, and she stopped beside him.

His jaw worked and he didn't look at her. Without speaking, he headed for the seesaw. Sat on one side, his legs braced to keep the plank of wood level.

She swung her leg over the other seat. Brendan stared down the length of the seesaw at her. Even in the darkness, she saw the wildness in his eyes.

"Jesus!" He dropped to the ground, making her rise with a whoosh. Her legs dangling in the air, she tightened her hands on the grips, knowing she was at his mercy. He was a lot bigger than her. She'd stay in the air until he let her come down.

"My God, Cilla." His face was shiny with sweat. From fear, she realized, a greasy lump of shame expanding in her stomach. "What the hell were you thinking to run at his car like that?"

"I was thinking we needed to see that license plate." She cleared her throat of the moisture that had collected. "And see if the trunk was unlocked."

"So you could grab the papers he took out of the house? Damn it, Cilla." His fingers flexed around the seesaw grips. "I got a look at him. We could have figured out who he was. You didn't have to do anything so stupid and reckless."

He pushed off the wood chips covering the playground, bringing her side of the seesaw slamming into the ground with a hard thump. "What if they'd seen you? What would you have done?"

Her instinct was to defend herself. Tell him she would have handled it. But she knew he was right. "Sorry, Brendan. It was a stupid, reckless thing to do. I wasn't being a good partner. I shouldn't have run off and left you alone."

"You think that's what's bothering me?" He stared at her, his eyes glittering in the darkness. "That you left me alone?" He dropped, sending her flying high again. Only her tight grip on the handles kept her from being launched into the air.

Staring at her, his eyes flashing in the darkness, he said, "They weren't going to see me. But they sure as hell were going to see you. Do you have any idea how I felt when they headed for the front door? While you were crouched behind their car, trying to pry the trunk open?"

"I..." she began, but Brendan continued as if she hadn't said a thing.

"Johnstone is a cop. He could have shot you and said you attacked him. Made up some kind of bullshit story. Internal Affairs would have investigated, but who cares? You would be dead." He let her drop to the ground again, then set her flying. "I thought I was going to watch you die, Cilla."

He stepped off the seesaw, sending her to the ground with a teeth-rattling thump. "Let's get out of here."

She followed him to the car and slid into the passenger's seat. Brendan turned on the ignition with a vicious twist of his wrist, then slammed the car into gear. The transmission jerked as he pulled into the street, and the engine rumbled as he drove too fast to the intersection.

His tires squealed as he rounded the traffic circle and burst onto a busier street.

"You shouldn't be driving when you're angry," she said quietly.

"No shit. But how do you suggest we get out of this neighborhood?" His fingers gripped the steering wheel so hard his knuckles turned white. "Because I don't want to be anywhere near Beverly right now. Don't want to take any chance that Johnstone spots us."

He rolled to a stop at a red light, leaned across the console, grabbed her face in his hands. Kissed her. Hard. All tongue and teeth and anger. "You scared the shit out of me tonight."

"Yeah. I can tell. I'm sorry."

"Not sure sorry's gonna cut it."

When the light turned green, he pulled away. Flexed the fingers of one hand, then the other. Took a deep breath.

Let it out slowly, then took another careful breath.

By the time they were back on the Dan Ryan, his shoulders had loosened. Hers had tightened.

God! What had she been thinking?

Whatever it was, she hadn't been thinking about Brendan. About him standing next to the house, watching her, knowing the two men would be coming out the door any moment.

"I'm sorry, Brendan," she said, her voice quiet in the rumble of the tires on the expressway. "I was so focused on getting that license plate, finding out what Johnstone had put in the trunk, that I didn't think about you. And that's inexcusable. You're my partner. I can't do boneheaded things without talking them through with you."

He didn't look at her, but his knuckles got white again. "I'm more than your partner, Cilla. I'm the guy who..." he swallowed. "The guy you're sleeping with. What would you have done if I'd run out there? If you knew they were leaving and had no way to tell me?"

She reached over and wrapped her hand around his wrist. Felt his pulse pounding beneath her fingertips. "I would be just as pissed as you are. Just as terrified. Brendan, I...I care about you." She swallowed. Facing Welles tonight had been easier than trying to tell Brendan what he meant to her. So much easier than getting the words out of her suddenly thick throat. "I...you...I've never felt like this about anyone. And it's scary. Makes my brain nervous. Turns me into an idiot. So, I'm sorry. I won't do anything like that again."

"Damn straight you won't. Because we are joined at the hip until this case is over. You understand? You're not out of my sight. I won't let you risk yourself like that again."

Warmth at his concern battled with prickliness at his words. "I don't need a keeper, Brendan. Just a partner."

He shot her a quick glare. "Then be a partner. Make plans with me, not by yourself. Don't throw yourself off a cliff and make me watch." He shoved his hand through his hair again. "Jesus! You scared ten years off my life."

She tightened her hand on his wrist. "And just for the record, I'm not complaining about the joined at the hip part. We need to figure out this case ASAP. And I..." She gulped. "I want to be with you, too."

He headed down the ramp to Belmont for the second time that night. Stopped at the light at the bottom. Sighed. "Okay. I'm sorry I lost it."

"You had a right to lose it," she conceded. "Thanks for yelling at me instead of stewing about it."

He glanced over at her and for the first time, she saw a tiny smile in his eyes. "I'm a yeller, not a stewer. Glad that works for you."

It worked really well for her. There had been way too much moodiness when she was growing up. "It does. Takes too much energy to brood and stew."

A car honked behind them, and she raised one eyebrow at him. "Green light. Guess I'm really falling down on the job tonight. Not being a good partner. Not being a good green light spotter. I don't know why you put up with me."

"Guess you're lucky I believe in second chances," he said as he turned onto Belmont.

"Yeah," she said quietly. "I am."

They didn't talk the rest of the way to his apartment. When they got out of the car, the street was deserted. It was three-o'clock in the morning, and only a couple of lights were on in Brendan's building. Suddenly, weariness washed over her, making her trip on the step into his building.

"You okay?" Brendan said as he grabbed her elbow.

"Tired," she said, sliding her hand into his again.

"Yeah. Long night." He gripped her hand. "We need to talk about Johnstone and the guy with him. But it can wait until tomorrow."

"Don't think I could focus on it tonight," she said.

Franny's tail thumped on the floor as they walked into Brendan's apartment, but she didn't get up to greet them. The dog watched for a moment, then laid her head down again.

The dog was in her bed. Brendan's desk sat in the corner, papers spread over his closed computer. The couch was shadowed in the light from the courtyard.

Brendan stood beside her. Solid. Warm. His scent enveloping her.

Everything was familiar. Comfortable. Comforting.

She'd been here only a handful of times, but already it felt like coming home. Like she could exhale, shut the door and leave the rest of the world on the other side.

Brendan's fingers curled around her waist. His thumb caressed her side. "Go ahead and use the bathroom. Get ready for bed."

Cilla nodded, too tired to speak. She stumbled into the bathroom, brushed her teeth, then walked into the bedroom. She was taking off her black jeans when she saw the room was empty.

"Brendan?" she called.

"Out here."

She walked into the living room and saw him covering the couch with a sheet. "What are you doing?" she asked.

"Thought I'd sleep out here," he said. He smoothed the sheet and avoided her eyes. "After what happened earlier, figured you'd want to sleep alone."

Her heart swelled at his thoughtfulness. "I don't want to sleep alone, Brendan. I want to sleep with you. Please put those sheets away and come to bed."

His hands stilled. "Are you sure?"

"Absolutely." As she helped him re-fold the sheets, she said, "It was scary and awful and made me sick to my stomach. Horrifying to think about what might have happened. But I didn't get hurt, he's sitting in jail, and...and I'm too tired to think about it. Okay?"

"Okay. If you're sure." He ran a hand down her back. "You can always kick me out if you're not comfortable."

"I want you in here. Close to me."

She lifted off her sweatshirt, shed her bra and panties

and slid naked between the sheets. Without taking his eyes off her, Brendan tossed his clothes to the floor, stepped out of his boxers and slid in beside to her.

"You need to tell me what you want, Cilla," he said, propped up on one elbow. Watching her, but carefully not touching her. "I don't want to make a mistake here."

"You, Brendan. I want you." She scooted closer to him and put her hand on his chest. "I want to make love with you," she whispered.

He stared at her, as if he couldn't believe what she'd just asked, so she pulled his head down and kissed him.

His body was hard against hers, all solid muscle and sinew. She melted into him, needing to wipe out the memories of this evening and replace them with Brendan.

She curled around him, and his arms wrapped around her and held her close. As if she was fragile. Precious.

He kissed her gently, tasting her lips, sliding his tongue along the seam of her mouth, patiently waiting for her to lead the way. To let him know what she needed.

"More," she whispered against his mouth. "I need more, Brendan."

He opened his mouth, welcomed her in. As she tasted him, he stroked her tongue with his. Slid one hand down to her hips, urged her closer. He stroked his other hand up and down her back, soothing her. Warming her. Relaxing her.

She shifted against him, enjoying the tenderness. But she knew she needed to make the first move tonight. So she brought one of his hands to her breast, then slipped one leg between his.

His body vibrated with tension. He was holding back, and trembling with it. Trying to let her lead, trying to be what she needed tonight. A wave of tenderness crashed over her for this sweet, careful man.

She rolled him onto his back and slid on top of him, straddling his hips. As he watched, she could see the wheels spinning inside his head. Take the lead? Lie there passively?

"It's okay," she whispered. "I'm okay. I want you, Brendan."

His hands tightened on her hips, and he lifted her up. Lowered her onto his erection. She closed her eyes and shuddered with pleasure as he slid into her.

She moved slowly, savoring every moment. He covered her breasts with his hands, thumbs brushing her nipples, and she began moving faster. She bent and kissed him, and as their tongues stroked and she moved against him, she felt Brendan trembling again. This time, trying to hold back. To wait for her.

"Let go," she murmured into his mouth. "Let go, Brendan. I'm with you."

She moved faster, feeling the tension build until it crested and she flew over the top. Brendan followed her over, gripping her hips tightly, groaning into her mouth.

She finally collapsed onto his chest, reaching for his hands and twining their fingers together. As their breathing slowed and the sweat on their skin cooled, she felt him lift her off his chest and settle her beside him. The last thing she remembered was the way he wrapped his arms around her and drew her close. As if he'd never let her go.

As sleep dragged her down, she murmured into his chest, "I love you, Brendan."

His breathing was slow and regular. He was probably asleep. Probably hadn't heard her.

That was okay, she told herself. It was a dry run. She'd tell him again. Tomorrow. Or the next day. Sometime when they were both awake.

But as she settled against him, his arms tightened around her.

CHAPTER TWENTY-THREE

An insistent buzzing filled Brendan's head, and he swatted above his ear with one hand. The other was wrapped around a warm body.

Cilla. The events of the previous night rolled through his mind, and he tried to get closer. But they were already mashed together along the whole length of their bodies.

His eyes fluttered open and he glanced down at the top of her head. Her face was snuggled into his chest, and her hand was trapped between them. Her leg nestled between his, and her warm breath wafted over his skin at slow but regular intervals.

The buzzing noise repeated, and he realized it was his phone. Without letting Cilla go to look for it, he stretched his hand for the table next to his bed, patting its smooth surface until his fingers closed around the cool metal.

"Do..." he began before he remembered it was his burner phone. Stupid. Caused by too much love-making and too little sleep. "Yeah?"

"Mr. Patton?" asked a female voice.

His cover name. He shook off the last dregs of sleep. "Yeah. Who's this?"

"Officer Sobieski. The responding officer last night when your partner was assaulted at The Pipe and Shamrock."

He reluctantly slid his hand away from Cilla and sat up, maintaining as much contact with her as he could. "Yes, Officer. What can I do for you?"

"We need to meet," she said. "This morning. As soon as you and Ms. Mason can make it."

"Why? What's wrong?" His hand gripped the phone until it cut into his fingertips. "Was Welles released?"

"No, he's still sitting in lock-up at the 22nd. Can you get to the Valois Restaurant in Hyde Park by eight?"

Brendan glanced at the clock. Six-thirty AM. Even in rush hour, they should be able to make it to Hyde Park by then. But they had cover stories, which included regular jobs.

"Cilla and I both have to work this morning. Can't we make it this evening?" His hand tightened around the phone. That would be a normal reaction from a guy who had a nine to five job. Sobieski would know that. So why would she ask to meet right now?

"Not sure it can wait until this evening," Sobieski answered.

What the hell was going on? His heart began to race, and Brendan pressed closer to Cilla. He nudged her, trying to wake her up so she could listen to this phone call. Help him figure it out. She didn't move.

He swallowed. "I guess we can check with our bosses. Since it's police business."

"You do that. Call me if you have a problem. If you don't, I'll see you at eight."

"I'll call my boss and have Cilla call hers."

"Thanks." Sobieski disconnected, and he set the phone back on the night table. She'd called Cilla his partner. He knew he'd referred to Cilla as his girlfriend last night. A curl of unease slithered through him.

It could be disastrous if someone from the 22nd realized

they were cops.

He slid down beside Cilla and smoothed his hand over her hair. "Hey, babe," he murmured. "You need to wake up."

Nothing.

"Cilla," he said in a louder voice. "Cilla, wake up."

She groaned and rolled onto her back, putting her arm over her eyes. "Too early," she said, her voice low and raspy.

"I know. But we have to get moving."

She dropped her arm to the bed and opened her eyes. Her expression softened into a smile. "Brendan." She searched for his hand and laced their fingers together. "We just fell asleep."

"Did you hear my phone?"

She frowned. "Just now?" When he nodded, she shook her head. "Didn't hear a thing."

"Sobieski called. We're meeting her in Hyde Park in an hour and a half."

Her eyes lost the sleepy, sated expression and she sat up. "What's up?"

"She didn't say. But she called you my partner. Not my girlfriend."

Cilla frowned. "Maybe she was just being PC."

"Maybe." He threw back the covers and stood up. "But I'm worried. You want the first shower?"

Her gaze swept over him, and he hardened immediately. She smiled and rolled toward him. "Maybe we could share," she murmured.

"Kills me to say it, but we don't have time." He stepped out of her reach. "Get up, Marini. Get in the shower before you make us late."

"Before I make us late?" She swung her legs over the side of the bed. Her hair was a tangled mass of curls around her shoulders, and her chest and neck sported red whisker burns. "If you don't want to be late, put some clothes on, Donovan."

She stumbled off the bed and grabbed his wrist. Held on as she pulled him closer and wrapped her arms around his neck. "If there's not going to be any fun in the shower, at least give me a kiss."

Five minutes later, panting and aching with need, he stepped away. "There's a reason the Sirens were women," he muttered. "Go get wet. I'll make some coffee."

"Already wet," she called over her shoulder as she sauntered toward his bathroom. "Too bad it's going to waste."

"God, Cilla." He shoved his hand through his hair as he watched the door close behind her. Why the hell did Sobieski need to talk to them so early, anyway?

He stomped toward the kitchen, then stopped in his tracks when Franny stood up and stretched. "Damn it, Fran. I suppose you need to go out."

He really needed coffee, and he bet Cilla did, too. But they didn't have time. Instead of making a pot, he dragged on an old pair of sweat pants, a sweatshirt and a pair of shoes. Then he grabbed the leash and called the dog.

"Has to be down and dirty," he told her as they walked down the hall. "If I don't get any play time this morning, you don't, either."

Ten minutes later, while he was feeding Franny after her quick walk, Cilla walked out of the bathroom. One towel was wrapped around her hair, and another covered her torso. With her hair out of the way, he spotted the bruise on the side of her throat from Welles's knife.

He'd forgotten all about her injuries.

"How's the cut?" He reached for the towel covering her chest, then hesitated. "May I?"

"It's good, I think. Aches a little, but it looked okay when I rebandaged it." She loosened the towel, showing him the rectangular piece of tape covering the sutures.

"You should have called me," he said, brushing his thumb over the bruise on her neck with its scabbed-over center. He wanted to grind Welles into dust. "I could have helped you with the bandage."

The towel dropped to the floor as she cupped his cheek. "I thought about it," she said with a tiny smile. "But we don't have time for your help this morning."

"Smart ass." He brushed a kiss over her mouth, then edged past her toward the bedroom. She was right. If he put his hands on her again, they'd be late.

He rushed through his own shower, then grabbed a pair of khakis and a blue oxford shirt. The kind of thing a computer programmer would wear to work.

Cilla wore the same skinny jeans, green silk shirt and boots she'd worn the night before. He studied her as he buckled his belt. "What do you think? Should you go home and change?"

She glanced at his clock. "If you think we have time. Supposed to be going to work, right?"

"Yeah. Your place is on the way."

As they hurried toward his car, he snagged her hand. He wanted to be connected to her. To feel the beat of her pulse in her wrist. It would steady him.

He stayed in the car as Cilla ran into her two flat. She emerged five minutes later wearing the same jeans and a light copper-colored sweater. Work appropriate. As she slid into the car, he glanced at his watch, calculating. They would make it, but just barely. Traffic would be heavy, but it would get lighter after they passed the Loop. If it didn't, they'd be late.

As soon as he merged onto Lake Shore Drive, he asked, "What do you think we should tell her about Johnstone?"

Cilla turned in her seat so she was half-facing him. "Hadn't thought about that," she admitted. "It takes me a while to get going in the morning."

Brendan's groin tightened as he remembered the moments before her shower. "Couldn't prove that by me," he muttered.

A wash of pink swept over her cheeks. "I wasn't completely awake. The filter between my mouth and brain hadn't booted up yet."

"Wasn't complaining." He reached for her hand, twined their fingers together. "Well, yeah, I was. But only because we didn't have enough time to take advantage of your missing filter."

She lifted her eyes from their joined hands and held his gaze. "I'm sorry about that, too." She squeezed his hand. "About Johnstone. I...ah..." She shoved one hand through her hair. "Sorry. I need caffeine to think."

She took a few deep breaths. "I don't think we can tell her anything," she finally said. "As far as she knows, we're a couple from the pub. And don't forget that Bates and Ward work out of the 22nd, too. We have no idea how deep this goes. We can't take any chances."

"Yeah." He smoothed his thumb over the back of her hand, then let her go reluctantly. Rush hour traffic on Lake Shore Drive wasn't a good place to be distracted. "I don't see any way around it."

"We should probably keep this as short as possible." She played with a strand of her hair as she stared out the windshield. "Tell her we have to get to work."

"I agree."

They were five minutes late when they walked into the Valois. The restaurant was legendary on the south side, and the line for the cafeteria-style serving area snaked almost to the door. Sobieski, sitting at a table in the corner, nodded when she spotted them.

She wore her uniform, except for the hat. Her blond hair was short and wavy, and made her appear far younger and softer than the cop they'd met at the pub.

He and Cilla got eggs, bacon, toast and coffee, then pulled out the chairs on the other side of the table.

"Morning, Officer," Brendan said. "What's up?"

Sobieski moved her tray to the side and set her coffee on the table. "Your bosses give you a hard time about missing work?"

Cilla took a long drink of her coffee and set her mug on

the table. "Nope. She said helping the police is more important."

Sobieski took a drink of her own coffee. "You tell her what the case was about?"

"No." Cilla pressed her lips together. "None of her business."

Sobieski turned her attention to Brendan. "How about you, Mr. Patton? You have any problems getting the time off?"

"I'll work late tonight," he said with a shrug. He hadn't looked at Cilla, and he was pretty sure she hadn't looked at him. But he pressed his leg to hers. "He was good with that."

"Glad to hear it."

Cilla leaned forward. "So what is this about, Officer Sobieski?"

Sobieski leaned against the back of her chair and crossed her arms. "For starters, you can stop jerking me around." She narrowed her eyes at Cilla, then at him. "I know you're both cops. Why didn't you tell us?"

Brendan struggled to hide his shock as he watched her. Sobieski didn't seem so young or soft anymore. "What makes you say that?" he said, managing to sound curious instead of stunned.

"Ran your prints." She circled her hands around her mug as she studied both of them. "Yours from your belt, hers from her phone." She switched her gaze to Cilla. "You're not a keyboardist, Marini." Back to him. "And you're not a player hanging around with a pick-up crowd, Donovan. What are you doing at the Pipe and Shamrock?"

"Lots of cops have second jobs," Cilla said calmly. "Why can't mine be in a band? I am a keyboardist. The Pipe and Shamrock wouldn't put me on the stage if I wasn't."

Thank God for his partner's composure under fire. "No rules about where cops can hang out," Brendan added. "I was there the first night Cilla played. Love at first sight."

Sobieski sighed. "Cut the crap, both of you. If your

presence at the pub is so innocent, why didn't you tell Welles you were a cop? Why didn't you flash your badge at him? Or pull your gun? You did have a gun in your purse, didn't you?"

"Knowing I was a cop wouldn't have stopped him," Cilla said. Her fingers closed around her mug. "Might have made it worse."

Sobieski shifted her gaze from Cilla to Brendan and back again. "You're both detectives. From different districts. You're on some undercover op, aren't you?"

Brendan pressed his leg harder against Cilla's. He needed to feel their connection. They'd figure this out. "Did you tell Johnstone who we were?"

Sobieski shook her head. "Didn't have a chance. He took off before I ran the prints." She frowned. "Said he was taking his lunch break, but it wasn't his usual time. And he grabbed the DNA swab from Welles and said he'd drop it off at the lab afterward."

"What's wrong with that?" Cilla asked quietly. Her calf pressed against his, as if she needed to be touching him, too.

"He hates going to the lab. Avoids it at all costs." Sobieski tapped her fingers on the white surface of the table as she watched them. "It's next to the morgue, and the morgue creeps him out. Wuss can't even watch an autopsy. So I wondered why he offered."

Brendan didn't look at Cilla. But he could feel the tension rolling off her. "Maybe he wanted a longer lunch break," he said.

"Wouldn't take one by volunteering for the lab run. And he knows I'm not going to bust his chops if he takes an extra fifteen minutes." She twirled the coffee cup on the Formica table. "Another thing. Welles's high-power attorney showed up pretty damn fast last night. Less than an hour after he was booked. He wanted to have Welles transported downtown for an immediate bond hearing. I refused, but it looked as if Derek would have said yes.

"I did some checking on Mr. Welles." Her mouth

tightened. "I'm guessing you did the same. Glen Larson was the night court judge last night. Sound familiar?"

"Oh, my God." Cilla leaned forward. "You noticed that in his court cases, too."

"Sure did. Larson and Peter Drake. He ended up in their courtrooms way too often. I wasn't about to let Larson grant Welles bail." Her jaw worked. "If Welles is our serial rapist, we need to keep him locked up. Six women have been raped in our district. That I know of." She glanced at Cilla. "You would have made seven.

"Beverly is a low-crime area, except for the serial rapist. And I suspect we've caught him, thanks to you. So were you two looking for him?" Her gaze shifted from Brendan to Cilla. "Or is there something else going on?"

"I'm sorry." Cilla's voice was quiet. Filled with real regret. "We can't tell you that."

Sobieski studied them for a long moment, then nodded. "Didn't figure you would. Thought it was worth a shot, though." She took another sip of coffee. "I took a second swab from Welles. Told him I'd dropped the other one. I took it to the lab on my way over here."

Cilla stilled beside him, then sat up straight. "Why did you do that?"

"This is a big case. We've been chasing this rapist for a long time. I don't want anything to screw it up," she said carefully. "That's what I told the tech at the lab. That we took two samples, the A and the B. The one I took was the B sample. She agreed to run both of them."

"How long will it take to get the results back?" Brendan asked.

"Shouldn't take long." Sobieski's smile was grim. "I told the tech it was a rape case. A friend of hers was raped a few years ago, and the guy was never caught. She said she'd rush it through. I'm hoping we can hold onto Welles until we get the results. I'm going to be in court today. Try to keep them from granting bail."

"Good luck." Brendan slid out of the booth, held out

his hand to help Cilla. "Keep us posted." He stood next to the table and stared down at Sobieski. "Can we trust you to keep your mouth shut about us? We don't want to have to start this op over with different people."

Sobieski nodded. "Yeah. I won't say a thing." She hesitated, looked from one of them to the other. "Not even to Derek."

"Thank you." Brendan felt Cilla's exhale of relief. "I wish we could tell you what we're doing."

"Yeah, I get it. Good luck." She smiled. "Maybe I'll run into you when this is over and you can fill me in."

"I'll make sure of it." Cilla paused, then said, "We can tell you one thing now, though. Watch your back."

The two women's gazes locked and held for a long moment. Then Sobieski nodded. "Thanks. I will."

She shook Cilla's hand, then Brendan's, and slid out of the booth. "Got to get to court before that asshole gets bail."

Brendan watched the woman weave her way through the tables and head out the door. Then he turned to Cilla. "You want to finish breakfast?"

"Cold eggs?" She shuddered. "No, thanks."

"Let's go, then."

Neither of them spoke until they were in his car and heading north. "What the hell is going on in the 22nd?" Brendan said once they were on Lake Shore Drive again.

Cilla was staring out the windshield. She didn't turn to look at him. "You want to bet on whether those two swabs from Welles are going to match?"

"God, I hope they do. Otherwise..." He shook his head. He didn't want to think about the implications if the swabs didn't match. Or if the first one never showed up at the lab.

"Jonhstone's a cop," Cilla said, her voice rising. "And he's helping a rapist get away?"

"Maybe he did drop off the sample," Brendan said. "Maybe he was just looking for some extra time to help Welles's lawyer."

"I hate this." Cilla stared out the windshield, her hands fisted on her thighs. "We started out looking for a drug dealer. Cut and dried. Now we don't know who to trust. We've got at least three cops from the 22nd and one DEA agent in our sights."

"I'm right there with you, Cilla. We need to get this drug case closed. Right away."

"So we can investigate Johnstone?" He heard the pain in her voice. "Other cops from the 22nd? Romano?"

"One thing at a time," he said. "We focus on the drug case."

They drove around the curve of the museum campus and straightened out next to the lake. A handful of sailboats skimmed across the water, and a flock of ducks paddled close to shore. Normal autumn sights. The sun glittered off the waves. He reached for his sunglasses.

"Get off the Drive," Cilla said suddenly as they passed Navy Pier.

"How come?"

"That guy who overdosed in the pub's parking lot. He's at Northwestern Memorial Hospital. Let's go see if he's awake. If he remembers anything."

"Sure, we can check." He changed lanes and got off at the stop light at Ontario. "But they'd have told us if he was awake," he reminded her.

"I need to do something."

"Yeah, I get it." She'd needed to do something last night, too. Today, though, he'd be prepared if she tried to pull a dangerous stunt.

Five minutes later they parked in front of the hospital and Brendan put a police ID on the dashboard. As he turned off the ignition, Cilla grabbed his arm. "Isn't that the girlfriend?" She nodded toward a woman walking slowly past their car.

"Yeah, I think it is."

He snatched the police ID card off the dashboard and slid it beneath the seat, then they hurried after the woman.

Cilla reached her first.

"Hey, Penny," she said. Brendan wondered how Cilla knew the woman's name. He didn't remember hearing it. "We were visiting someone at the hospital and we saw you. Do you remember us? From the pub the night your boyfriend got sick?"

Penny's face was pale, and dark shadows purpled her eyes. Her hair was pulled into a pony tail and looked as if it hadn't been washed in a few days.

She studied them for a moment, then her expression softened. "Yeah. You're the people who did CPR on him."

"How's he doing?" Brendan asked.

"A little better," Penny said, tucking a strand of hair behind her ear. "He's starting to wake up. I'm heading home to take a shower and get some sleep. Coming back this afternoon."

"Let us walk you to your car," Cilla said. "We've been thinking about him. What do the doctors say?"

Penny practically staggered across the street and walked into the parking lot. "They say his brain function looks okay. They're not sure why he's still in a coma, but they're hopeful he'll wake up soon." Her mouth quivered. "I'm holding onto that sliver of hope."

"Did you remember anything else about that night?" Cilla asked gently. "Anything that might help the cops?"

The woman swallowed. "Yeah. He told me he had taken some kind of sex drug. I didn't say anything to the cops who showed up because I didn't want him to get into trouble. I think he got it in the pub."

Being careful not to glance at Cilla, Brendan asked, "Did you at least tell the doctors?"

"I told them everything." Penny's eyes flashed as she met his gaze. "I love him. I want him to be okay. I don't know why he took that stupid drug."

"We all do stupid things sometimes," Cilla said.

The woman stopped next to a familiar-looking car and opened the door. Brendan held it for her as she climbed in.

A colorful pile of fabric pooled on the floor of the back seat. A shirt.

He remembered seeing the shirt on the floor of the car that night. And earlier that night, as well. On a tall, thin man talking to Tiffany.

He touched Penny's shoulder. "Drive carefully, okay? You look really tired."

"Thanks." She gave them a weary half-smile. "Thanks for asking about Jason."

"Glad to hear he's improving."

She nodded, then started the car and pulled out of the parking spot.

As he watched her drive away, he fumbled for Cilla's hand. "Thank God you suggested stopping here."

"Why? We didn't get any new information."

"Yes, we did. I think we found a solid link between the drugs and Tiffany."

CHAPTER TWENTY-FOUR

Cilla stared at Brendan, stunned, as he explained about the shirt in the back of Penny's car, and how he remembered seeing it on Steven earlier that night as he talked to Tiffany. "Thank God for loud shirts," Brendan said.

"And for observant partners," she added. She slumped in the seat as he maneuvered along Michigan and merged onto Lake Shore Drive. "At least this impulse of mine turned out well."

"Hey, we got some good information last night," Brendan said immediately.

"We were lucky," Cilla said quietly. She forced a smile as guilt thrummed through her. She'd been so damn reckless last night. She'd charged over to the lawyer's car without stopping to think. "You're supposed to be the impulsive one in this partnership. Since when did we switch roles?"

"Being impulsive isn't always bad." His gaze held hers for a long moment, then he switched his attention to the road. Her face burning, she remembered the first time they'd had sex. She'd been impulsive then, too.

It had turned out pretty well for her and Brendan.

Maybe she needed to take more risks in her life.

You already did.

Her face got hotter as she remembered the words she'd whispered to him early this morning as she fell asleep. Yeah. When she'd spoken, she hadn't been thinking again. Only feeling. It was probably just as well Brendan had been asleep.

For now, she'd keep these feelings locked away, where they couldn't get in the way of her job. And maybe, if she was feeling brave, she'd tell him again after the case was over.

Or maybe not.

She'd assumed all along this relationship of theirs came with an expiration date – the end of the case. If he was interested in continuing this...whatever it was, they could talk about it later. When they didn't have to focus all their energy on finding the people distributing this drug.

People who were likely to turn out to be cops.

She rolled her shoulders, feeling as if dirt clung to every inch of her. Filth she'd never be able to wash away.

"What's wrong?" Brendan asked.

It was a little scary how he noticed everything. Maybe because he was a writer. She leaned against the back of the seat and stared out the window. "I feel as though I need to take ten showers, and even then I'll never be clean."

"I know." His voice was so soft she could barely hear him over the rumble of the tires on the asphalt. "Everywhere we look, we uncover more slime."

"We need some help with this case, but I don't know who to trust," she said, pulling her feet onto the seat and wrapping her arms around her legs. "I'll be on the stage all weekend, so I can't help you watch Tiffany. You have any ideas?"

"Yeah. I do."

He sounded so confident. So sure, that her mood lightened a little. "You want to share with the class?"

"I think we should call Connor, Quinn and Mia. My siblings. I trust them completely. They could back us up at the pub this weekend. Between the four of us, we could watch Tiffany every minute."

"What would that get us?"

"We'd know if she met with Bates or Ward. We'd see if she passed something small, like a pill, to anyone. If we got hold of it, and it turned out to be that drug, we could pull her in and find out where she's getting the drug."

"No guarantees she's going to sell anything while we're watching," Cilla pointed out.

"Course not. But it gives us a chance. Do you have another idea?"

"No," she admitted. "But it seems like a lot to ask of your family. They'd potentially be giving up four nights. What if they have to work?"

"We'll figure something out. They can probably juggle their shifts so they're off at night this weekend." He pulled into a strip mall along Belmont. "I'm going to call Connor."

Brendan pulled out his phone and hit one of his speed dials. A few moments later, he said, "Hey, Con. You have a minute?"

Brendan put the phone on speaker and she heard Connor say, "Sure."

Brendan sketched out what was going on, then said, "We think there might be cops involved. You and Quinn and Mia are the only ones I trust right now. Except for Cilla."

He trusted her as much as he trusted his family.

Cilla's mushy heart stuttered, and pleasure swept through her. Her throat tightened and she turned to look out the window. Her eyes prickled, and she didn't want Brendan to see her stupid tears.

There was a pause. Then Connor asked, "Cilla from the hospital?" His voice sounded a little sharper. As if he was mining for information.

"How many partners do you think I have named Cilla? Yes, it's the woman you met in the hospital. Can you get away for lunch?"

"Absolutely." He must have covered the phone, because she heard his muffled voice say, "Hey, Q. Lunch with Bren?"

A few moments later he said, "Quinn's good. I'll give Mia a call. She's working tonight. Where do you want to go?"

Brendan glanced at her. "I was thinking a park. No one to overhear us."

"Sounds serious," Connor said.

"It is. How about Montrose Avenue Beach?"

"No," Connor said immediately. "It's fall. That place is a birding mecca. There will be crowds of people out there, all of them with binoculars. Don't want to take the chance one of them's an off-duty cop. How about North Avenue Beach?"

"That works." Brendan glanced at his watch. "Noon good for you?"

"Yep."

"See you then. We'll bring lunch."

He turned off his phone and grinned at her. "See how easy that was?"

She swallowed hard to dispel the lump in her throat. "Do your siblings always drop everything when you call?"

"Not always. Sometimes they're tied up with a case. Or busy with their girlfriends. But if one of us needs help, the rest of us try to make it." He shrugged. "We take care of each other."

A wisp of envy trickled through Cilla. She and her siblings didn't have that kind of relationship. Her brother and sister called her a lot when they needed help, but Cilla never asked them for anything.

She'd called Olivia last night. And Livvy had been glad to help.

Maybe she'd just needed to call all along. Maybe her siblings never stepped up because she never asked them to.

Maybe it wouldn't be as hard to change their family

dynamic as she'd thought it would be.

While she'd been thinking about her family, Brendan had pulled out of the strip mall parking spot. "Cilla. You in there?" he asked with a quizzical look.

"Yeah. Sorry. Just thinking about families." She made an effort to smile. "Yours sounds so different than mine."

"Doesn't mean better or worse," he said easily as he glanced at his watch. "We're meeting at noon. I need to take Franny for a walk. You want to come along?"

The thought of walking the dog with Brendan brought a prickle of longing to her throat. Last time she'd wondered how it would feel to be part of a couple with a normal life. Walking the dog. Coming home from work and fixing dinner.

After spending the last couple of days with him, she knew. It would feel pretty damn good.

But she couldn't go there now. Couldn't think about what she and Brendan had or what she was hoping they had.

She had to focus on the case. Not enough sleep the night before and the upsetting possibility of looking for dirty cops had made her emotional. Shockingly needy. Unless she wanted Brendan to see her usually-hidden clingy side, she needed to get away from him for a few hours. Steady herself.

"I should go home and change my clothes. Pay some bills." Her face heated. "I haven't been home much the last few days."

"Yeah." His voice was low and throaty in the idling car. "It's been great." He hesitated, and she wondered if he was going to tell her a little distance would work for him. "Do you, ah, want to pack a few things so you have clean clothes at my place for tomorrow?"

She stared at him, blood rushing through her veins so hard she heard it in her ears. He wasn't telling her he'd had enough closeness. "I could do that."

"Will you do that?"

She nodded. "Yes. I will."

"Good." He reached for her hand, squeezed it, then let her go. "Joined at the hip, remember? I won't sleep unless you're right next to me."

Her heart lurched. He was thinking about her safety.

She'd been thinking of something else entirely. "Drop me at my place, then?"

"Yes. I'll pick you up about eleven so we can grab some lunch first. Okay?"

"Sounds great."

When they reached her building, she leaped out of the car and hurried into the front door without looking back.

***

Brendan watched her rush into her apartment, wondering what the hell was wrong. Ever since he'd called Connor, she'd been acting weird. Quiet. He'd say she was brooding, except Cilla didn't seem like the type to brood.

That was one of the things he liked about her. She was straightforward. Told him what she thought and what she wanted. He didn't have to try and interpret hidden messages.

So he'd ask her when he picked her up, he promised himself. For now, he was going to spend some time with Franny, who had been neglected the last couple of days. Smiling in anticipation, he headed for his apartment.

An hour later, Franny lay on the ground in front of him, panting. "Give me the ball, Franny," he said, holding out his hand.

Instead of standing and dropping the ball in his hand, she set her head on the ground. Stared at him.

"Okay. I get it. You're done." He snatched up the ball and pulled her leash out of his pocket. But before he could clip it onto her collar, a voice behind him said, "Donovan? That you?"

He turned around to see Anson Bates strolling toward him.

Every muscle in his body clenched. He'd left his gun at the apartment. His first thought was, thank God Cilla was safe at home.

His second thought was, pull it together, idiot. You're an undercover cop. You know how to act. Pretend he's just an old buddy from the Academy, not someone you're investigating.

"Bates." He held out his hand as the other cop approached. "What the hell are you doing here?"

Bates shook his hand, squeezing a little harder than necessary. Brendan returned the pressure before he let go.

"Driving by. I saw you tossing a ball for your dog and recognized you. It's been a while. Figured I should say hello."

"Hey." Had Bates been following him? Brendan swallowed and forced a smile. "Glad you stopped. How the hell have you been?"

"I'm good. Keeping busy. How about you?"

Yeah, he bet Bates was keeping busy.

"The same." He shrugged. "We never lack for assholes to put away." Assholes like you, Bates.

Franny stood up and trotted to his side. Studied Bates for a long moment, then plopped herself down in front of Brendan.

Nice job, Fran. Don't think you can stop a bullet, but I appreciate the gesture.

"You on duty?" he asked Bates. "You have time to grab a coffee?" It's what they would have done if they bumped into each other in the past.

Back then, it would have been accidental.

"Sorry. On my way to court. But I have a minute to catch up with an old friend." He punched Brendan's shoulder. A little harder than a friendly thump. "Heard you were in my neck of the woods yesterday. Was disappointed you didn't look me up."

Thank God Brendan was used to keeping his cool in dicey situations. He made sure not a flicker of discomfort crossed his face. "Yeah, I was," he said easily. "Following a lead in a case. Didn't finish up until late. Figured you'd already be at home."

"Interesting case?" Bates asked.

He was fishing. Brendan smiled to himself. Two could play at this. "Run of the mill. Looking for a pimp who likes under-age girls. Got a tip he was in the Morgan Park area." He shrugged. "Spent way too much time looking for him. By the time I quit, I needed a beer. I heard there was a good Irish pub in Beverly. So I stopped in."

"The Pipe and Shamrock?" Bates crossed his arms over his chest. His right hand rested close to the gun holstered under his shoulder.

"Yeah, I think that's the name." He frowned, as if puzzled, as he stared at Bates's hand. Ready to act if it twitched even a little. "How did you know I was there?" Had Bates seen Cilla? Should he mention her?

"My partner Ward spotted you. He said it was one of the Donovans. Was pretty sure it was you. He remembered you from the hospital. When Cujo was shot."

So they'd been talking about him. Brendan wanted to leap at Bates and pound on him until he confessed what he was doing. Since that option wasn't on the table, he channeled his anger toward Cujo's shooting. "Damn bangers. You hear how Cujo's doing?"

"Out of the hospital. Doing rehab." Bates shook his head. "Won't be back on the job for months after that kind of chest surgery."

"That's too damn bad. They catch the guy who shot him?"

"Yeah. He's in Cook County Jail."

"One good thing, at least."

Bates stood in front of him, and the silence stretched uncomfortably. Brendan let the moment build, hoping Bates would reveal something. But the other cop finally said, "Guess I should be on my way. Good to see you, Donovan. Don't be a stranger. The next time you're chasing some shithead in my neck of the woods, give me a call. We'll grab a beer. Catch up."

"I'll do that. Take care, Bates."

Bates's gaze lingered on Brendan for a beat too long. "You, too, Donovan."

Brendan watched Bates walk across the park and slide into his unmarked. He glanced at Brendan, raised his hand once, then drove away.

When Bates was out of sight, Brendan bent and scratched Franny's head. "What a good girl you are," he crooned. "You were very brave to protect me."

He ruffled the dog's fur, then snapped the collar onto her leash. "Extra treats for you at home. Let's get going. I need to tell Cilla about this."

Maybe Bates had visited Cilla first.

Brendan began to run.

CHAPTER TWENTY-FIVE

Brendan stomped on his brakes in front of Cilla's building and leaped out as the car rolled to a stop. He was double-parked and the gumball was still flashing. He didn't give a damn.

He'd slammed the light onto the roof of his car and lit it up as he pulled away from the curb at his place. An agonizing eternity ago.

His breath sawed in and out as he sprinted for the door to her three-flat. He yanked at the doorknob with enough force to pull it out of the door. Didn't budge. So he pressed his finger on the buzzer next to 'Marini' and held it.

A few moments later Cilla's tinny voice came out of the speaker. "Who is this?"

She sounded pissed off. Or scared.

He wrapped his hand around the door knob. "Brendan. You okay?"

The door buzzed as it unlocked. Cilla's voice trailed behind him, but he didn't stop to listen. He was already half-way up the first staircase.

He skidded around the corner, pounded up the next set of stairs. Skidded and ran up the next set. Her door began to open when he was half-way there.

Banging the half-open door into the wall, he reached in and grabbed her. Crushed her against him. Breathed in her scent and the feel of her heart beating against his. She was alive. Apparently unhurt. He wrapped his arms her and squeezed.

"What's wrong?" She eased her face away from where it was smashed into his shoulder. He couldn't bear to let her go, and he pressed his fingers into her waist to keep her close.

"Brendan!" She cupped his face in her hands as she searched his eyes. "What happened?"

"You alone in there?" he breathed into her ear.

She wriggled away from him, grabbed his hand and pulled him inside. Shut the door and locked it. She didn't let go of his hand, though. Thank God. He needed to feel her fingers around his, needed to feel the play of her muscles as she clung to him.

"Of course I'm alone," she said. "You're scaring me, Brendan. What's going on?"

His gaze darted around her apartment. No one hiding behind the battered leather couch. No one crouching next to the Ikea bookshelves. No room for anything to hide among the hardcovers and paperbacks haphazardly crowding the shelves.

The faded Oriental rug was where it belonged. Not bunched up, as if there'd been a struggle. Bright blue, yellow and green pillows still neat on the couch. Small flat-screen television, scattered prints of the lake and the city hanging on the wall, were all straight.

Old, battered piano sitting in the corner of the room was untouched.

No signs of a struggle in Cilla's apartment.

For the first time since he ran from the park, he allowed himself to take a deep breath.

He pulled her close and buried his face in her hair. He'd been terrified, and he'd panicked. The thought of her hurt, or worse, had wrecked him. Knowing she was alone, and vulnerable, had made his stomach churn and his heart pound until it felt as if it would jump out of his chest.

He'd never been so scared in his life. Never felt so helpless. If anything had happened to Cilla...

He drew in a deep, shuddering breath. He never wanted to let her go. He wanted to make love to her, to prove to himself that she was okay.

He wanted to beg her to promise to never leave.

Oh, God.

Never leave.

What the hell did that mean? He wasn't a 'never leave' kind of guy. He wasn't about 'put a ring on it' and happily ever after.

He didn't know how the hell to do that. Where to even begin.

Cilla tugged on his arm. "Brendan! Stop it! You're freaking me out."

He focused his eyes and saw Cilla staring up at him, her hazel eyes dark and her face taut with fear. Still rocked by his realization of how he felt about her, he tried to steady himself.

He took a shaky breath. Then another. "Bates," he managed to say. "I was afraid he'd been here. Or that Ward had been. Or still was."

Cilla sucked in a breath. Grabbed his hand. "Why?"

Get it together, Donovan. Bury the personal stuff. Don't think about it. Focus on the case. On what's important.

He tugged her over to the couch and sat down. Pulled her down next to him, careful to keep a few inches between their bodies. So he wouldn't think about what might have happened. "I was throwing a ball for Franny, in that park we went to the other day. The one a couple of blocks from my place."

He swallowed, putting his arm over the back of the couch. Dug his fingers into her shoulder. To reassure himself she was there. "Bates showed up."

"What?" She straightened and swiveled to face him, dislodging his arm. Which was a good thing. "You saw him there? In your neighborhood?"

"Yes." Focus on Bates. On the case. "More than saw him. He got out of his car and came over to have a chat with me."

He told her what had happened, staring at her light blue walls instead of looking at her. Trying to remember every word. Every inflection of Bates's voice. "As soon as he drove away, I headed for my apartment. Then it occurred to me that he might have sent Ward to talk to you."

Cilla relaxed onto the couch. "I wouldn't have let Ward in," she assured him. She touched his face, scraping her palm along his whiskers. The rasping sound made his stomach clench. She was petting him.

"I always ask before I buzz somebody in," she added.

"He's a cop, Cilla." He took a deep breath, felt it shudder out. "He could have badged someone walking in and come straight to your door. Kicked it in."

Cilla leaned toward him and pressed her mouth to his. Lingered for a long moment. As if she knew he needed to be certain she was okay. "That's quite an imagination you have there, Mr. Cops and Robbers."

Brendan blew out a sigh and closed his eyes. Shoved his hands through his hair. "Didn't mean to scare you," he muttered.

He opened his eyes when he felt her hands smoothing his hair. "Got it all spiky," she murmured. "Makes you look like a goofball." She kissed him again, a quick brush of her mouth over his. "A sexy goofball, though."

He pulled her hands into her lap. "Sorry. Guess I went overboard. Built it up in my mind, you know? A whole novel. All of it bad."

"Don't apologize," she said, leaning into his shoulder. "I'm never going to complain about seeing you at my door."

Brendan froze. Shit! Exactly what he didn't want to

think about. Then he tried to smile. "Good to know, Marini." He glanced around her living room, scrambling for a way to change the subject. "I like your place."

"Thanks," she said, little squinchy lines between her eyes, as if she was confused. "It's nothing special, but it's comfortable."

Damn it. Now they were talking drivel about her apartment. His fault, for trying to duck the elephant in the living room. But before he could figure out a way to scramble around how he felt, Cilla saved his ass.

"Do you think Bates followed you home?" She sucked in a breath. "Did he see us at the Valois? Talking to Sobieski?"

"I don't know, damn it." He jumped up to give himself a little distance. He needed to think about this, about Cilla, but he didn't have time right now. "I wasn't looking for tails. I was thinking about what Sobieski said."

"Do you think he bought your story about chasing a lead in Morgan Park?"

Brendan stood at the windows, staring at the flashing light on top of his car. "Not sure why he wouldn't. He knows I'm a vice cop. Knows I chase a lot of pimps. Maybe it just made him nervous that I was on his turf."

"But we can't be sure." Cilla walked over to lean against him. He wanted to curl his arm around her, pull her closer. Instead, he stood stiff and still.

"Maybe he saw me, too," she said. "Maybe he's paranoid and we just made it worse. What now?" She glanced up at him, frowned and moved away. Put space between them.

Was that what he wanted? Space? He had no fucking idea. How would he know? He'd never felt this way before. He liked the weight of her against him, but the feelings it evoked terrified him.

He glanced at his watch. "Right now, we go pick up a bunch of Italian beefs from Al's and meet my siblings at North Avenue Beach. Maybe they'll have some ideas."

***

Cilla stared at the tense, edgy version of Brendan who stood in her living room, not quite meeting her gaze. What the hell was wrong with him?

He'd stormed into her apartment like he was claiming her. Grabbed her as if he'd never let her go. Now he was acting as nervous as a nun in a whorehouse.

He wouldn't even look at her, for God's sake.

Pain made her heart clench in her chest. Was he having second thoughts about the whole 'girlfriend' thing?

Or was distancing himself merely his default when he started to get too interested in a woman?

She'd seen the terror in his eyes when he'd rushed up the stairs toward her. He cared about her. Cared what happened to her. So was he pushing her away because he didn't know what to do about it?

The ache in her heart throbbed, like a sore tooth that you couldn't resist poking with your tongue. But watching the way he danced around her, avoided her eyes, made her pain morph into anger.

She couldn't fix whatever was bothering him. She couldn't make him want an adult relationship. She was so damn tired of fixing things for people. Managing other people's problems.

She loved him. Wanted to build something with him. But Brendan clearly wasn't ready for that.

They needed to finish this case. Catch Bates, or whoever was behind this drug. She and Brendan were good partners on the job. In their personal lives? Not so much.

So they'd do what whatever was needed to stop the distribution of this drug. And then she'd walk away.

Her heart might not be intact. But her pride would be.

She wouldn't beg him to love her back.

Her phone buzzed and she snatched it out of her pocket. "Marini."

"Hey, Cil. It's me. Livvy."

Cilla huffed out a breath. "Hey, Liv, what's up?"

"Wanted to fill you in on the Welles case."

She hesitated, and Cilla's gut clenched. Something was wrong. "What is it?"

"He got bail." Her sister swallowed. "Five million, which is practically impossible to raise, but if he can, he's getting out."

"Damn it." Cilla wanted to slam her phone to the floor, so she gripped it more tightly. "How did that happen?"

"Sorry, Cill. I tried. I really did. But he had some big-deal lawyer who told the judge he was an upstanding member of the bar, roots in the community, blah, blah, blah." Olivia hesitated. "The DA assigned to the case didn't seem to be trying real hard to keep him in jail. Even the cop who arrested him was there. Asked for no bail. Judge didn't pay any attention."

"What's the judge's name?"

"John Bolland."

Cilla would add his name to the list of Peter Drake and Glen Larson. "Thanks for letting me know, Liv. Keep me posted, okay? Let me know if he gets out."

"I'll do that, Cill." Olivia hesitated. "I feel really bad. You never ask me for anything. And the one time you did, I couldn't do it."

Olivia couldn't fix the impossible, Cilla realized. And neither could she. Brendan didn't want to be fixed, and she couldn't force him to change. "Don't beat yourself up, Liv. My guess? It was decided before it even got to court."

"That occurred to me. And I'm going to look into that. You watch yourself, Cill. I'll call you the minute I hear anything on this case."

"Thanks, Liv."

Cilla stared at her sister's name and phone number for a long moment. Then she pressed the key to darken the screen and slid it back into her pocket.

"Welles got bail. Five million. But that's only a half-mil if he gets the ten percent. He'll get out."

"He won't get near you." Brendan pulled her against him. "I'll make sure of it."

Cilla eased away from him. She tapped the bruise on her neck, brushed her hand over her side. "He gave me a couple of reminders that I'm not invincible. I'll be ready for him next time."

She turned on the phone and glanced at the time. "We have to get going or we're going to be late. Wouldn't want your family to get a bad impression of me."

"Not possible, Cilla." He stepped through the door to her apartment, waited for her to lock it, then followed her down the stairs. "They're gonna love you."

Just like you do, Brendan?

She shoved the snarky voice out of her head. Time to change the subject. As she reached the front door, she glanced over her shoulder. "You have your department car?"

"Double parked right in front."

"Great. I'll log into your computer and find out what kind of car Bates drives. I'll get the plate numbers of his personal car and his department car. So you can warn your siblings."

He bumped her shoulder with his. "Good to know my partner's on the same page."

"Yeah," she muttered. "We're a great team."

***

As they walked across the parking lot and onto the grass that bordered the sandy beach, Cilla saw two men and a woman sitting at a picnic table, their heads together. Talking.

Brendan's siblings. She recognized Connor, dressed in jeans and a black tee shirt. The man next to him wore black jeans and a white tee with the slogan 'Nurses do it standing up'. Their faces were almost identical. He had to be Connor's twin.

The woman had the same dark hair as the rest of the family, although hers fell in waves to her shoulders. Cilla wondered if all of them had Brendan's blue eyes.

Wondered what they'd all think of her.

Reminded herself it didn't matter. After they finished this case, she'd be gone. Wouldn't see any of the Donovans again.

They stopped talking and watched her and Brendan approach. All three of them were facing the parking lot. The closest they could get to the cop chairs in a restaurant. They might not have their backs to the wall, but Lake Michigan was a good second choice.

She tightened her grip on the bag of sandwiches, holding it carefully away from her body to avoid the grease stains already dotting the paper bag. Brendan carried two six-packs of Coke and a fistful of napkins. When he saw his family, he shifted one six-pack under his arm and took her hand.

Squeezed. As if reassuring her.

Of what? That his family wouldn't bite?

She could handle the Donovans.

He let her go before they reached his family, but all three stared at her. Assessing. Measuring.

They'd seen Brendan take her hand. Slide his fingers between hers.

Cilla wished they'd been able to ask someone else for help. Anyone but Brendan's family. Now they were all staring at her, their gazes assessing.

She didn't want to face them or their assumptions about her and Brendan. She wanted to turn and run away. But she forced herself to ignore the urge. She and Brendan needed help. And his siblings were the only ones they could trust.

"Hey." His sister was the first to speak. She trotted over to Brendan, hugged him for a long moment. Then leaned back. "Long tine, no see, Bren."

"Yeah." Brendan dropped the sodas on the picnic table.

"Not sure how I've survived not seeing you for a whole week."

"Smart ass," she said, punching him on the shoulder.

Then she turned to Cilla. "So you're Brendan's partner." She crooked one eyebrow at Cilla.

"Cilla Marini," Cilla said evenly. "And you're Brendan's sister."

The slender woman with Brendan's eyes smiled at that. "Touché. I'm Mia. Nice to meet you." She looked from Cilla to Brendan, as if expecting Cilla to explain their relationship.

Not going to happen. "Nice to meet you, too, Mia."

She dropped the bag with the beef sandwiches from Al's on the table, then nodded at Connor. Or at least the twin she was pretty sure was Connor. "Good to see you again, Connor."

He stood up and shook her hand. "You, too, Cilla." He slid back onto the picnic table bench. "Looks like you and Bren are doing well."

Cilla smiled, beginning to relax. She could do this. It didn't matter what they thought of her. They were no different than any group of nosy cops at the station. "We are. Your brother is a good partner." She turned to the man sitting next to Connor. "You must be Quinn. Nice to meet you."

"I am. And I'm impressed you could tell us apart after meeting Con once. Although it's pretty easy. I'm the good-looking twin."

She laughed as she shook his hand. "I'll remember that for next time."

"There's going to be a next time?" Across the table, Mia raised one eyebrow.

"Don't know. But this?" She gestured back and forth between her and Brendan. "It's our cover for this case. You never know who might be watching."

Brendan stepped closer, pressing against her from shoulder to thigh. "She's right. We have to sell the premise."

"You're doing a good job of selling it to us." Connor reached for one of the sandwiches. "Should have known it wasn't real, though. You don't do real, do you, Bren?"

Cilla felt him tense beside her. Without waiting for him to answer, she said, "You can't tell?" She smiled innocently. "That's because Brendan is a damn good undercover operator."

Mia popped the top on one of the cold, sweaty colas and smiled as she took a drink. "Looks like his partner is equally good."

"She is," Brendan said quietly. His fingers brushed her hip. "But we're going to need help. Let me tell you what's going on." He glanced over his shoulder. "You mind switching sides of the table?"

All three of the Donovans frowned. "How come?" Quinn finally said.

"I need to keep an eye on the parking lot."

They all stood up and slid off the bench. Edged onto the other side.

"Sounds pretty serious," Quinn said.

"It is." As Brendan unrolled the greasy paper around his sandwich, he told them about their assignment. About their suspicions of Bates. How he'd stopped at the park. His questions.

"We need to finish this. Cilla and I have an idea, but we're going to need your help."

As they ate, Brendan outlined their operation. He studied the parking lot every few minutes. When a car drove in, he tensed. Stared until he was sure the car didn't belong to Bates.

While he talked, his brothers and sister interrupted him repeatedly to ask questions. Finally, when all of them except Brendan had finished their sandwich, Mia reached for a napkin.

"So you need our help at your pub. When? I'm working nights this weekend, but I can probably switch with someone. How about you two?" she asked Connor and Quinn.

It took only a few minutes for everything to be arranged. All three of them would be at the pub on Thursday night. Connor and Quinn promised subtle disguises so they wouldn't look so much like Brendan.

As they all stood up to leave, Brendan said, "One last thing. You all know Bates and Ward?"

"I don't know either of them," Mia said.

Quinn didn't know either of them, either.

Connor said, "Ward made that scene at the hospital. I won't forget his face. Bates? Not sure I know him."

"Find pictures of them before Thursday night. But do it right away. Don't want any of you taken by surprise before then."

"Aren't you a little paranoid, bro?" Quinn asked. "Why would either of those dirtbags go after one of us?"

Brendan scanned the parking lot once more before he answered. "He saw me in the Pipe and Shamrock. If he's our guy, he has to be nervous. Worried enough to confront me in a park a couple of blocks from my apartment." He gazed from one of his siblings to another, then grabbed Cilla's hand. "Make sure you watch your six."

All five of them headed for the parking lot, dumping the trash in a garbage bin. Brendan's gaze combed the rows of cars as he pressed the 'unlock' button on his key fob. "Thanks, guys." He waved to his siblings as he opened the door for Cilla, then got into the driver's seat. "See you soon."

Cilla exhaled. That had gone...okay. At least they'd managed to deflect the nosier questions.

And even Connor's painful remark about Brendan not doing 'serious' had floated past without any comments. Thank God. She wouldn't have been able to handle a discussion of Brendan's past romantic entanglements.

She scanned the cars around them. Tensed. As Brendan closed his door and started the car, Cilla murmured,

"Burgandy Crown Vic, five cars down on our left." It was the color and model of the department car Bates drove.

Brendan didn't look in that direction. "We'll take a look as we pull out."

As they cruised slowly past the parked Crown Vic, Cilla turned to Brendan as if she was talking to him. She scanned the license plate. Wrong number. And the car was empty.

"False alarm," she said.

"Good catch. And keep paying attention," Brendan said, his voice grim. "The next one might be Bates. Or Ward."

CHAPTER TWENTY-SIX

Cilla's voice, singing Elton John's Rocket Man, washed over Brendan as he stood at the bar of the Pipe and Shamrock, drinking his fake Warsteiner beer. Her voice was haunting, and most of the people around him were staring at the stage. At Cilla.

Any other time, he would have lost himself in the music, in her, as well.

Not tonight. Tonight, he was watching Tiffany.

Dressed in another bright, flamboyant dress, this one a silver number that oozed sex, she was making the rounds in the pub. Talking to anyone who smiled at her or caught her eye.

Mia was behind her, wearing a red dress that was far too short and way too tight. It was matched with fuck-me black shoes that added three inches to her height. How the hell did she walk in those shoes?

It was the kind of outfit she'd go clubbing in. To dance with guys she didn't know. To pick those guys up. Brendan swallowed a too-big gulp of his half-warm beer. He didn't want to think about his baby sister that way.

But he had to admit, she was playing her role as the party

girl perfectly. Men crowded around her, offering to buy her drinks, trying to engage her attention. She flirted with all of them, but still managed to keep a close eye on Tiffany. Damn it. His little sister was good. She'd make a great detective one of these days.

Quinn was on Tiffany's other side. He wore a three-piece suit, with slicked-back hair and a fancy tie. Chatting up a lot of women, just like a real player would have done. Hoping Tiffany would see him and target him as a prospective customer.

Connor was the other point of the triangle surrounding Tiffany. He wore an old herringbone sports coat with suede patches on the elbows. Khakis and a blue dress shirt. He'd pasted a fake mustache on his upper lip and wore dark-rimmed glasses. A college professor, maybe. Or an aspiring writer.

Brendan felt some of his tension ease as he smiled into his beer at the thought. Writers knew they didn't need the suede patches on the herringbone sports coat or the dorky glasses to be real.

He could have given Con some tips about writing attire.

But in order to do that, he would have to share his secret. And he wasn't ready for that yet.

His brothers would tease him unmercifully. But they'd be happy for him. So why hadn't he told them?

He wasn't quite ready to shatter his cop image. The tough guy, the macho man who had the swagger to make it on the street. All of his brothers were cops. His father had been one, too. As the youngest boy, Brendan had equated being a cop with being a real man.

In his family, writers were way down on the scale of 'real' men.

Both of his brothers had chosen characters that were as far from their real personalities as possible. And since Con had chosen a writer as his avatar, it was clear that he bought into that pansy-assed image, too.

Finishing his fake beer, Brendan set his glass on the bar

and stepped away. This was not the night to brood about the choices he'd made and what those choices meant. Cilla was singing again, but he forced himself to ignore the sound of her voice. He had to concentrate on the job.

As he wandered toward the restrooms, he spotted Tiffany in the more dimly lit back room. The same room where she'd met with Bates and Ward.

She was talking to a man. Mia, Connor and Quinn were drifting in that direction, and Brendan slowed. Tiffany's customer was pulling a wallet out of his pocket. Handing Tiffany some bills.

She put something in his hand, smiled, and turned away.

Time for Drunk Guy to make an appearance. Brendan had honed this act on several previous undercover ops.

He staggered a little as he got closer to the buyer. Put one hand on the wall, as if steadying himself. Then pushed away and crashed into the other man. Hard.

The short, slightly stocky guy stumbled backward, his arms wind-milling. Something white fell out of his hand.

Keeping his eyes on the white capsule on the floor, Brendan grabbed the guy's arm and steadied him. "Sorry, man," he said, slurring his words. "Really sorry." Brendan gestured toward the floor and the capsule, a few inches away from a man's foot. "Saw you drop something. I'll get it for you."

He swayed for a moment, then dropped to his knees. Began crawling on the floor, patting it as if looking for whatever dropped. He didn't take his eyes off the capsule, a couple of feet away.

"Hey, buddy, it's okay." The stocky guy tugged on his arm. "Don't worry about it. It was just an allergy pill. No big deal."

"No, no. I'll find it," Brendan insisted with the stubborn focus of the really drunk. "Got to be here somewhere."

He got close enough to put his hand over the little white capsule, and he held it against his palm with his thumb. "Ouch," he yelled, flinching as if someone had stepped on his hand.

"Get off the floor," Stocky Guy said, a hint of panic in his voice. "It's not important. Get up." He yanked on Brendan's arm and Brendan staggered to his feet. He dropped the pill into the pocket of his jeans as he pretended to wipe his hands on the denim.

"Sorry," Brendan said, fumbling for his wallet in his other front pocket. "Lemme give you some money. For more allergy pills."

"Don't worry about it." The stocky guy backed away and held up his hands, palm out. "It's fine. I'm good." He backed another couple of steps, then turned and fled.

"You okay, man?" Connor grabbed his arm and steered him toward a booth. "Looks like you need to sit down."

"M'fine." He batted at Connor's arm, missing half the time. "Just need another beer."

"Looks as if you've had plenty." Connor pushed him down onto the padded bench. "I'll get you a cup of coffee. Okay?"

"Yeah, coffee's good. Irish coffee."

"Regular coffee." He stared down at Brendan, his eyes twinkling. "What's your problem, anyway?"

"Band stopped playing," Brendan said.

"Yeah. They're taking a break," Connor replied.

Brendan scowled. "They're all hitting on her. Trying to touch her. My gir...girlfriend."

"Who are you talking about?"

"In the band. Keyboards."

"You think that hot chick is your girlfriend?" Connor shook his head. "In your dreams, pal." A stifled laugh slipped out of Con's mouth. "You need to go home. Come on. I'll get you a ride."

Brendan pretended to resist until Connor hoisted him to his feet. "Gotta settle my tab," Brendan protested.

"I'll take care of it," Connor said. "What's your name?"

"You'd do that?" Brendan reared back and stared at Connor. "You're the best friend ever."

"Hey, keep your voice down. Don't want every drunk in here thinking I'll pick up their tab."

Connor fumbled in his pocket and pulled out his phone. Pretended to call for an Uber car. Slid the phone back into his pocket as they reached the front door.

Once they were outside, Connor let him go. "That was so good it was scary," Connor said. "Almost had me convinced you were drunk."

Brendan edged around the corner, away from the door. "Not the first time I've played a drunk." He walked down a row of cars until he got to the back of the parking lot. Then he pulled a plain white capsule out of his pocket.

"Chain of custody okay?" Connor asked.

"Golden. Had my eyes on it from the moment it left the buyer's hand until I picked it up." He rolled it in his palm, examining it. It looked like an ordinary drug. An allergy medication, maybe, like the buyer had claimed.

It didn't look like a drug that killed people.

Brendan curled his fist around it, then pulled a small manila envelope from his back pocket. He slid the capsule inside and sealed the flap. "I'm going to run this over to the lab."

He held out his hand to Con, who took a pen out of his pocket. Brendan scribbled his name, the date and time, the location on the envelope. "There's one tech who's done the analysis on the drugs from all the guys who've died. She works nights, so I'm going to give this to her. Want to get it in there as fast as possible.

"Stay close to Tiffany," he continued, tapping the envelope into his shirt pocket. "If she's got people she doesn't know hanging around, she might not try to sell another one tonight. I'll be back after I've sobered up." He slapped Connor on the back. "Thanks, bro."

Connor frowned. "You want to go in and let Cilla know you'll be gone?"

"Nah. Cilla's good, she knows the score on an undercover op. She won't worry if I disappear." He patted his pockets, looking for his keys. "You can tell her what happened if you get a chance, though."

"Will do." Connor brushed an imaginary piece of lint from his jacket. "Think she's the type to go for a writer?"

Brendan choked back a laugh. "You gonna read her some poetry, Professor? Not sure she'd be too impressed by that. Especially if you wrote it."

Connor grinned, flashed him the finger and strolled back toward the pub door. Brendan got into his car, waited until there was no one in the parking lot to see him leave, then turned onto the street.

***

Cilla slid off her stool at the end of the second set, anxiety making her palms sweat and her heart beat a little harder. What had happened to Brendan?

And why hadn't he signaled her?

During the first set, he'd followed their script to the letter – he'd hung around at the bar, watched her, watched Tiffany. Wandered through the pub, taking his beer with him, talking to people he knew.

Then suddenly nothing. He'd disappeared.

Mia, Connor and Quinn were still here. She'd seen them all in the last thirty minutes, hiding her smiles at their disguises. During the first break, none of them had approached her or tried to talk to her. They were too busy watching Tiffany.

The second break was when Brendan usually checked in. Bought her iced tea, stood close enough to give her the scoop on the evening. Pretending he was whispering sweet nothings.

Stepping off the stage, she scanned the thinning crowd, looking for Brendan. When she didn't see him, anxiety bloomed into worry. Morphed into anger.

His three siblings were here. If Bates or Ward had come in, Mia, Connor and Quinn would have had Brendan's back.

So there was no reason to worry.

Brendan wouldn't have left without telling one of them where he was going. So why hadn't one of them let her know?

Stepping up to the bar, she asked Rick for an iced tea, then watched as Connor rounded the corner. "Buy you a drink?" he asked with a friendly smile.

"No, thanks. I've got it."

"You're, ah, boyfriend asked me to keep an eye on you," Connor said, loud enough for other people to hear. "Or maybe I should say your 'so-called' boyfriend." Connor shook his head. "What do you see in a guy who gets wasted like that?"

Cilla took a deep breath, let it out slowly. Okay. Something had happened, but it was under control. She let her shoulders relax and took a long drink of her iced tea. "He has his good qualities." She made no effort to lower her voice, knowing people were listening. "Some big...strengths."

Connor choked on his beer and set the glass on the bar, coughing. "Good...ah, good to know." He took another drink and whispered, "Jesus. I'm gonna need to bleach my ears."

Then, more loudly, Connor continued, "If he doesn't show up in time to see you home, I'll do it. I have some big strengths, too."

An arm snaked around her waist and a familiar scent washed over her. Brendan. She turned, scanning his face for signs of injury. Nothing. "Hey," she said, making sure the people close to them could hear. "I missed you."

"Had some business to take care of," he answered.

Tightening his grip on Cilla's waist, he said to Connor, "Thanks for your help earlier. Really appreciate it. But I'm good. Sobered up. So Cilla will be going home with me." He pulled out his wallet and took out a few bills. "Here." He pressed the money into Connor's hand. "This should take care of my tab."

Connor held up his hands, the bills crushed into his palm. "Glad to see you made it back. You might want to pace yourself next time."

"Thanks for the advice."

He turned away from Connor and pulled Cilla closer. Nuzzled her ear. "Got one of Tiffany's pills. It's at the lab, being tested right now. We'll have an answer in the morning."

Cilla brushed her mouth over his neck. Bit down. A little too hard. "Glad to see you're in one piece."

He flinched and tightened his grip on her. "What the hell's wrong?"

"You've been gone for more than an hour," she hissed into his neck. "Didn't it occur to you to let me know you took off, partner?"

"I couldn't," he said. She felt his smile against her skin. He was a good actor. "Con was supposed to give you a sign."

"He didn't."

"We'll talk about this later." He pressed a kiss to her cheek, then urged her toward the stage. "Looks like you have to get back to work."

In a louder voice, he said, "Carry your keyboards tonight?"

"Don't you always?" She stared at him for a long moment. Her mouth smiled, but she knew her eyes held a different message. "You know I count on you."

His hand dropped away. "Good to know."

***

"What do you mean, we're going to your mom's for breakfast?" Cilla gripped the armrest on the car door and swiveled to face Brendan.

"No place else to go," he said calmly as he turned onto Belmont. "None of us have a big enough place. You want to take a chance and go to a restaurant?" He waited a beat.

286

"Didn't think so. At least no one will overhear us talking at my mom's."

"I'm not going to your mom's."

"Why not?"

"Because she'll think I'm your girlfriend or something."

"Aren't you?" He glanced at her, and she couldn't read his expression. "My girlfriend?"

"You tell me, Donovan. What am I? What is this we have going on? Because I have no fricking idea."

She'd intended to go home last night. Stay by herself. But with the possibility of Welles getting bail, Brendan was adamant that she not be alone.

He'd apologized for leaving her hanging last night. Didn't even try to blame Connor, which earned him some points. But she was tired of always being the one to fix things, always being the responsible one, tired of having everyone rely on her. She wanted someone she could rely on.

She'd thought she could count on Brendan. But she'd seen the panic in his face when he'd thought Bates had gone after her. Seen his horrified expression when he understood how much it upset him. Seen how fast he'd backed away.

It would take a long time to get the skid marks off her floor.

She'd been so sure she could count on Brendan. But after yesterday, she wasn't sure anymore.

She wanted sure.

Needed sure.

And she hated herself a little this morning. Even knowing there was no long term in the future for them, she hadn't been able to resist when he begged her to come home with him. Even though she knew it wasn't going to last, she wanted another night with him.

But she wasn't about to act all cuddly and girlfriend-y around his mother.

"Let's not do this right now, Marini." His knuckles whitened on the steering wheel. "Okay? Can we get through this case before we talk about feelings?"

The arrow hit her squarely in the chest. Cilla closed her eyes and sucked in a deep breath. Another. "I'm fine not talking about feelings, Donovan. But I still don't want to meet your mother."

"I can't change things now. Everyone is probably there already. With the food. So suck it up."

She bit her tongue before she could point out that if she hadn't 'sucked it up' that morning, they wouldn't have been late. They would have had time to change the plan.

"It's not a big deal, Cilla." His voice became conciliatory. Teasing. "We're being thoughtful kids and having breakfast with our mother," he said with a tiny grin that she wanted to smack off his face. "Quinn suggested it, and it was brilliant. Why do you have a problem with that?"

Because she was meeting Brendan's mother, and hadn't had time to prepare. Physically. But especially mentally.

She wore an old, faded pair of jeans with a hole in one knee and a short-sleeved, tunic top. No make-up. Way too casual.

But right now, that wasn't what worried her the most. Brendan's mother was going to think they were a couple. Cilla knew it was going to be awkward. Uncomfortable. Embarrassing.

"Your mother's going to think I'm a complete slob," she muttered. She knew it didn't matter. She probably wouldn't see his mother again after today.

Still. Easier to address those fears than the deeper ones. She wasn't going to reveal her vulnerability to Brendan. Not again.

"Cilla, relax." He reached across the console for her hand. "This is a business meeting. In a safe place. That's all. She probably won't even be there."

"Of course she'll be there." Cilla yanked her hand away from his.

"How do you know that?"

"Because your sister would have told her about our

lunch earlier this week." She shoved her hand through her hair, catching it on a knot. Great. After lingering too long in bed that morning, they'd rushed out of the house so fast that she hadn't even combed her hair. "She thinks I'm your girlfriend. She'll be there."

"The cool, always-together Cilla Marini is worried about meeting a guy's mom?" He reached for her hand again. When she slid it under her thigh, he glanced at her. "Wow. Can't wait to see this."

"I hate you, Donovan."

"I get that a lot."

"I bet you do."

Fifteen minutes later, Brendan pulled to the curb in front of a bungalow on a block made up of other bungalows. The silence in the car had gotten thicker as they got closer. Heavier.

By the time Brendan turned off the engine, Cilla's heart thundered against her chest. She closed her eyes and tried to take deep, steadying breaths as Brendan walked around the car. He opened her door, then lifted the rear gate to let Franny jump out.

The dog rushed up the front steps, then stood at the door, watching them. As if saying, "Hurry up. Why are you taking so long?"

Brendan slung one arm over her shoulders and steered her up the steps. "It'll be okay, Cilla. My mom's great. Stop worrying."

"Right." She whirled to face him. "If this is meeting-the-moms day, we'll go visit my mother after this."

He paled, and his arm tensed on her back.

"Yeah." She swallowed and shrugged his arm off her shoulders. "Figured that's what you'd say. So stop being patronizing. And don't give me that 'nothing to worry about' shit."

"Jesus. What crawled up your ass?" he muttered.

You did. And not my ass. You crawled into my heart. Now you're stuck there, and it's pissing me off.

Hurting me.

"Take a look in the mirror, Donovan," she said.

Damn it! She didn't want to be in this by herself. But clearly she was. Every time she'd mentioned the future, he'd frozen. She moved farther away from him. She could read body language as well as any other cop. And his was screaming 'I am so out of here after this case'.

Before Brendan could reach for the front door, it flew open. A dark-haired woman who looked like an older Mia stood there, smiling. "Brendan," she said, hugging him tightly. Then she turned to Cilla.

"You must be Cilla, Brendan's partner. Welcome." She held out her hand and shook Cilla's. Just as Cilla was relaxing, Brendan's mom pulled her into an embrace. "I'm Rose Donovan. Good to meet you."

"You, too, Mrs. Donovan," Cilla said, her face hot.

"Please. Call me Rose." She smiled. "We've been waiting for Brendan to bring someone to the house."

Cilla swallowed, her face on fire. "I'm here for a business meeting, Rose. That's all." She was burning up with embarrassed fury. At Brendan. For putting her in this position.

"I understand, Cilla." Rose smiled, sympathy and understanding in her eyes.

Cilla clenched her teeth to keep furious, mortified tears from spilling over. Damn Brendan for insisting they come here.

And damn herself for not putting her foot down and refusing.

She stepped past Rose, and the older woman bent to pet Franny. "Is Bren taking good care of you, Fran? Hmmm?"

"Shouldn't you be asking her if she's behaving herself for me?" Brendan retorted.

"Don't have to do that." Rose straightened and grinned at him. "Franny always behaves herself. You? Not sure about that."

She wanted to punch Brendan. The charmer. The guy

whose blue eyes and smile made women fall at his feet. The guy who took nothing seriously.

"Hey, Cilla, need some coffee?" Mia came out of the kitchen with a carafe and a couple of mugs.

"I'd love some," Cilla said, hurrying toward Mia. She lifted the mug to her face, breathing in the scent of caffeine. Steadying herself.

As they sat around Rose's large dining room table a few minutes later, eating bagels with cream cheese, smoked salmon, capers and avocado, she pushed her anger down deep. The five of them were discussing what had happened at the pub last night. She needed to focus on her job. Not on whatever was going on between her and Brendan.

She heard Rose in the kitchen, talking on the phone. Franny sat next to Brendan, staring intently at him.

"So," Quinn began. "Have you heard from the lab about the pill?"

"No." Brendan set his bagel on his plate. "She's supposed to get back to me this morning. Thought it would be before this."

Before anyone could respond, his phone chimed. Brendan pressed the call button, listened for several beats, then said, "Thanks for getting back to me so quickly, Jenny. I really appreciate it."

He ended the call and looked at all of them, a tiny smile on his face. "It's a match. Same drug that killed the five men." He glanced around the table. "We need to pick up Tiffany tonight and find out where she got those drugs. Who's in?"

CHAPTER TWENTY-SEVEN

Brendan sat in the observation room, watching Tiffany through the one-way mirror. She'd been sitting in the uncomfortable chair for almost an hour, and hadn't shifted once. Her hands folded on the table, she glanced around occasionally, as if it was the first time she'd seen the inside of an interrogation room.

As if she'd done nothing wrong and was waiting patiently for an explanation of why she'd been arrested.

Mia slid into the seat beside Brendan and handed him a piece of paper. "Crystal Everly," he read from the rap sheet. "Five prior arrests for possession or possession with intent to sell, and one for prostitution when she was sixteen. No convictions."

He raised his eyebrows. "No convictions after six arrests?"

"She had a good lawyer," Mia said, her mouth a hard line. "The prostitution arrest was in her juvie file. Usual horror story of an abusive stepfather and a runaway teen, hooking to survive. She was put in foster care, and apparently it worked. No more arrests.

"Until she was an adult. First possession bust when she

was nineteen. That one and all the rest were tossed." Her mouth thinned. "And you'll never guess who her attorney was."

"Henry Bennett." Brendan raised one eyebrow and waited for Mia to confirm it. The guy with the ATTY 1 license plate must have something going in the twenty-second. One of their cops was his errand boy. Welles, Cilla's would-be rapist, lived in the district. Bennett was Welles's lawyer. Follow the dots.

"Better than that." Mia swiveled to face him. "Michael Welles."

"Welles? Are you shitting me?" Brendan jerked his head around to stare at his sister, fury heating his face.

"Not shitting you. Cilla's rapist is Ms. Everly's lawyer for every one of her possession busts." Mia shifted to stare down at Tiffany/Crystal in the interrogation room. "Interesting district, the twenty-second."

Brendan turned to study Tiffany again. What the hell was going on in Beverly? A pair of cops running a drug ring in their own back yard? Their serial rapist turns out to be the attorney for the other dirtbags in the district? The rapist's lawyer is one of the biggest bigwigs in the city?

Brendan gritted his teeth as Tiffany studied her nails. As if she was waiting for a god-damned manicure. "Have to admit, she's got some cojones," he muttered.

Mia scowled. "She's acting like she knows she's going to walk. Like she knows you can't touch her."

"Then she's going to be disappointed." Brendan slouched in the chair and crossed his arms as he watched their suspect. "Quinn and Connor know what they're doing. And Welles isn't riding in on his black horse this time."

The door to the interrogation room opened and Brendan's brothers walked in. They sat down at the table, still wearing their 'disguises' from the pub.

"Ms. Everly," Quinn began. "We have the lab results from the capsule you sold to Mr. Quick last night. It's an illegal sex drug that's killed five men and put another into the hospital. Where did you get that drug?"

Tiffany frowned. "I have no idea what you're talking about."

Quinn pushed a picture of the capsule across the table to her, along with a picture of her customer, Sam Quick, handing her money in exchange for one. Connor had taken the photo with his phone. "You don't remember this transaction last night?"

Tiffany's gaze lingered on the photo for long seconds. Then she pushed it back across the table. "He needed an allergy pill. I gave him one. That's all."

"You sold it to him, you mean." Quinn tapped the photo of the money changing hands.

The woman shrugged one shoulder. "He wanted to give me money to buy myself another bottle."

"Are you betting that Mr. Quick told us the same story?" Connor asked.

For the first time, unease flashed in Tiffany's eyes. It was gone in a moment, but she shifted on the uncomfortable chair. "Why wouldn't he?"

"For starters, because he knows he'd have a hard time explaining his arrest for the purchase of an illegal sex drug to his wife. And he's nervous about the woman he'd planned to use that drug with. A woman who's not his wife. Who might tell his wife."

"He said that?" Tiffany frowned. As if she couldn't believe her customer would turn on her.

"Oh, yes, Ms. Everly. That and so much more. Apparently one of his friends is also a customer of yours. And that customer sang your drug's praises. And talked about how hot you were." Quinn smiled. "I'm pretty sure a guy like that would be able to pick you out of a line-up. You being so hot, you know?"

Tiffany chewed some of the bright red lipstick off her lower lip. "I'd like to speak to my lawyer now."

"Certainly." Quinn bared his teeth in a smile that made Brendan want to back away. "Give me his or her name and

I'll call their office."

"Mike Welles." Tiffany licked her lips. "He'll come right over."

Connor shook his head. "Afraid he won't, Ms. Everly. Mr. Welles is sitting in Cook County Jail as we speak." He leaned over the table toward her, and Tiffany reared back. "For attempted rape."

"What?" Tiffany stared at them, her expression morphing from bored tolerance to shock and fear. "He...he raped someone?"

"He tried," Connor said. "So who's number two on your lawyer list?"

"I...I don't have another lawyer. I've always used Mike."

"We can call the public defender," Quinn said.

"No." Tiffany swallowed and looked from one brother to the other, like she had just noticed them. "I need Mike. And who the hell are you two? Are you like, clones, or something?"

"Or something," Quinn said. "Welles is unavailable. So what's it going to be? Public defender? Someone else? Or do you just want to keep talking to us?"

"I...I don't know." Tiffany shoved her hand through her shoulder length hair. It made her look as if she'd just gotten out of bed. "Maybe we can work something out."

"What did you have in mind, Ms. Everly?" Connor asked.

Tiffany leaned forward, displaying her cleavage. "I've never done clones before. Might be fun."

Both Quinn and Connor froze. Quinn recovered first. "Are you offering us sexual favors in return for letting you go?" he asked carefully.

She shrugged one shoulder. "You interested?"

"No." Quinn leaned closer. "Attempting to bribe a police officer is a crime, Ms. Everly. We'll add it to our list. And since you're interested in working something out, we'll talk to the DA and try to get you a deal. We're not after low-level dealers."

Tiffany's eyes flashed at the words 'low-level'. Brendan smiled.

"We want the supplier of this drug," Connor said. "We want it off the street before it kills more people. So give me his name and we'll work something out."

Tiffany was shaking her head even before Connor finished speaking. "No way. I'm not ratting him out. I don't want to end up on the bottom of Lake Michigan."

Quinn raised an eyebrow. "Really? That's what happens if you cross this guy?"

Tiffany crossed her arms beneath her breasts and looked away. Didn't speak.

"We can protect you from him," Connor said quietly. "Put you in a safe house somewhere until we have him in custody."

She shook her head, a short, jerky motion. "There's no place that's safe from him. He has eyes everywhere."

Quinn and Connor tried logic, threats and flattery. They couldn't budge Tiffany. She wasn't giving up her supplier.

An hour later, Connor and Quinn emerged from the interrogation room, shaking their heads. When they joined Mia and Brendan in the observation room, Connor said, "That's one scared woman. We could keep her in the box until next week and she wouldn't give him up."

"Let's check into safe houses where we can stash her," Brendan said. "I don't want to let her back on the street. What if she tells Bates? Worse, what if she tells Bates and he doesn't believe she didn't flip on him? I don't want to get her killed."

"We'll find a place," Quinn said. "Keep her out of circulation."

"Yeah. Maybe we can get something on Bates and Ward in the next few days. Keep Tiffany locked up until then."

Connor elbowed Brendan. "Go back to the pub and stay with Cilla You tell her you were leaving this time? 'Cause she seemed a little pissed off at you at breakfast this morning."

"Yeah, I told her this time. She wasn't happy with me after last night." He swallowed, feeling his face turning read. "Which I guess you figured out."

God! Why did this have to be so complicated? Why couldn't they just do their jobs? How the hell could he have told her where he was going last night when he was playing a falling-down drunk?

He could have had Connor walk him past Cilla. So she'd know he was safe.

He hadn't thought of Cilla at all. He'd thought only of getting that capsule to the lab.

Brendan tugged at the collar of his suddenly too-tight dress shirt. He wasn't used to answering to a partner. Wasn't use to having someone worry about him.

He sucked in a breath as the suffocating sensation tightened his throat and banded around his chest. "She's fine. She knows the score."

Yeah, she knew the score. That's why she'd been acting off. More distant. Less open. Like she wasn't going to let herself go all-in.

Because he wasn't all-in. And she knew it.

How could he be? They had more important things to worry about than feelings, damn it.

"Cilla's good," Brendan told his brother. Trying to convince himself? "She's a cop. She gets it. She knows the job comes first."

"You poor, misguided fool." Connor shook his head. "Get back to that pub and pull your head out of your ass while you're at it."

Brendan scowled. "Who's side are you on, anyway?"

"Yours, Bren. That woman is a keeper." Connor shoved his elbow into Brendan's ribs. Hard. "Don't let her get away."

A keeper.

Was that what he wanted? To be tied down, like Connor and Quinn and Mac?

He didn't want Cilla to leave. Beyond that? He didn't know what the hell he wanted.

He'd think about it later. When the case was over. When there wasn't so much going on.

There was always stuff going on.

Damn it! Even his own fucking brain wouldn't cut him a break. "I'll catch you later," he muttered as he slammed out of the observation room.

***

Two nights later, Brendan sat at his desk, his fingers flying over the keyboard. The only light in his apartment came from his computer screen, but he didn't need even that. The pictures unspooling in his head were vivid and clear. It was like watching a movie flicker through his brain.

Franny snuffled in her sleep, and he glanced at her, lying in her bed next to his desk. Cilla slept silently in the other room. She'd been pretty silent for the last couple of nights, come to think of it.

When he'd picked her up from the pub two nights ago, after he'd watched Connor and Quinn interrogate Tiffany, Cilla had insisted on going to her own place. She'd wanted to stay by herself.

Just like she had last night and tonight, he realized uneasily.

His hands fell away from the keyboard. All three nights, he'd refused to take her there. Welles might have gotten bail. Bates and Ward were out there somewhere. All of them could easily find out where Cilla lived.

After the first night, she'd given in after a short argument. But she'd been distant. When he'd climbed into bed, she'd turned her back on him. Curled into a ball, as if protecting herself. From him.

He'd reached for her, but she'd shaken him off. Glared at him over her shoulder, and it hadn't been hard to read her expression. Really, Brendan?

Brendan squirmed in his chair. Even the last time they'd made love, several days ago, had been different. And not the good kind of different. She'd been holding back.

He swallowed. It was the way he'd had sex before Cilla. Fun and games. Pleasure. Release. Nothing more.

Was that what he wanted with Cilla?

His hands slid off the keyboard as he glanced toward the bedroom. Toward the woman sleeping there.

No.

He wanted more with Cilla.

What kind of more? A couple of months instead of a couple of weeks?

His foot jittered on the floor, making his knee bounce up and down. Not now. He couldn't do this at – he glanced at the clock on his computer – four-sixteen in the morning. He was working.

He needed to focus on the novel. On the characters and the action unfolding in front of him. There would be time for this...situation with Cilla later.

After they solved this case.

After he finished his book.

After he figured out what he wanted.

Brendan took a deep breath and re-read the last page he'd typed. Forced his mind back into the heads of his characters.

He'd just started typing again when Franny lifted her head. Cocked her ears. Stilled.

Stood up and walked to the door. Stood there, nose in the air. Sniffing.

The hair on the back of her neck rose. Lifted in a line down her back.

Brendan stood up and walked over to his gun safe against the wall. Removed his service weapon. Made sure it was loaded.

Then he crept into the bedroom. Put his hand over Cilla's mouth.

She jerked awake, flailing at his arm. Trying to push his

hand away.

"Shh," he breathed into her ear. He took his hand away when she focused on him and nodded. "Something's wrong. Find your gun."

By the time he returned to the living room, Franny's head was lowered. Her growl, deep in the back of her throat, sent a chill down Brendan's spine.

The dim light in the hallway spilled into his apartment from the gap at the bottom of the door. It cast two long, thin shadows onto the hardwood.

Two feet. Someone standing at his door.

The almost-silent snick of a pick inserted into the lock made Brendan take the safety off his Sig. The air moved behind him. Cilla stepped into the space at his left side, holding her gun. Steady as a rock.

He stepped to the right to give her more room. Then he snapped his fingers at Franny. Gave the 'come' hand signal when the dog glanced his way.

Franny stared at him, as if unable to believe Brendan was asking her to stand down. Brendan signaled her again, and she moved reluctantly toward him.

The click of the lock opening sounded like a gunshot in the silent apartment. Franny turned to the door as it opened slowly. Silently. A wedge of light from the hallway increased as the gap in the door widened.

A figure dressed in black stepped into the apartment. A black ski mask covered his head and face.

Before he could move far enough in to close the door, Brendan barked, "Stop. Hands in the air!"

The man's hand rose, holding a gun, and Franny leaped for his arm. Afraid he might hit Franny, Brendan held his fire. The intruder's gun flashed just before Franny hit him.

She yelped as the man stumbled backward. Franny fell to the floor. The intruder spun and fled down the hall.

"Stay here," Brendan ordered Cilla. "Take care of Franny."

As Brendan pounded down the hall after the intruder,

he watched as the black-clothed figure disappeared into the stairwell. By the time Brendan charged through the door into the courtyard, there was no sign of the intruder.

Cilla stepped out behind him, her gun raised. They stood back to back without speaking, completely in sync, scanning the courtyard. Brendan's gaze traveled over every bush, every tree, every possible hiding place. At his back, he knew Cilla did the same.

On the next block, a car engine roared to life. Tires squealed, then the rumble of the engine gradually faded as the car sped away.

Brendan lowered his gun. "I told you to stay with Franny," he said to Cilla.

She snapped the safety into place on her own Sig. "Figured you needed back-up more."

She reached for the keys she'd stuck in her waistband, unlocked the door and ran up the stairs, Brendan close behind. When they reached his apartment, Franny was struggling to breathe in short little gasps. Her chest was moving wrong. In when it should go out. A rapidly growing pool of blood spread on the floor beneath her. The dark, shiny puddle grew far too quickly in the light from the hall.

"Franny." Brendan's voice caught on the word. He pressed his hand to the hole in her chest where blood bubbled out. Her breaths became a little more steady.

Keeping one hand pressed against her wound, Brendan smoothed his other hand over her head, trying to steady her.

"Cilla," he called, and heard the panic in his voice. "I need...I need..."

Light suddenly flooded the room, and Cilla knelt at Franny's other side, one of Brendan's tee-shirts in her hand. She pressed it against Franny's side, and blood immediately soaked through.

Cilla lifted the shirt and studied the horrifying, bubbling hole on the dog's chest. Then she pressed the tee-shirt against the wound again.

"I think the bullet went into her lungs," Cilla said, using

her palm on the shirt to cover the hole. Blood streamed through her fingers. "Where's the closest vet?"

CHAPTER TWENTY-EIGHT

Cilla sat next to Brendan in the waiting room of the emergency veterinary clinic, watching his knee bounce rapidly up and down. He glanced at the time on his phone, then hit 'contacts'. Closed his contacts. Looked at the time again.

"What are you doing?" she finally asked.

"Steeling myself to call Lizzy and tell her I got her dog shot." He gripped the phone so hard his knuckles turned white.

Damn it! Cilla didn't want to watch the guilt in Brendan's expression. Over the past several days, she'd tried so hard to smother all her pain and anguish whenever she was around him. Focus only on the job. Wall off her heart from him.

But now that treacherous organ ached for him. She wanted to soothe the devastation in his expression. Ease the guilt in his eyes when he looked around the stark waiting room that smelled of disinfectant and fear.

She wanted to convince him that it wasn't his fault. Make him understand it was the fault of the bastard who'd broken into his apartment and shot Franny.

Most of all, she wanted to curl into his side and try to comfort him.

Instead, she sat stiffly in the chair next to his, careful not to touch him. The minutes on the clock above the reception desk ticked by agonizingly slowly. The door into the working area of the clinic remained firmly closed.

Waiting for news was almost unbearable.

When he pulled his phone out again, she couldn't help herself. She put her hand over his. Curled her cold fingers into his colder ones. "It's six o'clock in the morning," she said gently. "Maybe you should wait until you have more information before you call them."

"It's seven on the east coast," he said immediately. "They'll be up."

"They're on vacation," she reminded him. "Maybe they're sleeping in." Or doing the kinds of things couples did in the morning when they didn't have to rush off to their jobs.

The kinds of things she'd done in the past weeks with Brendan. Things she'd hoped to do with him in the future.

Damn it! She jumped up from the uncomfortable chair and began pacing the small waiting room. She had to knock it off. Stop mooning over Brendan and thing she'd never have.

She'd gone into this with her eyes wide open. She'd known what he was – a player. A serial dater. She'd gotten involved with him anyway.

So she didn't get to blame him when he broke her heart.

It had been her fault for thinking she could change him. Fix that place inside him that ran from commitment.

She glanced at him, still hunched over his phone. Staring at the screen.

Her fixing days were over.

She walked to the weary-looking receptionist. "Sorry, I know you get asked this about a million times every night. But do you have any idea when more information might be available about our dog? Franny Donovan?"

"My boy..." She swallowed the lump in her throat. "My partner needs to call Franny's owner. I want to wait until we have more idea what's going on."

The woman shoved a limp strand of hair away from her face. "I'll ask."

She stood and pushed through a swinging door. The whiff of air that wafted over Cilla smelled medicinal. Sharp. Vaguely unpleasant. A mixture of hospital and animal.

A few minutes later, the young woman came through the door again. "The doctor will be out in a few minutes to talk to you, Ms., ah..." She glanced down at the desk.

"Marini." Cilla forced a stiff smile. "Thanks for checking."

The woman nodded. "You're welcome."

Cilla plopped into the seat next to Brendan. He shocked her by putting his hand on her knee. "Thank you," he said quietly. "I couldn't have asked. I would have freaked out. Scared that poor woman."

In spite of her best intentions, Cilla put her hand on top of Brendan's. Twined their fingers and clung to him for a long moment. Then the door opened and a young blond woman in a white coat came out.

"Mr. Donovan?" she said. The doctor wasn't smiling.

Cilla's heart lurched in her chest. She dropped her hand from Brendan's and watched as he took two steps toward the woman. Then he turned and looked at Cilla. Extended his hand.

Cilla stood slowly and grasped his fingers. Allowed him to pull her close. Brendan wrapped his arm around her shoulders and leaned against her. As if bracing for the worst.

"The bullet went through Franny's chest," Dr. Winston began. "There were both entry and exit wounds. It didn't hit any major vessels, which is good news. If it had, she would have bled out before you could get her here.

"She still lost a lot of blood. I gave her two pints from our donor dog, and lots of fluids. She's alive. But I'm not going to sugarcoat this. It's going to be touch and go for the next twenty-four hours."

"You have a donor dog?" Brendan said.

The doctor's face relaxed. "My labrador retriever. She's a universal donor. I bring her with me every night in case we need blood."

"Thank you," Brendan said. Cilla watched his throat ripple. "So what next?"

"You need to take her to her regular vet. They'll monitor her today and continue to treat her. There's a drainage tube in her chest for the fluid that will accumulate. She'll need to continue getting fluids. Antibiotics." The doctor took a deep breath. "If she makes it through the next twenty-four hours, her chances of surviving are good."

"Okay." Brendan swallowed again. His expression was blank. As if he was numb. "I'll, ah, find out who her regular vet is and get her there. Can I leave her with you while I call my brother and get Franny's vet's name?"

"Of course. I gave your bill to Cindy. Take all the time you need."

Brendan stumbled backward and dropped into a chair. He stared as his phone and muttered, "Mac's going to go off on me. Use his FBI voice." He swallowed again and pressed 'call' on his phone.

After a few rings, someone answered. "Hey, Mac," Brendan began. "How's the visit with Lizzy's brother going?" Brendan pressed speaker so Cilla could hear.

"It was good. We're actually on the road, heading home. Lizzy's taking first driving shift."

"Good." Brendan cleared his throat. "Good that you're coming home."

"What's wrong?" a feminine voice said. "What happened?"

"I have some bad news, Lizzy." Brendan pressed his palm into his eyes, and Cilla reached for his hand. He glanced at her and tightened his fingers around hers. "We had a break-in at my apartment last night. Franny was shot."

A gasp. Then silence.

"Is she...is she...?"

"She's alive," Brendan interrupted Lizzy. "We're at the emergency vet. The bullet went through her chest. A lot of bleeding. She needed some transfusions. But she's alive. The next twenty-four hours are crucial. I need to take her to your regular vet."

Lizzy's voice broke as she recited her vet's name and phone number. "We'll be there as soon as we can," she said, now sobbing.

"Don't speed," Cilla heard herself saying. "We'll take care of her until you get here."

Silence. "Who's that?" Mac said. Cilla understood why Brendan called it his brother's FBI voice.

"That's Cilla. We're working an undercover op together. I'm pretty sure the guy we're chasing is the one who shot Fran." He cleared his throat. "When will you be home?"

"It's twelve, thirteen hours from Philadelphia to Chicago. We left about an hour ago. So late tonight," Mac said.

"We'll see you then. Drive safe."

He disconnected the call and let the phone drop onto the hard chair. "Why Franny?" he whispered. "She's the best dog ever. Lizzy loves her so much." A tear ran down his face. "We all do."

"She's going to make it," Cilla said, gripping his hand. "She's healthy. Young. And she was really lucky. She'll be fine."

Brendan gripped her hand. "She has to be. That dog saved my life. If she...dies, I'll never forgive myself."

"What do you mean, she saved your life?" Cilla swiveled in the hard chair to face him. "What are you talking about?"

"If she hadn't started growling, I wouldn't have heard the guy come in the front door. Even though I was in the living room."

Ah. He'd been lost in another world. "You didn't hear anything because you were writing."

"Yeah." He ground the heel of his hand into his eye and wouldn't meet her gaze. Picking up his phone, he called Connor and told him what had happened. Asked him to get the crime scene people out to Brendan's apartment.

***

She waited until they were in the car, heading for Franny's regular vet. Cilla was sitting in the back seat, Franny's head cradled on her lap. Neither of them had spoken since they left the emergency clinic.

The car bumped through a pot hole, and Franny whimpered. Cilla stroked the dog's head. Her eyes prickled as she whispered, "It's okay, baby. I know it hurts." She lifted her head and said to Brendan, "Watch those potholes, okay?"

"Sorry," Brendan muttered.

After a few more uncomfortable minutes, Cilla said, "You don't have to feel guilty because you were writing."

"How am I going to explain why I was so distracted that I didn't hear that guy until it was too late to get Franny out of the way?"

"You could tell them the truth."

He glanced at her in the rear view mirror, then looked away. "It's complicated."

She swallowed. "What's so complicated? Your writing is a huge part of your life. And you're hiding it from everyone. I don't understand why."

"Not everyone." He stared out the windshield. "You know."

"Everyone important to you," she retorted, her heart pinching when Brendan didn't correct her. "Your family. Their girlfriends. Your buddies in the district. Are you ashamed of your writing?"

"Of course not." He hunched his shoulders. "It's just that it's not...my image. As a cop, you know?"

"Which image is that? Your recklessness? Your

wildness? Your reputation as a player?"

"I'm not that guy anymore," he said, finally glancing over his shoulder at her.

"Really? Are you sure? Because if you're not, why can't you trash that wild image and admit that you want to write? That you are writing?" She tangled both hands in her hair, anger and frustration erupting. "Every cop I know raves about your blog. Talks about how great it is. I've seen comments on it from all over the country. People love what you're writing. But you can't own up to that?"

"It's not your decision, Cilla. Not your business. It's my business. So stay out of it."

Her heart twisted, and a band tightened around her chest. She couldn't breathe.

Brendan wasn't her business.

She took a ragged breath. Then another one. In and out. In and out. "You're right," she finally managed to say. "It's not any of my business. You're not my business." She glanced at her watch. Only eight in the morning. They had a whole day to get through.

She couldn't spend it with Brendan. "We need to finish this. We'll start hitting the clubs tonight. The ones where there have been deaths from the drug. I vote for The Seven Club first. It's the kind of place where people have sex against the walls in the corners of the room. Perfect place for someone like Tiffany to do business."

"I can't think about that right now, Marini." His voice cracked over her like a whip. "I almost got my sister-in-law's dog killed."

"You damn well better think about it. Isn't that what you've been telling me? 'We have to concentrate on the case. I don't have time to discuss personal stuff until we've closed it'. So we're going to close the damn case. We're going to the Seven Club tonight."

He swerved into the small parking lot next to the veterinary clinic. "I didn't realize you were such a heartless bitch, Marini. That dog almost died saving my life."

Her heart froze at his words. Stopped. Then jolted to life again, her chest aching with every beat.

"So make her pain mean something." Cilla's breath caught on a sob, but she ignored it. "Catch the bastard who shot her."

She slid out of the car and waited as he lifted Franny into his arms. Held the door open for Brendan as he walked into the waiting area of the clinic. As she followed him in, she stopped short.

His family was there. Connor, Quinn and Mia. Rose. And a short woman with blond hair who was holding Connor's hand. A taller woman with long red hair huddled next to Quinn.

"How is she?" Rose hurried over, smoothed a hand over Franny's head. "How's our baby?" Rose cooed. The dog's tail wagged once. "I have a Milk-bone for you." She held it up, and Franny sniffed it. "For when you're better."

"What the hell happened?" Connor barked.

There were two other people in the waiting room, both holding cats in carriers. They stared at the Donovan's clustered by the door.

"Someone broke in. Tried to shoot us. Got Franny instead."

A door opened and a man in a blue lab coat came out. "Is this Franny Monroe?"

"Yes," Brendan said.

"Bring her on back. Dr. Winston from the emergency clinic called me and filled me in."

Brendan disappeared through the door, and everyone turned to Cilla. "Come sit down, dear." Rose put her hand on Cilla's back and urged her toward a chair. "We brought coffee for everyone. Some doughnuts. Sounds like we could be here for awhile."

Mia pressed a hot cup into Cilla's hand, and she curled her fingers around its warmth. Inhaled the aroma.

She couldn't do this.

She couldn't stay here and pretend she was part of this

310

amazing family. This family that had come to a vet clinic at seven in the morning because their soon-to-be sister-in-law's dog was hurt.

She wasn't part of the close-knit circle of the Donovans and never would be. The knowledge made her heart twist. Left a desolate sadness in her empty chest. She backed toward the door as the rest of the Donovans picked up their coffee. Almost like they shared a brain, they all turned toward the door where Brendan had disappeared.

Several minutes later, Brendan walked back into the waiting room. "She's hooked up to an IV," he said. "They've got her on a heating pad to keep her warm, and she's in the treatment room, where there'll be someone with her almost all the time. They said we can come in and see her after they've had a chance to assess her."

He glanced at Cilla. "You sticking around?"

Her heart yearned to say yes. To sit with Brendan's family, share her grief and worry with them. Make sure Franny was okay.

But she couldn't. It was time to stop fooling herself. She didn't have a place in this family and never would.

"No, I'm going to take off. Pick me up at nine."

"Cilla, wait. I didn't mean what I..."

Ignoring him, she murmured good-byes to everyone, then pushed out the door into the cool autumn air. To the traffic and bustle of morning rush hour.

A bus passed by that would take her to her place. She ignored it and signaled for a taxi. She needed privacy. She didn't want to sob out her grief in front of a bus full of strangers.

CHAPTER TWENTY-NINE

Brendan scowled as they stepped into The Seven Club at ten o'clock that evening. The bass line of the electronic music was so loud that the floor vibrated beneath his feet. The dance floor was packed with people, most of them pressed close to their dance partners. The room was dimly lit, except for the scattered spotlights illuminating the dancers. Couples moved in and out of the lights appearing then disappearing.

He'd been to this club before. Been to others like it. The kinds of clubs that attracted men and women who wanted to hook up for a night.

He'd never come with a date. But Cilla was next to him tonight. And he didn't mind that. He liked it, actually. Liked having her beside him. As his...whatever.

But he didn't like the distance between them.

And he didn't like the way she was dressed.

She wore an outfit she'd used at the Pipe and Shamrock that first weekend. When she was establishing her 'hot chick in the band' persona.

Her shirt was the one that had driven him wild. The dark green, silky one without a back. The one that revealed glimpses of her creamy skin every time she moved.

It wasn't vulgar. Or obvious. The ends of the blouse hung together like a curtain, hiding her back. Except for when she moved. Then the silk rippled and flowed, flashing tiny peeks of her back that disappeared before a watcher realized what he was seeing.

Watching her dance tonight would be torture. Especially if she was dancing with someone besides him.

Which she wouldn't do. They were here to do a job. They would stick together.

Right?

He wasn't sure. She'd been cool and distant when he'd picked her up. She'd asked him how Franny was doing. Her lip had quivered and she'd stared out the windshield when he'd told her there was no change. But when he'd tried to apologize again for what he'd said to her, for his cruel and untrue 'heartless bitch' crack, she'd shut him down.

He'd seen the tears in her eyes as she'd walked out of the clinic. The devastation in her expression. But he hadn't gone after her. Hadn't wanted to face that conversation when he was still consumed by guilt over Franny. Guilt for what he'd done to Cilla.

The fact that he hadn't tried to apologize immediately?

He had no excuse besides cowardice.

He'd felt like shit all day.

Now a detached, impossible-to-read woman stood beside him. The one he'd met during that traffic stop on the Dan Ryan. A lot farther away than she'd been that night.

They needed to solve this case. Needed to get Bates, so they could work things out. Fix this mess between them.

He'd said that repeatedly. Now he wondered if it was even possible.

He wanted to kick himself. He knew how she felt. He'd heard her that night, when she'd thought he was asleep.

He wondered if it was still true. Or if, after this case, she'd walk away like this had been business and nothing more.

Because she thought that's what it was to him.

They stood a couple of feet apart, but the distance between them was a gaping chasm. While he was trying to figure out how to bridge it, his phone buzzed in his pocket.

Connor.

"Hold on," he yelled after he pressed the icon to connect the call. "I need to get outside to talk."

Cilla was scanning the crowd, and he reached for her hand. She glanced over her shoulder at him, nodded when she saw the phone. Leaned in close.

But she didn't take his hand.

"I'll wait here," she said into his ear. Her breath shivered over his skin and he sucked in a breath.

"No. Come with me," he said into her ear. "I don't want to get separated." A part of him was afraid that if she was out of his sight, she'd disappear.

He knew she wouldn't. She was on the job. But he inhaled her scent, holding in his lungs for a long moment to store it in his memory. Just in case.

Then he grabbed her hand and led her toward the door. He ignored the way her fingers rested limp against his. As if she didn't really want to hold his hand, but didn't want to make a scene.

Once they were outside, he said, "Okay, Con. I'm good to talk."

"Where are you?" his brother asked.

"At The Seven Club. We need a night on the town." He tugged Cilla closer, wrapping his arm around her. She tilted her head toward the phone, keeping her body carefully separate from his.

Irritated by her distance, he slid his hand over her black leather skirt. Pressed his palm against her hip, savoring her warmth through the soft, supple leather.

"Tiffany disappeared," Connor said.

"What?" He glanced at Cilla and met her eyes. For a moment, the spark jumped between them. The one that had burned like a flame from the beginning.

314

Then she lowered her gaze and shifted beside him. Moving farther away.

"We had her in a place in Bucktown," Connor continued. "Secure building. Someone with her twenty-four seven. She slipped out early this morning. When the idiot who was supposed to be guarding her woke up, Tiffany was gone."

His heart began thudding against his chest. Cilla tensed beside him.

"Any idea where she went?"

"Into thin air, as far as I can tell. No sign of her. I looked at all the street cameras in a three block radius. Thought I caught a glimpse of her in one, but couldn't say for sure."

"Better get a BOLO out on her. She's a loose end and I don't want Bates to snip her off."

"Already done. If we're really lucky, she might show up at one of the clubs where we know the drug has been sold. We've got people heading to all of them."

"Don't worry about Seven. Cilla and I have it."

"Got it. Keep in touch."

"Will do."

As he slid his phone into his pocket, Cilla straightened. Put more air between them. "You have a plan?" she asked softly. "'Cause I can't think of anything besides what we've already discussed. Keep our eyes open. Except now we add Tiffany to the mix."

"Yeah. That's the plan." He took her hand, aware of the bouncer close behind him. "Come on, honey," he said in a louder voice. "Let me buy you one of those drinks you like."

"Forget the drink," she said, playing her part perfectly. He was beginning to hate this job. "I want to dance."

God damn it. Dancing was the last thing he wanted to do with Cilla.

He needed to keep his mind clear. Needed to pay attention to what was happening around him. Dancing with

Cilla would distract him from anything but her.

But he knew dancing was a smart move. People came to Seven to dance. And hook up.

Gritting his teeth, he let her direct him to the dance floor. When she put her hands on his hips and pulled him closer, he swallowed hard and tried to smile. Stared at Cilla as he moved his eyes, studying the other dancers.

Cilla ground her ass into his crotch. Trailed her hands down his chest. Nuzzled his neck. Undulated against him as if they were having sex. After ten agonizing minutes, he couldn't take any more. He steered her off the dance floor. "We need to get a different perspective of the place," he said into her ear. "Can't see a thing from the middle of the dance floor."

"Yeah, but we had to dance." She glanced at him, cool and composed, as if their dancing hadn't affected her at all. She wasn't even breathing heavily, damn it. "You can't come to Seven and not dance."

"You've been here before?" He stared at her, knowing why he'd come to this club in the past. A stab of jealousy, ugly and hot, speared through him. Had Cilla come here for the same reason?

"Oh, honey, I don't want to talk about that," she said. Her simpering expression said 'I'm with you tonight, baby. Consider yourself lucky'.

She was a damned good actor. Anyone watching would think she was completely into him. Thinking about what would happen after they left the club.

But in the semi-darkness of the crowded room, her eyes never stopped moving. Assessing. "Let's find a place where we can see the crowd," she murmured.

Finally they found a spot along the wall. The club was circled by a raised platform holding booths. None of them were vacant, but there was a gap between two of them. They squeezed through the gap and leaned against the wall, plastered together from shoulders to knees.

Cilla took a sip out of the glass of water she'd gotten

from the bar and pretended to talk to him. The club was crowded, with people flowing in and out the door, moving from the dance floor to the booths to the bar. On the mezzanine above them, tiny tables overlooked the crowded floor of the club. A bouncer stood at the bottom of the stairs, barring the entrance.

"Must be for VIP's," he muttered to her.

"Yeah," she said. "Celebrities and their posses."

How the hell did she know that?

Before he could ask her, she grabbed his wrist. "Over there. On the left. Toward the corner. That looks like Bates."

His heart lurched and began to race. "It is. And Tiffany is with him."

***

"I'll circle around to the right," Cilla said, keeping her eyes on Bates and Tiffany. Cilla fingered the reassuring shape of the gun in her evening bag. "I'll stay between them and the front door."

"I'll go left," Brendan said immediately. "Not sure where the other exits are, but I'll make sure they don't leave."

"You gonna call your brothers and Mia? Get them over here?" Cilla asked, watching Bates and Tiffany.

"Not now. It's too hard to hear in this place." He had to lean close so she could hear him, and his scent washed over her. Adrenaline. Excitement. Recklessness. "I want to grab Bates before he gets Tiffany out of here."

"Then give me your phone." She held out her hand while she watched Bates. "We need some back-up."

"We don't have time."

"Make time."

She heard him cursing under his breath, but he pulled out his phone and stabbed a contact. "I won't be able to hear you, Con," he said. "So just listen. Bates is at Seven. Tiffany, too. Call everyone else and get over here ASAP."

He ended the call and shoved the phone in his pocket. "Satisfied?"

She didn't look at him. Couldn't. Why the hell did he think they could do this without backup? Reckless, a tiny voice whispered. "Thank you for taking five seconds to get us some back-up. Now let's get them and end this case."

Without looking back, she led with her shoulder as she crossed the dance floor. The smell of sweat and perfume filled the air. She bounced off one person, shoved against another.

"Hey! Watch where you're going." "What's your problem, bitch?" "Ow! What's in that purse?"

She ignored everyone as she focused on Bates and Tiffany. Bates glared at the woman. Tiffany hunched her shoulders and retreated.

Cilla opened her bag and slid her hand around the gun.

Suddenly, Bates grabbed Tiffany's wrist and dragged her toward the stairs. The bouncer stepped aside as they approached, then moved his bulked-up body back into place.

As Cilla changed direction, she scanned the crowd for Brendan. Had he seen Bates drag Tiffany up the stairs?

He had. Brendan stepped in front of the bouncer, argued for a moment, then shoved him aside.

The bouncer lifted his hand to his lapel. Brendan yanked something off the bouncer's jacket. Ripped something else from behind the bouncer's ear.

A mic. The bouncer was trying to warn Bates.

Cilla ignored the protests as she pushed harder through the crowd. She didn't slow down as she reached the stairs. Flashing her badge, she barked at the bouncer. "Chicago Police. Out of my way."

He hesitated, and Cilla pulled out her gun. "Don't make me use it."

The bouncer's gaze dropped to the gun in her hand. Back to her face. He moved away from the staircase.

Gripping the gun at her side, Cilla took the stairs two at

a time. As she reached the top, a gunshot echoed in the noisy club. A second one followed moments later.

Brendan.

Cilla charged toward the half-open door down a small hallway. The sharp, acrid smell of gunpowder swirled through the air. Her hand was slippery with sweat. She switched the gun to her other hand and wiped her palm down her thigh. Then gripped the gun again, her finger curling around the trigger.

Why the hell hadn't he waited for her?

She burst through the door. Brendan and Tiffany were both down. Tiffany wasn't moving. Blood poured out of her side. Brendan was struggling to get up, while blood ran down his head and dripped onto the floor.

Anson Bates spun around to face her. His features were contorted with rage, but his hand was rock-steady as he lifted his gun.

She didn't want to shoot him. They needed answers from him. But she pointed her gun at his chest. "Put the gun on the floor, Bates. Do it now."

Bates stared at her. Cilla watched his eyes. Saw the moment he made up his mind.

As he lifted his gun, she swept out her leg. Hooked one of his and brought him crashing to the floor. His gun clattered across the hardwood, and he reached for his ankle. For his back-up piece.

Cilla stepped on his wrist. Put more weight on it as Bates struggled. As he reached for her with his other hand, she put all of her weight on his arm. The sickening snap of a bone breaking echoed as loud as the earlier gunshots.

Bates screamed, and Cilla snatched a small gun from Bates's ankle holster. Tossed it in the corner with the other gun. Then she slapped handcuffs around his wrists. He screamed again, but she ignored him as she scrambled over to Brendan.

There was so much blood.

Brendan had staggered to his feet and stood there,

swaying. "Brendan," she said, wrapping her hand around his arm. "You need to sit down."

As she held onto him, she fumbled her phone out of her purse with one hand and dialed 911.

"Officer down," she said as soon as the operator answered. "Officer down. At the Seven Club. This is Detective Cilla Marini. We need three buses. Hurry."

"Where in the club are you located?" The calm voice of the 911 operator made Cilla swallow. Take a deep breath.

"Upstairs." Cilla exhaled. "There's a hallway at the top of the stairs. We're in a room at the end. Please hurry."

"Ambulances are on the way," the woman said. "Stay on the line."

Cilla touched 'end call' and dropped the phone on the floor.

Something moved against her leg. She spun around and saw Bates's foot kicking against her leg. Trying to trip her. Dropping Brendan's arm, she walked over to Bates and kicked him in the side.

"I told you not to move." She brushed the toe of her shoe over his broken arm. "Want a reminder?"

"Jesus, Cilla! Stop! What the hell are you doing?"

Brendan's arms closed around her from behind. He lifted her into the air and dragged her away from Bates.

Cilla struggled to separate herself from him. She shoved his arms away as she spun to face him, but he held onto her wrists. "He tried to kill you, Donovan! Or don't you feel that blood running down your face? Let me go, damn it." She tried to pry his hands away from her wrists, but they were like iron bands. Finally she crushed her fingernails into his fingers until his grip loosened.

"What the hell is wrong with you, Brendan? Why didn't you wait for me? I'm your partner. I'm supposed to back you up. But you don't want a partner, do you?"

She was shoving him back, back until he bumped into the wall. "You had to be a god-damned cowboy and go off on your own. You don't want anything from me, do you?

Not even my help on this case."

"Cilla." Brendan began to slide down the wall. "I need. I don't want...."

His eyes rolled back and he slumped to the side. Unconscious.

She pressed her fingers to his neck. Felt the flutter of his pulse. Saw the slow rise and fall of his chest.

The floor vibrated with the muffled thump of the music below them. "What were you thinking, dumbass?" She dropped to her knees in front of him and shuddered in a deep breath. "Taking off like that. Not waiting for me to back you up. I never was your partner, was I? Not really.

"I thought you'd changed. But you didn't. You're still reckless. Impulsive. You could have gotten yourself killed, you idiot."

Drops of liquid fell steadily onto his chest. Tears. She was crying.

She wiped her face on the sleeve of her silk shirt, praying for him to move. To wake up. But he lay motionless. She pressed her palm against the wound on his head, trying to stop the bleeding. But the blood continued to seep between her fingers and drip onto the floor.

He took ninety-seven breaths before she heard the approaching wail of the ambulance. Twenty more before she heard footsteps pounding up the stairs.

"Wake up, Brendan," she said, her voice shaking. She laid her hand on his neck, feeling the ragged beat of his heart. "The EMT's are here. You better wake up or they're going to haul your ass to the hospital."

Nothing.

Moments later, three men and a woman crowded into the room. The woman and one of the men crouched next to Brendan. The other two men hurried over to Tiffany.

More footsteps on the stairs. Another set of EMTs who headed for Bates. Moments later, Connor and Mia burst into the room. "What the hell happened?" Mia cried, dropping onto her knees next to Brendan. "Bren." She cupped her brother's face in her palm. "Wake up, buddy. Come on." Mia blinked, and a tear rolled down her face. "You're scaring your partner. And me, too."

"Ladies, please move away so we can treat him," the woman EMT said quietly. "Please," she said more firmly as neither of them moved.

Finally Mia took Cilla's arm and pulled her to her feet. Led her to the corner. "What happened?" she asked.

How could Mia be so calm? Her brother was slumped against the wall, blood pooling beneath him. Unconscious.

"Bates shot him," she finally said, watching the cuffed man on the floor. He was squirming toward the corner. Toward the gun.

She walked over and tore a piece off Bates's shirt. Used it to pick up the first gun. Handed it to Mia, then picked up the second one. "First one is the one he used to shoot Brendan and Tiffany. This is his back-up piece. It already has my prints on it."

Connor stepped between her and Mia. "Let's go downstairs," he said, herding them toward the door. "They're going to load Bren into the bus and get him to the hospital."

Cilla shook off his hand. "I have to take Bates in. Book him."

Connor cupped her elbow. "Bates is going to the hospital. So is Tiffany. Come on, Cilla. Mia and I will drive you over."

* * *

After what seemed like hours, the door to the treatment area of the emergency room opened and a young woman in a gray lab coat stepped into the waiting room. One pocket bulged with a stethoscope, and spots of blood dotted her coat.

Brendan's blood? Cilla swallowed the bile that rose in her throat.

"Family of Brendan Donovan?" she called.

His whole family had come. Just like this morning at the vet's. Now, they all hurried over to the doctor.

Cilla hung back, feeling awkward and out of place. Alone, even with Brendan's family surrounding her.

"I'm Doctor Carson." Her gaze skipped over the crowd, and she smiled. "Detective Donovan is going to be fine. He has a wound on the side of his head from the bullet, but it's basically just a graze. He also hit his head when he fell, and he has a mild concussion. I'm keeping him overnight as a precaution, but he can go home tomorrow."

Cilla's legs wobbled, and she sank into a chair. He was fine.

His family's voices rose as they all asked questions at once, and the doctor held up her hand. "We're transferring him to a room right now. Once he's settled, you can see him. The triage nurse will have his room number."

Cilla dropped her head into her hands and pressed her palms into her eyes. Brendan had been shot in the head. Because he'd been reckless and careless. Too impatient to wait for her to back him up.

A few more inches, and he'd probably be dead.

Her throat swelled and her hands shook. She'd fallen in love with a man who wouldn't grow up. Who didn't stop and think before he acted.

A man who couldn't deal with a real, adult relationship.

Her heart twisted in her chest with a physical pain that made her catch her breath. Her eyes throbbed and burned. She wanted to sob out her pain and her anger and her grief. But she wouldn't do it in front of his family.

She drew a deep, shaky breath. Then another. The murmured voices of Brendan's family flowed around her. The sound steadied her. One of them would take care of Brendan. They'd watch him tonight, check to make sure he was okay.

One of them would take him home tomorrow. Stay with him.

Knowing it wouldn't be her was a crushing weight on her chest.

She ached to be with him. She needed to watch him breathe as he slept. Hold onto that proof he was alive.

But she couldn't do it.

She loved him. And because she did, she couldn't sit beside him as he smiled at her. Flirted with her. Showed her the outer Brendan Donovan, but hid his true self, his heart, from her.

She had to protect herself. Sitting beside him as he further distanced himself would completely destroy her already-shattered heart. She needed to bury her anguish deep inside and focus on her job.

Bates needed to be interrogated. She had to find out who else was involved. Round them up. DEA agent Nick Romano from the pub was the first one on her list.

And Welles. She had to hound the lab for the results of his DNA test. See if it matched any of the victims. Make sure Welles stayed in jail until he could be tried.

She needed to talk to Internal Affairs about the twenty-second district.

It would take a while to tie up all the loose ends. She would focus on that and try to push Brendan to the back of her mind.

After that? She'd figure it out later.

Before she left, though, she had to see him with her own eyes. Make sure he really was going to be all right.

She'd allow herself one more moment with him.

A long hour later, the triage nurse approached them. "Detective Donovan is in Room 847. You can go up and see him now, if you like."

She held back when everyone else crowded into Brendan's room. Finally she stepped in, lingering at the back of the room. Brendan was in the bed, gauze around his head, smiling at his family. They were all talking to him, touching him, hugging him.

He was awake. Still pale, ragged, but awake.

His family was here for him. Every single one of them.

For a long moment, she watched and envied Brendan. The Donovans were the kind of family she'd always wanted. Warm. Loving. Caring.

She'd work on that, she vowed silently. She'd make sure that she, Livvy, Sam and their mom had that kind of mutually supportive relationship.

As she watched Brendan and his family, he looked around. "Where's Cilla?" he asked, frowning.

She stepped forward, staying behind his siblings. "Right here, Donovan."

He held out his hand. "C'mere."

Cilla slid past his brothers and their girlfriends until she stood beside the bed. Brendan wiggled his fingers, and she took his hand. It closed around hers, cool and dry. "You okay?"

"I think I should be asking you that. How do you feel?" she asked.

"Like I've been hit in the head with a sledgehammer. Other than that, just great."

She wanted to climb onto the bed and curl into his side. Hold him while he slept. Make sure he wasn't cold or uncomfortable.

Before she could succumb to temptation, she needed to get out of this room. Out of the hospital. So she took a deep breath. Focus on the job. On the case. "Bates is in custody," she began. "He'll be booked and questioned tomorrow, when he's released from the hospital. Tiffany is in surgery, but they think she'll be okay." Cilla swallowed and pasted a smile on her face. "We did a good job, Donovan."

Brendan frowned. "Wait. Why is Bates in the hospital?"

"He broke his arm. Needed surgery."

"How did he break his arm?"

"Resisting arrest."

"Tell me what happened." Brendan patted the bed, looking for the button that would raise the head of the bed.

"You don't remember?"

He shook his head, and she said, "Later. You'll hear all the details. Right now, you need to take it easy. Be with your family."

She squeezed his hand, leaned closer and whispered in his ear, "We could have been great together, Brendan." Then she stood up straight and let him go. "I'll see you around, Donovan."

She turned and walked out of his room without looking back.

CHAPTER THIRTY

In the ER waiting room, Cilla called an Uber car to take her home. When the car arrived, she slid in and gave the driver her address. He grunted and pulled away from the curb.

As the car merged into traffic, Cilla looked out the back window as the hospital receded. She was leaving her heart behind, and her chest was as empty as a dry well. Nothing but a vast space where her heart used to be.

And now she was going back to her quiet, lonely apartment.

Leaving her heart in that hospital room with Brendan.

Wrapping her arms around her shivering body, Cilla said, "Would you mind turning up the heat?"

"It's seventy degrees." The driver glanced in the rear view mirror.

"Cold in the hospital," she managed to get out, teeth chattering.

"Okay. No problem."

As he reached for the controls, she pictured her place. It would be cold there, too.

Cold wherever she went.

Maybe if she wasn't alone, she wouldn't be so cold. She leaned forward again. "I'm really sorry. It's been a bad evening. I need to go someplace else."

The driver shrugged. "It's your money."

Ten minutes later, she stepped out of the car at her sister's apartment. After handing the driver some bills, she walked inside the building.

The doorman recognized her from her last visit and nodded as she headed toward the elevator. Two minutes later, she was knocking on Livvy's door.

Livvy pulled it open, studied Cilla for a second and pulled her inside. "Cill. What's wrong? What happened? Is that your blood?"

Cilla swayed on her high heels and burst into tears. She pressed her fingers to her face. She'd scrubbed her hands, but dried blood lingered beneath her fingernails. The harsh, metallic smell reminded her of Brendan, lying in his own blood. She tried to stop crying, but sobs wracked her chest.

Livvy wrapped an arm around her shoulder and steered her toward the bathroom. "Let's get you cleaned up," she murmured. "Out of those clothes. Then you can tell me what happened."

A long time later, she lay curled up next to Livvy in her queen-sized bed. She was hollow. Barren. She'd told her sister everything. "What do I do, Liv?" she asked in a tiny voice.

Olivia smoothed a hand over Cilla's hair. "Not sure there's much you can do, Cill. You can't make him grow up. Can't make him love you." She squeezed Cilla's hand. "God, baby, I'm so sorry. He's an asshole."

"He's not," Cilla said immediately. "He's a good guy. We just want...we want different things, I guess."

"You've got it bad," her sister said. "He broke your heart but you're still defending him."

"I knew what he was," Cilla said, rolling onto her back and staring at the white ceiling. Picturing Brendan's smiling face. "I should have kept my distance, but I couldn't." God.

She'd wanted him from the moment he stepped out of his car on the Ryan Expressway. "It's not his fault. He never lied to me."

Cilla turned her head to study her sister. "Feels strange coming to you for help," she said quietly.

"I've always wanted to be there for you," Olivia replied. "But you never seemed to need our help. You were always so confident. So sure of yourself. I'm sorry I failed you, Cilly."

"No, I think I failed you," Cilla said slowly. "And Sam. And Mom, too. I guess I thought that was my role in the family. To fix stuff. But I was denying all of you the opportunity to fix stuff for me, wasn't I? Denying you the chance to feel as if you could help me."

"Yeah, maybe," Livvy said. "But it doesn't have to be that way. You came to me tonight, and I'm so glad you did." She nudged Cilla. "Ask Sammy to get you Cubs tickets. Make him come through for you."

"Maybe I will." She glanced at her sister, feeling a little lighter. "I'll start using all of you shamelessly. You want to go to a game with me?"

"Sounds good. We'll have hotdogs, beer and yell ourselves silly."

"I'd like that," Cilla said, her eyes prickling. It would have been fun to go with Brendan. Listen to his snarky remarks about the Cubs, tease him about the Sox.

"Think you can sleep?" Livvy asked quietly.

Cilla had talked for more than an hour, and she was numb. Completely drained. "I guess." She threw back the blankets and tried to stand up, but Livvy pulled her back.

"Where are you going?"

"To sleep on the couch."

"Don't be an idiot," her sister said. "Sleep here. It's a lot more comfortable. And it won't be the first time we shared a bed. Remember that trip we took to Florida when we were both in college?"

"Yeah. You booked us into a complete rat hole," Cilla

said, her mouth curling into a tiny smile. "With one bed. And roaches."

"No cockroaches here. So go to sleep, Cill." She waited until Cilla laid back down, then Livvy whispered, "Things will look better in the morning."

They wouldn't. In the clear light of day, it would hurt even more. But Cilla closed her eyes and tried not to feel. Tried to make her mind a blank slate.

Everything faded away except Brendan. Images of him ran in a loop in her head. Smiling. Kissing her. Holding her.

Her head resting on the wet pillow, she shivered until she fell asleep.

***

Brendan woke to the sharp scent of hospital disinfectant and the weak light of a hospital room. Lights flashed on a machine next to his bed, and out of the corner of his eye, he saw a woman sprawled in the chair beside his bed.

For a moment, he couldn't remember why he was there. Then the memories swept in. Running up the stairs after Bates. Leaping for the guy a moment too late to stop him from shooting Tiffany. Watching Bates lift his gun while Brendan reached for his own Sig. The sharp, searing pain in his head. The blackness.

Cilla, hours later, saying goodbye and walking out the door.

Was Cilla in the chair next to him?

He moved his head carefully to get a better look at her. The dim light in the room stabbed at his eyes, and he clenched his teeth at the pain. Drawing a careful breath, he turned again.

Not Cilla. Mia was the one slumped in the chair. Sound asleep.

His mouth felt as if the Russian army had marched through it. He reached for the glass with the straw sticking out of in on the table next to the bed and yelped when pain exploded in his head. Jesus!

"Bren?"

He opened his eyes to see Mia bent over the bed railing, her hair mussed and her clothes wrinkled. "Mia. What are you doing here?"

"I got the short straw," she said with a grin. "Overnight detail."

Cilla hadn't stayed. He'd really screwed up whatever it was they had.

Used to have.

He put his hand over his eyes to block the light. To hide his grief from his sister. If Cilla had been the one in the hospital bed, they couldn't have pried him away with a crowbar. "Thanks, Mimi, but you don't have to stay. I'm fine."

"You're an idiot, Bren." She plopped back down in the chair and edged it closer to the bed. "I had to fight off everyone else. We all wanted to stay. I won."

"You beat Cilla?"

Mia watched him for a long moment. "Cilla didn't stick around," she finally said. "What happened with you guys?"

"Hell if I know." He closed his eyes to hide the lie from his sister.

He knew damn well what he'd done. And Cilla had seen it. She'd understood he was terrified of what he felt for her. He'd burst into her apartment that day he'd thought Bates or Ward might have gotten to her. She'd seen him freaking out afterward, when he'd realized how he felt. How much he lov...cared about her.

For fuck's sake. He couldn't even say it now? Not even when he was alone in a hospital room with his sister instead of Cilla, the woman he loved?

For a guy who loved words, why was it so hard to use that particular one? To say it out loud. Hell, to even think it.

The men in his family never used words. They used

jokes. Teasing. Actions. They all knew their brothers and sister loved them. That their father loved them, too. Even though it was never actually spoken.

So he hadn't told Cilla. The woman who'd told him she loved him. Who'd said they could have been great as she walked away.

"I screwed up, Mia."

"There's a news flash," she answered, leaning against the back of the chair and propping her feet on the bottom of his bed rail. "What did you do?"

"Where do you want me to start?" he said, his head and his heart both aching.

"Wherever you want, Brenny," Mia said softly. She hadn't used his pet name in a long time.

Eyes prickling, he stared at the black screen on the television set attached to the wall. "I love her," he said out loud. No lightning bolt struck him, so he said it again. Louder. "I love her."

"A blind person could see that," she said. "So what's the problem?"

"I...I didn't want to love her. I was scared. And I pushed her away. The worst part? She knew what I was doing."

"So she bailed on you?" Mia scowled back. "Let you push her away? Doesn't have a lot of sticking power, does she?"

He scowled. "She did exactly what I intended. What I wanted her to do. Walked away." His stomach twisted as he remembered the ugly words he'd thrown at her. "I was reckless. Impulsive. Did shit that I knew would piss her off." His voice caught in his throat. "Hell, I got myself shot. Seemed to work, too, 'cause she's not here."

"You're a dumbass, Brendan Donovan." Mia's feet hit the floor, and she gripped the rail to stare down at him. "The biggest dumbass of all of my brothers, and that's saying a lot. You better fix this, genius. Find her and straighten this out."

"You're right." He pressed the button to raise the bed.

"Where are my clothes? I'm getting out of here."

She snatched the control from his hand and lowered the bed. "Relax, Bren. You aren't going anywhere tonight. If you're lucky, you'll get out of here tomorrow. You're coming home with me until you're back on your feet."

"I'm not staying with you." He needed to find Cilla. Make this right.

"Okay. Then you're staying with Mom." She studied him, and he squirmed. She knew what he was thinking. "You're not getting your car keys back until you're cleared to drive."

"What are you, the police or something?"

"Ha ha, Bren. Funny. You have a choice. Me or mom."

Mia wasn't going to back down. He swallowed, steeling himself to face another fear. "Fine. I'll stay with you. But I need my computer."

"Why? You can use my computer."

"I need my own."

Mia peered over the bed rail again. "Why is it so important to have your own computer?"

He drew in a deep breath. Let it out. Breathed in again. He needed to step up to the plate. Be true to who he really was. It was time to stop hiding.

"I've been keeping something from all of you, Mimi. I'm not just a cop. I...write. I'm a writer." It felt really good to say it out loud.

"What?" Mia stared at him, shocked. "What do you mean?"

"You know that Cops and Robbers blog?" When she nodded, he said, "It's mine. I write it."

"What?" She stared at him, her eyes wide. "Are you kidding me?"

"Nope. Not kidding."

"That blog is brilliant, Brenny. Every cop I know reads it."

"Yeah?" He let out the breath he hadn't realized he was holding.

"Oh, my God. My dumbass brother is a writer." She grabbed his hand and squeezed. "That's the coolest thing I've ever heard." She stood up and plopped down on the bed next to him. "How long have you been writing?"

Brendan shifted on the bed and studied his hands. Flexed them, the way he did when he'd been writing too long and they cramped up. "My whole life, pretty much. Started scribbling in notebooks in grade school. Writing stories in high school. I started the blog because I needed a way to...to deal with what happened every day on the job."

"That's amazing, Bren," Mia whispered. "I've never known a writer before. Tell me everything. Where you get your ideas. What it feels like to write something like your blog and get all those great comments. Where all those words come from."

She grabbed his hand and squeezed it. "Spill."

***

Cilla walked into the first district station at ten the next morning. Instead of Cook County Jail, Bates had been transferred to the closest station after his release from the hospital.

It was standard procedure after a cop was arrested – everyone knew what happened to police officers in Cook County jail.

She understood the reasons. The necessity.

But. Cops were still protecting Bates.

Cilla stopped at the desk and showed the Sergeant her badge. "I understand you have Anson Bates in holding."

He narrowed his eyes at her. "What if we do?"

"I'm Detective Cilla Marini," she said evenly. "The one who arrested him. I'd like to question him."

"Too late, Detective. The feds are on the job." The sergeant picked up his newspaper and snapped it open.

"What?" Cilla slapped her hand onto the sports section and flattened it on the desk. "What are you talking about?"

"DEA has him in the box. You're welcome to watch from observation." The sergeant slid the paper out from beneath her hand and pretended to read it.

"Police officer or not, Detective Bates is responsible for the deaths of five people." Cilla knocked the paper out of his hand. "Our job is getting murderers off the streets. No matter who they are."

The sergeant stared at her for a long moment, then jerked his head toward the door behind him. "Observation room is the third door down on the left."

Fuming, Cilla slammed through the door and strode down the hall to the third door. When she yanked open the door to the observation room, another man was already there, watching. Ignoring him, she sat down two seats away.

Then bolted to her feet. "What the hell?" On the other side of the glass, interrogating Bates, was Nick Romano from the Pipe and Shamrock pub. A guy they suspected was working with Bates.

"Henry at the desk didn't tell you the DEA was here?" the man on her left asked.

She spun to face Ryan Ward. Recoiled. "What are you doing here, Ward? Waiting for your turn in the box?"

Ward rubbed his hand across his face. Purple circles bagged beneath his puffy eyes, and his face was putty-gray. He looked as if he hadn't slept at all. "Romano's already taken his shot at me."

"If he already questioned you, shouldn't you be in holding?" Cilla stared down at him, waiting for the guilt. The defeat.

"Think whatever you want, Marini. I had no idea what Anson was doing."

"Right." Cilla rolled her eyes. "You're his partner. How could you not know?"

Ward turned his gaze back to the tableau beneath them. Romano leaned across the table, talking. Bates sat stone-faced and unmoving. His right arm was encased in white plaster from his hand to above his elbow, and a sling held

335

his arm immobile across his chest.

"A cop's partner is the person who knows him or her best," he said, not taking his gaze off Bates. "You spend more time with your partner than you do with your family. You tell him everything. He's the guy who has your back. You trust him completely. Otherwise, the partnership isn't going to work."

Cilla nodded once. She understood that. But..."At some point, you must have suspected something."

"How long have you had a partner, Marini?"

"Just for this undercover op," she said, clenching her hands in her lap. "After...after what happened with you, no one wanted to partner with me. And I was fine with that."

"I'm sorry about that," Ward said quietly. "I really am. You were right. I was too rough with that woman. I wasn't arresting her. She hadn't committed a crime, as far as I knew. But she'd accused Anson of stealing drugs from her. I was pissed off. Trying to make her recant."

He rubbed the back of his neck and rolled his shoulders. "I couldn't accept that my partner had done something wrong. Something illegal. I believed Anson was the best guy in the world."

"He's also a criminal," Cilla said, her voice cold as she watched the scene below. Romano wasn't getting flustered. Wasn't getting pissed. He sat across the table from Bates, calm and cool. As if he knew he had Bates.

"Yeah, I know that now. But I couldn't accept that everything I thought about my partner was wrong. I thought she was just trying to get him into trouble.

"That's why I'm here. Watching." He rubbed a shaking hand across his face. "I need to remember this day. Remember how I was so wrong about all the things I believed. About everything I thought was true. I thought I was good at reading people, but I was a spectacular failure. Don't know how I'm gonna function as a cop after this."

In spite of all the problems Ryan Ward had caused Cilla, she understood. She knew what the bond between partners was like. She bowed her head and took a deep breath. "Maybe we both learned some lessons, Ward. I stand with my fellow officers, too. I don't want to believe any of us is crooked. But we're cops. We're supposed to follow where the trail leads, even if it's to a place we don't want to go."

In the room on the other side of the glass, Romano stood up and exited the interrogation room. Cilla headed for the door, but Ward put his hand on her arm.

"I'm sorry about what I did to you," he said. "Sorrier than I can say. You're a good cop, Marini. You didn't deserve the shit I dumped on you. If I could go back and change what I did, I'd do it in a second. But I can't. All I can do is apologize."

Cilla nodded once, short and cool. He was sincere. She could see that. But right now, what Ward had done was just a blip on the radar. Compared to the devastation engulfing her, it was insignificant. "Thank you, Ward. I appreciate that."

Then she turned and exited the room.

Romano was coming around the corner as she closed the door behind her. "Hey," he said. "Marini, right?"

"Yes." She studied his expensive suit, blue shirt, dark tie. He looked like an ad for some big-name designer in an expensive men's magazine. "I thought you were working with him, Romano. I'm still not sure you aren't."

He smiled. "That's what you were supposed to think. And that's why you're a good detective. My name's Giuliani. Dominic Giuliani. You and your partner did a very nice job with this case. We've been looking for that shithead for a long time."

"Glad we could deliver him to you." She made a mental note to check on Giuliani. "Are you getting any information from him?"

"Not yet," Giuliani said cheerfully. "He's being the tough guy now. But he'll crack. He knows what's down the line for him if he doesn't cooperate."

"Good luck. I hope he goes away for a long time."

"Oh, he will. The only difference is whether it's on our terms, or his."

Cilla nodded. "I know you'll need to talk to me and my partner. Donovan is supposed to get out of the hospital today. He's from the nineteenth district. Belmont. You can get hold of him there. I'm in the sixteenth. Let me know when you need to talk to me."

"You two aren't permanent partners?" Giuliani asked, frowning. "I would have bet money that you were."

"Nope. Just for this job." Her heart ached, but she forced a smile. "Glad to know we fooled the feds."

The DEA agent studied her for a long moment, his mouth curling into a tiny smile. "Not sure you were fooling anyone, Marini. Good luck."

"Thanks." Cilla turned and walked away, blinking furiously. She rushed out of the building and gulped in deep breaths of the cool autumn air. God! Even the damn DEA knew how she felt about Brendan.

She pulled out her phone and called her sister. She needed more of the support that Olivia had provided the night before.

Hell, she might call Sam in Iowa, too.

And her mom.

CHAPTER THIRTY-ONE

Cilla pushed back from her desk and stretched, trying to ease tight muscles. Two straight days of paperwork had left her feeling as achy and sore as an old woman.

Her phone pinged. She picked it up, smiling grimly at the text.

Tiffany had decided to cooperate with Giuliani. And with his main seller spilling her guts, Bates had finally understood the case against him was rock-solid. He'd just agreed to cooperate, as well.

The bullet and casing from Franny's shooting had matched Bates's gun, so he'd be charged with attempted assault, as well.

She'd checked out Giuliani, and he was clean. She'd been convinced when she discovered Giuliani had enlisted Holly, the self-contained, aloof woman from the Pipe and Shamrock, to help him.

Holly's boyfriend had been one of the men who'd died after taking the drug. Giuliani had persuaded her to hang around the pub to try and identify the sellers.

Now that Cilla's paperwork was done and Giuliani was taking apart Bates's network, Cilla could focus on the rest of the loose ends.

She phoned the lab and requested the DNA results on Mike Welles. According to the technician, Welles's DNA from the second sample had matched saliva and skin cells on nail clippings from all of the rape victims from the Beverly area.

The first sample, the one Johnstone delivered, had been contaminated. Unusable.

Something else to share with Internal Affairs.

Cilla grabbed her phone. "Hey, Liv," she said when her sister answered. "Just got the DNA results back on Welles. Matches all the rape victims."

Cilla heard rustling, then a door opening. "I'm heading down the hall to the prosecutor assigned to his case," Livvy said. "The judge's assistant let me know that Welles's attorney was coming in this morning with the money for his bond. I'll make sure the prosecutor goes back to court to revoke the bail offer."

"Thanks, Liv," Cilla said softly. She smiled as she ended the call. Her relationship with Livvy had changed since the night she'd gone to her sister after Brendan's shooting. They talked more frequently. Leaned on each other after a hard day. And Livvy was doing as much for Cilla as Cilla did for her.

Finally. Last but not least. Sighing, she picked up the phone and made an appointment with Internal Affairs.

No police officer wanted to talk to IAD. But Cilla had no choice. Too much had happened in the twenty-second district.

As her partner on this operation, Brendan should be part of the conversation. She'd tried, unsuccessfully, to avoid thinking about him since the night she walked out of the hospital. But everything reminded her of Brendan.

Her station. His. Talking to Giuliani. At her apartment, where he'd freaked out when he thought she'd been hurt.

It had been three days since he'd been shot. Three days of wondering how he was, worrying about him, hoping he was okay.

Three days, and he hadn't called. He hadn't even sent a damn text.

Hadn't even let her know how Franny was doing. Afraid that meant bad news, Cilla had called the vet herself.

Franny was doing well. She was out of the clinic and recuperating with Lizzy and Mac. She'd be back to normal in a month or so.

Her hand had been shaking when she hung up the phone. Brendan hadn't even let her know about Franny. So he could talk to Internal Affairs by himself whenever he was ready. She didn't give a damn when that was.

When Cilla handed in her last piece of paperwork, her Captain said, "Nice close, Marini. You and your partner did a hell of a job. How's he doing, by the way?"

"He's out of the hospital." Cilla had called the following day to make sure he was okay. When the nurse on his floor told Cilla that he was scheduled to be released, she'd thanked the woman and turned down her offer to connect Cilla to Brendan's room.

Cilla had called the next day and found out he had, indeed, been released.

"Tell him congratulations from me on cracking this case." Captain Francisco studied her, assessing. "You two going to put in to be permanent partners? I heard you worked really well together."

"No, sir." Cilla swallowed the lump that swelled in her throat. "Our styles are too different."

"Sometimes, that's what makes good partners." Francisco leaned back in his chair, watching her. "A partnership is like a marriage, you know? Sometimes it's the pairs who are the least alike that do the best."

"Yes, sir, I've heard that." She swallowed the tears that wanted to fall. "In the case of me and Detective Donovan, I don't think that's true."

"Suit yourself." He sat up straight. "We like you here in the sixteenth, and we could make room for Donovan, if you wanted to work with him."

"Not going to happen, sir."

"Don't throw away a good thing, Marini, just because you disagree about a few things."

Her heart twisted and she forced herself to smile instead of sob. "Right, sir. I won't." She swallowed. "I'll get back to work."

"Hell, no, you won't." Francisco straightened and scowled at her. "Take Thursday and Friday and the weekend off, Marini. You must have a lot of comp time coming after working nights for so long. I don't want to see you in here until Monday morning."

"Thank you, sir, but I'm ready to get back to work." Four days off was a horrifying prospect. She'd have nothing to do but think about Brendan.

"No way. Now get out of here."

Gritting her teeth, she hesitated for a long moment. Watched Francisco's face for a sign of softening. When his gaze didn't waver, she nodded. "Yes, sir."

Grabbing purse from the bottom drawer of her desk, she walked out of the station, pulling her phone out of her blazer pocket. Nothing from Brendan. No missed calls, no emails, no texts. Clearly, he was perfectly happy with the way things had ended.

Hurt, anger and misery roiled through her, making her head ache and her stomach churn.

Eyes prickling, she shoved the phone into her purse. Damn it! She'd cried more in the last four days than she had in the last four years. Over Brendan Donovan, who didn't care enough to push a button on his phone and call her.

She drove home and pulled into her garage, staring at the tool chest against the wall in front of her. What was she going to do for four days? Maybe she'd go see Sam in Iowa. Catch one of his games.

Or maybe she and Livvy could drive up to Door County.

"You're pathetic," she said as she got out of the SUV and ran her hand over the smooth, lustrous surface of Betsy's hood. "Mooning around like some high school girl who's just broken up with her boyfriend."

Brendan had never been her boyfriend. What they'd had wasn't real. They'd been pretending. Part of the job.

It had been real for her.

Because she was an idiot. Expecting more than Brendan was willing to give.

As she trudged up the back stairs to her apartment, the sun warmed her back. The maple tree in the yard wore brilliant scarlet leaves, and the mums lining the fence were a palette of fall colors. A bird hopped through the branches of the crabapple tree, eating the small red berries.

The soft, warm air signaled Indian Summer. She'd take Betsy out and blow off the stink, just like she did after a hostage negotiation.

Running up the rest of the stairs, she charged into her apartment and changed into jeans and a tee shirt. Then, grabbing her Cubs hat and making sure her sunglasses were in her purse, she ran back down the stairs and slid into Betsy. She felt better already.

She ended up at North Avenue Beach. The boat house was closed, but the picnic tables were still there. She veered away from the one where she'd eaten lunch with Brendan and his siblings and found a table close to the sand. Slipping on her sunglasses, she sat on the top of the table, her feet on the bench, and stared out at the lake.

Whitecaps rolled in, leaving trails of wet, darker sand behind when they rolled out again. Gulls circled around her, looking for food to snatch. When they realized she had nothing to eat, they headed out to the lake again. Occasionally one of them landed on the water. Farther out, rafts of ducks floated on the waves.

The sun warmed her skin through her tee shirt, softening stiff muscles. The rhythmic motion of the waves and their soothing sound drained her tension. She eased down from the table top onto the bench, rested her back against the table and took a deep breath.

Red and yellow leaves fluttered to the ground from the trees close to the sand. Indian summer felt like spring, the warm air and sunshine promising new beginnings, but it was really an ending. A lead-in to a cold, dark, lonely winter.

Pushing away those bittersweet thoughts, she let her eyes flutter closed as the smell of water and the sound of the waves and the warmth of the sun worked their magic.

She must have fallen asleep, because the vibration of something jostling the picnic table startled her awake. She shot to her feet and instinctively reached for her gun.

She'd left it in the car.

She spun around and saw Brendan, sitting on the other side of the picnic table.

She stared at him for a long moment while her heart beat wildly in her chest. When she thought she could keep her voice steady, she said, "Donovan. What are you doing here?"

"I need to talk to you, Cilla."

A surge of anger made her suck in a deep, shaky breath. "Really? You want to talk? You could have called me any time in the past four days. Your head was broken, not your fingers." Feeding her anger, she added, "You didn't even call me to let me know how Franny was doing. I had to call the vet myself to find out she was okay."

Red washed over his cheeks. "Yeah, I should have called you. I'm sorry I didn't. But someone from my family was with me twenty-four/seven. I wanted some privacy when we talked."

"That's bullshit, Brendan, and you know it. If you really wanted to talk to me alone, you could have told them to leave the room."

Brendan shoved his hands into his pockets. "I know." His voice was almost too soft to hear. "I was too scared to call you. I was afraid you'd hang up on me. Tell me to go to hell. I wanted to talk to you in person. Face to face."

She wanted to hit him. She wanted to kiss him. "You don't think I'll tell you that in person?" She curled her fingers into her palms to keep from reaching for him.

"I hope not," he said, his voice muted. "Will you hear me out?"

She shrugged one shoulder, crushing the hope that wanted to spring to life. "You're here. So talk." She watched him swallow and search for the right words. "How did you find me, anyway?"

"You said you drove Betsy to the beach after a hostage negotiation when you needed to clear your mind. When you weren't home and didn't answer your phone, I called your captain. He said he'd told you to take some time off." He rolled his shoulders as if he were nervous. Anxious. "I thought you might be here."

"I never said which beach I go to." She mentally kicked herself. Of all the things she could have said, she picked that stupid response?

He shrugged. "I started at Oak Street and worked my way north. Spotted Betsy in the parking lot. Glad you chose this one. Didn't have to go very far."

"How did you remember what I said?" She scrambled for something insightful to say, like 'get the hell out of here'. But the only thing that came out of her mouth was, "I don't remember telling you that."

Brendan stood and untangled himself from the picnic table. Walked around to her side and sat down on the bench. Patted it, inviting her to join him.

She ignored him.

He held her gaze. "I remember everything you said, Cilla."

Her face flamed. The serious expression on his face, the hint of anxiety in his eyes told her exactly what he was talking about. Her I love you when she'd thought he was asleep. "Yeah, well, I said a lot of stupid stuff."

"None of it was stupid." The muscles of his throat rippled as he swallowed. She watched, remembering inhaling his scent from that space between his throat and his jaw. Remembering how he'd tasted there.

Not helping, Marini.

She looked away. "What do you want, Brendan?"

"I need to apologize for being an ass. 'The most flaming asshole in the history of assholes', is how Mia put it, and she was right. I did some stupid stuff. Stuff that could have gotten you injured." His jaw worked and he looked straight ahead at the lake. "Or killed."

She plopped down on the bench, as far away from him as she could get. "Like running after Bates without waiting for back-up."

"Yeah. Like that." His throat rippled again, and he stared at the waves. "Got myself shot. I deserved it."

"Yeah, you were a jerk, Donovan." Her mouth trembled, and it was hard to form words. Her eyes stung, too. "But I'm not sure your jerkiness deserved getting shot. So why did you do it?"

He put his elbows on his knees and rested his chin on his hands. Still not looking at her. "The thing is, Cilla, is that I was trying to push you away. Trying to make you dump me."

The words burned in her chest. Made her stomach churn. "Not breaking news, Donovan," she managed. "Figured that out a long time ago. And how could I dump you when we were never together?"

"We were together, Cilla." His voice was so low she barely heard him over the waves.

A ball of tears swelled in her throat. He didn't get to say that. Not after the way he'd acted. "No, we weren't. We fucked. That's all."

"You know it was more than that." He straightened and turned to face her. God, she wished he hadn't done that. She didn't want to see the naked longing in his expression. "You told me so, once, when you thought I'd fallen asleep. You said you loved me."

Tears burned her eyes but she stared at him and refused to let them fall. "It was the moment. Hormones. They make you say all kinds of stuff you regret later."

"Do you regret saying you loved me, Cilla?"

When had he slid closer? "Doesn't matter, does it? The case is over, our partnership is over, we go our separate ways."

She wanted to run to her car, get in and drive away. Away from the softness in Brendan's face. The hope.

"It doesn't have to be that way." He reached for her hand and curled his fingers around hers. She savored the feeling of his skin against hers for a moment, then eased her hand away. Slid a little farther away from him.

"I love you, too, Cilla." He edged closer. "I think I started falling in love with you when I stopped you on the Dan Ryan Expressway. You gave me that look – that cool, assessing stare that intimidates the hell out of people. And you were so beautiful. A wild, exotic woman I wanted to get to know."

"Pretty words. Guess I should have expected that from a writer," she said, her voice shaking. She looked down at her hand, curled into a fist on her knee. As she watched, Brendan took her hand, opened it and twined his fingers with her. "Words mean nothing. When I heard those gunshots, knowing I was too late to prevent them, I died a little myself." She tried to tug her hand away, but Brendan tightened his grip on her.

"I ran into that room and you were on the floor. Blood was pouring out of your head. I thought you were going to die, Brendan. I thought Bates had killed you."

She closed her eyes as she began to sob, ugly sounds she tried to suppress. But they poured out of her in a flood.

Brendan wrapped his arms around her and pulled her against him. Even though he felt so good, smelled so familiar and right, she shrugged him off. She couldn't show him her weakness.

"Words are all I have, Cilla." Instead of reaching for her again, he mimicked her pose on the wooden bench. Elbows on his knees, he stared out at the lake. "You said I'm an adrenaline junkie, and that's what I wanted everyone to think. But I was faking all the bravado, trying to fit the image that I thought I had to project. And I had to try even harder after I met you. Because I wanted you."

She jerked her head around to look at him. "Why? Why would you think I needed you to be some macho asshat?"

"Because I wanted you so damn much I couldn't think straight. And you were this tough, take-no-prisoners cop. A woman who was so good at her job. You were so competent. So alive." He rolled his shoulders. "What chance would a nerdy writer have with a woman like you? I had to try even harder to project that image if I wanted a chance with you."

"You're an idiot, Donovan." Her heart was melting. Her resistance crumbling. "And why should I think you're going to change?"

"Because if I have you, if you still love me, I don't have to put on a false front. I can be who I really am." He swiveled around to face her. "Do you think I'd still take stupid chances if I knew you were waiting at home for me? If we have kids? I wouldn't leave our kids without a father."

Kids? Swallowing the sob that wanted to burst out of her, she said, "Kind of early to talk about kids, isn't it?" She pressed her fingers to her eyes to hold in the tears. "Right now, you're still the jerk who ran into a room without any backup."

"Are you still going to be busting my balls about that after we've been married for thirty years?"

"Getting a little ahead of yourself, aren't you, Donovan?" Her heart was unfurling in her chest, growing and expanding until it felt as if it would burst through her ribs.

"I hope not." He lifted her hand, pressed it against his chest. "Do you feel that, Cilla? It beats for you. Only you. Always for you."

He held her hand there, put his other hand over her chest. "Does your heart call my name with every beat?" His fingers burned into her skin. Branded her.

The sob broke free of her throat. Made her chest hurt

with the force of her tears. The force of her want.

Brendan wrapped his arms around her and pulled her against him. She held herself stiffly for a moment, then folded herself into him. He felt so good. Smelled so familiar. So right. He stroked her back, and she never wanted him to stop.

He held her until her sobs subsided. Until she sniffled. Wiped her cheeks on his shirt. Then she straightened.

"Sorry." She brushed at his shoulder. "I got snot on your shirt."

"It's your snot," he said, wiping a tear from her cheek. "So I love it."

"That's disgusting," she said, swallowing hard.

"No. It's the truth," he said with a cautious smile. He reached for her hands. "Cilla, please forgive me. I know I hurt you. That day, when Franny was shot, I said horrible, untrue things about you. You're not heartless. You have the biggest heart of anyone I know. And you're certainly not a bitch."

He swallowed and she saw wetness in his eyes. "I was such a jerk. You made me want forever. You made me need you. And that scared me. I didn't know what to do. So I tried to push you away."

"Did a good job of it, too," she muttered.

"Will you give me another chance? Let me prove that I've changed?" He leaned toward her and kissed her wet cheek. Then he leaned back and held her gaze again. "You made me want to grow up, Cilla. You made me want to be a better person. A better man. Please," he whispered. "Let me try again to love you the way you deserve to be loved. With everything I have. Everything I am."

God! His words lodged in her heart, making it unclench. Grow. Come alive again.

Tears rolled down her face again by the time he finished speaking. They formed a thick ball in her throat, making it impossible to speak. So she cupped his face in her hands and kissed him.

She poured all her love into it, all her longing for him. All her need. He froze for a moment, then he wrapped his arms around her and pulled her onto his lap.

"I love you," he whispered against her mouth. "I'll always love you. You're it for me, Cilla." He stroked her hair, then buried his face in the wavy mass of it.

"You're the only woman I want." His voice vibrated against her skin. "The only woman I'll ever want. Please tell me you'll give me another chance."

"Yes," she whispered, wrapping her arms around his neck and holding him tightly. "Yes. I love you, too, Brendan. You're all I want. But I think we both need another chance.

"I'm not perfect either. I'm prickly and defensive and keep people at arm's length. Can you live with that?"

He pulled away far enough to grin down at her. "I'm going to piss you off sometimes. I'll get so wrapped up in my writing that I'll forget a date. Or I won't hear you talking to me."

"That's okay, Brendan, because I'm going to piss you off sometimes, too. I'll be snarky and snotty, say things I don't mean. But I'll always love you."

"We'll fight with each other," he said. "But I want us to fight for each other, too. Can we do that? Can we promise that neither of us will walk away? That we'll fight for our life together? Be partners in every way?"

"Yes," she whispered. "No more running. No more hiding our real selves. That's what I want, too, Brendan."

"Happily ever after, Cilla," he whispered, pressing a kiss to the side of her head. "That's what we're going to have. What we're going to work for. What we're going to make happen. Happily ever after."

EPILOGUE

One month later

Brendan gripped Cilla's hand beneath the table in his mother's dining room. She squeezed it reassuringly, and he flashed a smile at her. Thank God he'd found her. He never would have had the courage to take this step without her.

"Hey, guys," he said during a lull in the conversation. "Hey," he said a little louder when no one stopped talking.

"What is it, Brenny," Mia said with an innocent smile.

"I have some news, Mimi." He smiled when his sister frowned at him.

His mother put her fork down. "What's that, Brendan?" she asked, studying him.

Here goes. Cilla squeezed his hand, and he smiled over at her. "You all know about the blog I've been writing." Having Cilla at his side had given him the courage to tell them three weeks ago.

"Yeah, best damn stuff I've ever seen about being a cop," Connor said before forking another bite of lasagna into his mouth.

Brendan let his shoulders relax. "Thanks Con." He swallowed. Cilla slipped her arm into his. Hugged it to her side. "The thing is, the blog isn't the only thing I've been writing. I, ah, I've been working on a book, too."

"Yeah?" Quinn grinned at him. "What kind? I'm guessing a romance novel, since you and Cilla are so disgustingly happy together."

Cilla's fingers gripped his wrist. You can do this. "Nope, not a romance." He glanced at Cilla, felt his face soften into the smile that appeared whenever he saw her. "Maybe I'll tackle that next." He drew in a shaky breath. "It's a thriller. Set in Chicago." He swallowed. "An agent who read my blog contacted me and asked if I had anything else. I sent her the book – what I had of it – and it's, um, going to auction next week."

"What does that mean?" Mac asked.

"It's when more than one publishing house wants to buy it. They bid against each other for it."

"No shit!" Quinn reached across the table and slapped his palm. "Way cool, bro."

Everyone around the table was smiling. Congratulating him. Asking questions. Cilla leaned closer and said, "Told you so."

She'd been his biggest cheerleader. She nuzzled his ear. "Gonna tell them the rest of it?"

"Maybe I should wait," he muttered.

"For what? They're all going to be excited."

"Wait for what?" Mia, who was sitting on his other side, punched his shoulder. "You holding out on us, Bren?"

"If you don't tell them, I will," Cilla threatened.

"Tell us what?" Rose asked.

Brendan took a deep breath. "My agent sent it to another agent in Hollywood. It's making the rounds, and no one has said it stinks yet."

"What does that mean?" Connor asked.

"It means they're trying to get it optioned. That they'd make a movie out of it," Raine said.

"Maybe," Brendan said. "No one has made an offer yet. And even if it gets optioned, it's a long way from that to an actual movie."

"That's...wow. That's great," Mia said.

All of his brothers, their girlfriends, his mother, Helen and Jamie crowded around him. Hugging him. Slapping him on the back.

Even Franny nosed her way in, her stumpy tail wagging furiously. She looked thinner than usual, but that was because both sides of her chest had been shaved after her injury. To keep her warm, Brendan had bought her a child's red Blackhawks sweater.

He bent to pet her now, rubbing the sweater against her ribs. "If there's a movie, Fran, they'll get a very handsome Aussie to play the brave dog," he said.

Cilla slipped out of her chair and hurried into the kitchen. She came back moments later with three bottles of champagne and a tray full of champagne flutes. "We need to have a toast," she said with a grin.

"How the hell did you pull that off?" Brendan asked her.

Cilla smiled at Rose. "I had a little help."

"I thought you guys were getting engaged," Rose confessed.

"Mom!" Brendan rolled his eyes. "We've been dating for, what? A couple of months?"

Rose shrugged. "When it's right, it's right."

Brendan's gaze found Cilla. She smiled at him, and he smiled back. Even though it had only been two months, they'd talked about it.

His mother hugged him, jerking his attention back to the present. "I'm so proud of you, Brendan," she said quietly. "Your father would be proud, too. He'd be so happy you're following your dream."

"Yeah?" Brendan watched his mother, saw nothing but happiness in her eyes. "He wouldn't be disappointed if I was eventually able to quit the force and write full time?"

Rose cupped his face in her hands. "He'd want you to

do what you love doing. He'd want you to be happy. He'd be the proudest one here today."

"Thanks, Mom," he said, returning the hug. "That means a lot."

Rose reached out and pulled Cilla into her other side. "You two work on that engagement thing. I've never seen you happier, Brendan."

"I've never been happier." He picked up Cilla's hand and kissed her palm. "Cilla's the best thing that ever happened to me."

He'd already had plans for the first check he got for his book. He had his eye on an engagement ring he'd seen at Tiffany's. Seemed right to look there, since Tiffany had helped them crack their case.

And if he had any say in it, they wouldn't wait long to get married. He and Cilla had already started their happily ever after. They just needed to make it legal. Binding. Forever.

* * * * *

If you enjoyed **Cover Me**, pick up the next book in the series – **Protect Me**.

ABOUT THE AUTHOR

Two-time Rita finalist Margaret Watson published her first book in June, 1991. Since then, she has written thirty books for Silhouette Intimate Moments and Harlequin SuperRomance, as well as nine titles in the Donovan Family series.

Margaret's books have won or been finalists in many contests, including the Colorado Award of Excellence, Desert Rose Golden Quill, Holt Medallion, and National Reader's Choice.

When she's not writing, Margaret practices veterinary medicine. She lives in the Chicago area with her husband, three daughters and a menagerie of pets.

* * *

Thank you for reading Cover Me. I'm honored you chose one of my books, and I hope you enjoyed it!

- If you would like to receive an email newsletter when my next book is released, sign up at **www.margaretwatson.com**.
- Reviews help other readers find books they'd like to read. Please leave a review of Love Me at your favorite on-line retailer. I welcome all reviews.
- Please recommend Love Me to your friends and on discussion boards.